CALEB ROEHRIG

LAST SEEN LEAVING

SQUARE FISH **FEIWEL AND FRIENDS** NEW YORK

SQUARE FISH

An imprint of Macmillan Publishing Group, LLC
175 Fifth Avenue
New York, NY 10010
fiercereads.com

Square Fish and the Square Fish logo are trademarks of Macmillan and
are used by Feiwel and Friends under license from Macmillan.

Our books may be purchased in bulk for promotional, educational, or
business use. Please contact your local bookseller or the Macmillan
Corporate and Premium Sales Department at (800) 221-7945 ext. 5442
or by e-mail at MacmillanSpecialMarkets@macmillan.com.

Library of Congress Cataloging-in-Publication Data

Names: Roehrig, Caleb, author.
Title: Last seen leaving / Caleb Roehrig.
Description: New York : Feiwel & Friends, 2016. | Summary:
   Flynn's girlfriend is missing, and people are suspecting him of knowing
   something, so he struggles to uncover her secrets as he must also face the
   truth about himself.
Identifiers: LCCN 2015036480| ISBN 9781250129673 (paperback)
   ISBN 9781250085627 (ebook)
Subjects: | CYAC: Missing persons—Fiction. | Secrets—Fiction. | Mystery
   and detective stories. | BISAC: JUVENILE FICTION / Mysteries & Detective
   Stories.
Classification: LCC PZ7.1.R6397 Las 2016 | DDC [Fic]—dc23
LC record available at http://lccn.loc.gov/2015036480

Originally published in the United States by Feiwel and Friends
First Square Fish edition, 2018
Book designed by Liz Dresner
Square Fish logo designed by Filomena Tuosto

10 9 8 7 6 5 4 3 2 1

AR: 7.4 / LEXILE: 1110L

For Uldis,

*for all the dreams that have come true, and all the ones
that have yet to*

and

In memory of my grandmother, Helen Copperman

(aka "The Book Lady")—

Thanks for fueling this fire

ONE

Into the darkness they go, the wise and the lovely.
—EDNA ST. VINCENT MILLAY

THERE WAS A corpse in my neighbor's front yard. Sprawled before a hedge of juniper bushes, its twisted arms and legs flung out bonelessly, as if it had plummeted there from a passing helicopter, there was an enormous granite boulder where its head should have been. The gardening glove on its right hand was pulling away from the cuff of a flannel shirt, and a chunk of ghostly white foam rubber innards peeked through the opening.

It was one week until Halloween, and everyone on my block seemed to be already getting into the spirit. Across the street, the Harrisons had a series of tombstones lining the walk to their front door, each one engraved with a different "funny" epitaph. HERE LIES THE MILKMAN—HE PASSED HIS EXPIRATION DATE. That kind of thing. It was a gauntlet of terrible jokes, and if you survived it, Mrs. Harrison—dressed in a peaked hat and a warty latex nose—would award you a miniature Charleston Chew.

The last time I had gone trick-or-treating, which was nearly five years ago, I had skipped the Harrisons' house.

Up and down the street, you could see ghosts and skeletons, jack-o'-lanterns and candle bags, bats and black cats. Rubber spiders dangled from eaves, zombie hands thrust up from garden beds, and shrubs were cocooned in fake cobwebs as thick as cotton batting, my neighbors competing to see whose house could be the lamest and the "scariest." Mine had them all beat, however. Among that rogues' gallery of party-store clearance-sale showcases, my house alone on that chilly October afternoon was truly frightening.

My house had a cop car parked in the driveway.

"Dude, how much did your parents pay to rent that thing?" My best friend, Micah Feldman, was standing next to me on the sidewalk in front of my boring, two-story Colonial, and he was apparently being serious.

"They didn't, dumbass," I said, kicking up my skateboard—and if I sounded tense, it was an accurate reflection of my mood. *What the hell were the cops doing at my house?*

"Well, what the hell are the cops doing at your house?"

"How do I know?" I looked around nervously. The street was quiet, save for the rattling of dried leaves as wind shook the army of trees that occupied our neighborhood. A couple of weeks ago, my block had looked like a greeting card, the autumnal display of oaks and maples like jewel-tone fireworks in the midday sunshine. Now their branches were half bare, flocked intermittently with dried-out brown curls that as yet refused to fall.

"You don't think . . ." Micah's face lost a little bit of color.

"You don't think maybe they found out about that weed you bought?"

That weed you bought. Nice. "You paid for half of it, Micah."

"Yeah, but you were the one who actually, you know, held the money." My so-called best friend squirmed like the snake he was. "Maybe the guy fingered you."

"We bought, like, half an ounce! The cops have better things to do than bust some kids for buying two bowls' worth of pot"— *I hoped*—"especially in Ann Arbor."

"If you say so." Micah shrugged uneasily and then started backing away, down the sidewalk. "I gotta get home. Call me if you don't get arrested, okay?"

"Fuck off," I mumbled, but cold needles were pricking the back of my neck and drawing beads of sweat. *Were* the police here about the pot? If they'd arrested the guy who'd sold it to me, could he have given up the names of his customers in an exchange for leniency?

I shook my head to clear it. I was being an idiot. The guy had been the roommate of the brother of a friend of a friend; he didn't even know my real name. Still, if the cops were searching our house for . . . well, anything, they could easily find the little breath-mint box at the back of my desk drawer, open it up, identify the leafy contents as Not Altoids, and nail me for possession. My mouth felt dry and tacky as I tucked my skateboard under my elbow and started for the door. If the police hadn't found the pot yet, I wouldn't give them a chance; first thing I would do as soon as I got inside was find that box and flush the weed.

I didn't get to execute my plan. No sooner had I set foot in the foyer than I heard my mother call out from the living room, "Flynn? Is that you?"

She sounded . . . strained. Not angry, but anxious. *Was that better?* My palms were starting to feel a little clammy. "Uh, yeah."

"Come into the living room, okay?"

I glanced at the stairs leading to the second floor, where my bedroom was, and swallowed around an ungainly lump in my throat. The living room was dead ahead, and before I could pretend not to have heard her, my mother stepped into view. Standing in front of the sliding doors that let out into the backyard, she smiled at me, but it was a spooky, rigid smile that did nothing to calm my nerves.

"I'm just gonna go up to my room and put my stuff down—" I tried, but she cut me off.

"Don't worry about that right now, sweetie. You can leave your stuff there."

Sweetie. Uh-oh. My mom hadn't called me "sweetie" since . . . Actually, I couldn't remember the last time she'd called me that. Numbly, I dropped my bag and my skateboard, shrugged out of my coat, and shuffled into the living room. With the set of glass doors and a massive picture window, it was a space that received a ton of light, but my vision tunneled until I could see only two things: a police officer seated in my dad's recliner, and a second officer standing by the fireplace. The one in the recliner was a man with thinning ginger hair and a bulbous nose; the one by the fireplace was younger, twenties maybe, a black woman with eyes that looked straight through me to the marijuana hidden in my bedroom. They both wore heavy utility belts with holstered guns.

I swallowed again, and tried not to look like I was trying not to piss myself.

"Why don't you have a seat, son?" The male officer spoke, but it didn't sound like a suggestion so much as a command. My mom, not taking her eyes off me for a second, circled the couch and sat down first, patting the cushion beside her like I was a terrier or something. Obediently, I followed the implied order, and once I was situated the man said, "I'm Detective Wilkerson, and this is Detective Moses. We just have a few questions we need to ask you." He gave me a smile that fell somewhere between avuncular and "don't fuck with me," and my stomach gurgled. "I know it sounds silly, but since this is an official visit, I just need to confirm that you are Flynn Doherty—is that correct?"

"Yes, sir," I replied automatically, my voice sounding like it was coming from another room. *Sir?* I never called *anyone* "sir."

"Your mother tells us you're a sophomore at Riverside."

"Uh . . . yes?"

Wilkerson grinned. "My boy's going to be a freshman there next year. He's a wrestler, but I'm hoping I can convince him to try out for football. You guys have a pretty good team this year, don't you?"

"Sure," I said, trying to sound accommodating. I knew fuck-all about football, and even less about what our team was like. I'm a small guy, shorter and skinnier than most guys my age, and fifteen-year-olds who clock in at less than 120 don't exactly make for star athletes in contact sports. I figured out in the third grade that I was never going to bring home any such trophies, and every gym class since has been an exercise in sheer misery. Guys take sports incredibly seriously, and after getting slide-tackled six or seven times in a twenty-minute period of a middle school soccer game, I realized it was best if I focused my energies elsewhere.

A silence filled with apprehension stretched out, while Wilkerson and Moses stared at me. If they were expecting me to confess to something, I disappointed them. The older detective cleared his throat. "Son, your girlfriend is January McConville, isn't that right?"

Whatever I'd been expecting him to say, it wasn't that. My mom took my hand then, squeezing it hard enough to pulverize the boulder on the neighbor's lawn, and it was my first indication that whatever was going on was a lot more serious than a half ounce of pot. Licking my lips, I asked, "Why? What's happened?"

"Just answer the question, please."

My mom was still staring at me, radiating worry, and I decided not to overcomplicate things. "Yeah. Uh, yes, sir. Why?"

"Son, when's the last time you saw her?"

I looked at him uncomprehendingly. "Last Friday. Why?"

Wilkerson and Moses exchanged a look. "Last Friday. Are you sure?"

"Yeah, I know how to use a calendar," I blurted before I could stop myself. "Why are you asking me about January? What's happened?"

Acting like I'd said nothing at all, Wilkerson forged ahead with that avuncular/hard-assed expression on his face. "You didn't happen to see her on Tuesday night, did you?"

"He just told you that he hasn't seen her since Friday," my

mother interjected sharply. It was a tone that usually struck fear into the hearts of men—she once used it on my sadistic homeroom teacher in the sixth grade, and I got three tardies excused retroactively—but Wilkerson didn't even flinch.

"I'd like him to answer the questions, ma'am." Avuncular had given way fully to hard-assed. "Are you sure you didn't see her on Tuesday night?"

"Of course I'm sure," I insisted. My heart was starting to thud, and I felt something cold uncoiling in my gut. "I was here Tuesday night, writing a crappy history paper. The last time I saw January was Friday. Like I said."

Wilkerson's mouth shifted. "How did she seem?"

"Huh?"

"Was she upset? Angry?" Wilkerson made a revolving motion with one hand. "What did the two of you talk about?"

I flashed back to Friday night, January's breath fogging the air between us, her hands pawing at my jeans, her eyes a shimmering slick of tears, and I shifted on the couch. My mom was watching me like I was something under glass at the zoo, and I could feel my chest constricting. "I don't know. We talked about normal stuff."

I was sure they could see the sweat leaking at my temples. This was my worst nightmare. Why were they asking me about Friday night *in front of my mom*?

"Could you elaborate?"

It was like being called to the chalkboard to give a presentation you had forgotten you were supposed to prepare. I started talking, saying things that popped into my head, desperately avoiding the truth. I didn't *want* to mislead the cops—not if something bad had happened—but they wouldn't tell me what was going on, and I wasn't going to back willingly into this particular corner if I could help it. "We did some stargazing. January's really into that kind of thing, and it was a pretty clear night, so we went out and . . . you know, looked at stars for a while. And we talked about what we're going to do when we finally graduate, and we talked about her big, fancy new house and her big, fancy new school, and . . . and that's about it."

It sounded pitiful even to my own ears, and I could see the cops didn't believe me. Looking at me dubiously, Wilkerson asked, "Did she seem depressed at all, or preoccupied? Was she acting unusual in any way?"

Again, I flashed on January's torn expression, stark in the moonlight with bitter tears making silver lines down her cheeks, and I felt ashamed. "Not really."

Wilkerson frowned, and Detective Moses narrowed her eyes a little like she was trying to picture me in handcuffs. Then she spoke for the first time. "She's your girlfriend, but you haven't seen her in almost a week?" It was Thursday now, so technically she was right. "Not over the weekend? Not on Tuesday night?"

"Why do you keep asking me about Tuesday?" My pitch was climbing into the upper register and, like watching a cat run up a tree, I couldn't seem to stop it. "Why do you keep asking me about January? What's happened?"

Maddeningly, the detectives shared another glance, and then Wilkerson finally said, "January McConville is missing, son. She never came home from school on Tuesday night, and no one's seen or heard from her since." He watched me for a moment, as if he expected me to respond, but I merely stared back in quiet astonishment until he added, "So I think you can see why we'd like to know exactly what the two of you talked about the last time you saw her."

I looked from my mom's worried expression to the business-like ones of the cops, and I swallowed hard. *Oh, shit.*

TWO

TWO WEEKS TO *go before Halloween and the moon was full, a bone-white disc that glowed so brightly it rendered streetlamps redundant, so bright I actually cast a shadow over the waves of blond hair that trailed down January's back as she trudged quietly through the tall grass in front of me. A few small, wispy clouds hovered at the edge of the night sky, and the fields that stretched out around us were cast in a sharp, bluish relief. It was a startlingly cold night, and our breath streamed visibly into the air, white phantoms that vanished as soon as you looked at them.*

I hadn't heard from her in days—not a call, not a text, nothing—and then, out of nowhere, she wrote and asked me to come over. The second I arrived, she'd told her mom and stepdad we were going stargazing, and we'd be back later. "Don't wait up," she'd said sarcastically, knowing they probably weren't even listening.

Ever since her mom married Jonathan Walker, a rich-as-hell state senator with national aspirations, January had become increasingly, incongruously pessimistic about her life. She went from a tiny, rented condo to the biggest house I'd ever seen in real life—a house so big it could double as a hotel—and she hated it. It was an "estate" in the sprawling and largely rural Superior Charter Township area northeast of Ann Arbor, sitting on more acreage than my entire neighborhood, and she bitched about how far away it was. Her bedroom was enormous—her bed was enormous—and she'd already been promised a convertible when she turned sixteen.

Still, she complained. "Mom and I used to be close, you know? We used to actually talk. Now it's the 'Tammy and Jonathan Walker Show' all the time, and I'm the teenage daughter who gets reduced from 'starring' to 'recurring' because my character's no longer useful. Mom always takes his side, and she barely even sounds like herself at all!"

She was right, though. I could see it happening before my eyes. When I'd met January freshman year, her mom had only just started dating Walker, and January was convinced it wouldn't last. Tammy was a struggling office manager and single mother, and Walker was one of the richest men in the state; they had nothing in common. But then I watched as January's mom went from mousy brown to platinum blond, from Sears to Saks, and from "Tammy" to "Mrs. Walker." Mr. Walker had stamped a new identity on her, like a kid playing with a doll, and his girlfriend/fiancée/wife had been an eager and cooperative subject. January, however, resisted the interference every step of the way, becoming harder and pricklier until neither her mom nor her stepdad particularly wanted to handle her anymore.

She still hadn't spoken yet, and we were reaching the little stream that marked the back end of the Walker property. Beyond it, a garrison of black trees rose up toward the wispy shreds of cirrus clouds that drifted like torn gauze above our heads. Past the trees and to the left was a sloping meadow where January liked to watch the stars, far enough from any houses that you could easily pretend you were the only person left in the world, but instead of heading for it, she veered right.

We hopped the stream, shoved through a cluster of pines, and emerged in the moonlight only a few yards from what had once been a functioning barn. Now it was an abandoned, moldering shipwreck of a building, its boards hoary and warped with age, its roof sagging perilously in more than one spot, with an encampment of weeds spreading out around its foundation. Without a word, January headed for the wide doors, the lock on them long since rusted through.

"Uh . . . I thought we were going to look at the stars," I said uncertainly.

"We will," she answered, her breath vaporizing before my eyes. "I just want to go in here first."

"Why?" I halted in my tracks, eyeing the structure nervously, scared not of the building's safety rating but of what this unannounced stop might represent.

"Because it's cold," January told me simply, dragging one of the doors open with an ominous croak from its ancient hinges, "and I want to."

"Why?" I repeated, but she ignored me. Without waiting to see if I would follow, she walked through the dark maw of the doorway and was swallowed by the shadows within. Typical January. She knew I would follow; I didn't have a choice. Where else would I go?

Heaving an irritated sigh, I trotted obediently after her.

The inside of the barn was no cheerier than the outside, especially at night. Creepy stalls filled with petrified straw bordered a central passage, dust thickly coating every visible surface, and the sharp, rusted remains of farm equipment deemed too decrepit to salvage or sell hung from the walls like some kind of primitive armory. I'd been in there before, of course; immediately after discovering it, January had turned it into her own Fortress of Solitude, a place where she could get away from the Tammy and Jonathan Walker Show. As if she couldn't just go to the other end of that railway station they called a house and be equally as isolated.

Toward the far end of the barn was a ladder leading to the hayloft, and in the dim light I saw January already halfway to the top, the rungs giving little squeaks of protest under her feet. Frustrated, I called out, "Are you gonna tell me why we have to stop off in this haunted shithole first, or what?"

She didn't answer. She disappeared from sight, and then I heard her feet scraping through dirt and straw above my head, boards thumping and creaking until she came to a stop near the front of the barn. After a moment, I ascended the ladder and found her huddled in a little nest of hay near an open window that looked out toward the meadow and the woods, beside a stack of crates pushed up against the wall. The bright moonlight made a platinum halo of her pale hair.

"Sit with me for a little while, okay?" Her voice was scarcely above a whisper. "I'm cold."

I was still annoyed, but she sounded . . . fragile somehow. It was so unlike her, so out of character for the girl who had never had a sentimental word to say about anyone or anything, that I forgot to be wary of her motivation. I crossed the hayloft, skirting the weak spot in the floor, and settled next to her. She was shivering, so I opened my coat and let her move into my lap, then closed the coat around us both. We were silent for a moment, looking out the window at a sky rendered into a pointillist masterpiece by limitless stars, the moon shining like a beacon through the diaphanous lace of barely-there clouds.

"This is nice," January said at last. She looked up at me, the light picking out an icy reflection in the blue of one eye. "I've missed you, Flynn. I feel like . . . like we don't even see each other anymore."

"We kind of don't," I answered bluntly. It sounded rude, so I added, "I mean, we go to different schools now, you've got drama club every afternoon, you work every weekend—"

"It's not just that. I feel like—" She stopped abruptly, then changed gears. "I miss you," she repeated. "I want for us to be happy again, like before."

"We're not happy?" I asked carefully. "Or you're not happy?"

"You know I'm not happy. Not anymore." Familiar bitterness was in her voice, a rush of bile so strong I could almost taste it. "I fucking hate it here. I hate Jonathan, I hate Dumas, I hate fucking robo-mom. . . . I hate that you and Micah and Tiana and every-body else are all having your old lives and doing fun things, while I'm out here in Narnia with my brand-new wax museum family and nobody fucking cares."

"I care," I assured her automatically.

She was silent for just a moment. "Tell me about California, okay?"

This was a little game we played. We'd played it since before we started dating, but neither of us got tired of it. She rested her head on my shoulder and I looked out the window at the moon. "When we graduate, we're both going to California. I'll go to UCLA for English, but only until I figure out what I really want to do; your parents will make you apply to Stanford and you'll probably get in, but you'll choose Cal Tech instead just to prove a point. You'll major in astrology—"

"Astronomy," she corrected, and I could hear the smile in her voice.

"Same thing," I teased. "We'll go to parties every weekend,

alternating whose friends we hang out with, but pretty soon you'll join a sorority—"

"Fuck you!" She laughed, and I realized it was the first time I'd heard her laugh in weeks.

"—and I'll make friends with all these film school hipsters, and they'll get me to start drinking organic, fair-trade coffee and bitching about the Establishment. Your sorostitute friends won't like me, and my hipster friends won't like you, and nobody will understand how we ever got together in the first place—"

"—but we'll go to the beach every Saturday afternoon, the Sunset Strip every Friday night, and a different, trendy café-slash-bar-slash-restaurant every Sunday, and all of our faux-cool friends will wish they were those two awesome kids from Michigan," she fin-ished with a giggle, but her voice was quiet. "I really want that to happen."

"Me too."

She turned again, tilting her face up to mine, and then she kissed me. Her lips tasted like vanilla gloss and spiced rum, and I was sur-prised that I hadn't smelled the alcohol earlier. The kiss went from tender to serious in nothing flat, her tongue sliding between my teeth, her mouth pressing against mine with unmistakable urgency. Her right hand slipped underneath my sweater, moving over my stomach and up to my chest, and I jerked backward.

"What?" she asked, that one illuminated eye darting back and forth as she read my face. "What's wrong?"

"It's just—I mean, your hand is freezing cold!" I laughed awkwardly.

"It'll warm up," she promised, and she moved into me again, kissing harder, her left hand joining her right under my sweater. Her fingers clutched at my abs, the cold searing my skin, and then dropped

down to the waist of my jeans. She'd managed to get the button undone before I realized what she was doing and pushed her back.

"Wait," I said, a little panicked.

"The time is right," she insisted breathlessly, her hands twisting out of my grip like eels, and she reached for my crotch again. "It's finally the right time, and I want . . . I want you to be the first. I want you."

She was kneading me, tugging at my jeans, and I should have been enjoying it—I really wanted to be enjoying it—but the panic had escalated to a screaming tornado siren in my brain, and I pushed her back again. "Stop! Stop it!"

"Why?" Her voice was bleak, almost challenging. "What's wrong?"

"I'm not ready yet," I exclaimed, grappling my pants back into place and fastening the button like it was the seal on a bomb shelter. "We talked about this! I—. It's too early, and it—it needs to be . . . special."

It was the stupidest thing I could've said, and that fact did not escape my girlfriend. She drew away from me, her face disappearing into the inky blackness of the hayloft. Caustic as acid, she snarled, "And I'm not special enough for you, Flynn?"

"That isn't what I meant, and you know it," I snapped, nerves making me irrational.

"We've been dating for four months. You're supposed to want to do this."

"And you're supposed to be glad that I respect your body and stuff!"

"Is that what this is?" Her voice was completely hollow. "Is that what this is really about?"

My first instinct was to demand, What are you talking about?

But I knew exactly what she was talking about, and I didn't want the words to come out of her mouth. I'd have given anything to keep the words from coming out of her mouth. Sweat like ice water streaked down my spine as I retorted, "Sorry I'm not enough of a man-whore for you. Maybe I'm just old-fashioned."

"But I'm a regular, modern whore, I guess."

"I didn't say that!" I let her make me angry, because anger was safer. An objective listener would identify me as crazy, but I let wrath crowd out my guilt, my shame, and my rationale; I let it take over. "Don't put words in my mouth just because I'm not ready to have sex yet!"

January was quiet for a moment. "Are you afraid I'll be disappointed?"

"Huh?"

"In the size of your . . . you know?"

"There is nothing disappointing about my . . . size!" I exclaimed, offended and horrified by the delicate tone of the question, as if she truly believed I might have a tiny cock. Thing is, it felt like bullying, too, like she was trying to embarrass me as punishment for not wanting to get carnal in a haunted barn, or to goad me into whipping it out to prove my manhood.

"It's just that . . . Kaz said guys worry about stuff like that, and that maybe you—"

My anger swelled like a thunderhead as I interrupted her. "Why the fuck are you talking to fucking Kaz about my dick? Why are you talking to him at all about us? I don't talk about you behind your back!"

She leaned forward then, her face appearing again in the moonlight, and I was startled to see tears glimmering in her eyes and shining on her cheeks. Her expression was anguished, and in the blue-white illumination, she looked like a marble saint. "Can we not fight? Please? This isn't how I wanted tonight to go."

"Well, too bad. Guess you fucked up." I didn't sound balanced even to my own ears. I was being an asshole, but I wanted this to be over so badly that I didn't care.

If anything, January's marble face hardened further, anguish turning to resentment like milk curdling before my eyes. "You know what? I'm sick of pretending we don't both know the reason you freak whenever I touch you."

"Maybe it's because you always say stuff like that."

Her baleful glare was resolute. "I'm done letting you make me feel like it's me, like it's my fault. It's never been about me. It's always been about you."

"I don't know what you're talking about." I hugged my coat a little tighter. "You don't know what you're talking about."

"If you won't be honest with me, you should at least be honest with yourself."

"Thanks for the advice, Dr. Phil, I'll think about it."

She stared at me for another moment or so, and then hissed, "Fuck this! I'm tired of holding your hand and waiting for you to make friends with yourself, Flynn! I'm here, too—you're not the only one." She drew back again, into the darkness, and I heard her scrambling to her feet. "I'm done. I shouldn't have called you. It was a mistake." Her voice dropped to a whisper, catching, and I realized that she was crying again. "It was all a big mistake."

I shifted uncomfortably, suddenly freezing on the bed of hay in that pool of moonlight. "January—"

"I won't be your safeguard or your excuse or your problem anymore," she spat suddenly, venomously. "Either admit the truth, or find a new place to hide, because I'm done!"

Her feet pounded across the shadowy hayloft, then descended the ladder, and then crossed the barn underneath me. I heard the door creak open, and caught a glimpse of her glowing blond hair as she jogged from the barn back into the trees, heading toward the meadow.

It was the last time I saw her. Those were the last words she spoke to me.

THREE

I **SURE AS** hell couldn't tell Wilkerson and Moses about all of *that*, not in front of my mother. *Well, we had this huge fight, because she wanted to have sex and I didn't, because . . . because . . .* A trill of fear spiked through me, my head whirling and my stomach turning over just at the thought of it, and I announced in a haphazard way, "We broke up."

Moses remained impassive, Wilkerson shifted his jaw thoughtfully, and my mother looked at me in utter surprise. "You two broke up? Why didn't you tell us?"

"Because," I said, tempted to roll my eyes in spite of everything. My mom was acting as if it were a given that I should share news bulletins about my relationships. I couldn't think of anything that would make a breakup more awkward than having to dissect it after the fact with the help of my parents, like some kind of postgame analysis for the whole family. "It wasn't that big of a deal. It just kind of happened."

"Did you have a fight?" Wilkerson asked, like it was his business. All three adults were staring at me now, waiting for an answer, and I almost laughed.

Instead, I lied, dry-mouthed. "No. Like I said, it just kind of happened. I mean, we hardly ever see each other anymore, and I guess we both kind of realized that it wasn't working out."

"So it was mutual." Moses sounded as though she were trying to humor a loose-cannon conspiracy theorist. *It was aliens, hmm? Interesting point.*

"Well, yeah. I mean, sort of." I was getting flustered, and my body temperature rose about a million degrees until I was sure I was about to spontaneously combust.

Mom came to my rescue. "Does it really matter who broke up with who?"

"We'd just like to get a sense of her state of mind," Wilkerson explained soothingly, and then turned to me again, back in Avuncular Mode. "If you broke up with her, and she took it badly, it might be . . . illuminating."

It took me half a second to add that up. "You think . . . you think maybe she . . . hurt herself?"

There was an awkward, horrible silence before Moses stepped in, sounding kinder than I'd have thought possible. "Not necessarily—we just don't want to rule anything out until we have all the information. Was she upset about the breakup?"

I thought about January's tears, her angry, veiled accusations, and swallowed again. My tongue felt like a lump of sand in my mouth. "Maybe a little. But she wouldn't have *killed herself* because of me."

That much was true at least, I was certain. Our relationship hadn't been casual—we'd been inseparable for about a month before we'd even started dating—but we hadn't quite reached the Three Little Words phase before we'd started drifting apart; and even though she'd clearly been emotional that Friday in the barn, she hadn't exactly been devastated. *She* had dumped *me*! If that's indeed what had happened. *"I'm done"* had a pretty final ring to it, but she hadn't so much as changed her relationship status on Facebook.

"We understand there've been some problems at home for her," Wilkerson continued delicately. "Did she happen to confide in you about that?"

The phrase *problems at home* caused my mom to suck air in through her nose, and I was quick to say, "It's just normal stuff. She was annoyed because her parents made her leave Riverside and go to Dumas, and they argued about it. Plus, she doesn't really like her stepdad, and her stepbrother is a burnout and an assh—uh, a jerk, but it's not like . . . I mean, there's never been any *violence* or anything."

"In what way is he an asshole?" Moses asked seriously.

"I don't know. The normal way?" In reality, Anson Walker was the dickhole equivalent of a kung fu master, able to be a miscreant in so many ways it almost defied human understanding. His transgressions had made the news a couple of times—once when he got into a fistfight with a parking attendant, and once for pulling the *Do you have any idea who my dad is?* routine with someone who had the gall to treat him like a normal human—but he was adept at playing to the cameras, and his father's money frequently reduced criminal acts to "youthful indiscretions." His worst behavior he saved for behind closed doors, when he knew he wouldn't get caught. "He's got an attitude problem. He's nineteen and not in school, and all he does is sit in his bedroom playing *Call of Duty* and smoking po—" I caught myself in the nick of time. "Uh, ci-cigarettes."

"Okay," Wilkerson said, picking up the thread, "so January was unhappy at home. How about school? You said she wasn't thrilled to be going to Dumas?"

"Not really." Dumas was the most exclusive private school in the area, an institution accessible only to the richest of the rich kids. The January McConville I met at the beginning of freshman year would have laughed hysterically at the suggestion that she might someday attend the ivory-towered academy, but after Tammy married Jonathan Walker, they'd decided on January's behalf that she would upgrade learning institutions when the next school year started. It had been a bitter skirmish. January derided the Dumas kids as spoiled poseurs who cribbed their behavior from *Gossip Girl* reruns, and she wasn't interested in the least in leaving behind the friends she'd made at Riverside, no matter how prestigious the Dumas Academy would look on her transcripts.

"Here's the real fucking clincher," January had fumed to me one night over coffee at Starbucks, while the battle was still ongoing. "Neither of them actually care about my education, or my college opportunities, or any of the rest of that shit. Stepdaddy Dearest wants to be a fucking big-shot senator, and he needs me to go to the fanciest school in town so we all fit the part. Perfect house, perfect wife, perfect stepdaughter!"

"While Anson sits around the house jerking off and playing video games," I'd snarked.

"Anson is taking a gap year," January retorted in a sickly sweet imitation of her mother's newly acquired Stepford Wife speaking voice. *"He gets to decide what he wants to do with his stupid, worthless life. Me? Not so lucky."*

"So she wasn't happy at home or at school, and her

relationship had just gone bust," Wilkerson summarized bluntly, jerking me back to the present.

"Well, yeah, but she wasn't, like, *depressed* about it all—not like *that*." I shrugged helplessly. "I mean, she gets angry and unhappy about stuff, and maybe she blows up about it sometimes, but she isn't *suicidal* or anything. I'm pretty sure I would've noticed."

" 'Pretty sure'?" Detective Moses repeated.

"Well"—I squirmed again—"like I said, we've sort of been drifting apart. I haven't really seen her much for the past few weeks."

The woman surprised me then by saying, "She told her parents she spent most of the weekend with you."

"What?"

"They said that she's been with you four to five nights a week regularly, since about June."

I stared at her in blank astonishment. January and I had been together only four or five days total out of the past twenty, and I told the detectives as much. "I stayed at home most of the weekend."

"He did," my mother confirmed promptly. "He had a friend over on Saturday—Micah Feldman, who lives a couple of blocks over—and then we spent Sunday watching the football game as a family."

Ann Arbor was a college football town, and if there was a game on, my parents were guaranteed to be watching it. I'm sort of apathetic about the sport, as I said before, but I'm really into game-day festivities. Dad grills burgers, Mom loads up the coffee table with snacks, chips, and soda, and we spend the entire day pigging out. Even if it's just the three of us, it still feels kind of like a party, and if the game goes well, my parents will get celebratory enough that I can successfully sneak a beer. I like beer even less than I like football, but that isn't really the point of beer.

"So she was lying to her parents."

"I guess," I mumbled, feeling like a traitor. No matter how we'd left things, I still cared about January, and I didn't like selling her out.

"And you don't know where she might've been?"

I shook my head. "Like I said, I haven't talked to her since Friday night."

"Did she have any friends that her parents disapproved of?" Moses asked, and I shrugged again. Truth be told, I was pretty sure that Mr. and Mrs. Walker disapproved of *all* of January's friends on some level. "Can you think of anyone in particular, even people who live out of town, that she might've turned to if she was in trouble?"

"You think there's a chance she ran away?" My mother sounded almost relieved by this prospect, and I didn't blame her—it was a hell of a lot better than the alternatives.

"Frankly, there's a pretty good chance," Detective Moses affirmed. "Nine times out of ten in cases like this, that's the situation. It sounds like January wasn't dealing too well with all the big changes in her life, and it's possible she just took off. Maybe she ran away, or maybe she's lying low for a while, trying to scare her parents and teach them a lesson. That happened right here, a couple of years back: A boy about Flynn's age got in a fight with his parents, took the car, and vanished. The East Lansing police found him a week later, sleeping on the floor of a friend's dorm room at Michigan State."

It was an appealing suggestion, and I supposed it made sense. January *did* hate her life lately, and she was both impulsive and pretty obsessed with getting out of Ann Arbor. *Tell me about California, okay?* Was it possible she'd disappeared deliberately?

January wasn't stupid; she would've known she wouldn't get very far with no driver's license, no high school diploma, and no money of her own, but I could easily see her hiding somewhere for a few days to teach the Walkers a lesson. She was not above pulling such a stunt. When her mom was planning the wedding, January had fielded a phone call from the baker and, without a single pang of conscience, told them to cancel the order for the cake. She knew her monkey wrench wouldn't stop the marriage from happening, but disastrously fucking up the ceremony was, she'd stated with malicious satisfaction, the next best thing.

As it was, Tammy barely found out about what had happened before it was too late to rectify the situation, and January had been grounded for nearly a month as a result—the Wi-Fi signal was even turned off every night for three weeks, just to keep her from being able to reach the outside world—but January's anger at her mother had provided more than adequate insulation against any guilt she might have felt. She'd wanted to make her protest against the marriage impossible to ignore, and she'd succeeded.

Dutifully, I enumerated for Detectives Wilkerson and Moses the friends January had that might be candidates for Safe-Port-in-a-Storm status. Even as I rattled the list off, however, I knew my intel would amount to nothing; January's friends at Riverside were my friends, too, and if my girlfriend—or ex-girlfriend, as the case may be—were staying with one of them, I'd have certainly heard about it.

"I don't think she's really close with anyone at Dumas," I concluded with a shrug. January called Dumas "the Dumbass Academy," and referred to the students in a similar manner.

"This Dumbass girl is having a birthday party this weekend," she'd told me once when we were hanging out at the skate park Micah and I liked to use. *"I really don't want to go, but she asked me in front of Jonathan, and now he's insisting on dropping me off personally. I guess her dad has some kind of connections or something, and Jonathan wants to get the endorsement."* January gave me a nasty smile. *"Not only does he get to tell me where to go to school, now he gets to pick my friends, too!"*

"Don't worry about it," Wilkerson told me as he finished jotting down the last phone number I'd provided. "We're going to head over to the Dumas Academy tomorrow and ask around; if she had any friends there, we'll talk to them." *If she had any friends.* I supposed that meant her parents didn't know much more than I did. Wilkerson got to his feet. "Thanks for your time, Flynn."

My mom blinked in surprise. "Is that all you wanted to ask?"

"For now," Wilkerson said, making an effort not to sound too credulous. I guess they didn't want me to think they believed everything I'd said, just in case it turned out I was lying. "If we can think of anything else, we'll be in touch." The two detectives started for the short hall to the foyer, but then Wilkerson turned back and looked me square in the eye. "And, son? If you think of anything else you want to add to your story—or to change—I suggest you call us sooner rather than later. We suspect your girlfriend's probably fine, but . . . better safe than sorry."

And on that ominous note, they left, slamming the front door behind them.

FOUR

MY MOM SPENT the next couple of hours watching me watch TV, and asking if I was okay. When my dad got home, Mom told him everything that had happened, and then he joined her in watching me. Then, for about thirty minutes, we sat in a horrendously awkward silence at the dinner table while they watched me eat, periodically interrupting to ask how I was "dealing with everything." They didn't seem to want to let me out of their sight, just in case I had a mental breakdown or something and decided to swallow a handful of tacks to deal with the angst. Pleading an imminent math test, I excused myself from the table and fled to my bedroom to study. It was the first time I'd ever been grateful to have homework.

The truth was I had no idea how I felt about January's disappearance yet. On a certain level, I was aware that I was blocking myself from truly considering the different scenarios the detectives had presented. Moses had told my mom that, statistically speaking, it was most likely January had run away—and everything I knew about the girl jibed with that theory—and so I made a subconscious decision that this was indeed what had occurred. I didn't let myself dwell on the possibility that something actually bad might have happened to her.

I didn't let myself dwell on the fact that the cops had steered conspicuously clear of terms like "abducted" and "possibly killed," even though they were the two most unavoidable theories whenever a teenage girl disappeared.

After I went to bed, the sky cleared and a fiercely bright wedge of moon glared in through my window, throwing gray squares of light across my rumpled blankets and reminding me of that night in the barn. Each time I started to drift off, January appeared again in my memory, her white-gold hair glowing in the moonlight, those luminous eyes wet with tears, and her expression drawn tight with an anguish so alive it practically vibrated beneath her skin. The realness of the dream jarred me from sleep, over and over.

January was always kind of a drama queen, but she'd been more than just her usual, theatrically emotional self that night. Something serious had been bothering her. I'd sensed it in her strange silence when she'd led me across the fields to the barn, and in the faintly despondent way she'd asked me to talk to her about our plans of moving to California, as if it were a bedtime story—and there had been plenty of weird tension in her scrabbling desperation for us to deflower each other, too. If I'd been a better boyfriend, I'd have said something about it. Hell, if I'd been a better *friend*. But I had been on my guard from the beginning, and when she'd started kissing me, I'd let my defensiveness take over.

I'd become so scared that I'd lashed out at her, attacked to protect myself and deliberately started a fight. That was the worst part. My face burned from guilt and shame as I lay there in my bedroom, staring up at the ceiling and wishing I could go back in time and do everything over. January had been troubled by something, and I was so terrified of being honest that I'd made things worse on purpose. And now she was missing. *Missing.* What if the scenario was truly worst case? What if I could have done something to prevent it, but I'd let my secret get in the way?

And now I'd lied to the cops as well. It was a small lie, but still. What if January had killed herself? And what if part of the reason was because her boyfriend had rejected her? How would I live with myself?

What would have happened if I'd let her accuse me? If I'd finally blurted out the truth? It had been on the tip of my tongue—it was *always* on the tip of my tongue—but before I ever got near to speaking it aloud, terror squeezed my heart like a python. Once the words were out, they would never go back in again; everything would change. For better or worse, *everything would change*. The thought made me nauseated and dizzy.

You're right, January. It's not about you at all. The reason I don't want to have sex with you is because I'm gay, and I want to have sex with boys instead.

Fuck, what if I'd said it? Would it have made her feel better about being rejected, or worse, because then she'd think she had proof that I'd merely been using her as a smoke screen for the past four months? It wasn't true, that was the awful thing. I really *did* care for January, and had since the beginning. More than simply being my girlfriend, she was my *best* friend—just as much as Micah was, if in a different way. She and I knew each other so well that we could have whole conversations with nothing but meaningful looks, a volume of words exchanged in facial expressions; we liked the same bands, laughed at the same jokes, mocked the same bad TV shows; she was smart and pretty and easy to talk to. . . . She was everything a guy was supposed to want in a girlfriend. And I really, genuinely *liked* her. I'd thought, I'd hoped, that eventually I would also start to feel the *other* things I was supposed to feel for a girlfriend. The physical things.

But that stuff never developed. Incongruously, the more comfortable January and I got around each other, the less romantic our relationship became—to me, anyway. She started to seem like a sister or something, and the more I tried to find her sexy, the weirder it felt. Meanwhile, my penis would go up and down like a periscope every time I'd attend one of Micah's swim meets, where athletic guys strutted around the pool in tiny bathing suits, wet and glistening all over like hard candy. My body clearly didn't care what I wanted it to want.

Would January have hated me if I'd told her? Resented my lies forever? Or could she have maybe understood—laughed at the incredible awkwardness of the situation and resolved to stay my friend? I might never know, because I'd picked the safer option. I'd tried to make her feel bad for pressuring me, and now she was gone.

I burned with shame until my sheets were damp with sweat and I decided that, no matter what, I would do everything I could to figure out what had happened to her.

The heat had been punishing that summer, the air so thick with humidity that if you tossed up a blade of grass, you half expected it to get stuck on the way back down. That day in June, my bike's aluminum frame had become a deadly weapon as I pedaled my way across town, the blazing metal threatening to leave blisters on my flesh every time my knees touched it on a tight corner. By the time I skidded to a halt outside a nondescript brick building on Huron Street, my clothes were clinging to my skin and I could feel sweat dripping from the hair that bristled at the nape of my neck.

I grabbed my shirt at the bottom and started working it like a bellows, trying to circulate air across my torso, wishing I'd had the confidence to wear a tank top in spite of my skinny arms and glad that I'd remembered to put on deodorant. Biking that far had been sort of a stupid idea, I knew, but it had been either that or take the bus, and between the two options there was no contest. The last time I'd opted for public transportation, an eighty-year-old man had sat down beside me, popped out his false teeth, and stuck them in my lap before I knew what was happening. Anyway, it was silly for me to feel as self-conscious as I did; I was just there to meet up with January so we could go hang out at Starbucks or whatever, like always, and it wasn't as if she'd never seen me looking like shit before. The only difference on this occasion was that it would be the first time she'd see me looking like shit since becoming my girlfriend.

We'd been official for almost forty-eight hours, and even though we'd been friends for close to a year, my stomach still buzzed like an overtaxed electrical transformer as I made my way into the deep freeze of the air-conditioned building. The chill felt exquisite for about twenty seconds, and then goose bumps rippled across my exposed arms and legs as I spoke to the person behind the front desk and started down a corridor to the left. As nervous and excited as a musician taking the stage, I swallowed compulsively, baffled by my sudden case of the butterflies. There was no reason to freak out . . . was there?

I stepped into a cafeteria much like the one at Riverside, folding tables and flimsy chairs still in use despite appearing to be on the verge of collapse, with fluorescent lighting and colorless linoleum floors that had seen better days. The major difference was that most of the people I was looking at were adults; overdressed for the heat, their faces craggy and aged before their time by years of hard living, they were the city's homeless. A white-haired woman standing near the doorway, clearly someone who worked there, gave me a nakedly curious look. "Can I help you?"

"Actually, I'm . . . um, I'm just here to meet my girlfriend?" The G word sounded so important spoken out loud, and the woman's look turned doubtful, as though she found my claim suspicious. I was saved from having to explain myself further, however, when January appeared at that very moment through a doorway at the back of the room.

"Flynn!" Her face broke into a smile, her eyes lighting up, and I felt my cheeks redden as I grinned back, the reaction instant and irrepressible. We probably looked ridiculous, beaming idiotically at each other across the drab cafeteria like lovers meeting in a field of wildflowers, but it only lasted a moment before she darted to my side, tossing her arms around me and putting her lips to mine in our first-ever public kiss. After a moment, she drew back with an affectionate smirk and stated, "You're lucky you're so cute, because you are seriously gross right now."

"Get used to it," I advised her airily. "Now that we're a couple and I don't have to try so hard anymore, I've pretty much decided to just let myself go."

"Oh, thank God I'm not the only one." January rolled her eyes in exaggerated relief, adding, confidentially, "I haven't changed my underwear since Saturday."

"Well, I ate a whole tub of frosting for dinner last night."

"I ate a pack of raw hot dogs for breakfast," January countered, "and *I threw out all my body wash and shampoo, so I hope you're into chicks with BO.*"

"*Ah, young love.*" The white-haired lady interrupted our banter with a wistful sigh. "*So beautiful, and so darn weird.*"

January and I were holding hands, giggling stupidly with happiness and relief that our rapport remained the same as always, that altering the status of our relationship hadn't screwed everything up. I hadn't even realized until just then how afraid I'd been that crossing the boundary from Friends to Dating would somehow change us fundamentally, that the sudden new parameters and expectations that came with being a couple would make it impossible for us to be the way we'd always been together—relaxed, teasing, comfortable. The worst part of making that leap, of course, was that, much like those pop-up spikes at the entrance of a parking garage, it was a boundary you couldn't go back across without incurring irreparable damage.

January gave the woman a bashful smile and introduced me. "Carol, this is Flynn—my boyfriend."

"*It's very nice to meet you,*" *Carol said with a maternal air. "January is one of our favorite volunteers. It's such a blessing to see a young person who exhibits genuine care about the less fortunate!*"

Carol sighed rapturously at the end of this tribute to my girlfriend's sterling character, and January made a surreptitious face at me that I understood implicitly. It said: "Carol is harmless, if seriously corny and also maybe just a little bit crazy."

Volunteering at the Huron Street Homeless Shelter hadn't exactly been on January's summer vacation bucket list; rather, it was yet another decision that had been made on her behalf, and enforced, by Jonathan Walker. Once a week at the shelter and once a week at the Red Cross, the noticeably selfless commitment of her time to

Important Causes was guaranteed to be described in the most admiring of tones by journalists writing profiles of the aspiring U.S. senator's model family. The philanthropic activities actually appealed to my good-hearted girlfriend, but not even the threat of a face-first trip through a chipper shredder could have compelled her to admit as much to her parents.

"I'm almost ready to go," she told me, "but I still need to sign out and stuff. You want to wait out there?"

She gestured in the direction of the lobby, and I gave an affable shrug in reply. Knowing January, it would take a lot longer than she made it sound, but I'd be happy to hang out in the AC for as long as possible. Before I could take a step toward the hallway, however, the general peace in the room was interrupted by an angry shout that rose up from a table in a near corner.

Two men had lunged to their feet, chairs scraping across the floor and dishes scattering, and they squared off with rage-filled eyes. Before I even knew what the conflict was about, it had already escalated; one guy landed a blow on his opponent's nose, bringing forth a jet of blood that painted the man's graying beard a vivid scarlet, and the would-be victim immediately retaliated with an attempt at strangling his attacker. It all happened so quickly that we'd barely had a chance to react before the two men lurched abruptly in our direction, careening off tables and other diners like a runaway semi, a dangerous and uncontrolled burst of violence that promised a ton of collateral damage.

I was just starting to move, aiming to get in front of January, when she darted past me and in the next instant placed herself directly between the two furious combatants. Her expression calm and her voice low, she gently pushed them apart, forcing them to acknowledge her. Their chests heaving, they stared daggers at each other over her head, but as January continued speaking, the destructive energy that had erupted with such abruptness began to dissipate just as quickly. Other volunteers rushed in then, converging on the scene urgently if already too late, and led the two angry pugilists away from each other.

January sauntered back over to me, giving her hair a casual toss, acting like someone who'd just finished sorting out a mildly frustrating paper jam in the printer rather than stopping an honest-to-goodness bum fight in its tracks. I goggled at her, impressed. "I can't believe you just did that."

"Somebody had to, and I was the closest," she said with a verbal shrug, as if it were really that simple.

"They were huge and trying to kill each other," I pointed out. "They were, like, four times your size—you could've been stomped into the linoleum!"

"Please, me and the girls could've taken 'em easy," she blustered jokingly, flexing her biceps so I could see which girls she meant. "Fear is for suckers!"

"Seriously, though." I couldn't quite let the subject go. I was still worried about her safety, even in retrospect, and wanted her to admit she'd been reckless. "You can't honestly pretend that you weren't a little bit scared."

January gave me a bemused look that might or might not have been genuine, a knowing glint flickering in the depths of her placid blue eyes. "Flynn, haven't you figured it out by now? I'm not scared of anything."

The next day at school I learned that Wilkerson and Moses had wasted no time in following up on the names I'd given them: At least five of January's closest friends came up to me in the halls to tell me they'd received visits from the cops the night before. None of them knew anything, just as I'd surmised, and most of them tried to pump me for more information. The only person I'd held out any real hope of January's having confided in was Tiana Hughes, her best friend and—not coincidentally— Micah's girlfriend.

I caught Tiana at her locker after first period, where she was trying to fix the hinge on a heart-shaped locket that Micah had given her for their two-month anniversary the previous summer. She seemed to sense my arrival because, without even looking up from what she was doing, she groused, "This fucking heart keeps breaking and it's starting to make me homicidal."

"I hope that's no reflection on the state of your relationship," I said, and she smirked.

"Please. It'll take way more than Micah's questionable taste in jewelry to drive us apart," Tiana said, "although you might want to tell him, for future reference, that just because something's an antique doesn't mean it isn't also a piece of crap." Giving up, she tossed the necklace into her locker and slammed the door shut. Then she turned to face me for the first time, her brown eyes wide and frank. "Dude."

With just that one word, I knew the cops had spoken to her as well. Without any real hope, I asked, "You don't happen to know where she is, do you?"

"No." Tiana tossed her hands up and let them drop to her sides. "Do you?" When I shook my head, she bit her lip, looked away, and then met my eyes again, her brow furrowed worriedly. "Flynn . . . how freaked should I be here? Honestly."

The fact that she even had to ask sort of upped the Freak-Out

Quotient automatically for me. "The cops told me they think she's probably, like, hiding out somewhere, trying to scare Tammy and Jonathan. I mean, it kinda sounds like her, doesn't it?" I received a noncommittal hitch of one shoulder from Tiana, and continued, meekly, "I thought maybe she might've talked about it with you."

"She didn't, or I'd have told her it was a stupid-ass idea," Tiana replied in a level tone, and she was clearly being honest. The girl was not exactly known for keeping her opinions to herself for the sake of diplomacy.

"When *is* the last time you talked to her?"

Shifting her weight unhappily, Tiana made a strange face. "I don't know. Maybe a couple of weeks ago?"

"What, did your iPhones melt down from overuse or something?" I asked, only half kidding. January and Tiana sort of famously couldn't last five whole minutes without one of them texting the other; January once drowned a phone in the shower because she was trying to write Tiana something she'd forgotten to tell her when they'd been Skyping ten minutes previously. "I thought you guys talked, like, constantly!"

Tiana shifted again, and her strange expression became more pronounced, a mingling of unhappiness, embarrassment, and vulnerability. I had never seen Tiana—a girl who once chased a guy built like a linebacker across a Burger King parking lot, loudly and publicly denouncing him as a dick for knocking the cup of change out of a homeless man's hand—look the least bit vulnerable. "Actually, Flynn, she's kind of been . . . I don't know, icing me out lately."

"Did you guys have a fight or something?"

"No!" Tiana looked up at me, puzzled, more worried lines

appearing on her forehead. "That's just it! I . . . Flynn, did she say anything to you? Did I . . . do something to piss her off?"

"Not that I know of, but . . . to be honest, she's kind of been shutting me out, too. It's like, we would text for a bit, but then she'd blow me off whenever we'd try to make plans."

"Same here." Tiana slumped against her locker, her dark hair falling into her face. She brushed it back with fingertips painted a lilac hue that contrasted against her flawless sienna skin. "I mean, at the beginning of the year we made this huge pact that things would be exactly like always, that even though we were going to different schools, we would still talk all the time and that nothing would change. But, I don't know . . . it's hard to keep that up sometimes. It's one thing when you're just hanging out at rehearsals or whatever and talking shit, but it's another to write texts while you're supposed to be paying attention to other things. I guess I got lazy and sort of let things drift a bit."

"I can relate," I admitted.

"But for, like, the last few weeks or something, it's like she's barely bothered to respond to any of my messages. I was worried that maybe she was pissed at me." Tiana was looking at me with a doubtful expression. "It's weird, because Jan's the kind of girl who tells you to your face when you've crossed the line, you know? But she never said anything to me. Never even called me out for dropping the ball on our pact. I was always getting into it with her dipshit stepbrother, and for a while I thought maybe he'd gone crying to Mr. Walker and had me put on the Do Not Fly list, but Jan wouldn't have put up with that. So I don't get it."

"Me neither," I mumbled.

Tiana gave a nervous laugh. "I guess I also kinda worried that maybe she was starting to go native over there at Dumbass. You know? Like, she was spending all day rubbing designer elbows with her new rich-bitch classmates, and maybe it went to her head. Like suddenly I wasn't good enough for her anymore."

"I don't believe that," I said comfortingly. I couldn't think of a single nice thing January had ever said about her "rich-bitch classmates" that would lead me to believe she'd decided to cross over to the dark side, even if Jonathan Walker had forced her to socialize with them from time to time. "But while we're on the subject, what do you know about the people she hung out with at Dumbass?"

"Jackshit," Tiana answered promptly. "I know Mr. Walker forced her to go to some parties, but she never actually liked the chicks that threw them. I guess she *might* have made some friends over there once she joined the drama club?" Tiana's tone was skeptical. "I mean, she spent hours every single day after school hanging out with the same group of people, and she mentioned a few of them to me more than once, but that's about it."

"Who were the people she mentioned, specifically?" I was genuinely curious. January had never told me much about the drama club, except to say that the actors sucked, their play was incomprehensible, and the drama coach was a freak.

Tiana made a helpless gesture. "I don't know any of their real names, because she always used nicknames that she'd made up. Like, at the first meeting January went to, she texted me that this one girl was wearing a sparkly crop top that was apparently straight out of an eighties music video, so she called her Sparkles. It just kind of stuck, and after that, every time she talked about this girl she was just 'Sparkles.' 'Sparkles wants to know if Jonathan is hiring interns for his senate campaign,' and 'I wrote the quadratic formula on the back of my hand in math, and Sparkles literally just asked me if it was a tattoo.' Stuff like that."

"Sparkles," I repeated with deflating hopes. There went my plan to scrounge up new leads for the Missing Persons Unit.

"Yeah. I remember Sparkles for sure, and there was also Pube-stache, Pink, and FBA."

"FBA?" I asked, not caring for an explanation of "Pube-stache."

"Fake British Accent. Like, this bitch apparently lived in London for a year when she was twelve, and pretends it permanently made her sound like Kate Middleton or some shit."

Great. I could tell Detectives Moses and Wilkerson to head to Dumas and round up Sparkles, Pink, Pube-stache, and Fake British Accent. January would be home again by bedtime.

The bell rang for class, and the hall started pulsing with activity, people streaming in both directions while Tiana and I stayed right where we were.

Warily, I looked at Micah's girlfriend, my girlfriend's best friend, and watched her eye the passing crowd. I'd had no idea a rift had formed between her and January. I'd always thought of them as scary-close—the kind of close where I would tell January something in confidence and then hear it repeated back to me out of Tiana's mouth. It always made me wonder if January had told Tiana she suspected that I might be gay. Almost undoubtedly she had, which meant that, by extension, Micah had almost undoubtedly heard about it, too.

The three of them were closer to me than anyone on the planet, outside of my actual family, and for a moment my face burned and my heart twisted as I thought of them gossiping about me behind my back.

Over the rush of chaotic foot traffic, I finally asked, "Ti, what do *you* think happened to January?"

She didn't answer me right away—she didn't even *look* at me right away—and I felt a weird thrumming start up in the pit of my stomach. I wanted her to tell me not to worry, that it was no big deal, but her silence stretched out, unnervingly. Finally, Tiana sighed. "I don't know, dude. I want to believe she disappeared on purpose, and that everything's okay, but . . . I can't stop thinking about how rich her stepdad is. I mean, guy's *money* has money. That freaking palace they live in isn't even the biggest house he owns!"

"You think she was kidnapped?" Even though I'd thought of it already, it sounded almost surreal spoken out loud, a plot point from a soap opera, and I didn't like the way it made my palms feel cool and slippery. "The police didn't say anything about a ransom note, though."

"Maybe there hasn't been one," Tiana said, as if it were a significant point. "Don't forget her stepdad is probably on his way to Washington. People might want things from him that aren't money, and maybe he doesn't want the police to know what those things are."

"You think it might be political?"

"Maybe. I don't know. I don't know what I think." She looked like she did know what she thought, however, because her expression was even bleaker than it had been a minute earlier. Just then, the second bell rang, and Tiana straightened up, grabbing her bag from the floor. "I gotta get to class. Let me know if you hear anything, okay?"

"Sure, yeah," I answered mechanically as Tiana started down the emptying corridor, but I was distracted, thinking. January's classmates at Dumas came from families that Jonathan Walker had been eager to exploit for political gain; couldn't that street run both ways? As far as I knew, January had last been seen at school. An adult might have offered her a ride home on Tuesday, and then made demands of Walker after the police had already been called. . . .

I was so lost in thought that I didn't realize Tiana had doubled back until I turned and almost ran right into her. Her mouth tensed and her eyes troubled, she blurted, "Look, I didn't want to say this before, but you asked what I think happened to January, and the truth is . . . Flynn, there was something going on that she wouldn't tell me about, I know it. I could feel it in the way she responded to my texts. The way she *didn't* respond. She was keeping something from me. If she ran away, maybe she had a reason. And if she didn't . . . I think something *bad* happened." Tiana was shaking now, her voice a whisper. "And I have this awful feeling that . . . that we're never going to see January again. That she's just . . . gone."

And with that, Tiana turned and fled down the hallway.

FIVE

I SPENT THE rest of the day with Tiana's words ringing ominously in my ears, even while I tried not to let them get to me. I couldn't just give up and believe that January was never coming back. Like the cops, Ti had avoided using the M word—*murder*—but I knew she must have been thinking it. Kidnapping only ends one of two ways. I was still convinced that January had run away to freak out her parents, and that she hadn't bothered to let Ti and me in on the plan for two very good reasons: First, we would have spoiled it by telling the police, and second, she had obviously not felt like confiding much of anything in either of us lately.

I told myself this over and over, and by the time my mom was clearing dinner from the table, I had started to believe it. I met Micah at the skate park after, where we spent a couple of hours working on kickflips in relative silence. Micah had perfected his ollie the previous summer, and even though mine was still only about sixty-forty, my pride forbade me from letting him move on ahead without me. As a result, I spent more time rolling around on my ass than I did on my board, but the pain felt good in an elemental way.

The dark, portentous mood that had been gripping me all day refused to release its hold, though, even after Micah and I split the last of the weed that had been stashed in my desk. We ate Doritos to cover the smell, called it a night, and went home. My mom was still up when I walked in, sitting in the living room and flipping channels on the TV, and we had a short conversation while I rooted through the fridge for leftovers. I was too impatient to reheat stuff, but I'd discovered that almost anything can be eaten cold if you're open-minded enough. As I loaded a plate with chicken, potatoes, and macaroni that clung together in a congealed lump, my mom prattled on about "the decline of Western civilization," which meant she'd watched an episode of *Real Housewives*.

Finally, as I tried to leave the kitchen with my munchies, she moved in for the kill. I had a plate in one hand and a glass of water in the other, and no way to ward her off. She hugged me, hard, pressing her face into my hair for a long, awkward moment, and I tried to will any lingering trace of pot smoke to retreat into my scalp. If she smelled anything, though, she didn't mention it. Instead, she pulled back, looked me in the eye, and said, "I love you, Flynn."

"I love you, too, Mom," I mumbled. It's not like I was uncomfortable with the sentiment, but the way she was looking at me—like one of us was about to be dragged away by armed guards—made me feel a little put on the spot.

"I don't know what I would do if something happened to you."

Oh. "Nothing will, okay?"

"I'm sure Tammy thought the same thing," my mom said quietly, and then face-palmed herself. "I'm sorry, that was a low blow. I just . . . you hear about a thing like this and it turns you into . . . I don't know, a crazy person. The kind of hand-wringing helicopter parent you always swore you would never be." She sighed and rubbed her eyes. "Just . . . promise me you'll always be careful, okay?"

"I promise."

"Don't just say that to humor me, smart-ass." My mom gave me a shrewd look. "Promise me."

"Okay, I *promise*," I muttered again.

She didn't let me go. She was looking at me super seriously now. "You can tell me anything, Flynn. You know that. You're my son, and I will always love you and support you, no matter what. You know that, right?"

My breath caught, and I could feel the paranoid mayhem of nerves shimmering through my high. *Was she talking about what I thought she was talking about?* I squeaked out some kind of acknowledgment, and then rushed ahead before she could continue, "I really wanna go up and change my clothes, okay?"

"Okay, okay," my mom allowed, stepping back. "Just don't leave your dirty dishes in your room this time? You don't even have to wash them yourself, that's why we have that expensive machine." She gestured to the dishwasher while I sidled quickly for the hall leading to the foyer. I made it halfway before she called out, "Oh, and by the way, Flynn? If you're going to smoke pot, just *please* don't do it somewhere you could be arrested, okay?"

When I got up to my room, I texted Micah immediately about getting busted for the weed. I knew I hadn't heard the last of it from my parents, but I was hopeful that the punishment wouldn't be too draconian; Will and Kate Doherty were hugely pro-marijuana types, and there was a chance I'd get off with just a slap on the wrist. Still, I wanted to share the panic sweat with Micah a little bit.

I scarfed down my food while watching an episode of *It's Always Sunny in Philadelphia* online, checked Facebook, jerked off, and went to bed. That last step usually knocks me out, but that night, I couldn't get to sleep. Once again, January hovered in my thoughts, crowding her way into every corner of my brain like a catchy pop song, until I finally gave up and turned my attention fully to her.

Someone out there knew *something*. January hadn't been vaporized, or abducted by aliens or whatever—but who could I ask if not her friends? If her old clique at Riverside knew nothing, and I knew nothing about her associations at Dumas, who else was there for me to turn to?

And then it hit me: *Kaz*. Fucking Kaz. A freshman at the University of Michigan, Kaz was eighteen, gorgeous, and apparently right about every fucking thing he ever said. That's all I knew about him, and every bit of it was secondhand information from January, since I'd never set eyes on the guy myself. They'd met when he started working at the same downtown toy store where January had been employed part-time since the eighth grade, and from his very first day on the job I had heard stories about him.

"Kaz is soooo *cute! Girls are* always *coming into the store just to flirt with him, which is actually totally annoying because they never buy anything. He usually has to pretend that I'm his girlfriend, just to make them leave. Isn't that hilarious?"*

Yeah. *Super* hilarious. The stories were more pointed whenever January and I had been arguing. Like the time she'd bailed on a concert we'd been looking forward to for months, because Tiana's family was going to Chicago for the weekend and they'd unexpectedly invited her along.

"It's just a concert, Flynn! I can't believe how immature you're acting," she'd snapped. "You know, Kaz was right—I really should be dating an older guy."

Gee, I wonder if he might have had a particular "older guy" in mind?

"Kaz thinks we're going to break up," she'd announced on another occasion, completely out of the blue. "He says it's really hard to maintain a relationship when you can't see each other regularly, and since I'll be going to Dumas and you'll be staying at Riverside, we probably won't last."

Like, what the fuck was I supposed to say to *that*? That little pronouncement had come right at the time I was starting to realize that the all-important hot-sexy-time feelings I was supposed to have for my girlfriend were simply never going to develop—right at the time that I was beginning to really worry that I would never develop hot-sexy-time feelings for *any* girl—and I didn't react too well.

"Are you refusing to sex me because you have a micropenis? Kaz said that the reason you don't want to sex me is because you probably have a micropenis."

Okay, so the last one was paraphrased, but you can see why I disliked this guy whom I had never actually met. Even if I wasn't the most satisfying boyfriend in the world, I was *still* January's boyfriend, and it drove me insane that she'd take self-serving and manipulative advice from a dude who clearly had a thing for her, and that she used his words as a bludgeon whenever we argued. She was constantly reminding me that he was in her life, an enigma who was smart, cute, and supportive; an eager Prince Charming in the wings, ready and waiting to sweep her off her feet the second I screwed up. The fact that this dude was just trying to get into her pants was completely obvious, but January always became totally offended if I so much as suggested it.

The anecdote Detective Moses had shared with my mother came back to me as I lay there and stared at the moonlight angling across my feet: *A boy about Flynn's age got in a fight with his parents, took the car, and vanished. The East Lansing police found him a week later, sleeping on the floor of a friend's dorm room at Michigan State.* Sub Michigan for Michigan State, and maybe I'd just divined the solution to January's disappearance. Kaz was just the kind of douchewaffle who would encourage a high school sophomore to crash at his place for a week to teach her parents a lesson. *Nah, it's totally cool, babe! You can sleep in my bed, and I'll take the floor! Unless, like, it gets cold or something and you need a snuggle buddy. Did I mention the heater's broken?*

It wasn't until I resolved to track down Kaz and choke some answers out of him that I was finally able to drift off to sleep.

SIX

THE NEXT MORNING, I was treated to a pot lecture from my parents. It was awkward. They'd both campaigned pretty actively for the legalization of medicinal marijuana in Michigan, and they openly recognized that the situation with January's disappearance was a mitigating factor in my transgression, but they couldn't just let me get away with it. Ultimately, they said a lot about "respecting the law," and my punishment was a suspended sentence: If I did "community service" in the form of raking the yard and helping Mom with dinner, and I didn't get into any trouble of any kind for at least a month, they were going to let me off the hook *this time*.

After that, my mom dropped me off downtown with my skateboard, and I told her I'd take the bus home—a sword I was only willing to throw myself on for the sake of my missing girlfriend—in time to help with dinner. As soon as she drove off, I made my way to Old Mother Hubbard's, the toy store where January worked. Housed in one of the numerous nineteenth-century brick buildings on Fourth Avenue and just a couple of blocks from the municipal complex that functioned as Ann Arbor's civic center, the place was independently owned—which meant the prices were ridiculously high. Ergo, it was only a fierce commitment to buying local, on behalf of the city's fiercely loyal inhabitants, that kept the store in business.

Or so I was told. January had forbade me from visiting her at work, and I had no other excuse for going to a toy store, so I had never been inside. But I did know that she worked eight-hour shifts every Saturday and Sunday, as well as occasional weeknights after rehearsals.

The front window was cheerfully decorated for the holiday with cutesy jack-o'-lanterns and stuffed animals dressed like mummies, witches, and vampires, all gathered around a pyramid of Old Mother Hubbard's "spookiest" toys and children's books. A bell jingled as I pushed through the door, leaving the chilly outside and entering the oddly sterile inside. The place smelled antiseptic, like a new car, and the displays of shining, pristine toys ranged around the room seemed somehow uninviting, very *look but don't touch*. There was only one other person in the store besides me, an employee, and he was probably the hottest guy I had ever seen in person.

Lanky and square-jawed, his hair a carefully arranged crown of messy black spikes, he had at least five inches on me. Veins bulged like ropes under the olive skin of his obnoxiously toned arms, and the douchey-fratty lavender polo shirt he was wearing only made his startling hazel eyes even more striking. He was just about my age, not that it meant much. Pigs can live to be like twenty or so, but put one next to a male model who's *also* twenty or so, and the accomplishment begins to look less and less impressive.

In this particular analogy, in case you hadn't figured it out, I was the pig. And the male model who was smiling at me with

teeth that gleamed like a freshly whitewashed picket fence—
I was sure even before I saw the letters on his official employee
name tag—was Fucking Kaz.

"Hey, man, can I help you with something?" His cheekbones
were sharp enough to cut glass, and for a moment I had to
remind myself that I hated him.

"Yeah," I answered curtly, "I'm looking for January."

His smile dimmed a little. "She's not here."

"I know that," I returned, even more curtly. "I'm asking if
you know where she is."

His smile vanished completely. "Why would I know something like that?"

"You guys are pretty close, aren't you?" I couldn't stop it
from coming out as an accusation. Everything about this guy
bugged me, from his perfect face and body to his habit of
inserting himself in other people's business, and I had to work
to keep my temper under control. "I figured maybe she told
you where she went."

"Who are you?" he asked, crossing his arms over his annoyingly defined chest.

"Flynn."

"Oh. The *boyfriend*." His voice dripped with contempt, and
I felt my body temperature starting to rise.

"Yeah, I'm her *boyfriend*," I snapped, "and I'm worried about
her. So if you know where she is, just tell me, okay?"

His almond-shaped eyes narrowed, and one corner of his
mouth tugged upward. "If January's trying to duck you, she's
got her reasons, so what makes you think I'd rat her out?"

"Maybe I'm counting on you being at least half as smart as
you've been telling my girlfriend you are, and you'll figure out

that I'm being fucking serious here." I tried to stare him down, but it's hard to intimidate a guy who stands nearly half a foot taller than you.

Kaz actually laughed at me. "Get a load of you, the high school badass! You can't push your girlfriend around, so instead you come in here to push *me* around." He spread his arms out, and I could see the edge of a tattoo peeking out from under his sleeve. "Sorry, but the Skinny Little Tough Guy act doesn't really do it for me."

I was so surprised I just stared at him for a moment. "What the hell are you talking about?"

"I'm saying that if January's avoiding you, then good for her. She should've done it a long time ago."

His tone was filled with genuine distaste, and I just stood there, openmouthed, for what felt like about a year. Finally, I managed to reply, "You don't know dick about me! What the hell is your problem, dude?"

"My 'problem'? How about the fact that I've spent two months listening to January complain about what a shitty boy-friend you are? About how you make her feel unattractive, how you guilt-tripped her for having to go to a different school than you, how you make fun of all her new friends—"

"*What. The hell. Are you talking about?*" The things he was saying were so absurd that, for a moment, I was sure there'd been some kind of mistake; I'd walked into the wrong toy store, found the wrong Kaz, and was discussing the wrong January.

I was forced to admit that, in retrospect, maybe my unusu-ally strong aversion to even the PG-13-rated physical aspects of our relationship might not have had the most positive effect on January's self-esteem; but I *always* told her she was pretty, and I never once let her get away with calling herself basic or ugly or any of the other insults she hurled at her reflection. And as for making her feel bad about going to Dumas, *I* was the guy who'd held her hand for an hour while she cried, promising her that she would rule that snooty prep school like a dictator by the end of her sophomore year. The only snappy comeback that sputtered out of my mouth now, however, was, "I've never even met her 'friends' at Dumas—how could I possibly make fun of them?"

"I don't know, but I guess you found a way. She said you called them all 'spoiled, rich brats with disposable ponies' or something." Kaz glared at me. "Do you have any idea how that made her feel? Like she couldn't make any new friends because you'd hate them and think she was a sellout! You've got a chip on your shoulder about rich kids, and she *is* one now. It made her feel like absolute shit!"

I blinked in astonishment, the attack on my character landing like a barrage of grenades as I recalled the only exchange to which Kaz could possibly be referring.

"You have no idea what these bitches are like, Flynn," January had huffed incredulously after her first day at Dumas. She'd texted me during every break throughout the afternoon, giving me a progress report on her growing hatred for her new school and everyone in it, jokingly threatening to kill herself in increasingly elaborate ways to get out of having to go to her next class. Mimicking a blue-blooded accent, she whined, " 'Mummy bought me the Lambo in eggshell instead of cream, like, why is she trying to ruin my life? I am totally gonna go Menendez on her!' "

Laughing, I'd echoed her accent, replying with, " 'Papaw, my pony got dirty and I had to get rid of it—I need a new one!' "

How had that gotten twisted into me making January feel bad by deriding her so-called new friends? I'd been *commiserating* with her, for fuck's sake!

"Look, not that my relationship with January is at all your business, but I didn't do any of those things you said!" I seethed. "And if you've talked her into believing I did, then you're an even bigger asshole than I thought!"

"*I'm* the asshole?" It was Kaz's turn to be incredulous, his impossibly long black eyelashes fluttering dramatically.

"Yeah! Telling her she should break up with me because we weren't going to the same school anymore, telling her she should be dating an 'older' guy—like *that* isn't a fucking obvious douche move—and telling her that I probably have a *tiny dick*? Yeah! You're the asshole!"

To my satisfaction, that little counteroffensive took some of the wind out of his sails. Kaz's eyes widened and his lips parted just a little, his expression morphing from scorn into something like surprise. "Hey, look, I—"

"You know what? I don't even care. January already broke up with me, so I guess you got what you wanted. If she honestly thinks I was a shitty boyfriend all this time, and she's trying to punish me by disappearing, well, you can tell her she's succeeded and she can stop it." I was so worked up I was almost tripping over my words, seeing Kaz through a red haze of anger, and I could feel my throat tightening. *Great.* That's what I really needed: to start crying in front of Fucking Kaz. "And while you're at it, remind her that she's punishing a bunch of people who don't deserve it, too. Her parents are worried, *my* parents are worried, Tiana is completely freaking out, and now the police are involved, so wheth—"

"Waitwaitwait," Kaz interrupted, throwing his hands up, his eyes wide. "What do you mean 'the police'? What are you talking about?"

"I'm talking about the fact that January has been missing for three days and we've all been shitting our pants!" Swinging around to march out, to exit on a strong note, I snapped over my shoulder, "She's made her point, okay? And so have you. I hope you guys are real happy together."

It wasn't a very sincere wish. I actually kind of hoped that at the very least, Kaz got mowed down by a fire truck. I was halfway to the door before I felt his hand on my upper arm. "Wait a minute!" he implored, and this time he looked genuinely stunned. "What do you mean she's missing?"

"I mean she didn't come home from school on Tuesday and no one knows where she is." I gave him a pointed look. "At least, no one who's said anything."

He stepped back. "You think *I* know something?"

"Don't you?" I challenged bitterly. "You're her big confidant, the one giving her tons of relationship advice and apparently making her think that disappearing to get away from me was something she should've done 'a long time ago.'"

"I didn't—" He checked himself. "That's not what I meant by that."

He looked shaken, and even though his alarm didn't seem to be an act, I was feeling vengeful and didn't want to believe in it. "She's still a minor, you know, and if you're helping her hide, that's, like, aiding and abetting or something."

"I'm not," he said, quickly and convincingly. "I don't know where she is, man, I swear. I don't know anything about this!"

He looked me straight in the eye when he said it, and so help me, I believed him. Just like that, another crack spread across the already fragmenting surface of my hope that January was okay somewhere. I hadn't wanted to find out she was shacking up with Kaz, but I also realized that in a perverse way, I'd kind of been hoping for it, too. It would have meant that she was technically safe, it would have meant that the mystery was officially over, and it would have meant I was entitled to a little righteous anger rather than just confusion and guilt and fear.

"She didn't tell you she was planning to run away or anything?" I asked.

Kaz shook his head emphatically. "Is that what they think happened?"

I shrugged, my gaze dropping to the shallow vee of his polo shirt's open collar, to the little U-shaped dip where his collarbones met. His earnest concern was making me feel awkward; I wasn't ready to be nice yet, to have a serious and sympathetic conversation with him about January's disappearance. "They don't know. She didn't leave a note, or anything. I thought maybe . . . Did she call in today?"

It occurred to me for the first time, right then, that if January had planned her disappearance in advance—and intended to come back—she might have requested the time off from work so that her position would be waiting for her when she returned. Of course, she didn't need the money anymore, now that she was rich; gone were the days when Tammy couldn't afford to buy January anything that wasn't on clearance. But that wasn't the point. When she'd been forcibly enrolled in Dumas, her parents had pressured her to quit Old Mother Hubbard's so she could focus exclusively on her studies, and January had flatly refused.

"I'm not going to let Jonathan Walker fucking own me!" she'd *shouted at me once, after I'd foolishly asked why she* didn't *just quit and enjoy not having to work, like anyone else in her position would do.* "Don't you get it? He already owns my house, my phone, my mom! *I'm not going to let him start bankrolling my clothes and my movie tickets and my fucking Taco Bell, too, and let him control every single part of my life. Maybe I have to live with him, but I don't have to live* for *him!"*

Frankly, it wasn't a position I totally understood. Jonathan Walker wasn't exactly a warm and jovial father figure, but he didn't seem like one of those dead-eyed, militaristic tyrants from the after-school specials, either. The truth was, sometimes January was determined to cut off her face to spite her nose.

Kaz was shaking his head, though, still looking confused. "Well, no."

"So . . . what? You didn't think that maybe there was something wrong when she just didn't show up for work today?"

"No, you don't understand," he said, waving his hands agitatedly in the air. "She didn't call in because she didn't have to. She doesn't work here anymore, man."

I blinked. "What?"

"She quit a few weeks ago. Called in sick one day, didn't show up the next, and when I asked, the owners said she wasn't coming back to work." He turned his palms up to the ceiling, bewildered. "No reason, no notice—nothing. I don't know what to tell you, man. She hasn't worked here for nearly a month now."

SEVEN

I WAS STILL staring at him. Once again, nothing he was saying made any sense. *January quit her job?* It didn't compute.

I thought back to three weeks ago, Saturday, when Tiana and some of the drama kids at Riverside had organized a hayride at one of the many apple orchards in Washtenaw County. It was kind of a hokey fall tradition, but it was also kind of a *fun* hokey fall tradition. You sat on bales of gamy-smelling hay, bumping around on dirt roads in frigid air through row after identical row of trees; you picked shit-tons of apples, drank shit-tons of cider, and ate more powdered-sugar doughnuts than the human body was designed to withstand; and then you capped it all off with a bonfire where you made s'mores and sang dumb songs and somebody distributed crappy beer or wine coolers or a flask of bottom-shelf booze they managed to smuggle in under their coat, and someone barfed. It was awesome.

I'd texted January, asking if there was any way she could take the day off and join us, and she'd answered with a single, terse line of text: *the store is shorthanded this week and they need me sorry.*

Just under two weeks ago, five days before our showdown in the barn, one of the cable channels was running an edited-for-TV horror-movie marathon—basically, one of the things January and I used to live for. I'd invited her to come over to my house after rehearsal was over so we could laugh at the dumbed-down, fake-swearworded absurdity of it all, and she'd again demurred with another impersonal text: *rehearsal then work tonight sorry but have some popcorn for me.*

If Kaz was telling the truth, and January hadn't been working those nights, then where the hell had she been? And why had she lied to me? To all of us?

"She couldn't have quit," I contradicted Kaz, examining his perfectly structured face for proof that he was mistaken. "I mean, she told me she was still working here."

"She wasn't," he answered simply.

"Well, if she quit, then she must have given *some* kind of reason," I insisted. "You don't just quit your job and not say why."

"The lady who talked to her when she called said she wouldn't explain." Kaz ran a hand through his glossy dark hair. "I mean, obviously I asked her, too, when I saw her again, but she just said it was a long story, quote-unquote. She wouldn't give me any more than that."

"What do you mean, when you saw her again? I thought you said she quit and never came back."

"I said she never came back *to work*," he corrected me, "but she still had to come to the store to pick up her final paycheck. I was here the day she and that friend of hers dropped by to get it."

"What friend?" I was flipping through my mental Rolodex of January's known associates, wondering why no one at school had bothered to mention this particular errand.

"January didn't introduce us," Kaz said with a shrug, "and

her friend barely said a word the entire time they were here. She was Asian, with bright pink hair. Sound familiar?"

"Not really," I murmured, which was mostly true. It sure didn't sound like anyone from our circle at Riverside, but the description rang a bell nevertheless.

I remember Sparkles for sure, and there was also Pube-stache, Pink, and FBA.

Pink. As nicknames went, it wasn't especially telling. Considering that a girl could be branded "Sparkles" forever after having worn a spangled top on a single occasion, "Pink" could refer to a girl who'd worn pink shoes or a pink dress, drove a pink car, or was a great big stan for Pink. Kaz seemed to believe that January had actual friends at Dumas, however, and I knew of no one at Riverside who answered to the description of an Asian girl with bright pink hair.

I pressed Kaz for more information—any information—but he wasn't able to tell me anything illuminating. After I'd asked all the questions I could think to ask and gotten all the information I thought I would get, I started for the door again. Behind me, Kaz said, "Do you really think she just ran away? That she might come back?"

Without turning around, I answered, "I don't know."

The bell jingled above my head again as Kaz called out, "If you find her, let me know, okay? I'm . . . I'm starting to get kinda worried, too."

"Yeah, sure. You're first on my list," I returned sarcastically, and the door banged shut behind me.

All that night and for the rest of the next day, Kaz's words ate at me. The way he'd talked about me, the way he'd said *January* talked about me, had left me stunned, angry, and a little shaken. The real problem was that there was a grain of uncomfortable truth at the root of each ugly accusation. I *had* made fun of the Dumas kids—of course I had—but January had done so first; ironically enough, I'd played along because I thought it would cheer her up. Hearing Kaz describe it as if I'd been psychologically abusing my girlfriend was like looking into a fun-house mirror reflection of reality, the image so distorted that it might as well have been of something else entirely.

The same went for the claim that I'd made January feel bad for going to Dumas in the first place, when in fact I'd done everything I could think of to make her feel *better* about it. Micah, Ti, and I had put together a care package for her before the school year started: pictures of the four of us she could hang in her new locker, a mix for her iPod of songs that would remind her of things we'd done together, and special ringtones of our voices she could program into her phone. I'd told her a million times how much Riverside would suck without her, how much I would miss her when she went to Dumas, but I hadn't said any of it to make her feel *guilty*; I'd done it because I thought she'd want to know that it would be hard for me, too, that I wasn't happy to see her go.

How could she have misinterpreted my actions and intentions so extremely that when she talked about them to Kaz, I came across as a selfish, manipulative jerk? Could I have really made her feel so self-conscious with my lame joke about throwaway ponies that she believed I would judge her for making friends at Dumas? Clearly she *had* made friends there, and, just as clearly, she'd kept them from me with the same ease that she'd lied about still having her job at Old Mother Hubbard's. Or was *Kaz* the manipulator? Had he talked her into seeing my actions in the worst possible light as a way to drive a wedge between us?

Either way, I was beginning to learn there were a lot of things my girlfriend had concealed from me recently, and it was making me start to wonder if I knew her anywhere near as well as I thought I had.

When January was still missing on Monday morning, the halls of Riverside decorated with fliers bearing her brightly smiling face and a plea for information, I decided I needed to track down the girl with pink hair. Something must have prompted January to quit her job, and I was determined to find out what it was. "Pink" was starting to sound like the only one who might have the answers I wanted.

Micah and I had only one friend who could drive, Mason Collier, and even though he was a total asshelmet, I had no choice but to beg him for a ride to the Dumas Academy after school. Mason was one of those guys who believed firmly in a social hierarchy predicated exclusively on athletic accomplishments, and he considered the fact that he was built like the Incredible Hulk to be a sign from God that he was meant to be at the tippy-top of the pecking order. If it weren't for the fact that I'd broken Riverside's record in the 200-meter dash for the men's JV track team the year before, I doubted Mason would even bother speaking to me.

The trip out to Dumas took only twenty minutes, but it felt like forever. Mason filled every second of the drive with a running monologue about how awesome he was and about how, if I wasn't a total faggot, I would join the snowboarding club that winter. He said it in a joking way, like he wanted me to laugh and promise to join the club in defense of my manhood, but a cold, dreadful feeling slithered out of my heart and up into my mouth nonetheless.

If and when Mason learned the truth about me, what would he say then? Would he remember this moment with embarrassment? Would everyone remember the times they'd said stuff like "that's so gay" and "don't be a fag" in my presence, and suddenly be unable to look me in the eye anymore? Would they even care how it made me feel? Just how different would my life be if the truth got out?

When Mason pulled to a stop outside the massive brick pillars that marked the entrance to the Dumas Academy, I threw five bucks at him for gas and then fled the vehicle. From the gate to the front doors of the school was nearly a quarter mile, but I enjoyed every minute of the brisk air and total silence.

For an institution with a small and highly selective number of students, Dumas turned out to be a rather enormous complex of buildings. The campus sprawled over several acres of rolling, manicured lawns, with a main building that housed the administrative offices and cafeteria, and a handful of outbuildings that contained classrooms, segregated by subject matter. The architecture was spare and modern, all glass and travertine, and a network of walkways crisscrossed the landscaped green that stretched between the various destinations. A handy map outside the main office showed me where to find the theater, and I headed off to look for it.

It was a bit of a gamble, assuming the pink-haired girl would be there when I found the place, but I didn't really have a better strategy. I knew from Tiana that January had met the girl through the drama club, and I knew from January that the play they were working on had rehearsals every day after school. It was reasonable to think the girl might still be there—and if she wasn't, someone else would be, and I could at least get her name.

The theater was in its own building, it turned out: a fancy-looking, two-story edifice with a fountain out front composed of three bronze nymphs frolicking in a birdbath. A plaque on its base honored a couple called Harmon and Eugenia Davenport, presumably for having the most upper-crusty white-people names in the history of Michigan, and I wondered how much cash they'd donated to Dumas.

I passed through an immaculate lobby of gleaming white stone and followed the sound of voices into a vast auditorium. Cushy scarlet chairs swept down a gentle grade to the apron of the stage, which was set with ornate furniture, freestanding French doors, and empty picture frames that seemed to hover in space. It was a little abstract, maybe, but it looked expensive and professional, obviously meant to suggest a sitting room in some rococo *palais* somewhere. Meanwhile, over at Riverside, the drama club was struggling to build a set for *Hamlet* out of last spring's set for *The Glass Menagerie*.

The voices I had heard were coming from a clutch of students draped over chairs at the back of the theater, gossiping excitedly with one another in an overlapping cacophony I couldn't decipher. The second they took notice of me, however, they quieted and stared, making me feel self-conscious and unwelcome. Not one of them matched the description of my quarry. Clearing my throat, I ventured, "I'm looking for an Asian girl with pink hair . . . you guys know her?"

"Reiko?" A girl in a cashmere sweater blurted the name with a confused inflection, but I couldn't tell if she was surprised I was looking for Reiko, or if she wasn't sure *which* pink-haired Asian girl I meant and had guessed one at random.

"She's probably backstage," offered a boy with an effeminate voice. His eyes probed me from head to foot, like sonar equipment searching for sunken treasure, and I mumbled an awkward thanks before heading off. He was cute, and his obvious interest in me was simultaneously exciting and unnerving.

In the end, I literally almost stumbled over Reiko. Pawing my way around a velvet curtain that extended into one of the wings, I stopped just short of crashing into a low, moth-eaten sofa on which three girls were sitting and talking. Once again, the conversation died the second I appeared, and the trio stared up in surprise. The girl in the middle had bright pink hair and black nail polish, and when she saw me, her eyes first widened and then narrowed suspiciously.

"Are you Reiko?" I asked. She nodded but said nothing, while the other two stared at me vacantly. "Um . . . can I talk to you for a minute? In private?"

For a moment, she didn't react, as if she hadn't even heard me, and then she abruptly pushed herself to her feet. Speaking to her friends, and pointedly not to me, she announced, "I'll be right back, you guys. Don't go anywhere."

Still not acknowledging me, she marched straight to a door in the wall, shoving against a crash bar and pushing it open. Bright light from the hallway beyond skewered into the dim, cavernous space of the wing. When she turned and glared at me impatiently, I finally realized I was supposed to follow her.

"What do you want?" she demanded when we were face-to-face under the bright fluorescent lights in the quiet corridor, a huge poster for the fall show looming beside us. They were doing Molière's *Le Malade imaginaire*—in the original French, of course. Dumas was so fucking pretentious.

"My name is Flynn Dohe—"

"I know who you are," she cut me off abruptly, her voice cold enough to drop birds out of the sky. "You're *the boyfriend*."

"Well . . . yeah." Why did everyone say it like that? "How do you know me?"

"Well, let's see." She cocked her head and stared up at the ceiling, making an exaggerated performance out of pretending to think. "It wasn't from any of the parties you didn't come to, and it wasn't from the charity dance you made your girlfriend go to by herself . . . oh, wait, I've got it! January showed me some pictures to prove she wasn't lying when she said she really was dating someone!"

There was so much hostility flying at me that I actually took a step back, blinking in surprise. "What are you talking about?"

"I'm saying that maybe if January ever got any real support from the people she depended on most in her life, she wouldn't have gone off like this!"

I tried to ignore the aspersion. "So you think she ran away?"

"No," she returned condescendingly, "I think she disappeared because she was so fucking happy she just *exploded*."

"Hey, could you cool it for a second with the attack-dog routine?" I was starting to lose my patience with being pilloried by people I'd never met before. "I'm here because I'm concerned about her, all right?"

"About *yourself*, you mean."

"What the hell is your problem with me?" It was déjà vu all over again as I tried to defend myself against another one of January's friends.

Reiko stabbed a finger at my chest. "You were never around for January when she needed you. *Never*. You made her go to parties full of strangers all by herself because *you* didn't want to hang out with anyone from Dumas; she was the only person at that dance without a date, and she was so miserable she could barely smile in the pictures—"

"*What dance?*" I was shouting now, my voice rebounding loudly off the tiled corridor, and Reiko flinched.

"The charity dance," she repeated stiffly, and seeing that I needed more than that, she rolled her eyes. "The dance the Dumas Philanthropic Society puts on every year?" I was still looking at her blankly, so she huffily explained, "You buy tickets to attend, and all the proceeds go to a worthy cause, and everybody gets all dressed up, and it is literally *the* biggest social event of every single fall semester, and *your girlfriend* had to go *by herself* because you 'don't do dances'!"

She delivered the last bit with a remarkable amount of mocking sarcasm, and I assumed it to be a direct citation. It took me a moment to answer her, though, because the words conjured up no memories whatsoever. No conversation January and I had ever had came back to me at that prompt. Mystified, I put up my hands. "I may not be crazy about dances, but I would've gone if January had asked me. This is the first I'm even hearing about it."

"She said she *did* ask you, and you told her you weren't interested."

"She never invited me to anything at Dumas," I insisted. I don't know why, but all of a sudden it was really important to me that I repair my image in the eyes of this girl. "She told me that *she* didn't even want to go to those things, that her stepdad forced her, so why would she make me go with her? I mean, when even *was* this 'big dance'?"

Reiko was staring at me with naked suspicion, but she grudgingly answered the question. "Three weeks ago, Saturday."

"The day you picked up January's final paycheck together." I lifted a brow.

The girl shrugged uncomfortably. "Yeah. She wanted someone to go with her. I told her it was a bad idea to quit her job, but she wouldn't listen to me."

"Why did she quit?"

"I don't know. Maybe because of you," she shot back, her expression once more frigid and hard as an iceberg.

"Boy, I sure can't wait to hear where you're going with this."

"Well, you made her quit the play, so who knows what else you made her—"

"What do you mean she quit the play?" My head was starting to spin. It was like we were speaking two different languages that only sounded sort of similar. "She's been going to these rehearsals every day after school since almost the beginning of the year!"

Reiko cocked her head and stared at me like I was the crazy one. "No, she quit after the dance. She said you were giving her all this crap about how she was always busy with school stuff, and how she wasn't spending enough time with you! Once again, your great, big whiny needs came before—"

"I didn't say jackshit to her about the play, or about any of her other time commitments," I exclaimed heatedly, "and if she quit, she never told me anything about it! Two weeks ago, she was still blowing me off for rehearsals!"

Reiko was adamant. "No. No! She quit *for you*. We had plans for the Saturday before last, and January blew *me* off because *you* needed her to come watch you pop a wheelie on your skateboard or some dumbass thing like that."

"I've barely seen January since September, and ten days ago, she dumped me! So we didn't do *anything* together that Saturday," I declared firmly, deciding not to correct Reiko's egregious misunderstanding of what one does on a skateboard.

"She broke up with you?" The girl made a face. My announcement had disrupted the momentum of our argument, and for a long moment we just eyed each other in wary silence. Finally, Reiko ended the standoff with a noise somewhere between a sigh and a snort, her anger seeming to subside into irritable pensiveness. "Wow. So maybe she was planning it all along."

"Planning what?" I asked, bewildered, and Reiko huffed like I was an idiot.

"To run away!" She thrust both hands into the air, as if to say *Ta-da!* "January quit her job, she dropped out of the drama club, she broke up with your sorry ass . . . I mean, it kinda sounds like she was cutting all her ties, doesn't it?"

When she put it that way, that kind of *was* what it sounded like . . . but I wasn't sure it constituted proof beyond reasonable doubt. "Why, though? I get that she was unhappy, I even get that I wasn't always a great boyfriend, but January was a fighter, not a quitter. Something must have happened to make her do all this stuff—bail on her friends and her job and the play, and then lie about it all. What?"

Reiko's mouth twisted up in a frown, and her eyes wouldn't quite meet mine. A few seconds too late to sound convincing, she muttered, "I don't know."

I tensed. "Reiko? What happened?"

"There's nothing I can tell you," she returned evasively.

"What does that mean?" I demanded. "If you know something that might help the police figure out what happened to her, you have to say something."

"I *can't*—there are *rules*!" she shouted, and then clamped her lips together as if she'd just said something she shouldn't have.

"What are you talking about? What rules?"

Reiko dragged her hands through her hair, turned to leave, and then swung back around. "Look, January was surrounded by people who always let her down, and I won't turn into one of them. Anything I know, she told me in absolute confidence, and I will not betray that. If she doesn't want to be found, I'm sure as hell not going to drop a dime on her—and I'm also not about to blab her secrets to people she didn't trust with them!"

Turning her back on me once again, Reiko yanked open the backstage door and disappeared into the darkness of the stage-right wing. The door slammed shut behind her, and when the ripples of the echo had died away, I was left with one frightening question to which I would get no answer: *But what if January hadn't run away after all?*

EIGHT

IT WASN'T AN easy night. Reiko seemed to have been convinced that my ex-girlfriend was a runaway, but the point she'd made about January having cut all her ties wasn't particularly comforting. That kind of tidying up of loose ends was the sort of thing people did when they were preparing to shuffle off the old mortal coil—and hadn't that been the very first conclusion the detectives had implied when they'd come to my house? I still wanted to believe January had run away, but I didn't know what to think anymore. Things I'd thought I'd known about my girlfriend were suddenly coming into question, and it was making me insecure.

I didn't know how to process what I'd learned over the past few days, and the worst part was that I couldn't even confront January for an explanation. Why had she said I was never there for her, when the truth was that *she* had been the one pulling away from me? *I'm also not about to blab her secrets to people she didn't trust with them!* What did January feel she couldn't trust me with? Aside from the one significant issue in our relationship, what had I ever done to make her feel that she couldn't count on me?

She was one of the most important people in my life and had been since the start of freshman year; even if I'd bungled things by hoping I could make a romance work between us—and by panicking when I started to realize I couldn't—I still loved her in a very real way. I still wanted to be someone she could count on. Why hadn't she? And what else didn't I know about her?

On Tuesday morning, with January gone for almost a week, my mom called the school office and told them I would be out that day. A volunteer search party had been organized to comb the fields and wilderness that abounded in Superior Charter Township, and I had argued with my parents until they agreed to let me take part. A couple of church groups had spent the weekend tramping through the woods surrounding Dumas, the police had covertly dragged sections of the Huron River—the waterway that coiled through the center of town—and university students had canvased the Arb, a 123-acre arboretum near the center of campus. Not a trace of my ex-girlfriend had been found.

I had a lot of unresolved feelings about January—guilt, of course, and now a growing amount of confusion and anger as I learned of the way she had portrayed me to people who had nothing else to believe but her word—but the truth was that I missed her. I missed the nights we spent sharing popcorn and ice cream while watching old movies; I missed the IMs we sent back and forth nonstop during our conveniently simultaneous computer labs; and I missed the way she always had the perfect quip on the end of her tongue, an ability to skewer a moment so accurately that you couldn't believe it hadn't been scripted. I missed my best friend.

Even if January did return out of the blue, I knew we couldn't go back to the way things once were—but I couldn't just let things end the way they had, either. At the very least, I needed her to know that I was sorry about that stupid fight, about any hurt I'd caused her because I wasn't able to be honest with myself about what I really wanted. *Then* we could get into the issue of *her* dishonesty.

On his way to work, my dad dropped me off at January's new house. A gigantic campaign sign reading WALKER FOR SENATE greeted us as we left the road and made our way down a long, curving drive that wended through topiary on its way to the hopeful candidate's five-car garage. My ex-girlfriend's home was a colossal mansion of brick and stone, with four gables, three chimneys, and two enormous second-floor balconies. The elevated porch, complete with a low rail of carved stone, bowed gently to echo the shape of a massive fountain-slash-koi pond in the front courtyard. Harmon and Eugenia Davenport would have eaten their hearts out.

An impressive group of people had already gathered outside, including at least one TV news crew, and as I joined the crowd I looked around for familiar faces. There weren't many. Aside from January's parents and a handful of Jonathan Walker's stuffy political friends, the only adult I recognized was Mrs. Hughes, Tiana's mother. There was only one other volunteer from my own age group and, of course, it was Fucking Kaz. It was freezing out and I had a beanie pulled down over my ears, but Kaz—in a wool peacoat and Burberry scarf—had left his perfectly styled hair open to the elements. Without a trace of bitterness, I silently hoped he got frostbite and lost his ears.

He noticed me almost as soon as I arrived, but instead of

turning the other way, he actually waved at me, trying to get my attention like we were old friends or something. I ignored him, pushing ahead to the front of the crowd, and mounted one of the two sets of stone steps that converged on the stagelike porch. January's parents were standing there, attended by Detective Moses and Mr. Walker's campaign manager, Eddie Sward. Detective Moses was scanning the crowd and speaking into a walkie-talkie, while Mr. and Mrs. Walker did a lousy job of pretending to look interested in the words of an older man I didn't recognize.

I'd never exactly hit it off with January's stepfather. It wasn't that we'd argued or anything, more that he'd never seemed to consider me much worth relating to. When I would come over to see January, he would give me a perfunctory handshake, ask me a perfunctory question about my classes, and then excuse himself to take a phone call. I'd never heard him make a joke or laugh out loud—not a genuine laugh, anyway—and I didn't think I'd ever seen him without a necktie, either. His graying hair was combed back from his aristocratic face, and his expression was distant, like he was only vaguely disturbed by the weeklong, unexplained absence of his stepdaughter. He hadn't forgotten to affix a campaign button to the lapel of his trench coat, I noticed, and was clearly aware of the television cameras despite his attempts to appear oblivious.

In contrast, January's mother looked like a wreck. She'd lost some weight when she and Mr. Walker became serious as a couple, jumping quickly on board the latest diet and exercise trends that were being promoted on talk shows for Women of a Certain Age, but she'd lost even more since the last time I'd seen her. Her face was gaunt, her eyes puffy and uncertain, and her long fingers fiddled relentlessly with a strand of pearls at her throat. She wore an off-white pantsuit under an off-white jacket, her off-white hair pulled back in a tight French twist, and she looked startlingly like her own ghost.

"She's just a remarkable girl, so lovely," the older man was saying to them in a strangely mannered voice, as if he were reciting something he'd committed to memory. He was balding, with a white beard and rimless glasses, and gave off a professorial air. "I told her she was too pretty to be wasting her time behind the scenes—she ought to have been in the spotlight, I told her—but she was reluctant. Her modesty was quite becoming, as a matter of fact."

"Thank you, that's very kind," Jonathan Walker murmured with a clenched jaw, shifting slightly to be in better view of the cameras.

"She was quite engaging, January," the man went on earnestly, "she—"

"Flynn!" Tammy Walker caught sight of me, and her face lit up like a Christmas tree, genuine happiness splitting through a layer of grief, and the contrast was heartbreaking. "Flynn, I can't believe you came!"

"Hi, Mrs. Walker, Mr. Walker," I mumbled awkwardly as January's mother beckoned me into their uncomfortable little circle. Mr. Walker gave me the perfunctory handshake and a gruff, monosyllabic greeting, but Mrs. Walker dragged me into an intense, angular bear hug, her breath ragged and hot against my neck.

"I'm so glad you came," she repeated in a soft, strangled whisper, "I'm so glad you came, I'm so glad you came. . . ."

Mr. Walker separated us with a gentle but uncompromising

gesture, and I almost thanked him. January's mother was staring at me in a bewilderingly hopeful way, her hands flexing open and closed. I'd seen adults drunk from time to time, authority figures acting unpredictable and a little scary, but I'd never seen one who truly appeared to be on the verge of losing it. Tammy had always struck me as a little bit high-strung, prone to becoming emotional and melodramatic at the drop of a hat whenever she and January argued, but I'd never seen her so unstable.

Shuffling my feet self-consciously, I suddenly regretted climbing up onto the porch in the first place. Everyone in the courtyard was watching us, I realized, including the news crew. Clearing my throat, I mumbled, "I just . . . I've been really worried, since I heard . . . and I wanted . . . to tell you that."

It was the lamest offering of condolences ever, possibly in the history of the known universe, but I had no idea what was appropriate to say in that kind of situation. Nevertheless, mournful tears slipped from Mrs. Walker's eyes, and she said, "Of course, dear, of course you've been worried—"

"Flynn is January's boyfriend," Mr. Walker explained for the benefit of the bearded man, who then regarded me with some surprise. To me, Mr. Walker added, "This is Cedric Kaufmann, the director of the play January's working on at school."

"Hoffman, actually," the older man corrected gently. Shaking my hand, he stated, "I don't believe that I know you, son."

"Flynn goes to Riverside," Tammy said in a wobbly voice. "That was January's old school, before she started attending Dumas."

"No, you don't seem like the Dumas type," Hoffman informed me neutrally, and I couldn't tell whether I'd just been insulted or not. The look he was giving me, however, wasn't terribly friendly. "I don't recall January ever mentioning you."

"We started dating last summer," I said, because there was a very weird silence just then, and it felt like somebody needed to fill it before the world ended.

"She was a very lovely girl," he told me sternly. "Very lovely." The stagy sentimentality in his voice reminded me rather suddenly that January had called him a freak. I could see why. "I hope you appreciated her, son."

"Oh, he does, Mr. Hoffman," Mrs. Walker enthused softly, that crazy smile still plastered across her face. "Flynn is *wonderful* for January. They're so happy together." It was clear she, at least, hadn't heard any of the anti-Flynn propaganda that seemed to be going around town. "Isn't that right?"

Her look was expectant, Hoffman's was skeptical, and Mr. Walker's was detached. I was about to mumble an answer when Detective Moses interrupted and saved me from one of the most awkward exchanges of my life. "We're about to get started, so the two of you should probably go down there and join the others."

She was speaking to Hoffman and me of course, and with glad footsteps I retreated to the wide lip of the stone fountain. The fish had been removed for the season, but it had not yet been emptied of water, and when the wind shifted, an icy spray speckled my face. I kept my eyes on the porch, where Detective Moses stood, holding up a flier bearing a large photo of January. It was a picture that had been taken the previous summer, on a night when we'd been hanging out downtown. January was laughing, her long blond hair spilling over her shoulders. She looked confident. Happy.

"Listen up, everyone," Detective Moses began in a loud voice that carried clear to the back of the crowd. "We are all here today to search for January Beth McConville. For those of you who do not know her personally, she is a Caucasian female, fifteen years old, approximately five feet five inches, and one hundred ten pounds. She has blue eyes and long blond hair. Those are her vital statistics. They are printed out on this flier"—she held it up a little higher so everyone could see it—"along with a description of the last outfit she was seen wearing: a light gray hooded sweatshirt, dark jeans, and a pair of red canvas shoes.

"Also printed on the flier are contact numbers. If you find January today, call one of these numbers. If you find an article of January's clothing, a dropped cell phone, a footprint, anything that looks suspicious or out of place or like it might help us track January down, *call one of these numbers*. What you should *not* do is *touch* anything that looks like evidence, *move* anything that looks like evidence, or *photograph* anything that looks like evidence and then post it on the Internet. We all have the same goal here, and we need to work together.

"To that end: Do not go off anywhere alone. Ironically enough, people can and do get lost on search parties. Pick a buddy—or, better yet, a group—and stick together. Make sure at least one of you has a fully charged, functioning cell phone at all times. If possible, stay within earshot of other groups, and be aware of your surroundings. If you find January and she is injured, do not attempt to move her, and unless you are a trained medical professional, do not attempt to administer treatment. *Call one of these numbers*."

Detective Moses came down from the porch and began distributing fliers among the crowd, adults snatching them up and clutching them reverently, like church programs. Sympathetic mews rippled through the gathered volunteers as they examined January's bright, beautiful face, committed her outfit to memory, and programmed the contact numbers into their trusty cell phones. For a sickening moment, I felt as if I'd just joined the world's most macabre scavenger hunt.

My mouth felt tacky and dry as the flier found its way into my hand and I looked at January's vibrant smile. I'd seen dozens of similar smiles on TV and in the newspapers, on girls whose images usually accompanied a story of tragedy, abduction, or murder—girls you knew would never be seen again. It was surreal to me that the happy, likable girl in the news now was my ex-girlfriend. Would we really find her today? Did we *want* to? After all, if she were this close to home, and had been all along, then either she was camping in the woods somewhere . . . or she was dead.

And January had never been a big fan of camping.

Interrupting my thoughts, Detective Moses asked if there were any questions. When there weren't, she barked, "Okay, everyone. Let's bring January back home."

NINE

THE CROWD BEGAN to disperse, volunteers armed with flashlights, cell phones, and fliers heading in all directions, off into the relative wilderness that surrounded the Walker mansion. Detective Moses remounted the porch and herded January's parents back inside the house, through the massive front doors of carved and polished oak. I turned around and started looking for Mrs. Hughes. I wasn't especially anxious to tag along with a group of perfect strangers for the task ahead, and I was also sort of suddenly craving the comforting presence of a reliable and familiar adult.

I made it three steps before I heard someone call my name.

"Flynn!" It was Kaz. He was waving his hand in the air again, trying to draw my attention over the heads of the people between us, and I immediately turned the other way, pretending not to see him. I was screwed, though; the fountain created a huge barrier in front of me, and a gaggle of elderly volunteers bickering over a map formed an impassable obstacle on my left. By the time I got around to door number three, it was already too late. Kaz was upon me. "Hey, man, wait up!"

"What are you doing here?" I asked sourly, as if he had no business looking for my missing girlfriend.

"I wanted to help." He sounded a little embarrassed, and he gave me a crooked smile. "Listen, I feel bad about the other day. We kind of got off on the wrong foot, know what I mean?"

"You think so?" I deadpanned.

He shifted his weight nervously and ducked his head. "Yeah. Look, I've been thinking about some of the things you said on Saturday, because they didn't make a lot of sense to me, and I've been starting to wonder if maybe . . . I don't know."

"What?"

"I never told January she should be dating older guys," he blurted, glancing up at me as if he wasn't sure I'd believe him. "I mean, it sounded like you thought I was trying to move in on her or something like that, and that's totally not the case. I like January as a friend, but that's all. She isn't my type, and she knows that. I *know* she knows that."

"She told me you said it, though," I countered pedantically, even though I'd come to realize that my ex-girlfriend was perhaps the very definition of an unreliable source. "Why would she say it if it wasn't true?"

"I don't know!" he responded earnestly. "That's what I'm talking about. There was this one time that January was upset because you two were fighting about something, and she kept saying stuff like, 'Flynn is so immature,' and, 'Maybe I shouldn't be dating high school boys anymore, because they're all immature, maybe I should be dating college guys.' And she asked what I thought, and it was obvious she wanted me to agree with her, so I said sure. But that was it." Tugging awkwardly at the lapel of his peacoat, he mumbled, "And I never said any-thing about the size of your . . . size."

For clarification, he gestured to my crotch, and I could feel my face redden. "Did you tell her to break up with me?"

"Yeah, I did," he admitted, letting out a breath. "But the thing is, every time she talked to me about you, it was always some sort of complaint. She always seemed upset or depressed about stuff she said you did, so . . . yeah. I told her she didn't deserve to be unhappy, and that if things weren't good between you two, she should probably move on."

He looked down again and then up, waiting for me to say something. I was still pissed at him, nursing a grudge calcified from months of hearing how amazing Kaz was and how he was always making cases against me in absentia, cases by which my seemingly ever-credulous girlfriend was perpetually *thisclose* to being convinced. Now he was trying to reach out to me, and I knew the *mature* thing to do would be to reciprocate, and I knew I should *want* to do the mature thing—but I didn't. And the truth of that was frustrating. Irritated by the whole situation, I jammed my hands into my jacket pockets. "Why are you tell-ing me all this stuff?"

"Like I said, I was thinking. I guess I realized that if January told you things about me that, you know, misrepresented what really happened, then maybe the things she's told me about you weren't totally accurate, either." He shrugged uncomfortably. "I figured at the very least I owed you a chance to tell me your side of the story."

"Why?" I retorted. "Because I'm so concerned with what you think of me?"

"Fair enough." Kaz sighed. "I guess what I owe you is an

apology. January made you sound like this enormous ass who didn't care about her at all, but"—he gestured around the courtyard—"you're the only other one of her friends who showed up today. And you're the only one who stopped by the toy store to ask about her, other than the police. That's the other thing—I found out from the owners that the cops came by last week, and apparently January didn't tell her parents she'd quit, either." He gave me that crooked smile again, and his sheepish expression made him look about fifty percent less douchey. "I don't know why she said the things she said, but I wanted to set the record straight. I'm sorry, man."

It was a weird moment. Kaz had no reason to lie to me, and no reason to want peace with me unless he was telling the truth, but I was still annoyed at having to let go of my anger. I'd spent a lot of time convincing myself of my righteousness in hating Kaz, and I sure as hell wasn't ready to trust him, but I couldn't justify rejecting his olive branch, either. Reluctantly, I gave a curt nod. "Sure. Whatever."

Pointedly, I turned to walk away, only to discover that we'd been all but abandoned in the courtyard. Mrs. Hughes was nowhere to be seen, and the only adults left were the quarrelsome older people with the map, still arguing over who should hold it and which way was north, anyway. I let out a tired sigh, realizing my own fate a moment before I heard Kaz pipe up, "So, what do you say? Search buddies?"

We were silent for a long time, our booted feet swishing through grass that was silvered with a touch of frost left over from the morning. It was an overcast day, the sky a solid blanket of dove-white clouds, and cold, blunt light fell on the fields that rolled away from the back of the Walker mansion. We'd left the house far behind, and in the distance we could see groups of other searchers moving inexorably toward the thick woods that sprouted up to the southeast of the property. Without explanation, I veered southwest, and Kaz followed.

"You know, January told me that her parents were rich and annoyingly Waspy, but I hadn't really been expecting the whole Ken-and-Barbie-in-the-Hamptons routine," he remarked with forced amiability as he pulled up next to me, his long legs easily matching mine stride for stride. He was giving me that cute, crooked smile again, standing close enough for me to catch a mingled scent of herbal soap and sandalwood cologne, and it made funny things happen to my stomach. I gritted my teeth and tried to pick up the pace. I wasn't even sure I wanted to like Kaz as a person, let alone feel . . . *things* for him. Oblivious to my discomfort, he continued, "I mean, she makes her stepdad sound like some kind of animatronic, flag-waving caricature, but I always pictured her mom as a little more laid-back."

"She used to be," I said finally, my own peace offering. "Sort of. I mean, she could be kind of difficult sometimes? Like, if January said something even a little bit disrespectful, Tammy would start sobbing and going on about all her sacrifices and 'this is the thanks I get' and all that stuff. But she was usually pretty cool. She didn't talk down to you, and she didn't act like she thought you were too stupid to understand her. . . . She told jokes, and she laughed a lot, and she swore like a prison guard; she was fun." I could remember being at January's old condo, back before we were dating, sitting on the couch and watching Tammy blitz through the room, her mousy hair bundled up in a lopsided chignon. *Nobody look at me, I'm a fucking mess! I'm going to sue Sarah Jessica Parker.* Sex and the City *did not prepare me to be a single woman in her thirties* without *designer heels and amazing sex!* "Tammy changed a lot when she remarried. In their old condo, she had one of the walls in the kitchen covered with that chalkboard paint so people could write all over it? In their new house, she had white carpeting put down in one of the rooms on the first floor, and now no one's allowed to even go in there because she doesn't want it to get dirty."

"Fortunately, it looks like they have more than enough rooms to spare," Kaz remarked drily. "Still, though. Maybe January's *mom* is the animatronic one. Walker owns a software company or something, right? Maybe he built a replacement Tammy and installed the Anal-Retentive Rich Lady personality as part of the upgrade."

"Actually, January made almost that exact same joke." I smiled at the memory. "I wouldn't use the word upgrade when you mention it to her, though."

"I can't believe she hates it here so much!" Kaz exclaimed suddenly. Doing a one-eighty, he walked backward next to me, spreading out his arms to encompass the receding mansion and the expansive, landscaped lawn. Even in late October, under gray skies, it was pretty impressive. "I mean, sure, it's a little over the top, but it's still freaking amazing. If I lived here, I'd spend all my time walking around these fields with my camera."

"You're a photographer?"

"Yeah. Well, I mean, you know, not *really*." He swung back around. "I'm still a total amateur. I wanted to make photography my major, but my parents—*Doctor* and *Doctor* Bashiri—weren't too amped about the idea, and they're the ones paying my tuition, so . . ."

"So you're studying premed?"

"Yeah. And, I mean, I don't *hate* it; I always liked my science classes and stuff, and my parents have been prepping me for a medical career since I was, like, four, so it could be a lot worse." He sounded doubtful, though. "It's just . . . I don't *love* it."

"And you love photography."

"It's, like, my passion." He kept his eyes on his feet. "I got my first real camera for my tenth birthday, and I immediately went outside and took, like, a hundred super-close-up pictures of our birdfeeder. They were all totally out of focus, but I decided that made them 'artistic,' and I wanted to put them all over the walls of the dining room—because that was *our* feeder, get it?" He was laughing, but his face was pink with embarrassment. "I thought it was the deepest metaphor ever, and that if I took pictures of my pictures in the dining room, *that* picture could be put in a museum or something. *Ugh.*" He squeezed his eyes shut for a second. "I cannot believe what a freak I was. Thank God I didn't have a Tumblr account back then."

I was laughing a little now, too, in spite of myself. "I take it your 'human feeder' project was not appreciated by the curators at the Museum of Modern Art?"

"My genius is ahead of its time."

"I wanted to join the photography club at Riverside this year, but the only camera I have is this crappy little point-and-shoot digital," I admitted after a moment. "Even if I see something really cool, and get it framed just the way I want it, it always looks like total garbage when I upload it to my computer."

"Good equipment is really expensive." Kaz gave me a strange, tentative look. "You're welcome to use mine, if you want. I mean, it's probably the cheapest professional-quality camera on the market, but I can show you how it works, and I guarantee you'll get better results than with your point-and-shoot."

"Oh. Um . . . thanks," I managed to reply, surprised by and wary of his generosity.

"Well, I'll be getting something out of it, too." He smiled again, genially. "Don't forget that I didn't grow up here. I only just moved to Ann Arbor a few months ago for school, and I still don't know much about the area. You can use my camera, and I can use you as a guide to the spots that are worth photographing."

I mumbled something, honestly not sure how to respond to the suggested arrangement. I couldn't figure out why he was being so nice to me, why he seemed to want to be friends despite apparently only ever having heard bad things about me. He'd cleared the air regarding the misleading stories January had induced me to believe about him, but I hadn't returned the favor; he was merely taking it on faith that she'd depicted me unfairly as well. If anything, *he* should've been the one still intent on disliking *me*.

Even if he didn't feel the awkwardness between us, I did, and so finally I explained to Kaz the whole story behind the "disposable ponies" comment, and my strenuous efforts to make sure January hadn't felt bad about leaving Riverside. I didn't address her claims that I'd made her feel unattractive, because that was one can of worms I had absolutely no intention of opening—for anyone.

He was silent for a while after I finished talking, his perfectly sculpted features tensed and thoughtful. The grass we'd been trudging through had gotten much longer, the blades lick-ing at our shins, and I couldn't see any other volunteers any-more. Behind us, a grove of cypress trees blocked our view of the Walker manse, and a murder of crows swooped eerily above their dark spires. At last, he sighed. "I'm sorry, man. I can't think why she did it—why she made things sound . . . the way she made things sound."

Again, I mumbled a noncommittal reply, but the truth was that I had a pretty good idea. She'd made Kaz sound like a smooth, older guy trying to steal her away, because she wanted me to get jealous; she'd made him think I was a manipulative asshole because she was hoping that, in spite of whatever he'd said about her not being his type, maybe she could trigger his white knight reflex hard enough that he'd be willing to date her after all, if it meant rescuing her from me. If he'd responded favorably, maybe she'd even have dumped me for him and saved herself from my apparent romantic indifference.

When we reached the creek, the water burbling softly as it snaked along in its narrow channel, I jumped to the other side and waited by the trees for Kaz to follow suit. It was then that he finally asked me where I was taking him. Pushing past the limbs of a sharp-scented pine, I said, "Here."

The old barn loomed into view as we cleared the foliage, looking ominous and forsaken with its rotting gray face and the square black cavity of its hayloft window, and Kaz actually gasped. "Holy shit—this looks like Freddy Krueger's summer home or something! Does it belong to the Walkers?"

"They don't even know about it," I told him, starting for the door. "I'm not sure *anybody* knows about it. I guess you could say it's January's secret hideout."

I was valiantly maintaining a distant hope that I would find her safely ensconced in the abandoned, dilapidated structure, holed up with a sleeping bag, a stack of paperbacks, and an old transistor radio, camping out and laughing at the breathless news reports of her disappearance. In some ways, it was an explanation that made a lot of sense. I didn't think the police had searched out here yet, or they wouldn't be asking volunteers to comb the area; if January had been staying with friends or family, they would certainly have already found her; and if she'd been kidnapped, there'd have been a ransom demand by now. In other ways, however, it made no sense. Roughing it with no electricity, water, or indoor plumbing was not January's idea of a good time, and any point she had to make was surely made by now. Still, I clung to the possibility.

Heaving open the barn door, I stepped into the musty-smelling shadows, taking a moment to let my eyes adjust to the gloom. Light stabbed through gaps in the old boards, a constellation of pale slivers, and motes drifted in the haphazard bands of illuminated space, but otherwise the cavernous structure was as motionless and silent as a tomb. Not encouraging. Nevertheless, I called out, "January?"

There was no answer, my voice denied even an echo by the thick padding of straw that crunched underfoot. I was listening intently for the sound of movement or breathing, hoping that January was lurking somewhere and purposefully refusing to make her presence known, when Kaz barged in behind me. "This place is even scarier inside than outside. If that's possible."

"I'm gonna check the loft," I announced, heading for the ladder.

"What's in these stalls?" he asked, looking around as I gripped the rungs and started up. "Besides hay, I mean."

"I don't know," I called back brusquely. "Check 'em out."

Reaching the loft, my last vestigial hope died. In the light that washed the space through the open square of the window, I could see that no one had been staying there. Everything was exactly as I remembered it from the Friday night January and I had our big showdown: Bales of fusty hay were stacked against the walls alongside old, empty crates, the little nest where we'd argued was undisturbed, and there wasn't even so much as a candy wrapper or crumpled tissue to suggest a human presence. It wasn't until I took it all in, though, that I realized how badly I'd been hoping to find her up there.

"There's a big, rusty aerator down here, but not much else!" Kaz hollered from below as I got to my feet and set about searching the loft. "It looks like something you'd find in a medieval dungeon. I'm not going to touch it, because I'm not sure my tetanus shots are up to date."

"Keep looking around. See if you find anything that makes it look like someone's been staying here."

Sweeping my eyes from side to side, I slowly advanced from the ladder to the window, deftly sidestepping the weak spot in the loft floor; the wood groaned pitifully anyway, and it was one of the few times I was particularly grateful for being small and skinny. Kaz was still talking, shouting out to announce every piece of long-forgotten debris he uncovered in the stables, when I reached the nest and sank dispiritedly into it.

I looked out the window, staring at the spot where I'd last seen January, and let out a breath. It was clear that there was nothing to be found in the barn, and I suddenly felt overwhelmingly lost and defeated. Where else could I look? Who else could I talk to? I felt like I'd exhausted every lead I knew to check and had come up empty. Out loud, I mumbled, "Where *are* you, Jan?"

Down below, Kaz was moving toward the ladder, calling out and asking what I'd found in the loft. As I turned my head to answer him, something caught my eye. I froze. The bleached light of the early afternoon, slanting sideways through the barn, picked out an irregular pattern that seemed to be etched into the soft wooden boards of one wall. It was a strange assortment of grooves and bevels that emerged from the shadowy space behind a large crate. Scrambling to my feet, I pushed the obstacle aside and took a startled breath at my discovery.

"Kaz!" I shouted. "Get up here!"

Gouged into the soft wood, cut with a small knife or maybe even a house key, were a series of jagged hatch marks. I counted twenty-five of the spiky, uneven lines, which were organized in groups of five like someone keeping track of points in a poker game. I was staring at them, their furrows deep and emphatic, when Kaz scrambled up the ladder and popped into the loft.

"What is it? What did you find?"

"I'm not sure." I touched the marks with my fingers, feeling the sharp indentations. They definitely weren't old. "I think January carved something here."

"What's it say?"

Before I could answer, he was starting across the loft, feet banging down hard as he headed eagerly for my side. Instant alarm sent adrenaline streaking through my limbs, and I thrust my hands out in a futile attempt to stop him, words of warning on my lips at the same moment that I realized I was already too late. "WAIT, DON'T!"

Confused, he faltered, and one foot came down on the decayed floorboards. The wood wheezed and splintered, dropping sharply under his weight, and time seemed to slow as the horror of realization appeared in Kaz's eyes. The planks were buckling and giving way, breaking apart like dry twigs, and I launched myself at him with my arms outstretched. At the same moment, he pitched forward, hands grappling with the air as he fell, and we met somewhere in the middle.

Our combined momentum threw us sideways, Kaz's feet clearing the fracture in the floor only an instant before it turned into a gaping hole, and we crash-landed on a pile of dirty straw. Despite the padding, the impact was so great that it shook the entire barn, weathered timbers shifting and groaning under us until I was positive the place was about to collapse. But the shuddering slowed and finally stopped, the rafters creaking, until at last the only movement in the loft was the airy swirl of dust kicked up by the violent disturbance and the painful banging of my heart rebounding off my rib cage.

Kaz was on top of me, breathing hard, his gold-and-olive face gray with fright. "Holy shit, dude." He let out a shaky exhalation, his mouth so close I could smell coffee and spearmint gum on his breath. "I think you just saved my life!"

"I think you just broke my ribs," I joked weakly in return, my head whirling a little with the air I'd lost when he'd flattened my lungs.

"I can't believe you *dove* at me like fucking Batman!" He giggled a little bit, nerves escaping through laughter. "It was kind of badass, actually."

"That's me. The high school badass."

I'd meant it as another joke, but once I'd said it, the moment seemed to shift. Kaz's expression had transitioned from shock to relief to an emotion I couldn't quite put my finger on, and he was staring at me, his hazel eyes dark and intense. Something in his face softened perceptibly, and his eyelashes fluttered with a strange caution. "Flynn . . ."

He moved closer, hesitated . . . and then he kissed me.

The pressure was almost unbearably gentle at first, his lips soft and warm against mine, and an electrical storm erupted in my stomach as conflicting emotions rolled like thunder from my scalp to my toes. Then Kaz's bottom lip maneuvered my mouth open, his fingers tightening on the collar of my jacket; I felt heat and hunger, my head zooming like a carousel, and when his tongue touched mine, all the blood in my body made an immediate, mad rush to a certain point between my legs, like a horde of Black Friday shoppers at the opening bell.

Just like that I was *fully aroused*, zero to steel rebar in nothing flat, and a crazy jolt of destabilizing panic swept over me in the same instant. Our bodies pressed together the way they were, there was no chance that Kaz couldn't feel my physical response, and as electricity jabbed at every nerve ending in my skin, I jolted back. Fear, primal and absolute, jammed my lungs up into my throat. "Stop!"

Once again, Kaz looked utterly confused. "I—I don't g—"

"*Stop! Get off me!*" I shoved him to the side and scrambled to my feet, my heart slamming against my ribs again, and I struggled in vain to disguise my erection with the bottom edge of my jacket as I backed away from him.

"I—I'm sorry, man," Kaz stammered in a thin voice, look-ing startled and abashed. "I didn't mean for that to happen."

"Why did you do that?" I demanded crazily, pointing at him for no reason.

"I don't know. I just . . . the way you were looking at me, I—"

"*I'm not gay!*"

I don't know why I said it. It came out of my mouth before I could think about it. I could have admitted the truth then and there and at least allowed myself to have enjoyed that moment—and with one hand fumbling to hide the evidence of my lie, I don't know who I thought I was kidding—but I couldn't do it. It was easier to deny it, to put it off. Forever.

"I'm. Not. Gay!"

"I'm sorry," Kaz repeated in a small, flummoxed voice. "I shouldn't have—It was stupid. I just thought . . ."

He trailed off, staring up at me helplessly from the dusty pal-let on the floor, and I stared back, breathing hard. I was trying to think of what I should do next, to figure out what it meant that *Kaz* had *kissed* me, when we heard the screams.

High-pitched and wordless, they echoed against the downy blanket of the sky, an unmistakable distress signal that cut the tension in the loft like the blow of an ax. In an instant I was scrambling down the ladder with Kaz behind me, and when I burst from the barn I realized that the cries were coming from the adjacent meadow, where January liked to gaze at the stars.

My lungs and limbs stinging with alarm, I shoved through the thicket of trees that separated the barn from the former pasture; at the top of the rise in the middle of the vast field, with dark birds swooping portentously overhead, I could see a cluster of people. One of them was an African-American woman—Tiana's mother—and she was sobbing against the shoulder of the Dumas drama coach, Cedric Hoffman, her choked howl carrying across the empty space.

My thoughts splintered as I stumbled up the slope, abject fear making an icy slush of my bloodstream, certainty and denial kicking in simultaneously. I told myself, *No, no it isn't, it can't be, no*, but I knew. With every fiber of my being, I knew they had found her—that the search for January was over.

My eyes blurred and acid scorched the back of my throat as I reached Mrs. Hughes and looked down. I was so dazed with dread that at first I could make no sense of what I was seeing; it looked like nothing but a heap of old clothes—someone's trash, discarded where it didn't belong. When things at last swam into focus, the world beating around me in time with my heart, I was still blinking in total confusion. Laid out at my feet *was* a heap of clothes, and nothing more.

I spent another minute trying to conjure them into a body, trying to make the discovery fit my horrible expectations, before I finally understood exactly what I was seeing. The red canvas shoes, the dark jeans, the gray sweatshirt . . . they weren't just any clothes; they were *January's*. It was the same outfit described on the flier—the one she was last seen wearing—and then I recognized the familiar rip in the knee of the pants and the inky stain near the left elbow of the hoodie from a misadvised home attempt at dip-dyeing her hair. The clothes were hers without a doubt . . . but something was wrong with them. So wrong that I instantly understood Mrs. Hughes's breathless horror, and the frantic murmurs of the crowd of volunteers who had been drawn by her exclamations.

Trailing from the hoodie's cuffs and wrapped around the ankles of the jeans were long strips of silver tape; a dense, red-brown stain, so dark it was almost black, covered the front of the heathery sweatshirt. Starting at the neck, the stain stretched all the way to the bottom edge, and from one side almost clear to the other, stiffening the worn fabric to the consistency of cardboard. It was a grisly sight that made my head spin as my pulse thudded in my temples, some primal part of me already aware of what I was looking at a split second before my brain put the pieces together.

It was blood.

TEN

THE NEXT COUPLE of hours passed as if in a fog, time seeming to slip in both directions simultaneously. One minute, people were moving around me so quickly that I could barely see their faces; the next, things were so agonizingly slow that I was able to count every lash on Mrs. Hughes's right eye as she gripped my hands and prayed out loud through gasping sobs.

Reporters appeared on the scene with the swiftness of jackals, and everyone present was pumped dry of information by journalists wielding tape recorders and cameras. I stared at the trees, at the grass, at the ravens that zigzagged through the sky, my brain churning but refusing to process what I'd seen. With dulled ears, I listened as Cedric Hoffman gave an interview to a helmet-haired woman from a local news station, explaining how his group of volunteers had happened to make the discovery.

"She was such a lovely girl," he was saying in his distant, ruminative manner, "such a creative, thoughtful, and intelligent girl. She was interested in astronomy, you know, and she used to tell me of the meadow where she liked to watch the stars, and

I thought . . . well, I suppose that's what made me suggest we look there."

My feet went cold and then numb, but I couldn't move. I had a short conversation with my parents, telling them that I wasn't ready to leave yet, that I needed to stay, even though I wanted to be as far from there as possible. I just couldn't bring myself to walk away. It felt almost as if we *had* found January after all—and I could see decisions being made in the expressions of those around me, a closing of doors as the significance of the bloodstained clothing was interpreted.

I was watching hope dissolve in real time.

I felt it leaving me as well, and struggled to hold on, but how could I possibly explain what I'd seen, except by acknowledging the obvious? It was *blood*—and such a soul-shocking amount of it. I didn't know how much you could lose and still survive, but I did know that if January had made it to a hospital, it would have been in the news. Therefore, I knew that someone had to have taken her clothes from her and dumped them in the middle of that field. But who? And why? *And where was she?*

At last, January's clothes were surrounded by investigators while a growing cohort of uniformed officers pushed back the media and the congregated onlookers. People who hadn't even taken part in the search had appeared in the field seemingly from nowhere, watching the proceedings with the ghoulish curiosity of spectators who rubberneck at auto accidents. The helmet-haired reporter stepped into the empty space directly to my right, the odor of face powder and mousse suddenly filling my nostrils, and she began doing a stand-up for her nightly broadcast in a jarring, "newsy" voice.

"A short while ago, the search for fifteen-year-old January

Beth McConville took a dark turn in the field you see behind me. Scarcely a mile from the home she shared with her mother and stepfather, U.S. senatorial candidate Jonathan Walker, a pile of girl's clothes—*soaked in blood*—was found by members of a volunteer search party. The Ann Arbor Police Department has offered no official comment as yet, but multiple eyewitnesses have confirmed that the clothing discovered here matches the description of the outfit McConville was wearing the day she vanished. Speculation regarding the fate of the missing teenager has become understandably grim, and many of those I have spoken to today already fear the worst; but in the absence of a body, the question still remains: What happened to January McConville?"

I tuned her out, my eyes on the people gathered around my ex-girlfriend's clothes. The items were photographed and then collected by gloved technicians and tucked safely into plastic bags before the tedious enterprise of searching the meadow for trace evidence could begin. Finally, the earth released my feet and allowed me to stumble out of the meadow and back across the long, endless fields that spread between there and civilization.

She was dead. The thought hit me hard, bouncing inside my skull like a piece of shrapnel. I resisted it—but I couldn't exactly refute it, either. What other explanation could there be? Could I really continue to believe that January was just trying to frighten her parents? This was no petty prank, and no matter how much she resented the circumstances of her life, I could think of no reason she would resort to something this extreme, to staging something so horrific. Running away was one thing, but faking a *murder*? January was impulsive, but not irresponsible; and though it was true she could be vengeful, she had never been cruel the way she'd have to be to scare her friends and family like that. There would be legal consequences if and when she was found—possibly academic ones as well—and I simply couldn't see January risking her whole future like that just to teach Jonathan and Tammy a lesson.

I blinked in surprise when the back side of the Walker mansion abruptly reared up in front of me, as if having burst through the earth right in my path, French doors reflecting the bleak white sky and my bleak white face. I hadn't realized I had walked so far until that very moment, despite the fact that I had climbed the rear patio and was standing beside the vast, kidney-shaped pool.

Feeling shaky and exhausted, completely unsettled by what I'd seen and what I was thinking, I sank into one of the Walkers' custom-made Adirondack chairs and stared into the dry basin of the pool, emptied for the season. It was painted a pallid turquoise, and a handful of dirt and dead leaves had already gathered at the bottom of the gaping socket. There was supposed to be a tarp over it, I knew; Mr. Walker considered this sort of untidiness to be trashy and "low class." I wondered who had forgotten to take care of it.

The Jacuzzi, nestled into the pool's bend with its padded cover firmly in place, would remain operational all year long, I presumed. I'd spent a lot of time out here over the previous summer and early fall, and I could still easily picture January submerged across from me in the hot tub like she'd been one night in August, when we were lamenting the end of summer. The water had surged around us as the sky bruised and blackened with night, and she had tossed her head back over the lip of the tub so she could watch the stars blink to life overhead.

"I wish we could fucking move to California already," she'd said in a tone more wistful sorrow than complaint.

I looked around at the fancy deck furniture, the lanterns glowing in the gazebo, and the crescent moon reflecting brightly on the still surface of the pool. Music pumped from hidden speakers, and two sweating glasses next to the hot tub contained rum and Coke—heavy on the rum—that January had fixed from her stepdad's virtually bottomless and unguarded supply of liquor. There were always guests over at the mansion for cocktails, from political strategists to donors to politicians whose endorsements Jonathan was courting, and we'd discovered pretty quickly that unless we were caught red-handed, no one could tell if we had helped ourselves.

Add to all that the fact that the Walkers had a personal chef for their numerous parties, a fleet of sports cars begging to be driven by a newly licensed teenager, and enormous television screens in almost every single room in the house, and it was hard to compre-hend January's wish—no matter how many times she expressed it. Cocking a dubious brow, I asked her, "Do you really think that being a broke-ass college student in LA will be better than this?"

"Yes," she'd answered simply, eyes still on the heavens.

And then, as if to illustrate her point, the doors to the house burst open and a tall, imposing figure stalked out onto the patio. Glowering beneath a shock of stiff, dark hair, his broad face shiny and flushed with pique, it was Jonathan's campaign manager, Eddie Sward. The sleeves of his purple button-down shirt were rolled above his elbows, and his hands were clenched into fists. Without preamble, he barked, "Will you turn off that fucking music?"

"Hello to you, too, Eddie," January replied languidly, still looking up at the sky. She didn't move, and I felt tension coil in my gut. Flouting authority wasn't exactly my strong suit, and the man was practically vibrating with anger. "Want to join us?"

"Turn off the music!" he repeated, baring his teeth as cords sprang into view along the length of his neck. He thrust a finger in the direction of what Tammy called the "grand room," a wood-paneled den with a fireplace and cushy furniture that looked out over the rear of the property, where Jonathan had decided to conduct the bulk of his campaign-related business. "I can barely hear myself think in there with all this damned racket!"

"We were here first," January reminded him petulantly, and the man's eyes darkened. "You can always move your little meeting into the basement or whatever."

"Do you have any idea what we're trying to accomplish in there?" Eddie was practically spitting. "How critical things are at this stage? How important this actually is?"

"If this meeting is such a big deal," January returned slowly, "then maybe you should have set it up in the basement."

Eddie stared at her for a long moment, the darkness rolling in his eyes like storm clouds, his expression one of disbelief. Then, stomping closer, he grabbed for our things. "Where the hell is the remote?"

"Get your hands off my stuff!" January protested sharply, standing up in the tub. Her heated skin was pink around the white straps of her bikini, and she lunged for the pair of shorts Eddie was rifling through.

"Why don't you chill out for a second," I suggested to the man in a tone more bold than I felt, rising to my girlfriend's defense.

"You stay out of this, you little pothead punk—you're nothing but a bad influence," Eddie snapped. The minute he'd learned about

my parents' marijuana activism, he'd declared me a "political liability," and begun treating me like a case of campaign herpes. Giving
my towel a violent shake, he ejected from its folds the remote control
that operated the hidden speakers, and the device clattered across the
patio. Snatching it up, the man silenced the music immediately.

"Fine," January snapped, her voice a little shaky, "you got what
you wanted. Now leave us alone!"

But Eddie had discovered our glasses of rum and Coke, and as
he sniffed them, his eyebrows nearly blew into the stratosphere. "Is
this . . . are you drinking?"

Not waiting for a response, he hurled the contents of both glasses
out over the railing and into the darkness, and January shouted,
"Hey! You can't do that!"

Eddie spun back around, trembling all over, and jabbed a finger
into my girlfriend's face. "You listen to me, you ungrateful little bitch!
This is exactly the kind of dumb-shit teenage fuckery that we cannot tolerate. You get caught drinking underage and it's your father
who takes the heat! You could cost him this election!"

"He is not my father," January corrected him coldly, "and I don't
really give a shit if he gets elected."

Through his teeth, Eddie seethed, "If you were my kid, I'd belt
the sass out of your smart little mouth."

"Hey!" I jolted forward, putting myself between him and January. "Don't you threaten her!"

He ignored me completely. Still speaking to January, he snarled
over my shoulder, "Someone needs to teach you a little manners and
respect!"

"Manners and respect?" January laughed, the sound bright
and unpleasant. "You came out here to bully and curse out a couple
of teenagers, and you want to talk about manners and respect?"

There was a moment of charged silence, during which it looked as if Eddie might either blast off into orbit or burst into flames, and then he marched past us, toward the doors to the morning room, pocketing the remote. "Someone needs to do something about you—put you somewhere you can't fuck things up anymore! If you can't behave with even an ounce of class, you need to get out of the way."

The French doors slammed shut behind him, and silence descended on the patio, the only sound the turbulent movement of the heated water that roiled around our hips. January had turned away from me, her blond hair pasted to the wet skin of her back, her posture stiff and ramrod straight. For a long moment, we simply stood there while I tried desperately to think of something to say. "He didn't mean it" would be both inadequate and untrue.

Finally, my girlfriend turned around, her expression a studied blank, and she sank down into the Jacuzzi until the bubbles frothed around her collarbones. Tilting her head back over the lip of the tub, she returned her attention to the stars.

After a little while, in a thick, small voice, she whispered, "I really wish we could just move to California already."

ELEVEN

"FLYNN?" THE SOUND of my name snapped me back to reality, and I jumped up from the Adirondack chair with a start. Mr. Walker was standing in one of the French doors, his patrician features looking drawn and tired. He wore a white oxford shirt, and his necktie was loosened at the collar. "Why don't you come inside, son? It's freezing out."

Silently, I assented, following the man into the house. The door closed and locked behind us, and I found myself standing in the morning room, a squared-off space that housed an antique dining table with matching chairs, a nearly wall-to-wall throw rug, and a chandelier made from a wrought iron wagon wheel that threatened to bring down the ceiling supports. The grand room connected through a door to one side, and the keeping room—with its voluptuous armchairs, stone fireplace, and Impressionist art pieces—extended off to the other. I had no idea what the names of the rooms meant; only that the differences were apparently *very clear* and *very important* to January's mother, if to no one else.

For a terribly awkward moment, Mr. Walker and I simply stood there in silence, listening to a giant wall clock keep score of our discomfort from the keeping room. I didn't know what to say, wasn't sure if I owed him my condolences or if it was even appropriate; further, I was afraid to hear one more person assume the worst, out loud, about the discovery that had been made by the search team—even myself.

Self-consciously, Mr. Walker placed a wide hand on my shoulder and, nodding as if we had already shared a Deep Understanding, said, "Thank you for coming today, Flynn. It meant a lot. To both of us." I mumbled something in reply, and stared at the shining surface of the nearby table. I could see my own reflection in the gleaming wood, my face warped and elongated. "I . . . it's hard to believe that . . . well, it's just . . . awful," he continued, his voice sounding exhausted and uncertain. For the first time, possibly ever, January's stepdad seemed to be at a loss for exactly the right thing to say, and I could smell alcohol on his breath despite the fact that it was only the afternoon. "Mrs. Walker . . . Tammy is taking it pretty hard."

I mumbled a reply, scarcely able to imagine what Tammy must be going through, as I flashed on the bloody sweatshirt and its kite tail of twisted duct tape.

"She asked for you," Mr. Walker added, and I glanced up in surprise. His expression was both grave and removed at the same time, someone hearing a sad story that had nothing to do with him. "I would appreciate it if you'd talk with her a little. I think . . . I think it might make a difference."

I had no idea what this could possibly mean, but I nodded anyway, and Mr. Walker led me to the mahogany door that marked the entrance of the grand room. It was a spacious den that rose up two stories, one wall composed entirely of bowed glass windows that let in a flood of natural light and allowed a view of the pool, the gazebo, and the grassy fields that undulated off to the distant trees. A second stone fireplace dominated another wall, and above it hung a massive portrait of some whiskered military commander from the seventeenth century—probably an ancestral Walker. A third wall was open space, an unobstructed passage into the central hallway, where a double staircase swooped gracefully up to the second floor.

Eddie Sward leaned over an oak desk in a corner of the room, speaking forcefully into his cell phone; when he saw me he scowled unhappily but didn't miss a beat of his one-sided conversation. Slouched forward on an overstuffed sofa upholstered in creamy beige fabric, January's mother had her face buried in her hands. On the low table before her sat a half-empty tumbler of scotch.

As Mr. Walker shut the door behind us, he cleared his throat. "Tammy? Flynn is here."

Mrs. Walker looked up with a jerk, her eyes swollen and rimmed with red, and when she saw me she attempted a smile that fluttered like a leaf about to blow away in a stiff breeze. "Flynn."

She reached both arms out to me, and I moved forward to take them, sinking onto the sofa at her side. Her hands were cold, her grip viselike and desperate, and her once-precise coif of white-blond hair was a bristling mess. She looked like she'd aged a hundred years since the morning, and in her narrow, haggard face, I tried to find traces of the warm, scatterbrained woman I'd met when January and I first became friends. It was hard to believe she was even the same person.

"I d-don't—" I started to say, but just like that my chest ballooned, my throat squeezed shut, and the words stumbled out in a pitiful squeak as I began to cry. Tammy yanked me against her, smashing my face into her shoulder, and held on to me like we were on a plane spiraling into the Atlantic.

"What happened?" January's mother rasped plaintively in my ear, her voice a herky-jerky whine through the thickness in her own throat. "What happened to my baby? What happened to our precious girl?"

Her chin dug sharply into my shoulder as she began to sob, great, racking cries that wrenched her entire body, her fingers buried into my back so fiercely it was like she was trying to reach past my rib cage to my heart. After a moment, Mr. Walker intervened, prying us apart and placing Mrs. Walker's drink into her hand.

"Try to breathe, sweetheart." He guided the drink to Tammy's lips, and she swallowed a mouthful of booze, choking and then gasping for air. She slumped back against the cushions, and Mr. Walker set the glass on the table again.

"Why is this happening?" Tammy moaned at last, staring out the towering windows at the magnificent view. Her hand found mine, and she turned to me with glazed, forlorn eyes. "Why my baby? It isn't fair!"

"I don't know why," I whispered.

She let out an exhausted breath, squeezing my hand so hard I thought the setting of her baroque diamond ring was going to draw blood, and tremulously averred, "All I've ever wanted was for her to be happy. That's all a parent ever wants. It's the only thing. You . . . you have this perfect, little, tiny *person* in your hands, and you say, *I will never let anyone hurt you, I will never let you be sad, I will do anything in my power to make you happy.*

And then . . ." She shrugged, then shuddered, and then coughed violently. "I don't understand. I just . . . don't."

"We don't know anything for sure yet," Mr. Walker pointed out with automatic diplomacy, although even I could tell his heart wasn't in it. "Try to remember that."

"It was so hard when her father walked out on us." Tammy ignored him, speaking listlessly to the windows. "I was young and alone and scared, and it was such a struggle. The sleepless nights, the double shifts, the sacrifices . . . it took everything I had in me to hold us together, to give her the best life. And now . . . *this*. It feels like a punishment! What did I do to deserve this? Why is this happening?"

An uncharitable shadow passed across my sympathy for Tammy Walker as I watched her lay effortless claim to center stage in the unfolding drama—a move no less disappointing for its familiarity. I couldn't count the number of times her skirmishes with January had ended with the tearfully self-involved demand, *Why are you doing this to me?*—as if the girl's every quasi-insubordinate act were part of some grandiose revenge plot against her mother, rather than a simple expression of her own independence.

"It isn't your fault, Tams." Mr. Walker sounded exhausted. "You didn't do anything wrong."

Narrowing her eyes at her husband through a cloud of tears and alcohol, Mrs. Walker snapped, "She hated it here."

"That's not your fault, either," Mr. Walker returned, a little more firmly, "and it isn't the reason she . . the reason for . . . for any of this."

"I wanted her to be happy, and now she's—" Tammy choked

on the end of her statement and shuddered, unwilling or unable to finish the thought. "She hated this house, she hated her school, she hated *me* . . . and you tell me that I didn't do anything *wrong*?"

"All teenagers resent their parents," Mr. Walker returned shortly, his eyebrows drawing together. "It doesn't mean anything! I'm sure January knew—*knows* how lucky she is." His gaze turned to me, and I finally understood the real reason I'd been summoned into the house. "Isn't that right, Flynn?"

He wanted me to tell Tammy that January's anger was just a by-product of meaningless, pop-psych-approved Teen Rebelliousness, and that—deep down—she was truly appreciative of all the unstoppable changes overtaking her life. Maybe I didn't entirely get why my ex-girlfriend loathed this mansion and her gorgeous new school so much, but the fact was that I didn't have to spend any more time in them than I wanted to. No one had forced me to move and leave my friends behind; no one had demanded my gratitude for making peremptory decisions about the way I would live my life, and no one had treated me like my opinions on the subject were irrelevant obstructions. I couldn't pretend that January hadn't been filled with legitimate resentment, because she had.

Lucky for me, I didn't have to reply. Savagely, Mrs. Walker hissed, "She wasn't *all teenagers*, she was my daughter! My little girl! And she *hated it* here!"

"She was *difficult*!" Mr. Walker finally snapped in return, slipping firmly into the past tense while grabbing his own glass of scotch from the desk, where Eddie was still jabbering into his cell phone. "There was no making her happy, because she didn't *want* to be happy! I don't see why you can't grasp that."

He guzzled what was in his tumbler and then immediately refilled it, booze sloshing out of a bottle of Glenmorangie. "Nothing you did would ever be good enough, because she didn't want it to be."

"As if you know anything about her!" Tammy fired back, rings clacking against her own glass as she picked it up with her free hand, amber liquid nearly spilling over the side when she thrust it into the air at her husband. "You never even tried! She was just an object to you. Neither one of you made any effort—*I* had to do all the work." She turned to me then, her eyes almost manic. "*I* did all the work. Every peace that had to be brokered in this house fell on my shoulders, and not just the ones with January, either. Ask him about his criminal of a son! They're *bribing* him to stay out of trouble while the campaign is on, and he's *still* nearly impossible to control—"

"Tammy, calm down," Mr. Walker ordered through gritted teeth.

"Jonathan's never even here," Mrs. Walker continued acidly, still keeping her focus on me, even if her words were obviously for her husband's benefit. "Ask him where he was the night my baby didn't come home! The night I *needed* him! The night I spent all alone, sick to my stomach, until the sun came up and my daughter was missing and I finally had to call the police all by myself!"

"I have already apologized a thousand times for that!" Mr. Walker slammed his glass back down on the desk, making framed photos, campaign buttons, and other detritus jump with the impact. "I had drinks with some boosters and couldn't drive home, so I got a hotel room! I won't be made to feel guilty about it anymore!"

"That or anything else," Tammy retorted cryptically. Before Mr. Walker could respond, though, Eddie intervened.

Covering the phone with his hand, the campaign manager stated, "John, we really need to put together an official statement about this. Fritz is practically drowning in calls right now."

"I already gave a statement to the press this afternoon," Mr. Walker snapped.

"It's not good enough." Eddie was impatient. "You know what these situations are like; they need more, something substantial."

"For fuck's sake, Eddie!" Mr. Walker finally exploded. "They *just* found her clothes two hours ago! Can't we take a day to process before we start planning press conferences?"

"Not a week out from the election, you can't," Eddie replied bluntly. "You disappear now and voters start to wonder whether you can handle the pressures of the job."

"Yes, you certainly don't want to disappoint your voters, Jonathan," Tammy intoned frigidly, one finger circling the rim of her glass. Her husband eyeballed her for a moment before seizing his campaign manager by the shoulder and dragging him out of the room.

"Not in here, at the very least," he muttered brusquely. As the pair disappeared around the curving staircases, their dress shoes clacking loudly against the marble tiles, Tammy tossed back the remnants of her drink.

The footsteps died out immediately, and I suspected the men had disappeared into the carpeted library that opened off the foyer on the other side of the stairs; perforce, however, my attentions were now occupied by January's mother. Returning her tumbler to the coffee table with almost delicate motions, she placed her hand on the side of my face and smiled with muzzy fondness. "You're such a good boy, Flynn. You made my daughter happy."

It wasn't true, and I knew it. Guiltily, I mumbled, "I tried, Mrs. Walker."

"Call me Tammy," she implored. I always felt weird calling adults by their first names, but January's mother had insisted upon it at first, saying it made her feel young. Then, after she'd married Mr. Walker, she suddenly had to be called "Mrs. Walker" all the time, and I wondered what *that* had made her feel. Important, I suspect. Her rings were cold and hard against my cheek as she said, "You were about the only thing that still made her happy, you know."

Shame muddled my insides, and I looked down. "I think . . . I'm sure she—"

"Do you remember that night you came over to the condo and the three of us made cookies?" Tammy apparently hadn't heard me. "It was before you two were 'official,' but even back then you were all she talked about." She gave me a sly, maternal smile, and I felt myself blush. "We were all out of eggs, and January suggested we use peanut butter instead, remember? And everything stuck together, and the cookies came out like charcoal briquettes, and I nearly burned that damned condo to the ground when the third batch burst into flames in the oven, but you kept cracking all those jokes and I don't think I've ever laughed so hard in my life." Tears welled in her eyes and she swiped at them with a long, slim finger. "January was walking two feet off the ground for a week after that, she was so charmed by you."

"I remember that night." I smiled in spite of myself.

"Life was such a mess back then," Tammy said in a dreamy, agonized way. "It was a constant battle every day, trying to keep us afloat, trying to keep us *alive*. Jonathan was the best thing that happened to either of us in a long, long time." She gave me an apologetic look. "He really is a good man—an important man. He's done so much for us. I just don't understand; how could she be happy when things were so awful, and so . . . angry and destructive when they were finally going just right?"

January and her mother had competing ideas of perfection, of course, but I didn't think it was the right time to explain that to her. So, instead, I offered, "Sometimes it's just hard to deal when your life changes so much overnight. Even if it seems like it's changing for the better."

"I'm glad she had you, Flynn." Tammy beamed at me, her expression pitiful, and she clasped both my hands in hers again. "I'm so glad she had you, at least."

Again, it was like a knife in my gut. I loved January— honestly loved her—but I hadn't made her happy. And it hadn't been the kind of love she'd wanted, or the kind she'd had the right to expect from a boyfriend. There had been so much unsaid between us, and the words were an albatross around my neck as I looked at the expression on her mother's face. Finally, I said, "I'm the lucky one."

"Tell me about her," Tammy begged suddenly, her voice a broken whisper. "Tell me about January."

Tell me about California, okay?

I took a breath. "For our two-month anniversary, we planned out this big 'perfect date' evening." It was a story Tammy had to have heard a million times before, but she listened quietly anyway, a poignant look of grateful expectation on her face as I continued. "We rented a limo, and we made reservations at this fancy restaurant on Main Street, and January's favorite indie band—the Disasters—was doing a show at this place downtown. We got all dressed up, like for homecoming or something, and we couldn't stop talking about how awesome it was gonna be. And then the limo didn't show up.

"I called them, like, a zillion times, but the phone just rang and rang and no one ever answered, and eventually we realized that they weren't coming, and we ended up having to walk six blocks to the bus stop—all dressed up—and take this stinky, death-trap bus downtown." Tammy chuckled at the image, and I did, too, remembering the crazy old woman with facial warts and filthy hair who'd sat across from us the entire trip, telling January, *You look just like I did when I was your age!* "Anyway, by the time we got there, we were so late the restaurant had given away our table, and we figured maybe we'd just eat at the bar where the concert was going to be . . . only we didn't even get *in* to the concert because our fake—um, I mean, because we looked too young.

"So, our so-called perfect date is completely falling apart, and I'm starting to get really upset, but January won't give up. She leads me to this dirty little parking lot in back of the bar, where we find the band in the middle of unloading for their show. Without even stopping to think, January walks right up to them, introduces herself, and tells them that they're her favorite band in the world, and it's her birthday, but they won't let us into the show—and then she tells them about the limo and the bus and dinner and by the time she's done talking, they're pulling out acoustic guitars, and they do January's favorite song for us right there on the spot.

"Afterward, we went and got burgers and fries, and we took it all to the top of this parking structure and just had a fast-food picnic in our fancy clothes and watched the stars." Aside from a little awestruck blabber about how awesome it was that the Disasters had given us a private concert, we had eaten in a peaceful silence, listening to traffic and music and conversation drifting up from the street below. "She told me that it really had been the perfect date." I smiled. "That's what she was like, though. She could take the biggest catastrophe *ever* and somehow turn it into the perfect night."

"*Yes*," Tammy whispered, her eyes squeezed shut, a tear sliding down the pale skin of her cheek. Her lips trembled as she clung to my hands. "*Yes*."

TWELVE

TAMMY ASKED ME, sweetly and fuzzily, to refill her drink. By the time I turned back from the desk, however, she had sagged against the sofa cushions, her mouth open, with faint rattling sounds emitting from the back of her throat. Trying not to wake her, I set the tumbler down on the coffee table and stole into the central hallway, ready to go home at last.

I didn't make it past the library. The double doors slightly ajar, I could hear the voices of Eddie and Mr. Walker coming from within. I didn't intend to eavesdrop, but just as I reached the spot between the polished newel posts of the twin staircases, I heard January's name and it stopped me in my tracks. Through the slivered opening, I could see the back of one leather armchair and the mullioned panes of a window that looked out on the front of the house. It was Eddie who was speaking.

"—don't care if you don't want to hear it, John. You don't have a choice. And do you have any idea what kind of a golden opportunity this is?"

"I don't think—"

"Just listen to me!" The campaign manager was vehement. "We put together a proposal—we call it January's Law, or something like that—and we go public with it immediately. Right now, you don't just have the attention of Michigan's voters, you have the hearts of the entire *country*. You cannot *buy* that kind of PR, Jonathan!"

"Eddie . . ." Mr. Walker's low voice carried the edge of a warning.

"No! You hired me to do a job for you, and I'm doing it," Eddie persevered. "*This* is your calling card; *this* is what will get you into the senate! You propose harsher sentencing laws for any violent crime where the victim is a minor, mandatory jail time for first offenders, blah blah, whatever. No one will dare go against you on it. Nobody wants to be tarred with the 'soft on crime' label, and *now* they'd also get lambasted for not caring about *kids*, about *your daughter*. Even that asshole Torkelson will have to support you!" Andrew Torkelson was Mr. Walker's opponent in the race, and a relentless critic of the man's views. "If we could just figure out a way to pin it on that scrawny little pothead boyfriend of hers, we could throw a Reefer Madness angle in there, too, get the anti-drug crowd running to the polls next Tuesday. You'd practically be guaranteed a second term."

There was a silence, and my scalp prickled all over, goose bumps rising between my shoulders. I couldn't tell if that was sarcasm or not, and I suddenly wasn't sure if my alibi of studying at home the night January went missing was strong enough to withstand the irresistible force of the Walker campaign's financial influence. Then, with a disgusted undertone, Mr. Walker snarled, "What would it say about me as a father, as a *man*, if I capitalize on this for political gain, Eddie? I'll look like a monster! We can't treat this like just another platform issue."

"Well, we have to," the other man contradicted unapologetically. "*You're* going to have to, because in your line of work, everything is either a setback or an opportunity—and the only difference is whether you want the job or not. You're the candidate with the dead kid, now, John. That's the brass fucking ring!" He actually laughed. "No one has to know what an obnoxious brat she was when she was alive."

There was another long silence before Mr. Walker spoke again, his voice low and measured. "Eddie, I'm going to do you the favor of pretending that I didn't hear you say that—and, as far as our official position is concerned, no body has been found, and January is still only missing."

"Oh, come off it, Jonathan. It's just you and me here, and you're not paying me to blow sunshine up your ass. Everybody knows what blood-soaked clothes and *duct tape* means, and the whole Parent in Denial routine has short legs. That little bitch was your candidacy's Achilles' heel, a scandal waiting to happen, but now? She's your golden ticket to D.C. You can hate me for saying this if you want to, but you know I'm right. This shit is the best damn thing that has ever happened to your campaign, hands down."

There was another long pause, and I suspected—hoped, really—that Mr. Walker was about to throw the man through the window. But instead, I heard the sigh of air escaping through cushion seams as someone settled into one of the leather armchairs, and then Jonathan's voice again, bland and weary. "Let's start researching current sentencing laws and set up a press conference for the morning. There's no time to put a functional proposal together, but we can draft a position at least. Tell Jeff and Rachel to get a speech ready for me to look over by tonight."

I was stung, feeling betrayed and offended by the way Mr. Walker capitulated so easily to Eddie's plan—the way his only defense of his stepdaughter was a perfunctory rebuke. Maybe January wasn't some model child out of a 1950s sitcom, or something, but she wasn't the way Eddie made her out to seem. And it was almost scary how much the heartless campaign manager seemed to hate her—and disillusioning how little Mr. Walker cared to argue about the subject.

As I was turning toward the front door then, I finally sensed the figure standing at the top of the stairs, looming in the shadows of the upper hall. Watching me. Looking up, I stifled a gasp. With broad shoulders and meaty arms, eyes glowering down through a shaggy fringe of dull, greasy hair, he'd obviously been standing there the entire time, listening along with me. When he saw that I'd noticed him, he smiled. It was a smug, gleeful little smirk—like he was glad I'd heard what I'd heard, and equally glad I knew he'd heard it, too. Then, without a word, he turned and disappeared on silent feet down the upstairs hall.

It was Anson Walker, January's asshole stepbrother.

"You know, the only time I actually like *this house is when my mom and Jonathan aren't in it," January had stated frankly one night the previous July as we were cooking dinner in the Walkers' shiny, state-of-the-art kitchen. Mr. and Mrs. Walker were in Detroit for some kind of charity benefit so Jonathan could press flesh with moneyed donors and finagle a few photo opportunities for the media.*

"Maybe we can pull some kind of Scooby-Doo shit—you know, dress up like ghosts and make them think the place is haunted so they move out and let you stay here by yourself," I suggested with a loopy giggle, a little buzzed on the champagne January had opened when

I'd arrived. She was having most of it, though, drinking with a vengeance, like each swig from the bottle was a fuck you to her parents. "I can move into one of your many, many empty rooms and be your bodyguard, or something."

"Oh, are you going to guard my body from all the bad guys?" January batted her lashes at me seductively as she turned up the heat under a pot of water on the stove. The kitchen was bright and modern, with brushed steel appliances, marble tile flooring, pale granite countertops, and an overhead rack of gleaming copper pots and pans. The Night of Flaming Peanut Butter had dimmed our culinary ambitions, though, leading us to stick with spaghetti and store-bought marinara.

"I will guard your body from anyone smaller than me," I promised stoutly. "If any of the big guys show up, though, you're on your own."

"My hero." She rolled her eyes, sipped some champagne, and sighed happily. "I fucking love champagne, don't you?" She pushed the bottle into my hands and then dragged her loose-fitting top up over her head, tossing it onto the kitchen's wide center island. She was wearing her bikini underneath, as we were planning a soak in the hot tub, and the green-and-white triangles of fabric seemed dangerously insubstantial when coupled with the coy look in her eyes. "Doesn't it make everything feel, I don't know . . . sexy?"

"Maybe a little," I agreed nervously, taking a small sip and passing the bottle back. I had pretty well-defined abs—they came with the "skinny" territory—but I wasn't sure there was any power on earth that could make me feel actually sexy.

January hoisted herself up onto the island, right next to where I was using a long, serrated bread knife to hack my way through an uncooperative baguette. Behind me, tomato sauce simmered in a copper saucepan, and the water for the noodles was just coming to a boil. My girlfriend ruffled my hair. "You are so cute when you're in the kitchen, you know that?"

"I'm cute everywhere." I mugged at her, and she laughed. Then, as she lifted the bottle to her lips, champagne rushed and gurgled out of it, spilling down her chin and sloshing over her chest in a frothing, perfumed cascade.

"Oops! Shit." She laughed at her own clumsiness, but then her blue eyes quickly slid to me from under heavy lids, and her tongue swiped across her lower lip. Tossing her pale hair behind her, she arched her back, letting the recessed lights shine on her glistening, alcohol-soaked cleavage. "Flynn . . . would you help me clean this off?"

The bread knife stuttered over the crust of the baguette, and I felt a peculiar anxiety build up inside as I stared at her breasts. Did she want me to get her a towel, or . . . did she mean something else? I suspected the latter, and swallowed drily. At that point in our relationship, I was beginning to worry about my lack of sexual interest—in girls, generally speaking, and in January, in particular. This felt not unlike a test, and one that should be easy to pass. I was curious, which was a good sign, but I didn't feel especially excited. Weren't boobs supposed to be exciting?

I set the bread knife down and moved to where she was sitting, her legs dangling over the edge of the island's granite top. Standing there between her knees, I could feel her body heat, her breasts at eye level, and she didn't move. She wants me to look at them, I thought. But what the hell else does she want me to do? Tentatively, I leaned forward and swiped my tongue along a warm, wet inch or two of her sternum, just grazing her breasts with my chin, but otherwise staying in what felt like safe territory. I tasted wine and salt, and January purred happily.

"That is soooo hot," she whispered, and then she put her hand in my hair again, tilted my face upward, and kissed me. I tasted more champagne on her mouth, mixed with vanilla lip gloss, and despite the awkward position of our bodies she really seemed to be enjoying this particular make-out. Little sounds escaped the back of her throat as she sucked at my lips and dragged her fingers across my shoulders, and when she drew back again, her eyes were soft and dilated. "Maybe . . . you know, I've been thinking—" She broke off all of a sudden, her gaze snapping to something in a corner of the room, and she jolted upright. "What the fuck?"

"Don't let me interrupt," came a deep voice from over my shoulder, and I jumped away from January, spinning around with a start. Standing in the dark rectangle of the open pantry door was Anson. His stringy hair was tucked under a snapback, which laid bare the acne-scarred skin of his elongated face, and the tank top he wore revealed the similarly pockmarked flesh of his wide, powerful shoulders.

"What are you doing down here?" January demanded unevenly, sounding both annoyed and a little perturbed.

"It's my fucking house, remember?" the older boy replied, his voice thick with contempt. "You're the one that doesn't belong here."

He sauntered forward from the pantry and started poking at the things we'd left sitting on the counter—the food, January's iPod, my phone—and instead of telling him to fuck off, I found myself frozen to the spot. He was twice my size, and it was like having a bear prowl your campsite: You didn't want to upset him, or draw any attention; you just wanted him to get bored and leave. It occurred to me, too, *that he had to have come down from upstairs, where he'd been when I'd arrived, and circled through the dining room to access the pantry without our having seen him. He'd been deliberately spying on us. I tried to remember if we'd said anything blackmail-worthy.*

"Why don't you just go back upstairs and play with yourself." January slid down from the island, crossing her arms self-consciously over her chest.

"Why? So you two can go back to fucking in my dad's kitchen?" He glared at us, and that's when he saw the champagne bottle next to the cutting board. His eyes lit up with glee, and he whooped, "No way!" Laughing, he grabbed the bottle and sneered nastily at his stepsister. "You picked this *bottle—that is* priceless! *Dad's been saving this bottle for a special occasion for, like, five years, and then White Trash Barbie goes and pops it open so she can slut it up with her faggot boyfriend. I can't wait to tell him about this. You'll be back in your shitty trailer park by next week!"*

"What's your problem, dude?" I demanded. He eyeballed me for a moment, and then took a long gulp of champagne. Turning back around, he picked my iPhone up from the counter and started messing with it. It was alarmingly easy to picture him smashing it against the floor out of spite, just to prove he could, and I felt a spike of anxiety. "Leave our stuff alone!"

"Go back to licking her titties again," he commanded. "I'll take some pictures for you, and January can start her porn career early." She gave him the finger, and he grinned malevolently. "Your gold-digging mom whored her way into my dad's bank account, but I bet you can do even better than that. You could be the next Sasha Grey or something!"

"You are so disgusting," January said quietly as Anson made a point of pushing my phone's camera at her cleavage. Uncomfortable,

she reached for her discarded top, but Anson anticipated the move and darted forward, snatching it out of her hands and holding it up so neither one of us could reach it. "Give me back my shirt!"

"Show me your tits first," he goaded, leering at her image in the view screen of my iPhone. "Push 'em together and say, 'I'm a big slut just like my whore mom,' and then you can have your shirt."

"Fuck you, you demented asshole!" I had finally had enough. Without thinking, I lunged for my phone, yanking it from his hands. "You think you're such hot shit, but all you do is jerk off and spend your dad's money, so what does that make you? How come you're not in college, anyway, Anson? Are you seriously so fucking stupid that even your dad can't buy you into a halfway decent school?"

The instant the words left my mouth, I regretted them. Anson was at least seven inches taller than me, and his left bicep had to be as big around as my left thigh. His pitted face darkened with rage, his eyebrows knotting together in an ugly scowl, and I saw sinews ripple tightly in his bared shoulders. I swallowed a rueful lump only a half-second before the muscle-bound freak dove forward, his fist speeding toward my face like a truck with no brakes.

Then it stopped, two centimeters from my nose. It was a fake-out; one of those obnoxious Tough Guy things that boys do to make you flinch and prove that you're a pussy—and, of course, it worked. I lurched back about a mile, crashing into the center island and almost knocking the cutting board to the floor. Anson laughed uproariously, pointing at my comically fearful expression, and finally turned to leave.

It was then, when I let my guard down, that he spun back around and decked me. He moved so fast that he didn't really have time to aim, but even for a glancing blow it felt like I'd been hit by a steam shovel. January let out a surprised shriek as I crashed down hard on the marble floor, stars popping and sparkling around me like Mr. Walker's special champagne. It felt like the left side of my face had been cut off, set on fire, and then stomped out. Towering over me like a sequoia, Anson snarled, "Watch your fucking mouth, you punk-ass bitch."

And, just like that, the bread knife was in January's hand, aimed right at Anson's thick, bullish neck. It didn't have a sharply pointed tip, but it was extremely long, and its jagged teeth were plenty dangerous. Shaking all over, she said, "Get the fuck out of here, you steroidal! Mutant! Psychopath!"

"Oh, are you gonna cut me, White Trash Barbie?" He was taunting her, but he didn't sound entirely sure of himself. "I'm so scared."

"You don't know anything about me," January hissed in a tone I'd never heard before, ruthless and confident and deadly serious. "You've got no idea what I'd do. Maybe I will cut you, or maybe I'll wait till you're asleep and chop off that little pencil dick of yours . . . or maybe I'll just show Eddie and your dad where you've been hiding your weed. And your oxy. And your coke."

Anson's expression changed, his sneer becoming a deep frown. His face a volatile shade of crimson, the boy took a step back, fixing January with a hateful glare; then, without saying another word, he hurled her shirt into the bubbling pot of spaghetti sauce on the stove, and stalked out of the kitchen.

It wasn't until we heard his feet banging up the stairs to the second floor that January sheathed her improvised weapon in the knife block on the island, and dropped to her knees by my side. "Flynn, are you okay?"

"Some bodyguard I turned out to be." I tried to smile, but I still felt like the aftermath of a natural disaster.

We rescued her shirt from the saucepan, though it was pretty clearly ruined, and decided we weren't really into the idea of spaghetti for dinner anymore. Eventually, I called my dad to see if he could come get me early, and began preparing a cover story to explain the ugly bruise beginning to spread across my cheekbone. The last thing I needed to do was give my parents a reason to complain about Anson to Mr. Walker—who would do nothing about it anyway—and make myself an even more irresistible target for the sadistic burnout's rage problem every time I came over.

It wasn't until January asked me if I thought we could drop her off at Tiana's house on my way home, however, that I realized how unnerved she'd been by the scene in the kitchen—and how much she didn't want to spend a night alone in the house with Anson.

THIRTEEN

I'M NOT SURE what the hell I was thinking—maybe I wasn't thinking at all—but I started marching immediately up the stairs to the second floor, my emotions turbulent and sharp. The self-satisfied look on Anson's face when he'd realized I'd overheard the awful things Eddie was saying about January had hit me just as hard as the nineteen-year-old's clumsy fist that night in the kitchen. She'd stood up to him for me once, and I needed to return the favor.

I was still totally outclassed, of course; Anson could easily pound me into the hardwood floors until the maid would need a putty knife to scrape me up again, and there was no one around to stop him this time. But his little smirk had made me just angry enough to ignore common sense and, at the moment, the rage felt really good.

The head of the upstairs hall formed a horseshoe around the curving staircases, opening in the front on the gaping cavern of the Walkers' foyer, with its triptych of stained-glass windows and wedding cake chandelier that dangled from the high ceiling like a flamboyant spider. To the back, there was a view over an ornate rail down into the grand room, where Tammy was still asleep on the sofa. Twin doors of paneled wood set into the east wall guarded the entry to the master suite, but a long corridor into the west wing of the mansion gave access to the remaining bedrooms on this floor.

Anson's room was at the end of the hallway, the farthest one from the master suite and therefore the one with the most privacy. Not only was it massive, and situated in a corner with views in two directions, but he even had an adjoining, bay-windowed study with access to a roof-level balcony. I'd seen the inside of his private quarters only once, when he was out of town visiting his mother for the July Fourth weekend, and his were undeniably the best quarters in the house after his parents'—despite being so filthy and disordered that even a dedicated slob such as myself had to think twice about touching anything without rubber gloves on.

That's why I was startled nearly out of my righteous fury when I discovered that it had not been his own spacious sanctuary to which Anson had retreated.

The door to January's bedroom, which always, *always* remained closed—no matter what, under penalty of gruesome torture—was standing open. I drew up short, then advanced closer and peered in, eyes wide with mounting outrage as I watched Anson Walker casually rummaging through his stepsister's private belongings.

It was not a girly bedroom, because January was not a girly girl; she'd even fought a determined, if quixotic, battle to paint the whole room black. Not a glossy black, either, but a sepulchral, matte-finish, emo black that would have made the place look like a satanic chapel with a walk-in closet and sunken tub. I was ninety percent sure that the crusade had merely been about getting under Tammy and Jonathan's white-bread skin, though; January really couldn't have cared less what color her walls were, but the very suggestion of an "all-black bedroom" made her *Town & Country*-obsessed parents squirm with horror, and that's what really mattered.

They compromised by letting her cover one whole wall with blackboard paint, like the project Tammy had undertaken at the condo, which was thereafter forever covered with chalked messages, song lyrics, and drawings in pastel hues. Another wall was plastered with impossibly detailed photographs of the night sky, the Milky Way glowing like phosphorescent mold above mountains, lakes, and glaciers. Elsewhere were pictures of me, Tiana, and Micah, as well as some of her other friends from Riverside; album art from Panic! At the Disco, Fun, and the Disasters; and images of Luke Hemmings, the lead singer of 5 Seconds of Summer. January didn't actually like 5SOS, but thought Hemmings was hot enough to rise above the group's musical failings—an opinion I'd secretly shared.

None of her old furniture made the trip up the tax bracket from the condo; her twin bed had been traded for a queen with a satin-upholstered headboard, the Ikea dresser for a hand-crafted bureau of cherrywood, and her refurbished PC had become a brand-new MacBook Air as quickly and easily as a rotting pumpkin turned into a set of designer wheels before Cinderella's very eyes. This particular Cinderella, of course, had far preferred the scullery to the ballroom.

Anson was rooting through an open drawer at January's desk, another of her new acquisitions, pulling things out and tossing them aside as he examined them and grew instantly bored. Letters she and Ti had passed to each other in class freshman year, a deck of tarot cards, and a box of colored pencils hit the floor while I stood there in disbelief. "What the hell are you doing?" I finally found my voice. "This is January's room!"

"Fuck off," Anson countered lazily. He sounded as drunk as Tammy had, only I didn't think he had the same excuse; for him, this was just another Tuesday. "Hey, you know if she keeps anything good in here? Weed, or cash, or whatever? I already checked her laptop for nudes, but I couldn't find any, and I don't see her phone around."

From the top right drawer of the desk, he pulled out a small, dried flower—the rose I'd given January on the night of our fateful two-month anniversary date. Until that very moment, I hadn't even realized she'd kept it, but I recognized it immediately because of the little heart she'd painted on one leaf in silver marker. Anson gave the flower a disinterested glance and then tossed it to the floor, where the fragile, blackened petals crumbled like charred newspaper.

"What the fuck is wrong with you?" I took two unsteady steps forward. "We *just* found her clothes out there covered in *blood*! Her mom is totally losing it right now, and you're ransacking her room for weed and selfies?" I was getting angrier by the second, just hearing it out loud. "Who do you think you are?"

"How 'bout I promise to cry myself to sleep tonight?" He

turned to face me with a sardonic chuckle, but his expression was flat, most likely deadened by controlled substances. As if to confirm my impression, he pulled a joint out of his back pocket and lit up right there, standing beside January's desk. "We both know she's dead, so you can just save your breath. It's too late to impress her with this pussy-ass white knight routine."

"You're an asshole," I fumed as the pungent, earthy aroma of pot unfurled from his mouth in a smoky tangle. "What the hell did she ever do to you, anyway? You've been nothing but a grade-A dick from the minute your dad started dating her mom, and she never deserved that. You call her trash, when you're nothing but a spoiled fuck-up sponging off your dad!"

"Oh, ouch! Your dumbshit opinion matters so much to me." He clutched at his heart, the joint clamped between his teeth. Then he crossed heavily to the bureau and began searching among January's underwear. I could feel brain cells starting to burst like popcorn as I watched this callous asswipe simultaneously smoke up and paw through his maybe-dead stepsister's panties; the injustice of it all was suffocating. Downstairs, Eddie was off on his insulting rant about January's having been Jonathan Walker's "Achilles' heel" because she drank sometimes and spoke her mind, while the man's own son was a deviant sleazebag without even a hint of a moral compass.

"Get out of her room," I ordered, as if I really expected Anson to listen to me.

"She have a diary, or anything, dude? Might be good for a laugh."

"Should I tell your dad you're getting high up here?" Threatening to tattle was a bitch move, but it's not like I stood a chance of intimidating him on my own.

"Shit, would you just go back to your Section 8 apartment already? You're like one of those yappy little dumb-ass dogs that nip at your ankles till you kick 'em," Anson grumbled dismissively, his dirty hands bunching up piles of silk and lace as he looked under and around January's lingerie. "You don't even know who it is you're up here trying to defend."

"What's that supposed to mean?"

"Sorry to break it to you, but your precious little Saint January was a dirty, lying slut. And I mean that literally. She was fucking around behind your back. So that's whose honor you're all worried about right now."

"Screw you."

"You think *I'm* the liar?" He yanked a particularly insubstantial G-string out of the drawer and held it up for my inspection, his rough, knobby fingers stretching out the dainty fabric. "Why'd she have these, then? She wear 'em for you?"

"It's just underwear," I said uncomfortably, feeling my face heat up.

"Nuh-uh." He grinned maliciously. "All this lace and shit? A chick doesn't buy these to *wear*, she buys 'em to *take off*. You only get sexy panties for one reason, and it ain't keeping skid marks out of your jeans." He tossed them aside and then leered at me. "So? How 'bout it, chief? Was she a good fuck?"

"Like I'd tell you anything about that."

Anson laughed as if I'd just supplied the punch line to a cruel joke at my own expense. "She didn't even let you hit it, did she?" He snorted blithely, stepping on the G-string as he shifted his huge feet. "She bought them slutty little panties to wear for somebody else, and you didn't even know about it!"

"Sure." I gave the word a bored affect, to let him know he wasn't getting under my skin and, predictably, he became annoyed.

"Fuck you, I know she did," Anson snapped, his thick brows coming together. Somehow, my doubting him seemed to have struck a nerve where my direct insults had failed. "She was never gonna settle for banging your broke, skinny ass. She was like her mom—she was only gonna spread her legs for money. Serious money."

It was my turn to laugh. The thing that January had disdained the most about the Walkers and their rarified social echelon was their obsession with wealth—their pride in having it, their greed for more of it, and their snobbish attitude toward those without it. I didn't know who Anson was describing, but it sure as hell wasn't his stepsister, and the more I thought about it, the funnier it seemed.

"You don't want to believe me, shit-smear?" Anson snarled, slamming the underwear drawer shut and yanking open the next one. "Fine. It's the damn truth, though. Your girlfriend was a dirty fucking whore who tried to Lolita my dad."

The suggestion was so twisted I almost choked. "That's bullshit."

"You wish." Seeing he'd scored some kind of a point, Anson's reptilian grin returned. "I came home one night from a friend's house and caught her trying to get him to do her in the kitchen. She was deep-throating a banana and everything! Guess the kitchen gets her gears running, huh?"

"That is such a load of crap," I snarled, disgusted. "You need mental help."

"They were making sundaes," he elaborated, still giving me that obscene, cold-blooded grin, "or at least she was. She was wearing her little bikini, like always, and she had all this shit all over the counter—whipped cream, peanuts, potato chips, maple syrup . . . I don't even know what she needed all that junk for, but it was everywhere." As he was talking, a hairline crack appeared in my confidence. Potato chips with maple syrup was January's favorite topping combo for ice cream, a quirk I'd sometimes teased her about, and one Anson couldn't possibly have hit upon by accident. "And my dad's like, 'That looks good, I haven't had a sundae in forever.' And January goes, 'This one's my specialty,' and then she deliberately gets syrup on her fingers and starts slobbering it off like a porn star.

"And my dad says, 'You know, we have bananas in the fruit bowl, if you want a banana split,' and she says, 'Oh, girls can't eat bananas!'" He did a breathless Marilyn Monroe voice for January. "And my dad asks what she's talking about, and she's all, 'Men think every cylindrical object is a proxy phallus, and if a girl eats a banana in public, she's automatically a slut.' And my dad says, 'Freud said sometimes a cigar is just a cigar,' and she goes, 'A cigar is only just a cigar when a *guy* is smoking it; if a girl is smoking it, it's a dick.'" Anson laughed maliciously and my lips tightened against my teeth. "And *then* she goes, 'No guy can watch a girl eating a banana without breaking out in a cold sweat, wanna see?' And she grabs this banana from the fruit bowl and starts giving it a blow job right there! She put whipped cream on it and everything, and just went to town like Jenna Jameson. Then they finally noticed I was standing there, and my dad told her to quit."

He was smirking at me triumphantly, arms folded across his chest so that his massive biceps nearly ripped the seams out of his shirtsleeves, and the joint trailed a long ribbon of smoke that threatened to strangle us both. All kinds of thoughts and emotions were running through me—the strongest of which was the desire to kick his asshole pelvis out from under him—but I felt rooted to the spot, affronted and horrified by the scene he'd just described.

"What are you doing up here?" The stern, unhappy voice came from behind me, and I spun around with a start. It was Mr. Walker himself, standing in January's doorway with a deep frown, his gray eyes zeroed in on me with a distinct lack of friendliness. "I thought you'd gone home, Flynn."

"I—I was on my way out, and then . . ." *And then?* I had no idea how to finish that sentence without explaining what a foul-mouthed, sex-obsessed muckraker his son was, and the moment didn't seem right for that.

"It isn't appropriate for you to be in January's bedroom," the man went on, blatantly ignoring the fact that Anson was right there with me—and the fact that the older boy was openly smoking weed. "Our family has suffered a terrible shock today, and we are entitled to a little privacy. I appreciate your help from this afternoon, but now I think it's time for you to leave."

And then, as if he hadn't been the one who'd invited me into the house in the first place, he escorted me brusquely back down the stairs and through the elaborate foyer, his hand on my back the entire time as if to prevent me from turning around and running upstairs again. He was acting like a bouncer ejecting a combative patron, despite my having offered no resistance, and his demeanor was stiff and frosty as he deposited me onto the front porch. Then, without even a word of farewell, he slammed the massive oak doors shut in my face.

FOURTEEN

FOR A LONG moment I just stood there on the windswept stone, the chill October air wrapping itself around me while my mind reeled like a punch-drunk boxer.

Anson was a liar, I reminded myself. January would never have done what he'd described—fellated a piece of fruit to seduce the stepfather she outspokenly disliked. Those were gross fabrications, fantasies spurred on by classism, resentment, and an overweening obsession with porn. He didn't have an ounce of scruples, and fondled his missing stepsister's underwear for thrills; who could believe a thing out of his mouth?

Which thus gave rise to the obvious question: Why was I having so much trouble shrugging the story off as nothing more than an obvious attempt to rile me? "Sundaes with potato chips and maple syrup" formed part of the answer. It was a detail that was so specific, so *her*, that I couldn't just dismiss it. That feminist theory stuff about proxy phalluses and the male gaze also had a distinctly January-esque sound to it—it sure as hell hadn't come from the primitive, misogynistic imagination of Anson Walker, at any rate. He would never have invented that on his own.

I also couldn't pretend that, just twenty-four hours earlier, I hadn't been grappling with my own growing realization that I didn't know my ex-girlfriend nearly as well as I thought I had—that she'd told lies that couldn't be easily justified, for reasons I didn't understand. What else had she kept secret? The shock of seeing her bloodstained hoodie, of realizing that she might have been *killed*, had sent me into a tailspin of emotional memories . . . but the girl who'd dried and saved a rose from our "perfect date" night was also the girl who'd told her friends I was an emotionally abusive jerk who'd tried to make her feel bad about leaving Riverside.

Anson could easily have cherry-picked some details from a random exchange between January and her stepdad and then used them as set dressing for his bullshit story, but I didn't think he was that conniving. His preferred method of warfare was direct and physical, not psychological. More likely, he'd embellished the hell out of an innocuous conversation, because he was a dick and a pervert, and he got off on offending people. Either way, there was really only one solid truth I felt he'd exposed, even if it had come as no surprise: He liked to spy on his stepsister.

I descended the stairs into the courtyard, walking toward the fountain as I fished in my pocket for my phone, and then stopped short when I saw a black Lexus parked at an angle across the long drive leading back out to the road. It was the only vehicle left, now that the volunteers, media, and police had all departed. Leaning against the driver's side door in his long, dark peacoat was Kaz.

When he realized I'd noticed him, he gave me an awkward wave. "Hey."

"What are you still doing here?" I asked, surprised. In the numbness and mind-wiping confusion that ensued after the discovery of January's clothes, I'd completely forgotten about him.

"I . . . I thought you might need a ride home." It sounded lame, and he offered me a clumsy smile that would have been endearing if I weren't so annoyed.

"I was just about to call my parents," I reported in a surly voice. This had been an awful and confusing day, and the last thing I really needed was to revisit the scene in the hayloft— not after everything else that had gone down since. "You shouldn't have waited around."

"I wanted to." He had his hands jammed in his pockets, shoulders hunched against the cold, and I wondered if he'd actually been standing there staring at the door all this time, like a dog waiting for its owner to emerge from a grocery store. "I thought . . . it's been a shitty day, right? I just wanted to." He gestured at the Lexus, which was shiny and obviously a recent model. "Come on, get in."

With an irritable sigh, I looked down at my phone, and then back at the mansion. Eddie Sward was watching me through the library windows, arms crossed and jaw tight, and although I couldn't see him, I was positive Mr. Walker was behind him. Did I really want to sit down on the freezing-cold fountain and wait twenty to thirty minutes for one of my parents to drive all the way out here to the middle of nowhere, with both men staring daggers at me the entire time?

"Fine," I said resignedly, moving around the front of the vehicle to the passenger side. As I belted myself in, I forced out a grudging "Thanks."

"No problem," Kaz said. The engine purred to life with barely a whisper, and the car did a weightless three-point turn before cruising down the drive through the topiary. The seats were covered in soft leather, still smelling like a showroom floor, and some bass-heavy music thumped at a low volume from the speakers.

We were quiet until we reached the road, by which point the silence between us had begun to feel like a third passenger. Unable to bear it any longer, and anxious to take preemptive control of the conversation, I blurted out, "This is a really nice car."

"Compliments of the Doctors Bashiri," Kaz replied with a self-conscious smile. "I won't pretend I don't like driving it, but sometimes it makes me feel really conspicuous. Like, people look at it and immediately think that I'm spoiled, you know?" Then he laughed a little. "Well, okay, I guess I *am* kind of spoiled, but I try not to act like it."

"I hope this doesn't sound rude, but if your parents are paying for your car and your tuition, why are you working at the toy store?" I was genuinely curious, although the second I heard the question out loud, I realized it really *did* sound kind of rude.

Kaz didn't seem to mind, though. "My parents . . . I love them, but they think that if they give me money, they have the right to tell me how to spend it. I got sick of having to justify literally every purchase I ever made—like if I wanted to eat McDonald's or download an app, I had to clear it first. Try explaining to your mom why you want to buy sexy underwear, you know?" He shot me a grin, and the image that rushed into my mind made my face feel hot. "Having a crappy job means having money that's just mine, that I can spend on whatever I want to. I can't tell you how good that feels."

"I think I understand," I said. It sounded an awful lot like what January had said when I'd asked her the same question—working at the toy store was a way she could take control of her life away from her stepfather. I was starting to see why she and Kaz could relate to each other.

Almost as if he could read my thoughts, Kaz then asked, "How are her parents doing?"

"About as you might expect," I answered, because getting into detail was too much to unpack at the moment. "Her mom is having a breakdown in a Munchausen syndrome kind of way, and her stepdad is worried about the political ramifications."

Kaz screwed up his mouth for a moment, but even the strange look on his face couldn't detract from how hot he was. I felt my annoyance becoming more entrenched. What is it about effortlessly good-looking people that is so aggravating? Gently, he then asked, "How are *you* handling it? I mean, it must be hitting you pretty hard, too. After what we saw in that field . . ."

"I'm okay," I said quickly. I didn't want to think about it. I wanted to believe that there was a happy ending out there, that I could find an explanation for the blood-drenched hoodie that meant January was still okay—and if it turned out I couldn't, well, I sure as hell did not want to have to face those particular demons in the passenger seat of Kaz's fancy car. "I'm just tired."

I gave him my address, which he programmed into his GPS, and then we drove in silence for a time before Kaz cleared his throat and said, "I hope you don't mind my asking, but how did you and January start dating?"

Considering the events of the afternoon, it sounded like a loaded question, but I decided to answer anyway. "She was—is best friends with my best friend's girlfriend, so we all just started hanging out a lot, and then . . . I don't know, we decided to take things to the next level."

The thing was, January and I had always been something that was a little bit more than "just friends." I couldn't totally explain it. When I flirted with her freshman year, it wasn't just camouflage; I *felt* something. I felt connected to January in a way that I didn't feel connected to other girls, even if the physical part of the equation was always elusive. When Madison Reinbeck shoved us into the kitchen pantry at the Walker mansion for a lamest-of-the-lame round of Seven Minutes in Heaven at a pool party the previous June, I'd actually been really excited to make out with her.

"Um, I hope it won't make you uncomfortable if I admit that I've actually wanted to kiss you, like, pretty much every day since the beginning of last year," January had confessed breathlessly when we'd finally come up for air. My head was spinning, and I was so relieved to feel something for a girl that I actually giggled.

"You're really good at it," I'd said, which was probably the stupidest, lamest thing any guy has ever said, ever—but January didn't seem to mind.

"Does that mean you want to go out with me?"

It was an uncompromising question and, emboldened by the dizzying head rush of the previous seven minutes, I took it by the horns. "Yeah."

"Well then, ask me, *dumbass!"*

And that was January, in a nutshell. And now . . . was she ever coming back? Would I ever see her again? I'd made a mess of things in our relationship—maybe we both had—but a sharp pain speared through my chest as I considered the possibility that she might really have disappeared from my life forever.

"Listen . . ." Kaz began, and even though I was grateful to have my thoughts suddenly interrupted, I recognized immediately where he was heading with this particular opening gambit and briefly considering forcing open the door and rolling out into traffic. "I'm really sorry about what happened in the barn."

"Let's not talk about it, okay?"

"No, I think we have to," he insisted obliviously, and I committed my gaze to the roadside. Trees and shrubs rose on both sides of the car, the season slowly whittling their limbs down to the bone as more and more leaves dropped away. "I mean, I guess now you understand why I was so surprised when you made it sound like you thought I was trying to hit on January. She knew I was gay. It's not like it was some big secret, or anything, so it kind of threw me for a loop when I realized that you didn't know, that she'd never told you." I remained silent, and after a moment, he added, "I guess that's really why I wanted to apologize this morning. If January was keeping that from you to make you jealous of our friendship, then I realized I couldn't exactly trust that she'd been totally honest with me about you, either. The truth is, some of her complaints about you sounded really . . ."

"Fake?"

"Indulgent. Like she secretly enjoyed being upset about them. Obviously I didn't know enough about you at the time to know they weren't true, but milking the pathos of having a selfish boyfriend seemed to make her weirdly satisfied."

I thought about my theatrical ex-girlfriend, and how her

personal drama meter had always seemed perennially stuck at ten. Certainly she'd had enough legitimate reasons to complain about her life; why had she needed me to be a villain, too? I took a breath. "I'm sorry I was rude to you that day I came into the toy store. It goes without saying that I didn't know better, but I wish I had."

"Thanks." There was a tense moment then that seemed to last about fifty years before he spoke again. "I'm sorry about the hayloft, too. I—I don't know what the hell I was thinking." His eyes were riveted on the road ahead of us, but his face was turning pink. "I got caught up in the moment, I guess, but I was a complete idiot. It was the wrong time, and the wrong situation, and I should've known."

"You made a mistake. Forget about it," I said, sincerely hoping he would.

"You know," he continued lightly, as if it would make me feel better, "January actually told me that sometimes she wondered. She said she wouldn't even have been mad, she'd just have wanted to know."

I gritted my teeth. "Wanted to know *what*?"

"You know. That you're gay."

"I'm not gay, though."

"Flynn—"

"I'm not gay!" I insisted defensively and, it must be said, a trifle hysterically. "I've already told you that I'm not gay, Kaz. How many times do I have to say it? What do I have to do to get the point across? I'm! Not! Gay! Get it? Understand?"

The dark slashes of his eyebrows drew downward, and in a peevish voice he stated, "You kissed me back, Flynn. It wasn't all one-sided up there. I understand if maybe you're freaked out about it, but you can't pretend that it didn't happen. I was there, remember? And it was a really good kiss."

"I don't know what you're talking about," I said desperately. "Okay? I don't know what I did or didn't do—I was surprised, and it all just happened really fast!"

"It didn't happen *that* fast," he countered pedantically. "I kissed you, and you didn't stop me. Instead, you stuck your tongue in my—"

"I DIDN'T STICK *ANYTHING ANYWHERE*," I declared shrilly. I was sweating, and I wanted to be anywhere else in the world but inside that car at that moment. If a chasm in the earth opened up in front of the Lexus right then, and we plummeted straight down to hell, I would have cheered.

"I know what happened. I know what I *felt*," he said quietly, moving on from my tongue to the other body part that had betrayed me in the hayloft. "You don't have to be ashamed, Flynn."

"I'm not ashamed, I am *straight*," I lied, clutching tightly to the leather cushion of the seat. "I'm not talking about this anymore, so just drop the subject!"

"I'm sorry. I didn't mean to upset you," he replied in a sober way, and was then mercifully silent for the remainder of the drive to my house. Still, as he pulled up to the curb, he said, "Let me see your phone for a second."

"Why?" I asked suspiciously.

"I want you to have my phone number, in case you ever want to talk."

"That really won't be necessary," I said breezily, and tried to let myself out. The door wouldn't open, though, and the buttons on the armrest wouldn't respond, either. I glared at Kaz. "The child locks are on."

"I know." He smiled, pleased with his own cunning, stomach-melting dimples appearing in his cheeks. "Let me see your phone."

"Are you kidding me? You're holding me hostage?" I gave him an imperious look, but he merely held out his hand, palm up. Annoyed, I slapped my phone into it. If that's what it took to free myself, then fine. "I'll just delete it the minute you let me out of the car."

"At least I can say I tried." He entered his information into my contacts list, returned the phone to me, and disengaged the safety locks. Impatiently, I shoved the door open and started up the walk to my house. Behind me, Kaz called out, "You know you can call me anytime!"

"Don't hold your breath," I retorted, jamming the phone into my pocket and hurrying to the front door, every step an excruciating exercise in self-consciousness, aware that he was watching me the whole way. I could have erased his entry right there, while he was looking, and driven my point home—but I didn't.

He'd said I was a *good kisser*; he'd said he wanted me to call him. I was embarrassed and confused and upset and thrilled all at the same time.

That fleeting kiss had been more intense, more exhilarating, than any kiss I'd ever shared with a girl—more exciting even than my seven minutes in heaven with January—and I could still feel my lips tingling where Kaz's had touched them. The memory made my heart speed up and the pressure build in my groin again, and no matter how complicated it made things, I could at least admit to myself that it had been incredible. I wasn't going to call Kaz, but having his number in my phone was like a souvenir of that intoxicating moment in the hayloft. It was something I couldn't talk to anyone about, not even Micah, but it was an event I could relive over and over in my head as often as I wanted, and his number was my proof that it had happened. I couldn't bring myself to get rid of it.

FIFTEEN

IT WAS 4:00 A.M., when I ran out of excuses for staying up and finally had to crawl into bed, that I could no longer stave off my encroaching apprehensions. The second I closed my eyes, the darkness in my room filled with swarming ravens, black feathers flashing as they were drawn by the scent of my ex-girlfriend's blood.

The hoodie burned like a sun in my mind, its hideous red-black stain a depthless tattoo etched into my memory. No matter how many ways I tried to argue it with myself, no matter how many angles I viewed it from, my hopes lost ground against my ascending conviction; unable to blank my mind, the thoughts trampling the air from my lungs, I was forced to admit to myself that I'd known—from the second I'd recognized what lay at my feet in that meadow—that January was really dead. There was no other explanation.

Regardless of her bitter antipathy to the Tammy and Jonathan Walker Show, I simply couldn't see January doing something as diabolical and operatic as tossing fake blood all over her clothes and then hiding somewhere, calmly watching an entire community go into an uproar when they were found. If it *were* a hoax, the police would figure it out in very short order, and my girlfriend would go from being a tragic figure to a national pariah in the blink of an eye—at which point no university of any esteem would want to have her as a student, no matter the outcome of Mr. Walker's election. It would unquestionably mean the end of her California dreams, and she was too smart and too driven to compromise that goal for such short-term satisfaction.

But if she hadn't left her things in that meadow, tangled in duct tape and soaked in blood from who-knew-what, then someone else had. *Someone else had.* Her clothes hadn't been deposited somewhere obvious, somewhere they'd be found immediately—and they hadn't been sent directly to the Walkers like a severed finger, accompanied by a demand for payment, either—which meant they were not a message. They had simply been dumped, an inconvenience, abandoned there by someone who had apparently first spilled January's blood, *so much blood*, and then . . . *what?*

My pulse raced, my palms were clammy and damp, and I gasped for air as I began to face that she was gone—really gone. We'd shared so much, and it seemed impossible to me that I would never again be able to tease her about the warty old lady on the bus—*you look just like I did when I was your age!*—to fantasize together about life in California, to listen to the familiar rhythms of her bitching about her rags-to-riches life story. I'd never be able to apologize for hiding from myself in our relationship, to confront her about the lies she'd told Kaz and Reiko, or to ask her just what Anson had really overheard between her and Jonathan. There was a hole in my life now where January Beth McConville used to be, and a year of friendship, four months of dating, and a lifetime of inside jokes and little memories had vaporized irrecoverably.

Finally, at 6:00 a.m., a wrenching, unearthly howl erupted from deep in my throat. I curled up in the fetal position and sobbed until my stomach ached and I couldn't breathe. I cried like that for an hour or so, and finally, numb all over, I fell asleep as the morning sunlight was at last beginning to dispel the ravens from my bedroom.

My parents let me take the next day off from school, and I spent most of the morning trying to figure out what I could do with myself besides playing *BioShock*, trying not to think about the day before, and wishing I had more weed hidden in my breath mints container. Micah and Ti came over in the afternoon, their parents having called them in as well, and the three of us spent several emotional hours sharing our favorite memories of January. Micah wouldn't look either of us in the eye when saying her name, and it was clear he believed she was dead; Tiana was defiant, however, and refused to let either of us get away with using the past tense.

The afternoon was cathartic, grief and doubt erupting in stormy bursts; but Ti did eventually get us laughing when she reminded us of the time that Señora Findlay, our erratic Spanish teacher from freshman year, had been haranguing the class about our collective failure to pass a pop quiz, while January, standing unseen in the doorway behind her, had simultaneously mimicked the woman's every exaggerated physical movement to perfection. She'd received detention for a week when she was discovered, but it had been worth it.

We ordered pizza, made root beer floats, told more stories, and seesawed between laughter and tears for the rest of the day.

By 8:00 p.m., I was physically and emotionally exhausted, my body hurting all over like I'd been dragged six blocks by a panicked horse, and I fell asleep in the living room.

It rained torrentially the next day, and school was a gloomy affair. A makeshift shrine to January had been set up outside the theater: a picture of her mounted on a blank paper canvas underneath enormous letters reading BRING JANUARY HOME; all around her photo students had written personal messages. Half of them said *we miss u!* or some idiotic variation thereon, and many of them were from kids January had hated unabashedly. That afternoon Jonathan Walker gave his press conference demanding harsher sentencing laws in cases of crimes against children, and received the very outpouring of support that Eddie had predicted. Even teachers were talking about it.

Then, later that evening, all hell finally broke loose.

I thought there'd been a horrible glitch in the matrix when I got home from school, and Micah and I found ourselves standing outside my house and staring at the cop car parked in my parents' driveway. It was as if the previous Thursday were being repeated all over again; with a wave of nausea, I tried to think if I had any other friends who were suddenly unaccounted for. Micah and I stuttered our good-byes, and I walked stiffly to the house, feeling chilled straight through to the bone as I pushed open the door and let myself inside.

Two detectives that I'd never seen before were positioned in our living room, exactly where Moses and Wilkerson had been a week ago, while my parents sat facing them on our sofa. One had a mustache, and was introduced to me as Garcia, and the other was a tall, gangly blond man called Becker. Before I could ask about the unexplained change in the lineup, my dad indicated the cushion between him and my mom, and said, "The police had a few more questions to ask you about January."

When I was seated, Becker turned his horsey countenance on me. In a mild voice, he asked, "I understand you participated in the search party out at the Walker place the other day. How're you holding up, Flynn?" It was a meaningless question, and I offered a meaningless reply. Nodding, he started getting to the point. "We've read over your statement from when you spoke to our colleagues, and we'd like to talk a little more about the last time you saw your girlfriend."

"What do you want to know?"

"We'd like you to think some more about how she behaved that night."

"Um . . . what do you mean?" I asked, even though I was pretty sure what he meant was, *this is your chance to change your story before we call bullshit—with consequences.*

Becker gave me a bland look. "Are you sure she wasn't acting strangely in any way? Angrier or more upset than usual?"

"Not really," I prevaricated, thinking once again about January's hands urgently fumbling at the waistband of my jeans. What had made her want to take that step, that night? My secret made me feel like I'd been acting unreasonably, but now that I thought about it, I couldn't figure out why she'd been so insistent about it. "I mean, yeah, she was upset. . . . Like I said before, we had kind of an argument and broke up."

"You said it was mutual," Detective Garcia interjected coolly, and I froze. "When the other detectives were here last week, you said the breakup was mutual. That it"—he glanced at some notes in his hand—" 'just happened.' "

"Well . . . they asked if we'd had a *fight,* and we didn't. We argued a little bit, but that's all," I said, sounding like a complete ass. My temples were immediately damp with sweat, and I knew the lie was written all over my face. Suddenly I couldn't remember the details of all the half-truths and obfuscations I'd related to Moses and Wilkerson the week before, and *why were there new detectives, anyway?* "I mean, she'd been acting kind of distant for a while already and, technically speaking, breaking up was her idea, so it wasn't, like, you know . . . a *fight.*"

"So the breakup was *her* idea," Becker repeated, making a note of it, and I nodded vigorously. "When you say she was *distant,* what does that mean?"

"I don't know . . . she'd ignore my texts, or she'd make excuses not to get together, or we'd make plans and she'd blow them off . . . that kind of stuff."

"And this was unusual for her?"

"Well, I mean, yeah, I guess." I shrugged miserably. "I just sorta figured maybe she was mad at me about something I didn't know I'd done."

"That happen a lot?" Garcia asked. "She get mad at you and not say why?"

"Sometimes." It had been known to happen; although, truth be told, January's episodes of icy, silent resentment had synchronized almost perfectly with the moments when I had gracelessly terminated some increasingly passionate interlude without any explanation. She'd never needed to say why she was upset, because the reason was obvious, even if I didn't dare acknowledge it.

"Prior to when she started 'acting distant,'" Becker began,

in a way that suggested air quotes, like he was barely humoring the notion, "you two were still pretty close, though, right? Spent a lot of time together?"

He made it sound like a loaded question, but I couldn't figure out where the trap was, so I just said, "Yeah, of course."

"There isn't anyone else in the picture, is there?" he asked suddenly.

I hated repeating myself, but the only thing I could think to say was, "Huh?"

"I mean, if we ask around a bit, we're not going to find out that maybe one of you two was seeing someone else on the side this past month or so?" His tone dripped with fake confidentiality, very come-on-you-can-tell-me, and I bristled at the question.

"No, of course not! And what does that have to do with what's happened to January, anyway?"

"Just answer the questions, please," Garcia ordered sternly, and my mouth snapped shut. Sometimes I might fancy myself a bit of a rebel, but I had no desire to piss off the cops. "I'd like to discuss the last night you saw your girlfriend again. What exactly did the two of you talk about?"

I felt heat welling up inside of me, my mouth drying out like an old sponge. Omitting facts was one thing, but downright lying to the police felt especially wrong, a cardinal sin against an innate sense of order. Furthermore, I wasn't even sure I was capable of inventing a convincing and benign argument out of whole cloth on the spot; but how could I possibly answer this question truthfully without turning my entire life upside down? *Why were they asking about this?* Licking my lips, I began uncertainly, "We . . . we talked about California."

"California?"

"We both wanted to move to the West Coast after graduation, and so sometimes we'd tell each other stories about what it'd be like, hanging out in LA together and stuff."

"You went from talking about your future together to breaking up, but there was no fight?"

"Well . . ." I was hoping a bunch of brilliant words would come flying out of my mouth at the end of that self-conscious ellipsis, but instead I just looked at Garcia in silence with a growing sense of desolation.

My dad, God bless him, stepped in just then to save me. "Detective, I'm afraid I'm going to have to ask you to get to the point. What does my son's breakup with January have to do with her clothes being found in a field behind her house?"

Garcia and Becker looked at him, and then at me, and then at each other, and seemed to come to some unspoken agreement. The ball appeared to have been passed to Becker, because the slender detective eyed me very seriously and then asked the question that changed everything. "Flynn . . . were you aware that your girlfriend was pregnant?"

SIXTEEN

FOR A MOMENT, the room lost focus and my ears filled with feedback, the couch swaying like a catamaran as I tried to make sense of what I'd just been told. My parents were staring at me, white-faced, and I was staring at Becker. Finally, I laughed, a little wildly. "No she wasn't!"

He continued to stare at me, his face serious, his mouth clamped into a taut little line. Uncompromising, he asked again, "Did you know?"

"Know what? Of *course* I didn't know! There was nothing *to* know!" I turned to my parents for support, but they were looking at me like they'd never seen me before. The sweat at my temples started to roll. Did they not *believe* me? "She was a virgin!"

"We're very careful," Garcia explained smugly, as though he rather enjoyed my escalating agitation. "We have to be. As soon as we realized it was blood we were dealing with, we had it analyzed and compared against a DNA sample taken from January's bedroom, crossing our Ts and making sure the facts were the facts. The specimens matched, Flynn; there's no question about it. Your girlfriend lost a ton of blood, and somebody tried to wipe it all up with her sweatshirt." His eyes bored into me like an oil drill. "And I mean it was a *lot* of blood. Enough that we just don't see how she could have survived without medical attention—which we know she didn't get, at least not at any licensed emergency room in this part of the state. That's why we're here. We're from Homicide. This is officially no longer a missing persons case, Flynn."

Homicide—official now. *Everybody knows she's not just missing anymore.* But I couldn't even process that part, couldn't find any spare room in the mosh pit of crazy thoughts squirming and crashing about in my head. *Pregnant?* They were wrong!

"Confirming that it was January's blood and that she's most likely dead wasn't all we learned when we had the samples tested, though." Becker took over seamlessly, their interplay a well-choreographed routine. "The analysis also showed the presence of hCG—human chorionic gonadotropin—a hormone excreted during pregnancy. It surprised us, too, but it's one hundred percent accurate: Your girlfriend was pregnant."

"*She was a virgin!*" I insisted, instantly aware of how unhinged I sounded. I knew from TV that sometimes cops lied to suspects to get a confession—*your partner's in the next room right now, spilling his guts out*—but I could see no reason they would lie about this. No reason to fabricate the detection of "human chorionic gonadotropin" in January's blood. I could practically feel all the color drain out of my face, and the room slid and throbbed around me. When I spoke again, my voice sounded tinny and small. "I don't . . . there has to be . . . I don't understand."

"Is that what the two of you fought about?" Becker asked gently. My mother wouldn't look at me anymore, her hand over her mouth, but my father continued to stare. "Did she tell you she was pregnant?"

"She wasn't," I maintained irrationally. Then, "We never even had sex!"

"Flynn," my dad began in a strangled voice, "we're not going to be upset—"

"There's nothing to be upset about! We didn't have sex!"

"Maybe you tried to talk her out of having it, but you couldn't," Garcia suggested next, almost cajoling. "We understand January was pretty headstrong. Maybe she told you she was having the baby, and she expected you to step up to the plate."

"That's a lot to have hanging over your head," Becker chimed in sympathetically. "Being a father at fifteen? No one would blame you for being angry—even a little desperate. You'd have to tell your parents, her parents . . . and her stepfather isn't the kind of guy—"

"*No*," I gasped, my eyes huge. "No! That's all wrong!"

"It could be someone else's," my mother finally managed to suggest, but her tone was so dubious it both enraged me and broke my heart at the same time. Coupled with that, the austere, skeptical looks on the detectives' faces felt like a kick directly to my solar plexus.

"None of this makes any fucking sense!" I exclaimed manically. "I'm telling you the truth—*we didn't have sex*. She was still a virgin, she said so!"

Garcia moved closer, interest piqued. "When did she say that, Flynn?"

"Friday!" My entire body felt raw and hot, and I was answering the questions without thinking about where they were going, the need to clear my name suddenly urgent. "The night we broke up. She said she wanted me to be her . . . you know, her *first*."

"And afterward, you realized she had been lying to you?"

"What? No! There was no afterward! I'm telling you that we didn't do it!" I was emphatic, everything coming out with exclamation points. "She wanted to, and I wouldn't, and she got mad, and then . . . and then she said it was over."

"She broke up with you because you wouldn't sleep with her." Garcia seemed disappointed in me for thinking he might be stupid enough to buy such an absurd story.

"*She* wanted to have sex and *you* didn't?" Becker asked, sounding even less credulous than his partner, if that were possible.

"Yes! We—we'd agreed to wait, and then she didn't want to wait, and I told her I still wanted to wait. . . ." My voice petered out pathetically. I felt like I had floodlights pouring into my eyes, and my chest was constricted, the air too thick and hot to breathe.

They stared at me. Just stared. I thought I was going to lose my mind, my body burning all over, my parents rigid on either side of me, and these two cops sizing me up for an orange jumpsuit while I tried not to speak the words that were crawling up my throat like stomach acid. Becker shifted. "Son, we know you claim you have an alibi for the night she disappeared, but you need to be honest with us—"

"I'm gay!"

The words burst out of me like they were spring-loaded, and I'm not certain, but I think my soul left my body for a moment. It was like I was looking down at myself, damp and stricken at the center of that ridiculous tableau, everyone blinking at me with saucered eyes. The room was dead silent, and it was far too late to stuff the genie back into the bottle, and my entire life had just changed—completely, totally, irrevocably, and so fast it wasn't fair, *I still needed more time*—and then more words poured out like a river of barf, because I couldn't stop them anymore. "She wanted to have sex, and I said no, and I guess she'd figured out the reason why I never wanted to . . . *do* anything with her, because she tried to make me admit that I . . . that I don't like girls, and I got mad, and we started fighting, and she said . . . she told me I needed to 'admit the truth,' because she was done. And then she stormed out, and it was the last time I ever saw her. It was the last time."

I couldn't look at my parents, and I couldn't look at the detectives, so I stared at the coffee table. A hiccup jerked at my esophagus and I tasted bile, but I bit down against the impulse to vomit. I was struggling to breathe, waiting for my mom to start crying or something, but the room was so quiet it was like I'd been struck deaf. Finally, after an interminable length of time, Becker cleared his throat. "So, it's safe to say she was pretty upset that night."

I actually laughed. "Yeah. Yes. It's *safe to say* that she was upset."

"I don't understand," my dad said, his voice steady but unnatural, and I still couldn't look at him. "If she was pregnant, it obviously wasn't Flynn's—and you yourself just pointed out he has an alibi—so what's the point of all these questions? What difference does it make?"

"Kind of convenient, you suddenly realizing you don't like girls anymore, right after finding out a piece of news like this,"

Becker remarked, almost casually, and I gave him a poisonous glare in response. Did anything about the situation actually seem "convenient" to him? Tossing a look at his notes, he continued, "And about that alibi . . . you say you were doing homework the night January disappeared. Can anyone else confirm that?"

"He watched TV before dinner, right in this room, and then sat at that table and worked on his history paper until he went to bed," my mother reported, her tone as cold and stiff as a corpse. The question didn't make any sense to me; did they really think I could have hopped on my bike, gone off to *kill January,* and then dumped her clothes in a field behind her own house before cycling back home? It was insane. The whole thing was completely insane.

"And you're sure that we're not going to find out about a secret girlfriend—or boyfriend—when we ask around about this?" Garcia pressed. "Someone who might have gotten jealous?"

My heart tripped and fell over. *When we ask around about this.* Naturally, they couldn't just take my word for it, and soon—the next day? The day after?—they would start talking to my friends. Micah, Ti, Mason, the guys on the track team . . . one by one, they'd all get asked if I might have been cheating on January. If I might really be gay. My stomach dropped like an anchor as I pictured it, all their faces flashing through my mind in high speed as they reacted to the question. I couldn't speak, my tongue felt like it was coasted in paste, so I just shook my head in response.

"We understand that the field where her clothes were found

had some particular significance to her," Becker noted, direct-ing the comment to me.

"She watched the stars there." My voice was barely above a whisper.

"Do you think that's where she was . . . Do you think . . . it happened in the same place?" my father asked, still strug-gling with the unnamable act, as if saying it out loud might upset someone. As if the night could possibly become more upsetting.

The detectives ignored him, scribbling down some notes, and then Becker inquired, "Flynn, if you weren't the father, then do you have any idea who was? Any guesses as to who else your girlfriend might have been seeing on the side?"

"No," I replied rigidly. "I really don't know."

It was the truth, but it was also somewhat misleading. I didn't *know*, but I was starting to have a suspicion, and it was one that made the taste of bile flood the back of my throat once again. It was sick and twisted and wrong, but I couldn't stop thinking about Anson sneering at me in January's bedroom, a lacy G-string in his hands. *Your girlfriend was a dirty fucking whore who tried to Lolita my dad.*

It was bullshit. It had to be. January would never ever have had sex with Jonathan Walker—*ever.* Like I'd said to myself the day Anson made the preposterous allegation, it was nothing but a perverse fantasy, invented by the most fantastic pervert of all time. January loathed her pompous martinet of a stepfather and, until that night in the barn, had agreed with me that sex was a Big Deal and shouldn't be rushed. Beyond all of that, there was simply no way I could picture her trying to seduce her mom's husband. It was as insane as everything else that was happening.

And yet. I couldn't rid myself of the image of ice cream with maple syrup and potato chips, of January complaining about sexual objectification while gesticulating provocatively with a banana. The details were too *real* to be wholly false.

And what if, somewhere at the bottom of it all, there was a grain of truth in Anson's claims? *It's finally the right time, and I want . . . I want you to be the first.* What if January had known she was pregnant that night in the barn, and the reason she'd been so desperate to sleep with me was because she was hoping to convince me that the baby was *mine*? If, somehow, she really had been carrying her perfect, politically ambitious, image-obsessed stepdad's baby, the man couldn't possibly afford to let anyone find out. Jonathan Walker would have had an excellent motive for wanting her to disappear—and that desolate field behind the mansion would have been a really convenient place to dump the evidence.

In a flash, I heard Eddie's voice in my head: *That little bitch was your candidacy's Achilles' heel, a scandal waiting to happen.* Had he known something? Had they both? Could it be true? And did I dare mention any of it to the police?

I was overwhelmed, my thoughts cacophonous and out of control; I wasn't even sure that I was completely *compos mentis*, and I didn't want to make an enemy of Jonathan Walker by slinging accusations when I barely had my head on straight. Not when the cops were already making veiled observations to the effect that my coming out was possibly just a lie to divert suspicion. Besides, at the end of the day, all I really had to show for myself was the dubious word of pathological shit-starter Anson

Walker—who would no doubt deny everything if he were asked. No; I had to keep my own counsel for now, and trust that the cops were already considering Mr. Walker a possible suspect.

A million or so questions later, most of which I had no real answers for, the detectives finally left, the front door slamming on their perfunctory have-a-nice-evenings. The air in the house had been suffocating in their presence, but without their gun belts and threatening demeanors to distract me, the echo of my unplanned confession suddenly rang throughout the empty rooms as loudly as a church bell.

I was standing by the kitchen island, one hand jammed in my pocket and the other clutching the counter's edge so my fingers wouldn't visibly tremble, when my parents walked quietly back from the front door. Their expressions were concerned, but otherwise indecipherable, and my throat seized with another hiccup as I managed, "I'm s-sorry I didn't tell you earlier—"

I was cut off midsentence when my mother wrapped her arms around me, so tightly that the air whooshed out of my lungs, and she spoke gruffly into my ear. "I love you. I will always love you and support you, no matter what. *No matter what.*"

"Me too," my dad said, and engulfed both of us in a bear hug. I was already sort of crying and laughing at the same time, overwhelmed with relief, when he added, "And I am really, *really* glad that you didn't get anybody pregnant."

SEVENTEEN

THE REST OF the night was surreal. The atmosphere in the house was supercharged by my admission, and while I was constantly aware of the almost shocking relief of finally *not* having to edit myself—of not having to think twice about every statement that left my mouth, fearing I would betray myself with a slip of the tongue—I was also painfully aware of the stilted way my parents were behaving around me; the three of us were trying so hard to act normal around one another that *nothing* felt normal. The roller coaster went up and then down as the realization crept over me that I was going to have to get to know my own parents all over again, to forge a brand-new "normal" after fifteen years of struggling to be comfortable in my own skin, and the same would be true with all of my friends. The thought was both exhausting and a little scary.

Once the detectives were gone, their intimidation fading into memory, I was able to let go of the fear that had first gripped me when they'd implied that I was a suspect. My alibi was solid, and anyone I knew—no matter what they thought of me after learning my secret—would tell the cops I could never hurt January. Not ever, for any reason. But when at last I went to bed, all I could seem to think about was that she had been *pregnant*. With child. Expecting. *Enceinte*. Who was the father? The idea that she might have been planning to claim that *I* was disturbed me even more than all the lies she'd told her friends about me. Would she really have done that? Conned me, used me as a cover rather than taking me into her confidence?

On the other hand, I hadn't trusted her with my own difficult secret, and mine would only have effected temporary upheaval in our lives. I hoped. I couldn't begin to imagine what she must have been going through, how scared she must have been.

Had she really known? And for how long? She'd been in real distress, that night in the barn. I could see it so clearly now, looking back; the emotion I'd mistaken for frustrated desire had actually been desperation. I had been her last hope. But why? Why had she felt the need to conceal the identity of the guy who'd gotten her pregnant?

Unless the truth would've caused an even greater shitstorm than if she'd succeeded in passing the baby off as mine. And when I'd turned her down? If I knew January at all, a take-no-prisoners girl who stepped in the middle of fistfights and once threatened her meth-head lumberjack stepbrother with a freaking bread knife, she would have gone straight to the would-be father and confronted him.

And after that, she'd disappeared.

The next day was Halloween, and ironically the first day I was going to set foot in the halls of Riverside High without my mask. When I hadn't been dwelling on January and my troubling thoughts about the baby she'd been carrying, I'd been sweating cold bullets as I thought over what I would say to my best friend when I saw him again. Between the two problems, I got almost zero sleep.

I'd known Micah Feldman since we were two years old, and our moms decided to start a toddler playgroup in the neighborhood—a generous-sounding pretense for beefing up their own social lives. For a couple of hours in the afternoon, Micah and I would bang toy cars together in a room full of squalling little kids while the adults drank coffee and shared embarrassing stories about our bodily functions. As it turned out, one of the only things the playgroup adults happened to have in common was being parents, and once the kids started kindergarten, the coffee klatch moms and dads drifted apart.

Micah and I, on the other hand, became friends for life. We did T-ball together, peewee soccer, summer camp, science fair projects; we learned to ride bikes, skate, and play *Call of Duty*; we talked about philosophy and people and nothing at all; sometimes we just sat in my bedroom or his and listened to music for hours without any pressure to fill the empty space. We'd even talked about girls—who was hot, who wasn't, and who maybe just possibly *like*-liked one of us. The only subject we'd never really discussed in any amount of depth was ourselves.

Half the night I'd spent telling myself that I didn't have to do this so soon, that I'd gotten the news out to my parents—arguably the bigger hurdle—and could let the dust settle before purposefully upending my life again. My coming-out experience hadn't exactly lacked for drama, and with everything that was going on at the moment, there was an appealing argument to be made in favor of taking some time to breathe before I notified the student body at Riverside.

The problem with that was that I was facing a great, big, ticking time bomb in the form of Detectives Garcia and Becker, who would sooner rather than later be making the rounds to double-check my story; I couldn't let that be how the news got out, and I couldn't just sit around and act natural while waiting for the blow, either, knowing it could come at any moment. Plus, I wasn't exactly sure how to deal with having the cat only halfway out of the bag, being honest at home while still pretending to agree with Micah when he went on about how much he really, *really* liked watching Megan Fox in *Transformers*, even though he really hated *Transformers*.

Simply deciding to move ahead with Operation Surprise-I'm-Gay did not, however, bring me a huge sense of relief. While it was great to know that my parents weren't going to disown me or—worse—try to "fix" me, they weren't my *friends*. If Micah freaked out, who would I bitch to *about* my parents? Who would I practice my kickflips with, buy weed with, and sneak into R-rated movies with?

I found him in front of his locker, kneeling on the floor and trying to reorganize the contents of his backpack to accommodate his chemistry book. A hoarder-in-training, Micah had filled his bag with a staggering quantity of useless crap he was afraid to throw away: old tests, receipts, a beanie in case it got cold, a thicker beanie in case it got cold*er*, a canister of awful body spray he used after swim practice, and actual, honest-to-goodness trash he'd stuffed in there because he refused to litter, but which he never remembered to throw away.

"Hey, dude," I said, sure my voice was quivering like a guitar string. Micah didn't notice, glancing up at me, his eyes popped open wide.

"*Dude!*" He abandoned the backpack, springing to his feet. "You never texted me back last night, head case! What did the cops want this time?" I blinked. I'd been so focused on my errand that I'd forgotten he'd seen the police car in my driveway. Thrown off-balance, I explained what Detectives Garcia and Becker had told me and my parents, and watched my best friend cycle through the same series of extreme reactions I'd had the previous evening. "*Pregnant?* Dude. *Dude.*"

"I know."

"You didn't even tell me that the two of you 'sealed the deal,' asshole!" he admonished, sincerely annoyed in addition to being genuinely shocked.

"We didn't," I said uncomfortably, and his eyes bulged even more.

"She was *cheating on you?*" He was flabbergasted at the very idea and, feeling more awkward by the moment, I didn't tell him I believed it might not be quite as simple as that. For the moment, it was probably best if he went on thinking that January had maybe simply hooked up with some rich Dumas kid behind my back. Micah frowned worriedly. "You don't think Ti knew about it, though, do you?"

"No, I really don't," I answered honestly.

He looked a little relieved. "Man, I'm sorry. That pretty much sucks." We stood there in silence for a moment, but it wasn't one of our normal, congenial silences—this one was thick enough to write your name in. "Is something else going on? You're giving off this weird *vibe* right now."

I swallowed, my throat so dry I tasted sand. "Yeah. Um, actually, there's something I need to say."

He waited, but I was frozen, struggling to force the words

off the end of my tongue. I stared at the dirty linoleum floor until he gave a nervous laugh. "What is it, dude? Don't tell me you're pregnant, too."

I was so anxious I couldn't even crack a smile at the joke. My joints were starting to vibrate and my brain was speeding and I took a deep breath that rattled ominously in my chest. "The fact is, man, I'm, um . . . I'm gay."

He stared at me for a beat, totally expressionless, and then he let out another laugh. "Ha! Good one. You almost got me."

He dropped back to his knees, struggling with his backpack again, and I looked down at the top of his head, confused. "I'm not joking, man. It's true."

"No it isn't," he said crossly. With a grunt, he forced his chemistry book into the Dumpster that was his bag and yanked the zipper closed. "You're just saying it to fuck with me. I've known you since you were potty training, Flynn. You're not gay."

He stood up again, slung the bag over his shoulders, and slammed his locker door shut. His expression was angry now, and I was starting to sweat. "I am, Micah." My voice was a foreign squeak, and I was grateful that the halls were emptying out so that there wasn't anyone around to hear it. "I swear it's not a joke or anything. I told my parents last night, and I . . . I wanted to make sure you were first after that."

"Stop it, okay?" He put up his hands. "Just stop."

"Micah—"

"You think I wouldn't have noticed something like that? Something like my best friend being into dudes? You've had girlfriends, Flynn! Plural. We've watched porn online together and talked about . . . *doing things*—*you* talked about doing *things* with *girls*—and now, all of a sudden you're gay, just like that?"

"No, not . . . just like that," I mumbled, feeling cold all over. "I've kinda known for a while, but I didn't—"

"I said stop!"

"You need to listen to me, okay?" I exclaimed. "I've been dealing with it for a long time, Micah—maybe even since eighth grade, but I just—I kept hoping that it was some kind of a phase, or that I would—"

"You've known since the *eighth grade* and you never told me?" His manner shifted abruptly, unchecked anger flooding his tone. "Dude, I tell you *everything*!"

"No you don't," I said. I could feel pressure building behind my eyes and I tried to stay calm. This wasn't going the way it was supposed to.

"I tell you all the important shit!" he countered hotly. "I told you when I thought my dad was having an affair, when I had IBS and had to wear a fucking diaper to school . . . you were the only person I came to that time I thought I'd gotten genital warts!"

"You knew you didn't have genital warts," I pointed out, distantly hoping that maybe he would see the humor in it now. "You were still a virgin."

"*I showed you my dick!*"

I stared at him blankly for a moment while my fear and dismay curdled together and produced alarm. "Is that why you're so pissed?"

"I've spent the last thirteen years changing my clothes in front of you and whatever, thinking it was no big deal, and now I find out that the whole time you . . ."

"I what?" I challenged, spreading my arms out. "That I was secretly *lusting* after you? That I was jerking off at night thinking about your IBS and your maybe–genital warts? Just because I'm gay doesn't mean I'm into you, Micah! You're like my *brother*! Trust me—I'm not hot for your body." Insistently, I added, "I'm still the same fucking person!"

"No you're not!" he fired back indignantly, leveling a finger at my face. "You are *not* the guy who bragged about seeing Brittany Cole's boobs fall out at my bar mitzvah; you are *not* the guy who helped me draw nipples on my sister's Barbies so we could take porny pictures of them; and you are *not* the guy I thought I knew for my entire fucking life! I don't know *who* you are."

We stared at each other, breathing hard, and then the bell rang, splitting the dense air of the hall like a meat cleaver. Stiffly, Micah stated, "I have to get to class."

With that, he turned and marched down the corridor, while a wave of panic, disbelief, and sorrow rose up and forced all the air from my lungs.

EIGHTEEN

NEEDLES STABBED AT my tear ducts, my vision a whorl of light and color. *What had I been thinking?* How could I have been so stupid as to expect that Micah would just take my little announcement in stride? Of course he'd freaked out—I'd lied to him for *years*.

I hadn't left myself enough time to collect my books, so I trudged to my first class empty-handed and stared at the board for fifty-five minutes without hearing a word of Mr. Pierce's algebraic musings. Could my life get any worse? It felt like I'd finally hit an iceberg that had been in front of me forever, but which I'd been too stupid to take seriously. Every day I was finding out things about January that I'd never known, things that had been there beneath the surface all along, but which I'd managed not to see; now I'd blithely steered myself into the first real fight I'd ever had with Micah, thanks to the same reluctance to recognize what was right in front of me. What if he couldn't get over it? What would I do without my best friend? *Either* of my best friends?

Micah avoided me the rest of the day and didn't respond to

the text messages I sent, apologizing some more and asking if we could talk. Even though he wasn't speaking with *me*, however, it appeared he was in communication with just about everyone else at Riverside. No fewer than three people approached me in the hall to confirm the rumors going around, and I struggled to look okay with the casual invasion of my privacy. Even Mason Collier, asshelmet extraordinaire, wanted to let me know how open-minded he could be.

"I've got a cousin who's gay," he confided, kind of like it was a big secret he was sharing because I might understand. "He's actually pretty cool. Really funny. But you guys are always funny, I guess."

Then he waited until I obliged his perspective with a humorous remark, while inside I groaned and died a little. I had cousins, too, and I wondered if this was the sort of thing they were going to say to *their* gay friends when they found out about me. And how funny was I going to have to be in order to fit in, anyway?

To my surprise, Tiana approached me after fifth period and gave me a hug. "I heard the news—obviously—and I'm totally proud of you, Flynn. I know you didn't tell me, personally, but still. It's a really big deal, and I know it's probably scary, so I wanted to make sure I said that I support you and that I'm happy for you."

"I'm glad somebody is," I mumbled.

"Yeah, well." She didn't need me to spell the reference out for her. "He's freaking out, but you know Micah: Shoot first, ask questions later."

"You think he'll get around to asking questions?"

"Of course he will, dumbass! You guys have been best friends since you were zygotes—he just needs a minute to get used to it."

"He was really pissed off, though." I could feel my throat swelling up, moisture beginning to glaze my eyes, and my face heated with embarrassment. Ti was making it sound like it was no big deal, but she hadn't been there; she hadn't seen the look on Micah's face when he told me he didn't know who I was anymore.

"He's not *pissed*, he's just . . ." Tiana sighed. "You have to understand that he kinda thinks of the two of you as the dynamic duo or something. It's nerdy and pathetic, in a totally adorable way, but that's my boyfriend." She tossed up her hands, resigned to her fate. "He's confused right now, and he's not sure how to make sense of it. You being different makes *him* feel different, and he's . . . scared."

"Scared of me?"

"Scared of *life*." Tiana gave me such a serious look that I finally realized she'd also heard the news about January. "I mean, aren't we all? Just a little?"

By the end of the day, I'd made up my mind. My coming out might not have been the heartwarming Very Special Episode that TV shows made the experience out to be, but the fact was that it was behind me now. Micah had saved me the trouble of having to repeat it to everyone I knew at school, and my parents were sure to tell my grandparents and all other assorted relations, and that meant the hard work was effectively over. It hadn't been easy, and the shit was far from done hitting the fan, but at least the truth was out in the open.

Having accomplished that much, it still left one unresolved problem to deal with: January's mysterious pregnancy. Though I didn't want to implicate Jonathan Walker without something real to back it up, I wasn't just going to let it drop, either. If he was the father, he wasn't likely to confess, but there was one person I could think of who might already know the truth.

I prevailed upon Mason for another ride after school, and he spent most of it rather nervously telling me more about how comfortable he was around gay people—paradoxically proving the opposite. He kept sneaking glances at me when he thought I wasn't looking, and finally fell silent. When he spoke again, he cleared his throat first. "Uh, look, just to be totally clear, I'm not a homo or anything."

"Sorry?" It came so out of left field I wasn't sure how to respond.

"I mean, I'm not giving you a ride because I'm into you, or anything. I'm just trying to be cool." Judging from his tone, he seemed to feel the importance of this distinction could not be overstated. "Like I said, I don't have a problem with gay guys, but I'm not one, so . . . you know. Don't get any ideas or whatever."

"Ideas about what?"

He rolled his eyes impatiently. "About *me*. I like girls, okay?"

"No one said you didn't," I pointed out with growing irritation.

"Right." He was firm. "Just so we're clear."

"We're clear," I assured him coldly. He was such an egotist he couldn't even entertain the possibility that I wasn't attracted to him—and although he wasn't exactly hard on the eyes, Mason Collier, with his Bieber-inspired wardrobe and douche-inspired personality, fell somewhere below a wax dummy of Jack the Ripper on my list of Guys I Might Want to Date. His car then came to a stop outside the gates of the Dumas Academy, and I disembarked with a friendly—but not *too* friendly, lest he think I was getting "ideas"—good-bye.

This time I found Reiko sitting at the back of the auditorium, quietly drawing on the top sheet of a high-quality sketchpad, her hands moving with careful, confident strokes across the heavy paper. Arranged beside her were a collection of professional-looking colored pencils and a lumpy gray eraser that resembled a wad of chewed-up food. Near the apron of the stage, Cedric Hoffman stood, offering nebulous directions to a pair of scowling actors. "Cléante, I'm not believing that you *love* Angelique. Be more *in the moment.*"

"But I don't even understand the script!" the actor playing Cléante snapped.

"That's not the point," Cedric answered in his calm, airy way. "The audience won't understand it, either. You have to make them *feel* it."

I rolled my eyes, and interrupted Reiko's concentration. "Hey. Um . . . I need to speak to you."

She looked up. Her eyes were swollen, her face blotchy from crying. When she recognized me, she emitted a sigh and said, tiredly, "I thought I made it really clear that I can't tell you anything."

"You did." I crossed my arms over my chest, trying not to be moved by her obvious grief. The local media had been relentless that week, salivating over descriptions of duct tape and bloody clothes, and January's smiling picture had been making hourly appearances above block-letter captions reading PRESUMED DEAD. "That was before, though, when you thought she'd run away because I didn't want to go to a dance with her."

Her mouth twisted unhappily. "Yeah, well. I guess I was wrong. If that's what you wanted to hear, there you go. You're not the reason she disappeared; you're just part of the reason she felt so *alone* all the time."

"That's not fair," I said, annoyed. "*She* shut *me* out—not the other way around. I told you that."

"Fine." Her commitment to arguing the point seemed to have drained away, and she uttered the word as if she were truly willing to concede the matter.

She returned to her sketch, pointedly tuning me out as she selected a pencil and applied it to the paper with short, deft strokes, angling the pad so I couldn't see what she was working on. A little louder, I stated, "That's not what I came all the way out here for. There's something I need to ask you."

"Excuse me." The interruption, peremptory and reproachful, had come from Cedric Hoffman. "I hope our little rehearsal here isn't interfering with your conversation."

I turned around, and when the man saw my face, his expression shifted from irritation to surprise to some unfriendliness that I couldn't quite read, his lips folding together into a thin, flat line. It was clear that he recognized me, and he didn't seem particularly thrilled to renew the acquaintance. I didn't have time to puzzle about it, though, because Reiko thrust her sketchpad down and got to her feet, shoving past me and heading for the door to the lobby. Before I took off after her, I glanced down at what she'd been working on and almost gasped; it was a portrait of January, so accurately detailed that its realism startled me. It was hard to believe a person could produce something so exact by hand; Reiko's talent was humbling.

She was ready for me when I emerged into the lobby, Cedric's glare still burning holes in my back like a surgical laser, and as the door shut behind me she hissed, "I've already told you twice that I've got nothing to say to you—"

"I'm aware of that," I cut her off disdainfully. "You said you couldn't tell me anything because 'there are rules.' What does that mean? Rules about what?"

She blew out air, her brow knitted, like she was trying to decide if she could even tell me enough to answer the question. "I'm a peer counselor," she said finally, her tone clipped and resentful. "I got to know January because she came to see me about . . . stuff she was going through, okay? Part of being involved in the counseling program means I can't just go blabbing things that people tell me in confidence. January came to me because she needed someone to listen, who wouldn't judge or spread her private business all over school. I gave my word, okay?"

"Well, she might be dead now." The statement took me by surprise, even as it came out of my mouth. It was the first time I'd really acknowledged it aloud, and it felt like someone had just wiped their feet on my soul. "So your secrecy isn't helping her any."

"It doesn't matter." The pink-haired girl was resolute, and it was my own composure that was beginning to crumble. I'd been on the verge of an embarrassing meltdown since my argument with Micah that morning, and once again my chest grew tight as I tried to form my next question.

"Was she . . . was it rape?" I asked in a strained voice. The word came out with difficulty, disgorged painfully from my heart, and I felt my hands begin to tremble. It had been hard to picture January cheating on me, impossible to imagine her seducing her stepfather, but this . . .

"I can't tell you that," Reiko whispered, but confirmation was written in the stricken rigidity of her expression.

"Oh, fuck, it's true." The sudden distance, the lying, the distress; it made sense.

"You should go," she said thickly, starting past me for the door to the theater. "I shouldn't have said anything. I should've told you to fuck off! What is wrong with me?"

I grabbed her arm. "Why didn't you go to the police?"

"January didn't want to. She hated the thought of everybody knowing. I told her . . . I told her the guy belonged behind bars, but she refused to come forward, and there was nothing I could do."

"You could've gone to them yourself!" I practically shouted, aghast at the thought of what she was telling me, trying desperately not to picture January being . . . *attacked*. "Fuck your *confidentiality*! Don't you have an obligation to report a *crime*?" Reiko struggled against my grip, but I held firm, outrage building like a feedback loop. "January was raped, and you're letting the guy get away with it because you 'gave your word'?"

"*Fuck you!*" she screamed, striking against me with more strength than I would have thought she possessed. I stumbled back as her face twisted up with tears. "You have no idea what it's like! How *dehumanizing* it is, how it feels to have everyone look at you afterward! And God help you if the guy who did it was popular, or an athlete or something." She must have seen the comprehension dawning in my eyes, because she let out a sharp, caustic laugh. "Yeah. Me too. Why do you think my parents took me out of my old school and moved here? I made the mistake of getting raped by a lacrosse player, and when I reported it, I immediately became the town slut. The town *liar*. A psychopathic whore who just wanted attention. 'She totally wanted it!' 'It was probably a pity fuck, and she just said it was rape to get revenge!' 'Boys will be boys!'" She spat the words out, pain glimmering in her eyes. "Even the friends who believed me stopped hanging out with me, because suddenly I was a liability—a social leper. How could I tell January that was worth it?"

"I'm sorry," I said sincerely. "But, look, it's just . . . it's not *right*. I get that she didn't want to go through all of that, but it's crazy to stick by your promise now! This guy might have killed her, Reiko, and he can't just get away with it! He *can't*. January would never have wanted that, either." I knew that as surely as I knew anything. January would want her rapist to pay the price—he *deserved* to pay—and someone damn well had to see that he did.

"There's no way to prove it." She shook her head. "There were no witnesses, the guy slipped her something so she was unconscious when it happened, and by the time she came to see me all the bruises were gone. There was no evidence left."

My jaw felt stiff, my eyes swimming. "He got her pregnant."

Reiko blanched and her knees seemed to give out; back to the wall, she sank down, whispering, "*No . . .*"

"She must have been scared shitless when she realized it." I felt heat on my cheek as a tear slipped toward my chin. "She didn't know what to do, or who she could count on. And I think he found out. I think she confronted him, and he killed her to keep it a secret." I got down so I was eye to eye with Reiko. "Even if you didn't see it happen, you can tell the cops what January said to you. Don't let him get away with it, Reiko. Tell me who did it."

"I . . . I can't," she said in a strange, anguished way. "She never said his name."

It sounded like the truth, but I'd picked up on her brief hesitation. Quietly, I said, "You figured it out, though, didn't you? Or you suspect?" Stomach acid stinging in my mouth, I asked, "Was it her stepdad?"

Reiko looked back at me for a long time, her expression tortured but undecipherable. I waited her out, trying in vain to detect whether I'd hit the target. Finally, in a soft, rocky murmur, she promised, "I'll think about what you said."

Then she stood up and slipped through the door into the theater, leaving me alone in the silence of the lobby.

NINETEEN

MY STOMACH BUMPED and rolled like a barrel going over Niagara Falls as I took a city bus home, kids in costume streaking past on the sidewalks in the settling dusk. A ghost was swinging a pumpkin-shaped pail filled with colorfully wrapped candy, a diminutive witch with a pointy hat and a green face dragged an old broom along the ground in her wake, and two fairy princesses screamed and hugged each other when a plastic skull at the end of someone's walk lit up and started laughing when they got too close. It made my heart hurt, nostalgic for a time when cheap Halloween decorations were what girls feared most.

I dropped my head into my hands. January had been *raped*. The instances of her aloof and inexplicable behavior erupted across my memory like painful sores, their timing suddenly significant in retrospect. The weekend before the hayride, she'd just stopped showing up for work, giving no explanation . . . was that when it had happened? With growing unease, I recognized that that was just about the same time the distance between us first truly became apparent; and, as I counted backward, I gave a sudden start, my blood turning to cement as another realization dawned: The Saturday Kaz said January had called in sick to Old Mother Hubbard's was exactly twenty-four days before she'd vanished. In an instant, the bus dissolved into nothingness, replaced before me by a vision of twenty-five hatch marks carved emphatically into the rotting wall of the hayloft.

Twenty-five. Was it possible? Barricaded in the isolation of her secret hideout, had she really *marked the days* she'd endured after her assault? Twenty-five days was almost four weeks. . . . Was that long enough for her to realize she might be pregnant? To become panicked enough to take a test and confirm the answer?

Long enough to learn the truth and begin spiraling?

She'd quit her job and then she'd dropped out of the play . . . each move a decision that Reiko had argued against. She'd probably told January it wasn't healthy to distance herself from other people, that she shouldn't allow her trauma to get the upper hand and take over her life; in response, January had lied and said she was doing it so she could spend more time with me. Reiko had probably been outraged because January was hurting and she believed that I was making demands, either oblivious of or apathetic to my girlfriend's horrific ordeal.

You were never around for January when she needed you. It was starting to sound like Reiko had been right. It hurt like an open wound that January felt as if she couldn't tell me what had happened, as if she thought that maybe I would judge her or look at her differently; I wasn't a good boyfriend, but I'd *loved* her, and I would have stood by her no matter what. But the pain I felt, knowing that instead of asking for my support she'd lied and said I was selfish, was dwarfed by my shame; there had been signs, and I'd missed them because I was too busy using the rift in our relationship as a place to hide from the intimacy she'd wanted from me.

It finally occurred to me, though, that there might have been more behind her attempt at seduction that night in the barn than just a simple ruse to disguise the baby's paternity. Maybe she really did want me to be her "first." Rape was violence, not sex, and after what had been done to her, maybe she wanted to be with someone who cared. Another sharp pang shot through me. The fact was, I would never know.

By the time I got home, I was heartsick and restless. I didn't feel like I could tell my parents what I'd learned; the thought of saying the words out loud again filled me with dread, and in any event, I had no evidence to back it up. It was a conversation I wouldn't have been sure how to initiate under ordinary circumstances, let alone the current ones, where it seemed like even the simplest interactions were awkward and laden with subtext. My mom rambled for a long time about how she and my dad had joined PFLAG that afternoon, and then they proceeded to have a conversation for my benefit about Annette at my dad's office, whose daughter was a lesbian. They even started recommending gay-themed movies they'd read about and thought I might enjoy. As touched as I was by the effort they were making, the whole experience was mortifying, and I fled to my room as soon as I could to drown my embarrassment, grief, and related emotions in several mind-numbing hours of Xbox.

I'd been supposed to go to Madison Reinbeck's Halloween party with Micah and Tiana, but I wasn't exactly in a partying mood—and I wasn't sure they wanted me to go with them anymore. I texted Micah several times after dinner with no response, and then finally tried Ti. A while later, she wrote back, telling me that the two of them were already at Madison's house. *Sorry for the mix-up!* Right.

Even though I'd no longer wanted to go, even though I had anticipated Micah not wanting to see me that night, I felt miserable knowing they'd gone without even bothering to tell me they wouldn't be picking me up after all. A week ago, Micah and I had been skating together and getting high, wondering where January was; now I was sitting on the floor of my bedroom, staring at a paused game of *BioShock*, feeling lonelier than I'd ever been in my life.

Knowing I had to either do something or risk being sucked through a metaphorical air lock into an oxygen-free wasteland of bad juju, I grabbed my phone and called the only person left.

A half hour later, my phone buzzed, and my feet barely touched the floor as I raced down the stairs and out the front door, calling a hasty good-bye to my bewildered parents with a promise to return before my midnight curfew. The black Lexus was purring at the curb like a contented panther, and when I yanked open the passenger door, I was greeting with the scent of sandalwood and soft leather. The combination made me embarrassingly weak in the knees.

"Hey," Kaz said with his crooked smile as I buckled myself in. He was wearing his peacoat again, his hair constructed into that perfect crown of soft, messy spikes, and his stunning hazel eyes were filled with curiosity. "Where are we going?"

"I don't know," I said, flushed and a little flustered. I was looking at his lips, thinking again about the kiss in the hayloft, and I suddenly felt so electrified I was afraid the air would start crackling around me. "Downtown, I guess. Maybe coffee?"

"Okay." Kaz sounded mildly amused, as if he could tell that a caffeine fix wasn't at all what I had in mind. "Coffee it is." He put the Lexus in drive and pulled away from the curb, turning when we reached Plymouth Road and heading for the center of the city. "I have to admit I was surprised when you called. I know I gave you my number and all, but I kinda thought you were really pissed at me."

"I . . . I mean, I wasn't *pissed*, exactly—"

"Yes you were," he corrected me, but in an understanding way. "I was really pushy and presumptuous. I didn't have the right to say the things I said. For the record, I'm sorry again. And I'm really glad you called." He shot me another cockeyed smile, glancing at me across that perfect Grecian nose. "Why *did* you call, by the way? I mean, it's a Friday night— Halloween, even. How come you're not going to some huge party somewhere?"

I squirmed a little as we coasted to a stop at a red light, feeling my neck get warm. For some reason, I'd thought it would be easier to tell Kaz than either my parents or Micah, but the same nerves were spiraling through my limbs again. "I—I told my parents that I'm gay."

"Wait . . . what?"

"I told everyone, actually. Well, I told one person, and *he* told everyone, but—" I was cut off when Kaz lunged across the center console and dragged me into a tight embrace. I was enveloped by the scent of laundry detergent, hair product, and rich cologne, and heat spread through the pit of my stomach. Even through his coat he felt warm, and for the first time I put my arms around a cute boy without having to act guarded or nonchalant about it.

"That's incredible, Flynn!" he gushed, his cheek pressed against mine. If I was expecting some kind of "toldja so," it wasn't forthcoming. "That's huge! I'm so proud of you—no, wait, scratch that. 'Proud' sounds kind of condescending, doesn't it?" His arms loosened their hold just a little, then tightened again determinedly. "No, actually, you know what? Fuck it. I *am* proud of you, because it takes a lot of guts to come out. Like, a *lot*. Good for you."

"The light is green," I said, my throat compressed against his shoulder.

Kaz let me go and started driving again, his mood buoyant, verging on giddy, and the excitement in his tone was infectious as he said, "Okay, coffee is on me. If I was old enough to buy alcohol, or if I had a fake ID, I'd get us some champagne or something, but you'll have to settle for coffee. Tell me how it happened."

"It was kind of unplanned, actually," I admitted. I gave him an edited recap of the Big Moment, not ready yet to relinquish his warm attention by mentioning the purpose of the cops' visit, and concluded with the hair-raising tale of my Gay-Friendly Dinner From Hell. "My dad said something about *Glee*, and then something about us all going to a Pride march in Chicago as a family thing this summer, and then I went hysterically deaf and blind and had to excuse myself."

Kaz laughed. "That's hilarious—they sound really cool."

"I don't think you understand," I said seriously. "They mean it about this Pride march. You know how kids are supposed to be embarrassed about getting driven to the mall by their parents? This is going to be like that, only ten times worse. It'll be like taking your grandmother to the prom. With drag queens."

"I think you're lucky," he replied, but I noticed a bit of the spark had left his voice. "Where are your other friends, by the way? I thought you said you told everybody."

"I did," I answered uncomfortably. "Not everybody was as humiliatingly supportive as my parents. My best friend isn't . . . he's not exactly talking to me right now."

"I'm sorry." Kaz was quiet as Plymouth became Broadway and Broadway became Beakes. "Listen, no matter what, you made the right choice. I think your friend will come around, but even if he doesn't, you're so much better off living honestly than pretending to be someone you're not just to fit in." The blinker made a soft clicking sound as Kaz navigated a left turn onto Main Street, gliding under lampposts and past Victorian-era homes that had been converted into offices. "I know it's easier to say that than to go through it—trust me—but you'll never be happy if you have to spend the rest of your life lying to people. And if he can't accept you for who you are, then he's not really your friend to begin with. Besides, there's always a little bit of pain when you grow."

As platitudes went, these were very nice, but they didn't make me feel any better about possibly losing Micah forever. He wasn't a homophobe. There were two guys in the drama club who were already out and proud, and Micah had never said a bad word about either of them—his problem wasn't with gay people, but with *me*, and I couldn't console myself by saying I was better off without him in my life, because I didn't believe that was true. Maybe someday in the future I'd be able to look back and think in lame clichés about how lucky I was to have been cut off like a gangrenous finger by my best friend of thirteen years, but that day was not today.

"I don't think I'm ready to be that optimistic about it just yet."

"I get it. But don't be discouraged, okay?" Kaz refused to let me wallow in my depression. "I went through it, too, and look at me now!"

He flashed me a cocky grin that positively dazzled under passing streetlights, and I laughed in spite of myself. "Top of the world?"

"Top of the world," he agreed. "Believe me, Flynn—someday you are going to look back and realize that this was the best decision you ever made." I felt my blood start humming when he looked over at me, his arresting jade-and-copper eyes warm and soft. "Just think about all the things you don't have to be afraid to do anymore."

"Such as?"

"Such as finally saying out loud what guys you think are hot," he answered mischievously. For a moment, I was sure he was giving me an opening to say, *You, duh,* so he could pull the car over and we could make out, but then he commanded, "Sexiest male celebrities: Go!"

"Dave Franco and Colton Haynes," I confessed, and the weird thing was that it felt kind of incredible to verbalize such thoughts for the first time. I'd spent years bottling up any admissions that might be construed as "gay," and it was both scary and liberating to finally let those words come out of my mouth. "Actually, pretty much all the guys in the cast of *Teen Wolf.* Every time they take their shirts off, it's like Christmas or something. Micah makes fun of me for being so obsessed with the show, and I've never been able to tell him that I'm not watching it for the plot."

"I thought guys taking off their shirts *was* the plot."

Kaz parked on Washington and we walked from there to the Nickels Arcade, a picturesque passageway with a vaulted glass ceiling that ran between State Street and Maynard. The Arcade housed an eclectic group of local businesses, including an artisanal coffee shop where discerning adults and students liked to hang out. Kaz ordered two cappuccinos from a cute barista with tattooed arms and geek-chic glasses, and we took a seat at one of the tables out front.

"Here's to Flynn Doherty, whose future begins today," Kaz announced, clinking his mug against mine and giving me another adorably giddy smile. "By the way, you never really said why you just kind of blurted it out in front of your parents like that. I . . . I hope it wasn't because you felt pressured or anything by what I said on Tuesday?" He winced apologetically, and I shook my head to assuage his guilt, but the Good News part of the evening was clearly over. With a heavy sigh, I explained about the police visit—January's pregnancy, Reiko's subsequent bombshell, and even my theory about the hatch marks. When I finished, Kaz was staring at me with wide, troubled eyes, his face pale. "Holy shit, Flynn. That's . . . I mean, I don't even know what to say."

"I tried to convince Reiko to go to the police, but she acted like there wasn't any point. She says there isn't any evidence, and January never told her who the guy was in the first place, but . . . I mean, I can't just drop it. I won't."

Kaz looked down into his rapidly emptying mug with a

frown. "I'm with you. But this kind of situation . . . I mean, it'd be one thing if they'd found her body, and had DNA from the fetus or whatever to compare against possible suspects' . . . but if there's *really* no evidence—no witnesses, no weapon—what do they have to go on?"

"Not to state the obvious, but maybe that's exactly the reason they haven't been able to find a body. If this guy killed January to cover up what he'd done, he sure as hell couldn't risk letting the police perform an autopsy." I leaned forward, closing in on my hypothesis, and felt steel in my veins. "You ever ask yourself how January's stuff got out into that field in the first place? The last time anyone saw her, she was at Dumas, like ten miles from home. If she really went missing from there, how'd her clothes end up in her own neighborhood?"

"I have a feeling you're about to make a guess."

"Tammy said Jonathan never came home that night," I finally announced, the words coming out with heat and relief, "but what if he did? What if he just never came into the house?"

Kaz's slanted, dark eyebrows shot up. "You think *Jonathan Walker* did it?"

"He could have picked her up at school, no problem," I began intently, barreling ahead with my theory despite the skepticism in Kaz's tone, "overpowered her, taken her somewhere to kill her, and then dumped her things in the meadow after Tammy was asleep. Or maybe he did it out there—it's far enough away from anywhere that no one would've heard a thing."

"So he kills her in the meadow and leaves her clothes for the police to discover, then conceals the body somewhere nobody's been able to find it?" Kaz gave me a dubious look and I frowned reflexively, embarrassed that I hadn't thought of that inconsistency myself. "I mean, why not hide the clothes *with* the body?"

I shifted in my seat, feeling wrong and disloyal to be referring to January as *the body*—symbolically giving up on her, reducing her to a thing, an obstacle someone else had been forced to deal with. "You sound like you have a theory of your own."

"Maybe the clothes were misdirection." Kaz rubbed a thumb along the curve of his spoon, thinking out loud. "Maybe someone wanted to implicate Walker—or one of the Walkers—and left her things there to put the cops onto the wrong trail."

The idea floated briefly in my mind. Torkelson? Mr. Walker's opponent in the senate race would probably love to see his competition suspected of murder . . . but the facts didn't fit. What politician would rape and then—weeks later—kill his opponent's underage stepdaughter, just for the incriminating evidence? And Kaz didn't know yet about the scene Anson had allegedly witnessed in the kitchen. I was sure I was right about Jonathan. What had happened to January was personal rather than political, and there would be an explanation to account for the issue with the clothes; I just had to find it. We were quiet for a short while until I felt I could no longer ignore the *other* subject that had been eating at me.

"I don't understand why she didn't trust me." I was staring at the leftover foam of my cappuccino, a frothy glob that clung to the bottom of my mug. "I mean, it kills me that she didn't give me a chance to help her—and that she told all those lies. That she apparently thought it was better to make me sound like a douche who didn't care rather than to talk to me about what was going on. Why would January want people to think all that stuff about me, anyway?"

"Maybe she was lonely," Kaz suggested softly. "She was separated from all her friends, she didn't fit in at Dumas, she despised her stepbrother—and she couldn't talk about any of it with her parents, because they were the ones orchestrating it all. Telling people her boyfriend was an asshole probably got her sympathy and attention. It worked on me. I was always asking how she was doing, when she was finally going to break up with you, etcetera." He hunched his shoulders unhappily. "It's easier to relate to a girl with a lousy boyfriend than a girl who got rich overnight and hates it."

"I guess." I still couldn't tell how to feel about it. Part of me was hurt and angry, but another part of me kind of understood. She'd used me to create a false image for herself; hadn't I used her for the same reason? And I couldn't imagine how hard it must have been for her, how much she must have been suffering. How could I hold anything against her, knowing what I did about what had happened?

We finished our coffee and walked around for a bit, drinking in the cold night air, making fun of the lame, Halloween-themed deals advertised in storefronts along State Street, and talking about things that didn't really matter. Kaz described interning at his father's medical practice over the summer, and how he'd accidentally screwed up the filing system so badly they'd needed to hire two temps to sort it out; in response, I told him about the time my mom paid me to stuff envelopes for a day at her real estate agency, and how I'd managed to not only bungle a task that could've been accomplished by any well-trained monkey but also proceeded to flood the break room by knocking over the watercooler. He was laughing so hard there were tears in his eyes when we finally reached his car.

"So . . ." He put his hands in his pockets, swiveling nervously. "What do you want to do now?"

It was still early, nearly an hour left before my curfew; not enough time for a movie, but plenty to do what I'd been dying to do all night. My lips were tingling again, nerves fizzing just under my skin. A couple laughed somewhere up the street, and an overhead light made a halo of bronze highlights in Kaz's dark hair. I felt like he'd been waiting the whole evening for me to make a move, and even though my stomach was twisted up like a balloon animal, my heart thumping as I gazed up at his strong jawline and impishly cocked eyebrow, I was going to do it.

I stepped close, breathing in his intoxicating scent, my lips parting. I had to stretch onto my toes, angling my face upward to cover the distance, but I made contact, my mouth touching his in a blissful, electric kiss.

And he jerked away from me, so suddenly he smacked into the Lexus, his expression both surprised and concerned. "Whoa, wait."

I blinked, totally confused. "I don't . . . What's wrong?"

"This probably isn't a good idea," he answered, uncomfortable and apparently serious. I stared at him blankly.

"Are you kidding?" The distant couple's laughter grew louder, and I suddenly felt as if it were directed at me—only Kaz was clearly not joking, his face tense and his eyes downcast. Insecurity and indignation were suddenly playing tug-of-war in my muddled brain. "I don't understand. You seemed to think the idea was just fine on Tuesday."

"Yeah, I know," he muttered humbly, "and, like I said, it was a mistake. I shouldn't have done it."

Just like that, the tears I'd been warding off all day punched the back of my eyes and I felt my face grow warm. Struggling to sound in control, I said, "Fuck. You already have a boyfriend, don't you?"

"No, it's not that." His reply, strangely enough, made me feel even worse.

"Oh, great. You're just not attracted to me." My humiliation felt almost complete, and the tears were rolling now, making me grateful for the darkness. "Why the hell did you kiss me, then? Were you just fucking with me? Was it some game you play where you try to get guys to admit they're gay?" I was ranting and losing that tenuous image of control, but I couldn't help myself. In a way, he was partly responsible for my finally coming out; if I'd never felt his lips against mine, if I hadn't been made aware of what I was missing by staying in the closet, maybe I'd have been more able to bite my tongue in the face of the detectives' questions. "I cannot believe what an idiot I am!"

"You're not an idiot, Flynn," Kaz stated. He moved closer, as if to comfort me, and I stepped back. "Look, I *am* attracted to you, okay? Seriously, you have no idea. Why do you think I tripped all over myself apologizing for the fight at the toy store? Why I wanted to talk to you again in the first place?" He ran a hand through his hair. "I've been thinking about that kiss all freaking week!"

"Then what the hell?" I demanded with a pitiful sniffle, tossing my hands up and letting them slap down against my thighs. "What's wrong with me now?"

"Nothing! I just . . . I don't think you're ready for . . . this."

"*I'm* not ready?" I was offended and incredulous. "What the hell does that mean? Don't I get to have any input on what I'm ready for?"

"You just came out of the closet yesterday, and you've got a lot of turmoil in your life right now. I mean, do you really think you want to jump into, like, dating or whatever? Now?" He let out a breath. "My family is Muslim, and totally conservative. It took everything I had to get up the courage to come out to my mom and dad—I mean, I was terrified that they were going to kick me out, or refuse to let me go to college or something. But what they told me was, 'Don't you dare say anything like that in front of your grandparents!' And then they totally changed the subject. The end. To this day, they refuse to acknowledge that I'm gay—the whole topic is off-limits, like the conversation never even happened!" He gave a helpless shrug and stuffed his hands into his pockets again. "It was so hard to talk to them after that, about *anything*. There were so many things I couldn't say because they'd just completely shut down if I tried. It was awful. I was sort of dating this guy at the time, too, a guy I really liked, and I totally blew it with him because I wasn't ready. He wanted a relationship, and I was losing my shit! I was terrified that if we went out together one of my cousins—a couple of whom are *really* religious—would see us and freak, I couldn't even *think* about introducing him to my parents, and I was way too mixed up to be anybody's boyfriend in the first place. I didn't have anyone to talk to about what I was feeling, about *who I am*. There was no one who would listen to me, no one I knew who'd gone through it and would just *be there* for me while I went psycho a few times a day. . . . I felt totally alone, and what I really needed was a *friend*. I want to give you that, be someone you can count on for support without any pressure. I mean, you get what I'm saying, right?"

"Yeah, sure," I answered emptily, miserable and defeated. I didn't want Kaz to be my "friend." I wanted *Micah* to be my friend, and I wanted Kaz to be . . . well, something else. Sure, his position sounded all noble, but that was *his* experience—not mine. How could he decide for me what I could and couldn't handle? And how could I just turn off all the things he made me feel even when he wasn't trying? I would never be able to look at him without thinking about how much I wanted to kiss him, and how much he *didn't* want to kiss me back. What the hell kind of friendship would that be?

It was not without a trace of irony that I then recognized how much my situation was like January's had been: alienated from my friends, unable to talk to my parents, and attracted to a guy who didn't want me in the way that I wanted him. I was suddenly so depressed I didn't even have the energy to resent Kaz for flirting with me when he had no intention of following through. If this is how January had felt—even before the sexual assault that had precipitated everything else that happened—maybe I really could forgive her for seeking a little sympathy at my expense.

"I should probably get home," I mumbled, surreptitiously swiping tears out of my eyes with my sleeve. It was barely 11:15, but I couldn't face forty-five more minutes of being "friends." "My parents have been freaking out about safety and stuff ever since January disappeared, and they're probably waiting up for me."

It was a lie, and an obvious one, but Kaz didn't challenge

me on it. Instead, he blipped the locks open on the Lexus and we got inside. Just as the seat warmers started to kick in, my phone began buzzing in my pocket.

When I saw the name and image on the display, shock took my breath away and I dropped the device at my feet as if it had burned me.

The call was coming from January's phone.

TWENTY

"DO YOU BELIEVE in ghosts?" January asked me. It was late June and we were upstairs in her room at the mansion, the windows open wide to let in air that smelled like lilacs and freshly cut grass. Her iPod was on shuffle, and I was looking up movie times on the Internet while she paged through a gossip magazine. The question seemed to have come out of nowhere.

"No," I said, confident it was the response of any sane individual. "I think people see what they want to see. I read this thing online once that said humans are basically programmed—on, like, an evolutionary level—to detect faces. When you encounter something random, your brain automatically scans it for a pattern it can recognize, and that's why there are all these weirdos out there who think the Virgin Mary appeared to them on a potato chip, or whatever. It's the same thing with ghosts."

January set the magazine aside and stared ruminatively up at the ceiling. After a moment, she said, "I believe in them."

I was sitting on the floor beside the bed, and I craned my neck around to look at her with a bemused expression. "January McConville, the future CEO of NASA, believes in the supernatural?"

"NASA does not have a CEO, it has a government-appointed administrator," she retorted smartly, "and it's not as if I believe in, like, vampires and shit. Just ghosts."

"Same thing."

"They are not the same!" She sat up, giving me a serious look. "I just don't think that you die and it's, poof! You're gone! Like someone flipping off a light switch. I think people leave energy behind. Sometimes, I'll be sitting in class, taking notes, whatever, and I'll just suddenly feel my grandma next to me. It's not like I'm thinking about her so hard I magically convince myself that I sense her presence—I'll be completely focused on something else and, out of nowhere, it's like she walks up and taps me on the shoulder." Tossing back her long straw-colored hair, she went on, "Okay, maybe I've never seen a ghost myself, but haven't you ever walked into an empty room and immediately felt sad, or nervous, or like somebody was watching you, and you couldn't figure out any reason why?"

"Maybe," I said. In truth, I had experienced something like that before—I just wasn't sure I was ready to identify disembodied energy as the cause. "When they make you CEO of NASA, maybe you can dedicate the budget to holding séances and developing those proton guns they use in Ghostbusters—"

"Shut up," she said with a laugh, hurling a pillow at my face. "You better be nice to me, or I'll dedicate the budget to breaking down the barrier between this world and the next, and when I die my ghost will haunt the shit out you!"

"Just stay out of the bathroom when I'm pooping, okay?"

"I'm not kidding, Flynn Doherty," she said, leaning toward me across the bed with a mischievous smirk. "You're never getting rid of me."

For several heartbeats—once my heart started up again, that is—I was prepared to believe it really was January calling me. Not from beyond the grave, but maybe from somewhere in California, having faked her death after all. If anyone could've pulled off something like that, it was her. Her body was still missing, her clothes disposed of in a place where they would have to be found sooner or later . . . it could have been true.

Only I had seen the amount of blood on her hoodie with my own eyes, had heard the police confirm that it was hers, beyond question—*enough that we just don't see how she could have survived without medical attention*—and when I looked again at the display, I felt my hopes escape like a breath of air when I realized I'd made a simple error. The call wasn't coming from January's cell, but from her home number—the landline at the mansion. It was still unexpected, of course, but it wasn't my ex-girlfriend, either calling me *or* haunting me. I answered, and the subsequent conversation I had was both short and baffling. When I hung up again, I turned to Kaz and asked, in a perturbed voice, "Can you take me to January's? I mean, right now?"

"I . . . sure, why? Who was that?"

"It was Jonathan Walker." I was still rattled at hearing the man's voice in my ear, and perplexed by what he'd said. "He practically begged me to come over there. He told me it was an emergency."

"And you believe him?" Kaz oozed doubt from every pore, even as he redirected the Lexus in the direction of Superior Charter Township. "Flynn, just a little while ago, you said you thought he had raped and killed his stepdaughter!"

"And what was my excuse supposed to be for refusing

to go? 'Sorry, but I'm pretty sure you raped and killed your stepdaughter?'" I was still clinging to my phone, half hoping for January to call for real this time and clear the matter up. "I'm not sure what's going on, but he sounded pretty sincere."

"I'm not leaving you there alone," Kaz said decisively, his hands tightening on the wheel. "I'm coming in with you."

I didn't fight him on it. I didn't want to go there alone. Maybe I should have said no to Mr. Walker in the first place, but he'd sounded urgent, almost panicked. *Flynn? Listen, I . . . could you please come out to the house? Right away. Please. It's . . . it's Mrs. Walker, she's . . . honestly, it's kind of an emergency. Please come?* He'd offered no details, hadn't explained what kind of an emergency Tammy might be having that I could help with, but I wasn't sure how to say no.

The interior of the Lexus was silent on the drive out to where the Walkers lived, the residual tension of the embarrassing almost-kiss mingling with a sense of foreboding about where we were headed and what we might find when we got there. Eventually, though, we were turning onto the drive leading to the mansion, headlights sweeping across another small shrine to January that had sprung up since Tuesday. Candles, flowers, stuffed animals, and other mementos had been piled under a prominent photograph of my ex-girlfriend smiling into the darkness.

At the end of the twisting lane, we pulled to a stop in the mansion's forecourt, stepped from the car, and started for the front porch. The door opened before we even reached the top of the steps, and Jonathan Walker appeared, backlit by the blazing glory of the crystal chandelier that floated in the foyer.

"Flynn! Thank you for coming." The man's voice was thin and anxious, and from behind him, out of the depths of the enormous manse, I heard alarming sounds: animalistic wails and sobs punctuated by the noise of shattering dishes. As we stepped into the glow of the porch lamps, Mr. Walker seemed to notice Kaz for the first time. "I'm sorry . . . I believe we've met, but I can't remember your name."

"Kaz Bashiri, sir. I worked with January at Old Mother Hubbard's, and I was here on Tuesday for the . . . um, the search." He shifted his weight uneasily and seemed to have trouble looking Mr. Walker in the eye.

"Of course," the man returned with a nod, though he still appeared distracted, radiating an aura of jittery carelessness. "Thank you for taking part. I . . . I hope you don't think I'm being rude, but I would appreciate it if you would wait out here. This is . . . it's a private matter."

Kaz looked to me, and I gave him a short nod before Mr. Walker ushered me quickly into the foyer, slamming the door shut on Kaz's worried, watchful gaze. While I wasn't anxious to go inside without backup, I didn't believe that the man wished to do me harm; he couldn't possibly know what I suspected. Besides, he would have to have assumed someone would bring me, and would therefore be waiting to take me home. Not the slick move of a criminal plotting his next kill.

"What's going on?" I asked with trepidation as he herded me along. "Is it . . . Why did you ask me to come over?"

"You were so good with her the other day," he answered indirectly, guiding me past the rounded staircases and toward the kitchen, from whence the dramatic and destructive sounds emanated. When we passed through the doors into the once immaculate and exquisitely appointed space, my mouth dropped open and I gazed in a state of horrified fascination at the source of the emergency.

Tammy Walker was down on her hands and knees, sobbing and babbling incomprehensibly, her hair disheveled and her silk robe in disarray. It hadn't been dishes I'd heard breaking from the front door, but stone; in one hand she gripped a claw hammer, and was bringing it down over and over against the expensive marble that paved the kitchen floor. The creamy tiles were cracked and smashed, gaping holes revealing the glue where Tammy had torn up large fragments and flung them aside.

The diaphanous, Martha Stewart–y window treatments had been pulled down, copper pots pounded against the floor until they were bent and twisted, and a silverware drawer yanked out and emptied over the center island, its rectangular socket gaping in the otherwise impeccable white facade of the below-counter cabinetry.

Mr. Walker rushed forward, grabbing Tammy's wrist before she could bring the hammer down again. His wife began to shriek like a madwoman as he struggled to wrest the tool from her grasp. "Let it go, Tammy, let it go—*let it go!*"

He jerked the hammer free at last and tossed it to the side. As Tammy began to flail in his arms, striking his chest with wild, ineffectual blows, he directed her—without warning—to me. The handoff was seamless, however; as Tammy fell against me, her frenzied rage segued immediately into paroxysms of hysterical grief. Clutching me in a fiercely tight embrace, she wept into my ear, tears wetting my neck as her fingers dug into the flesh of my back.

"She's gone," January's mother gasped, almost uncomprehendingly, her voice thin and ragged. "She's really, really gone. . . ."

"I'm sorry." It was a stupid thing to say, but the first thing that came to mind.

"She hated those tiles," the woman choked out in a defensive, almost childish tone that was also tinged with regret. "She said they were . . . pretentious. She hated this kitchen, Flynn. She hated this *house*, this *gilded cage*."

"I know."

The sobbing started again, and she seemed to melt against me, sagging gradually as though her life force was depleting bit by bit with every tear. She cried for a long time, shaking and sniffling, her hair clinging damply to my face, until she was able to form words again. "I thought this was going to be the happy ending. I thought this was going to be our reward! I wanted her to have everything, the most wonderful life, and this was supposed to be *it*. How could it turn out this way?"

"I don't know." The robe had slipped off her shoulder now, and I was terrified that if I looked down, I would see mom boobs.

"He never tried," she said with sudden contempt. "Even when he was around, he never tried! He looked at her like she might detonate at any second—how was she supposed to feel?"

"I don't know." I didn't even know what she was talking about.

"She was always so angry, Flynn, always so hurtful, so 'me against the world'! Why?" The question came out so despondent and confused it nearly broke my heart, and as Tammy's grip weakened, I moved her around the center island to one of the tall stools at the counter that faced the morning room. She slumped onto it, a husk of a woman, her face haggard and swollen with anguish, and pulled her robe together with trembling fingers. "Why did she always want to hurt me?"

"I . . . I don't think . . ." I trailed off, unsure how to approach this question, how to manage Tammy's combined grief and narcissism with any kind of finesse.

Then, bluntly, the woman asked, "Was it yours? The . . . baby?"

"N-no."

She studied me, as if trying to read my face, to see if I was lying, and then rasped in the same desolate tone, "I don't understand how life turns out like this."

I had nothing to say to that, and therefore just nodded my agreement. I didn't understand, either. Completely worn out, January's mother hunched over the counter and buried her face in her hands, her shoulders shaking gently and silently. A shoe scraped against the ruined floor behind me, and I turned to see Mr. Walker standing by the edge of the counter, half consumed by the shadows that filled the central hall. I wondered how much of our exchange he had heard. Nothing particularly private or sensitive had come up, and yet I felt a thrill of unease, thinking that he'd been eavesdropping.

With a blank face, the man beckoned, turned, and then disappeared from sight without waiting to see if I would follow. Clearly, the ambitious state senator was used to giving orders and having them followed without question.

Tammy had tuned me out, and for the moment it looked like she was finished with her kitchen demolition project, so I heeded Mr. Walker's summons. He was waiting for me in the grand room, pouring scotch into two cut-glass tumblers that sat on his desk. One serving he knocked back immediately; the other he thrust into my hands. I looked at it with wide eyes, wondering if he was seriously expecting me to have a drink with him, and then he finished swallowing and spoke. "Give that to Mrs. Walker. She needs a drink—and she'll take it, if it's from you."

Why wouldn't she take it from you? I wanted to ask, but couldn't find the courage to do so aloud. "Is she going to be okay?"

"She will," he said tiredly, pouring more scotch into his tumbler, "eventually." He took a sip, closed his eyes, and exhaled. "This has all been . . . exceedingly difficult for her, as I'm sure you can imagine. I'm afraid she hasn't been herself since January disappeared. Her outburst on Tuesday was just the tip of the iceberg."

It was both an apology and a rebuke of his wife, and I squirmed uncomfortably. "I think she's calmed down now."

"She'll start up again." He rubbed his mouth ruefully. His hand looked raw and chapped from repeated washings, and I wondered if he was a germophobe. "The election is Tuesday. What am I going to do with her?"

The question was both crass and rhetorical and, once again, I found myself disappointed to see Mr. Walker's selfish priorities cast in such sharp relief. I didn't have the balls to call him on it, though—especially in light of what he might well have done to the last teenager that pissed him off. "Maybe she needs some help? Like, professional help, I mean."

"That reminds me," Mr. Walker said suddenly. Putting down his glass, he reached into his pocket and withdrew an orange plastic vial. Popping off the cap, he turned it over into the palm of his hand and a cascade of blue capsules tumbled out. "She'd better take some of these, too."

"What are they?"

"Sedatives," he replied. He noticed my reaction and, with a faint smile, added, "I know, I know, you shouldn't mix pills and alcohol. Believe me, though, Mrs. Walker can handle a lot more than this. She'll be fine, don't worry."

"What if she won't take them?"

"Good point." With obviously practiced skill, he broke two capsules open and emptied their contents into the whiskey I held in my hands. "Swirl that around a bit—she won't even notice."

I did as I was told, my stomach feeling unsettled and queasy, and then carried the concoction back into the kitchen. Stiffly, aware that I was being watched, I slid the drink in front of January's mother. She looked up at me with a feeble smile.

"Thank you, Flynn." She downed the whiskey in two gulps, then closed her hand over mine on the counter and expelled a breath that rattled like an old car with a busted muffler. "You're a sweet boy. January was lucky to have met you."

"I . . ." I blushed, feeling miserably unable to accept the compliment.

"The truth is," she admitted, letting out another sigh, "I wish it *had* been yours." There was absolutely nothing to say to this, so I sat stock-still and allowed her to continue. "I was young when I had January. Too young. Everyone told me it was a big mistake, to have a baby at seventeen, but I thought I knew everything. Kids always think they know everything. Sure, I understood that childcare was challenging—I had younger siblings, I'd been a babysitter—but I never had any doubt that I could hack it as a mom. I'd always landed on my feet before, why would this be any different?" She was staring at the black windows of the morning room, our faces reflected in the overlaid glass. Tammy's voice was already starting to get soft around the edges. "I didn't use to believe in having regrets, but maybe I should have listened. Maybe I was selfish."

"Don't say that," I offered weakly. "January loved you. She said you weren't just her mom, you were her friend, too, you know?"

Tammy sobbed a little, then squeezed my hand. "Such a sweet boy."

Her eyes were dreamy and unfocused, her movements becoming lethargic, and Mr. Walker seemed to take this as his cue to reenter the scene. "Come along, Tammy, let's get you to bed."

"Flynn is a sweet boy," she told him faintly as he pulled her up from the barstool and put his arm around her waist. "A good boy."

"Of course," Jonathan responded, his tone perfunctory and meaningless, and the smell of bullshit seemed to have an adverse effect on his wife.

Pushing out of his grasp with an unsteady stumble, she snapped, "You don't care. You only care about yourself, about your *election*."

"Tammy—"

"You want everything to be perfect, and even then it's still not good enough!" Her words ran together like watercolors. "The more I try to do what you want, the less shits you give.

My unhappiness is an 'inconvenience'! My contributions are *unappreciated*! Look, sweetheart," she announced, with a sadistic cackle, "I fixed the kitchen for you!"

"I noticed." Mr. Walker's tone was as remote as the surface of Pluto.

"*Where were you when I needed you?*" she demanded accusingly.

His face turned beet red. "We have been over this at least a dozen times: I had an important meeting with some people from the PAC, I had too much to drink, I got a hotel room—"

"I'm talking about tonight!" Tammy slurred furiously. "Where were you *tonight*?"

Something rippled across her husband's face and disappeared, leaving him rigid and icy. "You're confused, and it's time for you to go to bed." He took hold of her again, roughly this time, and hauled her purposefully toward the stairs. Tammy didn't look happy, but she didn't have the strength to fight him. Over his shoulder, he called back in an unfriendly manner, "You'd better go home now, Flynn. And I trust you'll have the sense not to discuss this sordid little scene publicly."

They were halfway up the stairs, and me halfway to the front door, when Tammy's broken whisper echoed in the airy foyer. "I was talking about *tonight*. . . ."

The next day was Saturday, and I got up late—not only because that is a teenager's primary moral imperative on weekends but also because I'd spent the night tossing and turning, thinking about Jonathan Walker. I was starting to see that he had married Tammy McConville not out of love but out of strategic necessity. She was young and still beautiful—"the quintessential MILF," Micah had once dubbed her—so she looked good by his side, and with her he'd leveled up from being a Divorced Single Parent to being a Family Man, thereby increasing his political cachet.

If he'd truly cared for Tammy, it wouldn't have been his fifteen-year-old stepdaughter's ex-boyfriend that he'd have called to the rescue when his wife had a mental breakdown and started renovating the kitchen with a claw hammer. Again, he'd thought strategically, using unimportant me to defuse the problem, and then casting me out indifferently once I had served my purpose. He viewed the people around him as either resources or problems, and acted accordingly.

I already knew he thought of January as a "problem," and that he had no issue with resorting to devious means when it came to controlling difficult McConville women. I also knew he'd made at least one mistake.

On Tuesday, during the first argument I'd witnessed between him and Tammy, he'd said that the night January died he'd been having "drinks with some boosters"; but last night, when Tammy shifted from self-destruct to attack mode, the alibi he'd spit out was "an important meeting with some people from the PAC." I didn't know much about politics, but I knew from my U.S. government class that a political action committee raised money through donations and then funneled it to a candidate, while boosters were more like goodwill ambassadors dedicated to promoting said candidate. Unless Jonathan Walker had said "boosters" when he meant to say "donors," I was pretty sure I'd caught him in a discrepancy. Not that I could do much with it. It was circumstantial, a slip of the tongue, and hardly enough to incriminate a man with Mr. Walker's level of power and influence.

Still half-asleep, I got out of bed and started down the stairs, surprised when I reached the ground floor and heard the indistinct bleating of the television. Typically, my parents are never around on Saturdays, choosing instead to get up at some ungodly hour so they could exercise, run errands, and do whatever it is parents do before finally coming back in time for dinner. When they *were* home, it was invariably so that they could engage in some conspicuously constructive activity and pressure me to join in. The only time they watched television in the afternoon was on Sunday, a special dispensation issued for the sake of college football.

The second my footsteps sounded in the hallway, the television went off. When I entered the living room, I found my mother staring at me from the couch with the worried, guilty expression of a little kid who's just been caught drawing on the walls.

"You're up," she informed me with a painfully false attempt at cheer.

"Yeah." I scratched my head, my hair a stiff mass in its usual state of morning disarray. "So are you." We stared at each other some more. "So . . . what's going on?"

"Nothing," my mom responded automatically, and then squeezed her eyes shut, embarrassed by the obviousness of the lie. "There was—" She stopped herself, shook her head. "Something awful has happened."

"Oh, shit, what now?" It was a testament to the seriousness of the situation that she didn't even offer a cursory cluck of the tongue in response to my four-letter word.

"Sweetie, they found a body today," she began, and I felt the room do a complete barrel roll, my stomach going as cold as the ocean floor. My vision fogged over, and my mom's voice was hollow and far away when she added hastily, "Not January." I was still frozen stiff, trying to process this, when she delivered a piece of news that was even more shocking. "It was another student from Dumas. A girl named Reiko Matsuda."

TWENTY-ONE

MY MOM SAID some things for a while, all of which were drowned out by the clamoring buzz that filled my brain, and then she turned the television back on so that I could see the news program she'd been hiding from me.

The gist of things was this: Early that morning, two kayakers had discovered the body of sixteen-year-old Reiko Matsuda floating in the Huron River. A gifted student and talented artist, the Dumas Academy junior had been "stabbed and mutilated" before being dumped in the water. She had been last seen leaving school, where she was involved in the drama club and frequently stayed late for rehearsals. Police were still seeking the whereabouts of her car, as well as anyone who might have knowledge of her movements.

Dazed by the time the report ended, I then numbly endured my mother's delicate questions about whether I had known this Reiko Matsuda, who was reported to have been a "friend of January McConville's." It was impossible not to connect what had happened to the two girls, and silly to pretend like they might not be linked. Two Dumas students, both sharing the same secret, meeting tragic fates within as many weeks? The odds of that being a coincidence were so slim they weren't even worth calculating. As my mom's sympathetic probing continued, though, I was thinking: *Is* that *what happened to my girlfriend?* Had she been "stabbed and mutilated" and dumped in the river? Is that why they still hadn't found her? And what, exactly, did "mutilated" *mean*, anyway? Or maybe I didn't even want to know; just thinking about it made the room swim around me.

And through the din of my morbid thoughts, I kept hearing Tammy's insistent voice in my head: *I'm talking about tonight. Where were you* tonight?

I was still sure Mr. Walker was guilty, but the news gave me pause nonetheless. If he had indeed forced himself on January and gotten her pregnant as a result, he would have the strongest motive out of anyone for wanting her gone; a powerful man on the cusp of gaining national importance, what would happen to him if the story came out? Reiko had known the truth, and had promised to consider going to the authorities, which would have made her a serious threat as well. It all fit. The only catch was, I couldn't figure out how the man could have possibly gotten wind of a conversation that had transpired in the lobby of the Dumas theater building the previous afternoon.

I tried to expand my thinking. Eddie? Anson? Same catch applied. *Tammy?* It seemed far-fetched, but . . . she'd never exactly been the steadiest boat in the harbor, and her assault on the kitchen had not only revealed a mania I never knew existed in her but also made it clear she was capable of doing real damage when she wanted to. Anson had implied that January tried to seduce Jonathan; no matter what the facts were, if Tammy had believed it to be true, could she have killed her own daughter in a fit of manic rage? I rubbed my temples; it sounded like a soap opera—and *still* there was the issue of how Tammy could have known that Reiko was a potential problem.

Maybe Jonathan had known or suspected that January had told Reiko about what happened, and maybe he'd been planning to kill her all along. Or maybe Reiko, believing she could intimidate him into confessing, had confronted the man, and he had seized the opportunity to silence her.

How it had happened almost didn't matter; obviously I couldn't prove that Mr. Walker had killed Reiko any more than I could prove he'd killed January, but I had to tell the police about the conversation I'd had with the pink-haired girl, regardless. I'd been seen with her at Dumas the afternoon of the day she was murdered, and they were bound to find out about it, so I had to report it first and trust that they would eventually nail the man, even if I couldn't.

Taking the initiative, I called the station and, after explaining myself, was directed to Detective Garcia. I left out my speculation about Jonathan Walker, even the stuff about the changing alibi—the police would already be checking into the whereabouts of the Walker family, and I was pretty sure that hearing the theory from a breathless teenager would make them less inclined to take it seriously—but I explained that I had spoken to Reiko the day she was killed, what it was that the girl had revealed to me, and how I had tried to convince her to come forward.

"She said she would think about, and then she got killed!"

"And you think there's a connection." It was a statement, flat and stark, and the way Garcia said it made it impossible for me to answer yes without looking nuts.

"I'm not saying they're connected for sure, I'm just saying that it happened," I explained with some difficulty, annoyed at having to deny what felt obvious. "Did she come forward, though? Did she report the rape?"

Garcia sighed. "Listen, Flynn, I can't give out infor—"

"Look, I just want you to take this seriously, okay?" I was aware immediately that my outburst had cost me some credibility. "I think that the guy who raped January is the one who killed her. Maybe she told him she was pregnant, or that she was going to make a report about it. I mean, it can't be a coincidence that the only other person who knew about it just turned up dead, too!"

"Look, I promise you that we take all of our leads seriously, and we know how to do our jobs. Leave the speculation to us. *If* there's a link between the deaths, we'll find it." After this reassurance, Garcia added, "And don't let anyone tell you there's no such thing as a coincidence. They happen all the time."

And he hung up. For a minute, I sat and stared out my window at the trees that ringed our backyard, feeling powerless and annoyed. That couldn't be the end of it. I kept seeing Reiko's face, puffy and wet with tears, just before she vanished back into the theater. *I'll think about what you said.* How could her death be a coincidence?

My phone buzzed again on my desk, and I saw that the call was from Kaz. I was so anxious for someone to agree with me that I decided to—temporarily, at least—ignore how hurt I still was by his rejection. I answered immediately. "Did you hear what happened?"

"Of course!" He sounded hushed, like he was trying not to

be heard. "I couldn't believe it. It *is* the same girl, right? Not a different Reiko, maybe?"

"Same girl," I said. "Listen, I told the police about the rape, and it barely seemed like the guy cared! I left out names, but I'm starting to think maybe I should just go ahead and implicate Mr. Walker after all." Kaz tried to interrupt me; irritated, I talked over him. "I'm going to write it out so they can see it all together, and they won't be able to pick the story apart while I'm telling it to them and make me look like a paranoid wack job."

"Flynn!" Kaz finally exclaimed. "You have to listen to me, man! I've been doing some research, and I found out . . . well, you really need to hear this."

I frowned. "What?"

"Look, based on what you figured about the hatch marks, we're thinking the assault must have happened right around the last week of September, right?" he asked rhetorically. "That's when January's strange behavior really started: quitting her job, dropping out of the play, blowing off her friends. Well, here's the thing: I got this idea to check out the calendar of events on Jonathan Walker's website, and . . . Flynn, he wasn't even in Michigan at the end of September."

"Huh?"

"He was in D.C. for almost two weeks on some campaign-related tour, getting endorsements from political big shots and having his picture taken at important-sounding charity functions." There was a pause. "He couldn't have done it."

I was thrown completely off-balance. "But . . . just because the trip was on his calendar doesn't mean he actually went, Kaz."

"There are pictures online confirming each of the appearances listed."

"D.C. is only a couple of hours away by plane," I returned stubbornly, "and it's not like he doesn't have the money to charter a private jet. He could have come back to Ann Arbor at any time and then returned to Washington without being missed!"

"You think he made a supersecret emergency trip back home just to rape his stepdaughter?" Kaz sounded even more doubtful than Detective Garcia.

"Maybe we're wrong about the time frame! Maybe it happened earlier . . . like, a couple of weeks earlier, and the trauma just didn't set in—"

"Flynn?" He cut me off decisively. "Face it. It doesn't sound like Jonathan Walker could've been the one who raped January, which means he had no reason to kill her." He let out a breath. "I don't think he did it, Flynn. I think Jonathan Walker is innocent."

TWENTY-TWO

IT DIDN'T MAKE any sense, and for a long while I couldn't internalize what I was being told. I started arguing back, talking about the alibi screwup, reiterating all the points I was going to make in the theory I'd planned to submit to the police, but my case against Mr. Walker was taking on water faster than I could bail it out. Calmly, Kaz pointed out that even if Jonathan *had* lied about where he was the night January disappeared, it didn't mean anything without a motive. He could have been having an affair, or tying one on in a nudie bar or something, and simply didn't want his wife—or the media—to know about it. What I had against him was a house of cards, which was starting to look flimsier with every passing moment.

After I hung up, I sat listlessly in my room for a while, feeling worked up and unable to concentrate on anything. To avoid my mom's constant checking in to see if I was "okay," I grabbed my skateboard and went to the park, where I could work on my ollie in private, hoping that maybe Micah would show up so we could talk. He didn't, though, and I remained alone with the tumult of my frustrated thoughts, attempting the same stunt over and over again and expecting different results.

The sun faded in and out through a bank of clouds, a cold wind blasting through the inadequate insulation of my sweatshirt, but I scarcely noticed any of it.

I still wanted to believe Mr. Walker could be guilty, that the hatch marks were meaningless after all, and that the assault could have taken place either before or after his trip to D.C.; but "after" didn't sync with January's sudden behavioral changes, and "before" fell within a time period that January and I had still been talking pretty regularly. If she'd gone through something so traumatic, I was positive I'd have noticed. As it was, she'd only managed to hide it from me by icing me out.

But if it hadn't been Jonathan Walker, then who? The obvious runner-up, to me, was Anson; he was a pervert with anger management issues, and I could easily imagine him forcing himself on a girl. Add to that his habit of lurking and spying, and the fact that January was afraid to be alone with him, and you had another compelling—if circumstantial—case for a potential rapist-slash-murderer.

The possible details coagulated in my thoughts like drying blood as I picked up speed on my board, wheels rattling loudly over the uneven pavement—and my distracted concentration cost me when I launched into the air. My takeoff was clumsy, and I came back down on all fours when my skateboard and I had a difference of opinion about where to land. I brushed myself off, savoring the sting of a skinned elbow, brooding.

Anson. Violent and impulsive, he would have killed January without thinking twice and panicked afterward about how to clean it up. An explanation for why the clothes had been removed from January's body occurred to me, and it made my stomach revolt as I kicked my board up into my hand: What if

Anson had decided to dismember her to make the remains easier to hide? I could picture it with terrifying ease, and it would explain why she still remained unfound; maybe that's what "mutilated" meant—an aborted attempt by Anson to do the same thing to Reiko. However, if he'd killed January, why had he waited until everyone else believed she was dead before ransacking her room for treasure? Why was he still looking for her phone, which she always, *always* had with her? And there was also the matter of how he could have known about Reiko in the first place, unless *she'd* been the one to go to *him*. And if she'd known anything about Anson, heard any of the stories January had to tell, she wouldn't have dared do something like that alone.

I shoved myself into the air again, managing to keep my skateboard underneath me this time as I sailed over a set of shallow steps, but my mind still wasn't clear; the board shot sideways when it hit the ground, and I stumbled hard for several feet, struggling to catch both my balance and my breath. Cursing, I pulled myself back together and mounted the steps again, wrestling with the same oppressive question the whole time: *If it* wasn't *Anson, then who* else *could it have been?*

Eddie Sward? He was yet another foaming-at-the-mouth rage monster—but while I definitely believed he would stop at pretty much nothing to protect himself and his client, I didn't think he would have actually assaulted his boss's stepdaughter. He wasn't like Jonathan, who was powerful enough to buy away the consequences of his actions; and he wasn't like Anson, either, who routinely got away with whatever he wanted, because the rules literally didn't apply to him. Eddie would have had too much to lose. And again, I couldn't fathom any way he'd have become aware of the knowledge Reiko had been privy to, or what she might have been planning to do with it. For her to have confronted Eddie, she'd have had to track him down first, which would have involved phone calls to campaign personnel, which would have created an official record so easy for the cops to follow that Eddie would have to be an idiot to think he could kill Reiko and get away with it.

A car horn blared as I landed hard again, my skateboard careening out from under me and into the road, escaping certain doom beneath the wheels of a speeding SUV by mere inches. The driver flipped me off, shouting something hateful and indistinct through his closed window, and I jumped back to my feet with just enough time to return the favor as he raced away. My knees were both scraped raw from my collision with the sidewalk, and I was almost certain that I was bleeding under my clothes; I ignored the pain as I started across the street to retrieve my board, too consumed by my dark meditations on the subject of January's disappearance to care.

Who else was left? Tammy? She certainly wasn't January's rapist, and with Jonathan all but excused from that particular role as well, I was now even further from a convincing motive for her than ever. Protecting the security of Mr. Walker's campaign? Not likely. Having a pregnant, unmarried, teenage daughter was no longer political kryptonite, as Sarah Palin had so adeptly proved, and—after all—news of the pregnancy had come out anyway. I'd invoked Munchausen syndrome as a joke on Tuesday, but I couldn't quite see it as a real possibility; Tammy's grief might have arrived with an unappealing side order of *why is this happening to me?*—but as the wife of a promising senatorial candidate, she was already getting plenty of attention even before her daughter went missing.

After six more miserable attempts at the ollie, each one a slightly more embarrassing failure than the last, I finally acknowledged that my head and feet were not going to work together and gave up. In a black mood, I sat down on the edge of a low brick wall and watched some kids play soccer while I struggled to think.

More than ever, I wanted to believe that January was still out there somewhere—that her body hadn't been found yet for the very simple reason that there *was* no body. Maybe her rapist had been some Dumas dipshit, a random, low-life asshole whose name I'd never even heard. Maybe, caught in the tailspin of trauma and weighed down by her dismal home existence, January had simply decided to cash in her chips and leave town; she could have faked her death so no one would search for her, and fled to someplace where she believed she could start over again.

Only that tempting fantasy had more holes in it than a silhouette at a gun range. The blood that drenched her hoodie, confirmed to have been hers beyond question, was no mere "trace evidence." To shed so much of it, she'd have had to injure herself seriously; she'd have been weak and dizzy, dehydrated and possibly confused, by the time she'd lost enough blood to stage the scene we'd stumbled across in the meadow—and then she'd have had to stop the bleeding and close the wound before it was too late, and then rest for hours to recoup the strength she'd need to proceed to step two. She was too smart to hazard such extreme risks just for a little set dressing.

And then there was Reiko, who absolutely had not faked

being "stabbed and mutilated" after considering going public with January's secret. Any daydreams about my ex-girlfriend's survival hit a hard brick wall as I tried to mentally navigate them around the gruesome killing of her only friend and confidant at Dumas. I couldn't pretend, even to myself, that the pink-haired girl's death did not comprise the most obvious and likely blueprint for what had become of January.

After hours of thinking, I was still left empty-handed, confused, and utterly depressed. It wasn't like I'd developed some kind of hero complex, determined to solve the mystery myself, but with everything in my life seeming to collapse all at once, having the answer to January's disappearance fall apart as well was too much to accept. I had poked at my ex-girlfriend's life for over a week, and found myself with nothing but a bouquet of loose ends to show for it; maybe it was time to start over.

Micah was still avoiding me on Monday—and now Tiana was, too, presumably because she felt awkward about being in the middle—and I felt the silent, painful erosion of my spirit as I began to accept that things might never again be the way they had been. With some effort, I decided to redouble my investigative endeavors, hoping that might distract me from my melancholy.

My plan involved cadging another ride out to Dumas after school, but a monkey wrench was introduced to the machinery in the form of Ashley Sobol, a popular-clique girl who unexpectedly sat down next to me in fourth-period study hall and gave me a ravenously inquiring look. "Flynn, is it true that you're gay?"

"Yes," I said tersely. I was getting tired of answering this question, especially when it came from people who had barely acknowledged my existence before.

"I knew it!" she squealed happily, as if my inclination toward kissing boys was somehow a personal accomplishment of her own. "Listen, just between us? You can do way better than Mason Collier."

I cocked my head to the side. "Excuse me?"

"Well"—she drew the word out for a good five seconds—"he *happened* to mention how you tried to hit on him the other day, and how he had to shut you down? He's being kind of a dick about it, actually. I know he's pretty, but, Flynn? The boy is both straight *and* undateable." She tossed her flame-red hair over her shoulder and leaned in, her manner both gossipy and familiar. "Here's what, though: Like, three different guys have told me they think you're cute, and all of them are A-double-pluses. If you're not too hung up on Mason, just say the word, 'kay?"

I spent the rest of fourth period burning with embarrassment until I was certain my chair would melt underneath me. As flattered as I was that Ashley wished to play matchmaker for me—and that there were three mysterious guys out there who maybe *actually* wanted to kiss me—the whole situation felt weird. I wasn't used to this kind of attention, and I hated being the subject of gossip.

One thing was clear, however: I needed to stop asking Mason for favors that he could misconstrue. That meant that there was only one person I knew who both had a car and would probably be willing to enable my errand, and again it was the last person I wanted to call.

Kaz was waiting for me after the final bell, though, leaning against the Lexus in the looping drive on the side of the school that faced the river; I'd tried to give him an out when I'd asked if he was free, but he'd assured me he had no afternoon classes and was more than happy to be of assistance. Surrounded by minivans, soccer-mom SUVs, and thirdhand lemons, he stood out like a tuxedo at a hootenanny, and about a hundred curious eyes followed me as I headed his way. I was starting to get used to being tracked in the hallways like some kind of exotic migratory bird, and I wondered what Ashley and her friends would do with this piece of news.

I made a beeline for the passenger seat, hoping we could just get out of there, but Kaz intercepted me en route, drawing me into a "friendly"—and utterly clueless—hug. "Hey! So this is where you go to school, huh?"

"Uh, yeah," I confirmed, writhing from his grasp and darting around the front of the vehicle.

"It's pretty big." He took his time looking the building over while a bunch of idle students took their time looking *us* over, and I tugged futilely at the door handle. It was locked. "Makes me realize how much I miss my old high school. Which is to say, not at all."

"Great story. Can we go?"

He blipped the locks open, and just as I was about to get in, I caught sight of a familiar face staring back at me from a group on the sidewalk. Micah. He was frowning, and when I raised my hand to wave, he pointedly turned his back to me and pretended to engage in conversation with Tessa Horton, a girl I happened to know for a fact he couldn't stand. With a heavy sigh, I climbed into the posh, climate-controlled environment of Kaz's luxury auto, feeling another small piece of my spirit slip back away with the tide.

"Buckle up," Kaz advised cheerfully, putting the car in drive, "because it's gonna be a long ride!"

"You said it."

The ride was actually just long enough for me to explain my plan to Kaz—which amounted to: find some of Reiko's friends and ask them if they knew anything—and for him to try, unsuccessfully, to talk me out of it. I didn't flatter myself with the notion that I could figure out something the cops couldn't, but I had my own inquisitive nature to appease, and who knew? Maybe I *would* detect something significant that they had missed. I knew the players better, *and* I believed that Reiko's death and January's disappearance were related, so I might have something of an advantage after all.

I left Kaz in the theater lobby, where a new poster exhorted students to attend an assembly there the next day after school to remember their two departed classmates, and made my way along the side corridors leading to the backstage door. I didn't want to go in through the audience and risk being intentionally embarrassed for interrupting rehearsal again, and I figured I might find some people hanging out on the dingy sofa where I'd first seen Reiko.

As it turned out, I didn't even have to go that far; rounding a corner, I nearly tumbled over a trio of girls who were sitting on the floor, speaking in hushed voices. Two of them were the ones I'd seen Reiko with on my initial visit to Dumas, and although I didn't know the third, it was immediately apparent that all three of them had been close to the dead girl: Each one

sported a bright pink streak in her hair—presumably as a tribute to their friend's memory.

"I'm sorry to interrupt," I began timidly, "but you guys were
friends with Reiko, right?"

The question got one of the girls sobbing, her cries almost
absurdly loud and expressive, while a second girl—with
feather earrings the same pink as the streak in her hair—
huddled next to her, stroking her back. The third girl stood
up and looked me over. She was tall and thin, with black hair
that contrasted against a starkly pale face, her blue eyes dry but
red-rimmed. "We are. Wait, I know you . . . you were here
last week, yeah?"

Her voice was still shaded by grief, but she nevertheless
sounded like she was doing such a preposterously bad imper-
sonation of Hermione Granger that I had to struggle not to
laugh. Clearly, I'd just encountered the girl January had dubbed
FBA—Fake British Accent. "Uh, yeah. I had dropped by to see
Reiko."

"Right. And she was bloody well brassed off when you left,"
FBA replied imperiously. "What did you say to her, anyway?"

"I asked her some questions about January McConville," I
revealed, and the sobbing died out almost immediately as
both girls on the floor turned their attention my way. I looked
from one wary face to the next. "You guys knew her, too,
right?"

"Yeah," FBA answered suspiciously. "We weren't *friends*
with her, though."

"Why not?"

The girl who had been crying answered with a congested
snort, "Because she was a bitch."

"Melanie!" her comforting friend admonished. Then, quietly, but still deliberately audible, "What if this guy is, like, her brother?"

"I don't care," Melanie snapped. "If he is, then he probably already knows she was a stuck-up bitch—I'm not ruining the surprise."

"You guys thought *January* was stuck-up," I stated, beginning to feel angry on my ex-girlfriend's behalf. I'd had it from Reiko's own mouth that January had been ostracized at Dumas, and her commitment to despising Jonathan Walker's wealth made Melanie's claim ludicrous, to say the least.

"Well, yeah," FBA said defensively, crossing her arms. "She acted like she was better than us or something, just because she came from a public school." She said *public school* as if it might be some kind of cult. "Like it made her more authentic than us. We all tried to be nice to her at first, but she was really rude. She made fun of the way we dress for school, the things we like to do, and just . . . the whole way that we live! It was insulting and, honestly, nobody wanted to put up with it."

I looked at what FBA was wearing—a little black dress, four-inch heels, and diamond teardrop earrings—and I could hear January's voice in my head: *Who wears diamonds to school? Does she think she's fucking Beyoncé?* My ex-girlfriend might not have been a snob in the way that these girls were snobs, but that didn't mean she never felt or acted superior to others.

What I said was, "Reiko seemed to like her just fine. She told me that she and January were best friends."

"Well, that whole situation was bizarre," Melanie put in disdainfully from the floor, sniffling and wiping her nose with the heel of her hand.

"How do you mean?" I asked. "Why was it bizarre?"

"Before we answer any more questions about Reiko," Feather Earrings interjected shrewdly, "maybe you better tell us who you are?"

Obligingly, I introduced myself. "I just want to know what happened—to January *and* to Reiko."

FBA's mouth shifted. "Well, look, I'm sure she was the dog's bollocks back at Riverfront or wherever, but January . . . she didn't belong here. She didn't *want* to belong here, and she let everybody know it."

"It was impossible not to make fun of her," Melanie cut in bluntly. "She wanted it that way. She'd arrive at school in a Mercedes or a Porsche or a Rolls or a Lambo—a different car every single day—and she'd get out wearing a ratty sweatshirt and some beat-up old hobo shoes! If you tried to be polite to her, she'd just *glare* at you until you shut up and went away." With a pert smile, she added, "We all talked shit about her. *Including* Reiko."

"And then one day, out of the blue, the two of them come into rehearsal together, all arm in arm like long-lost sisters or something." FBA picked up the thread with a tone of wonderment. "We all thought it was some kind of a joke or whatever at first, but . . ."

"But when we asked about it, Reiko Hulked out on us," Melanie concluded. "She said that January was 'actually really cool,' and that we 'just didn't understand where she was coming from.' Whatever the hell that meant."

It meant that January and Reiko had something terrible in common, but if these girls didn't know the details, I wasn't going to share them. Trying to sound neutral, I asked, "What about guys? Were there any guys here who were into January? Anyone that, like, Reiko maybe didn't like in particular, for some reason?"

Melanie gave a sour laugh. "Not unless you're talking about—"

"He isn't talking about that," Feather Earrings interrupted under her breath.

"About what?" I jumped on it. "Who?"

The eagerness in my tone made them abruptly cautious, and the silence in the hallway rose to a deafening crescendo as they seemed to be considering whether to respond. The three of them were trying desperately to communicate in thought waves, their eyes flicking back and forth as they struggled to keep their faces blank, until at last Melanie gave a loud huff. "OMG, gimme a break, you guys! This is the same shit we've been talking about all over school for the last two months, and all of a sudden you're acting like we're guarding the CIA kill list or something!"

"Melanie . . ." Feather Earrings warned, but her friend was not to be deterred.

"The only 'guy' at Dumas who was into January was *Cedric*," Melanie blurted with a malicious giggle.

"*Melanie.*"

"Oh, whatever." Melanie rolled her eyes. "I'm not saying they were secret lovers or anything, but he paid *way* too much attention to her. Like, he basically told her that if she agreed to audition for the play, he would just *give* her the part of Angelique! It was such bullshit. Sylvie is a senior and she deserved that part, and then just because Cedric got a boner for some *sophomore* who wasn't even an actress, he offered it to her on a silver platter! Total bullshit."

"Cedric?" I repeated stupidly.

"He talked about her all the time." Melanie was really warming to the topic. "'Perhaps we can style Angelique's hair like January's,' and 'January had a brilliant idea the other day,' and 'Sylvie, try to smile like January'! I mean . . . *gross*."

"*Cedric?*"

"He was always trying to talk to her during breaks, telling her what kind of clothes she should wear, offering her rides home from school . . . I mean, Cedric's always been kind of Uncle Bad-Touch, but she *really* brought it out of him."

"'Rides home from school,'" I repeated, barely feeling my lips. Just the other night I had challenged Kaz to explain how January's clothes could have gotten from Dumas to the mansion, and his response had been *misdirection*. Had he been right? It finally occurred to me that Cedric had been the one who'd found January's things in the meadow. I could still picture the first time I met him, on the front porch of the Walker mansion. *She was a very lovely girl. I hope you appreciated her, son.* Was I remembering correctly? Had he really used the past tense before anyone else thought she was dead? "Do you really think Cedric was . . . that he wanted to . . . with January?"

"Considering the way he left his old school, I wouldn't be the least bit surprised," Melanie replied with malevolent sweetness.

"That's not fair, Mel," Feather Earrings said with a troubled frown.

My head was spinning. "Why? What happened at his old school?"

"Nobody knows, that's the point." Feather Earrings was

clearly unnerved, glancing around like she feared we were being spied on. "People just make stuff up."

"Whatever it was, it was bad enough that he's not allowed to be a teacher anymore," Melanie revealed triumphantly. "*That's* the point." To me, she elaborated, "My sister's friend's cousin went to Hazelton, and apparently Cedric taught English there; then, all of a sudden, he left and moved here. He had an actual job at one of the most prestigious private schools in the state, and now he coaches a drama club for a living? Either he had a total nervous breakdown, or he did something awful."

"He's not a teacher here?" The information was coming almost too fast for me to soak it all in.

Melanie shook her head. "Nope. I asked him about it once, and he acted like he didn't even understand the question. The whole thing is fucking weird."

I had to agree. I'd encountered Cedric Hoffman only twice, and both times he'd made me uncomfortable; he gave off a strange vibe, with his soft, edgeless voice and probing eyes, and hearing about his fixation on January made my skin crawl like a swarm of millipedes—but it didn't necessarily mean anything. Mr. Walker had always rubbed me the wrong way as well, and my suspicions about him had turned out to be off base. I needed to know more.

"Do you guys happen to remember what time Reiko left school on Friday?"

"It was after us," FBA announced. "She was in kind of a weird mood, and she had this drawing she was working on for January's memorial thing—the one outside her house? She said she was going to stay until she finished it."

The girl's throat closed on the end of her sentence, and the words came out as a hoarse, uneven whisper. She swiped at her eyes, and I waited for her to regain control before I asked, "Did anyone else stay after?"

They all looked at each other again, and then Feather Earrings spoke up. "Some of the tech guys end up being here pretty late if there's a lot of equipment to put away after the rehearsal, but I don't think there was much to do that night. And it was Friday, so everybody wanted to just go home, you know?"

"What about Cedric?"

"Oh. Well, yeah, I mean obviously he stayed. He has to lock up once everyone is gone." She shrugged. "I think he told the police that Reiko left while he was putting away some tools that were sitting out, and that he offered to walk her to her car, but she said no thanks." It was her turn to tear up and Melanie took the girl's hand and squeezed it comfortingly while she cried.

"What about the night January went missing?" I asked. "Do any of you know who saw her last?"

"It might have been me," FBA surprised me by saying. "While they were running one of the scenes, I came outside to have a fag, and I saw January sitting by the fountain." Knowing fag was slang for "cigarette" in England, I decided not to interrupt her narrative to take offense. "I was surprised, because she'd quit drama club, and I couldn't figure out what she was doing there. And, I mean, school had been over for an hour already. I'd have asked, but she'd have just snapped at me."

She made a sulky face, as if she expected consolation or perhaps an apology, but I forbore to indulge her. "What was she doing? How did she seem?"

"I don't know." FBA appeared bewildered by the question.

"She wasn't *doing* anything—just sitting there. And I don't know how she seemed. Thoughtful, maybe? Depressed? I told the constables who interviewed us that she looked sort of unhappy."

It took every ounce of willpower I had not to roll my eyes at her use of the word *constables*. "And she wasn't there when rehearsal ended?"

"No. I don't know where she went after that."

Distractedly, I gave the girls my phone number, asking them to call if they thought of anything else, and then turned around on clumsy feet. As I made my way back to the lobby, my brain was revolving like a pinwheel, thoughts spinning endlessly. *Cedric?* Was it possible? I'd been so focused on January's miserable home life that her drama coach hadn't even registered as a possible suspect—but if these girls were telling me the truth, maybe I'd been barking up the wrong tree all along; maybe January's attacker really had been at Dumas the whole time. All of a sudden the sterile, acoustic hallways of the theater building were giving me the heebie-jeebies, and I wanted to get out of there as quickly as possible.

Barreling back into the lobby, I stopped short. The vast room, clad from floor to ceiling in broad squares of spotless travertine, was empty. Through the bank of glass doors fronting the building, I could see the Harmon and Eugenia Davenport fountain—where FBA had last seen January before her disappearance—still spewing arcs of frigid water into the early November air. The little plaza surrounding it was vacant, though, and I could see no signs of life in the gathering dusk that spread across the well-tended grounds of the school beyond. Where was Kaz?

Reluctantly, I ducked through the door to the auditorium, peering around to see if maybe he had decided to take himself on a little tour. A group of students gathered in a back corner of the room looking grave and subdued, while three more sat in a pool of light on the stage and conversed inaudibly. The drama club was clearly on a break, and I could see no sign of Kaz. Antsy to get gone, I turned to head back into the lobby, thinking maybe I would go outside and see if he had wandered out there, and ran straight into a solid wall of flesh.

"Mr. Doherty. We meet again." His voice cold and reproachful, Cedric Hoffman himself stood in my way, glaring down at me with an irritated frown on his grizzled face. It was the expression of a man who'd just caught a pickpocket in the act of stealing his wallet. "For someone who isn't actually a student, you seem to spend an awful lot of time at this august institution."

"I just dropped by to . . . see some friends," I replied, disconcerted, when a better excuse failed me. His flat black eyes, warped by bifocal lenses, bored into me like he was trying to read the truth in my brain, and his resentful expression was as fixed as a mannequin's. It gave me the creeps.

"I don't believe you have any friends here, Mr. Doherty," Cedric stated in that soft, formless way of his. "I told you once before that you weren't Dumas material. You don't belong here, and I doubt any of the students care for the way you constantly disrupt their rehearsals any more than I do."

"I've only been here three times!" I retorted before I could stop myself, stung by the petty nature of his remark. I'd been scolded by teachers before, and talked down to by dismissive adults, but this man seemed to dislike me personally, and it was unnerving.

"Three times too many," he said briskly. "I shouldn't have to remind you that this is not a public library, nor is it a parking lot or community center where you may come and go as you please. These students are working toward something, and their parents pay good money to see that they are not distracted. If I find you here again, I will be calling campus security."

"Actually, I was already on my way out when you stopped me," I said, mustering up my dignity. Then, proud of the way my voice almost didn't shake at all, I asked with a belligerent bravado I didn't feel, "Do you mind if I leave now?"

It occurred to me that both girls had stayed late after school on the nights they disappeared; and no one, I had been told, stayed later than Cedric. Had January lingered that day, waiting for an opportunity to confront her rapist? Had Reiko done so for the exact same reason? Did I have the guts—or the stupidity, depending on how you looked at it—to ask him about it point-blank?

Of course, in Reiko's case, a confrontation might not have been necessary for him to have known what she had in mind. Our conversation on Friday hadn't exactly been in secretive tones; for all I knew, the Dumas Academy drama coach might have suspended rehearsal the second he banished us to the lobby, and then stood behind the door and listened in to everything we said. Cedric would have seen the writing on the wall, and possibly he'd already been planning his next move when Reiko played right into his hands by choosing to stay late. Looking up at his dour countenance now, I suddenly realized that I had been mistaken in what I'd told Detective Garcia;

Reiko was *not* the only other person who knew what had happened to January. I knew it, too.

Without a word, Cedric Hoffman removed his bulk from the doorway, allowing me to slither past him. I tried not to break into a sprint as I shoved through the glass doors with his black eyes on me like a pair of hands.

TWENTY-THREE

THE NEXT DAY, the same day as Mr. Walker's much-anticipated election, I did something I'd never done before: I skipped school. It wasn't like I'd never been tempted to ditch in the past, but I'd always been too paranoid about the consequences, and too unswerving in my certainty that I would be caught in the act. My parents weren't puritans or anything—neither in the rigidly moralistic sense nor, thankfully, in the public-flogging-builds-character one—but they could apply heartbroken disappointment like Torquemada applied thumbscrews, and I liked to avoid that whenever I could. But questions were eating at me like acid, demanding to be answered, and I had to take the risk. If I got busted, I would have to play the emotional/psychological trauma card again, and hope it still had some juice left.

It had been Kaz who, after hearing the details of my visit to the theater building at Dumas, had suggested the impromptu day off—he'd even volunteered to skip a couple of classes of his own to help me. I don't think he was particularly in favor of my amateur investigation, but I think he *was* eager to prove to me what a supportive friend he could be in this Time of Great

Upheaval, and I rather shamelessly intended to milk that impulse for everything it was worth.

I went to my first few classes Tuesday morning, but when lunch period rolled around I was waiting outside the school, glancing about as nervously as a junkie looking to score at a convention of undercover cops. As the Lexus pulled into the traffic circle, I darted to the passenger door before it came to a complete stop, grateful that I had almost no audience this time. Riverside's administration didn't encourage students to go off-campus to eat, but it wasn't specifically against the rules, either, so no one stopped us as we cruised back down the drive to the road.

The Hazelton School was located in Birmingham, a city tucked into a group of posh Detroit suburbs roughly forty-five miles northeast of Ann Arbor. The midday traffic seemed light to me, and we made excellent time, sailing under gray skies and billboards urging the over-eighteens to vote for Walker. I watched the dashboard clock and odometer with a mingled sense of excitement and dry-mouthed panic as my chances to call off this insane errand and return to school without incident became ever more remote. Finally, when my lunch period drew to its official close as Kaz negotiated the hair-raising interchange at I-696—breakneck drivers crisscrossing our path with the brutal, unyielding determination of charioteers in the Circus Maximus—I accepted that we were past the point of no return.

Hazelton wasn't a big school, but it had a big reputation—or so its website boasted, anyway. Its list of distinguished faculty and alumni went on and on, although most of the so-called luminaries were people I had never heard of. There were doctors, judges, authors of books I'd probably never be interested in reading, and a slew of individuals whose names were followed by initials like CEO, COO, EVP, and the like. One individual I could find no mention of whatsoever, though, was Cedric Hoffman. If his exit from Hazelton's esteemed halls had carried any whiff of scandal, the Internet seemed to have missed it.

The school's architecture bespoke the same sense of inflated self-worth as its promotional materials. Pulling through a soaring, wrought iron gate that wouldn't have been out of place at Downton Abbey, we were confronted by a Gothic pile of stone turrets, peaked windows, and pitched roofs, all wrapped in an endless skein of ivy. During the warmer months, I'm sure the clinging vines ennobled the place and invited visions of Harvard and Dartmouth and Yale; now, though, leafless and dung-heap brown, they looked like the desiccated veins of a flaying victim.

Hardwood floors—scuffed, waxed, scuffed, and waxed again in an apparently endless cycle—resounded underfoot as we made our way to the main office. It was easy to find; Hazelton cultivated a deliberately intimate atmosphere, the dark, wood-paneled walls seeming to press against you with concern for your academic well-being, and it took only one sign with a single arrow to guide us to our destination, twenty feet beyond our first right-hand turn.

Unbelievably, it wasn't until I stood face-to-face with the general secretary, a battleship of a woman with charcoal hair, tortoiseshell glasses, and an aubergine sweater set, that I started to doubt the wisdom of coming there. Beyond the counterlike desk, as solid and imposing as the woman who occupied it, were a bank of filing cabinets, a warren of wall-mounted pigeonholes for mail, a Xerox machine, and some cupboards. A girl about my age, with long sandy hair and an austere school uniform, stood at the copier, but she didn't even glance up as Kaz and I shuffled uncomfortably into the stuffy room.

"May I help you gentlemen?" the secretary asked, although her starched tone suggested doubt on the subject.

"I, uh . . . we had some questions," I said, trying to sound confident. It was dawning on me that what I intended to ask would probably strike this no-nonsense woman—the nameplate on the counter read V. BAGLEY—as completely outrageous, and I wanted to sound as if I believed the information was owed to us.

"About enrollment?" One eyebrow, plucked almost to extinction, rose into a skeptical arch.

"No, about a teacher here." I corrected myself, "A former teacher."

"That sounds rather unorthodox," she replied in a way that suggested we ought to be ashamed of ourselves for asking, and frowned. "What sort of questions?"

"Primarily," I began, pleased with how mature the word sounded, "we were interested in knowing why this teacher no longer works at Hazelton."

The secretary's frown deepened, grooves as ominous as fault lines spreading on either side of her downturned mouth. "I'm afraid it is not our policy to hand out information like that. Why are you asking? To which instructor are you referring?"

I thought it was rather unfair of her to demand answers of her own without first offering up even a token bit of information, but I decided to indulge her anyway, hoping her reaction might tell me something. "Cedric Hoffman?"

The name had a definite effect, and not just on the secretary: The girl at the copy machine jerked up with a startled glance, her brown eyes wide and riveted on Kaz and me for the first time since we'd entered. The secretary's expression had gone from guarded to serious in the blink of an eye, and at her young assistant's reaction, she cast a look over her shoulder. "Klara, why don't you take a break now? Come back in fifteen minutes."

It was not a suggestion, and after the briefest of hesitations, the girl gave a quick, birdlike nod, set down the papers she'd been holding, and made a hasty exit. Skirting the counter, she darted past Kaz and me with her chin tucked low, closing the door to the main hallway soundlessly behind her. Once Klara was gone, the secretary waited a while to make sure the girl was no longer in earshot before she spoke again. "Why are you two boys asking about Cedric Hoffman?"

I wouldn't say that her demeanor had softened, exactly, but a mixture of genuine concern and curiosity suddenly showed through the veneer of disciplined imperviousness. Her hands were folded together on the surface of the desk, and I watched as the skin around her blunted nails turned white with pressure. Carefully, I offered, "He's working in Ann Arbor now."

"Teaching?" Her tone was agitated, confused.

I shook my head. "No. He's a drama coach at a private school."

Ms. Bagley's troubled gaze darted to the desktop, skittered sideways, and then moved back up to Kaz and me. One hand reached reflexively for a discarded stress ball, which she proceeded to idly strangle the life out of. "Why did you come here?" she asked at last. "Did he . . . Has something . . . happened?"

"Something like what?" I pounced, unable to temper my zeal, and watched as she immediately retreated into her armor again. "What do you think might have happened?"

"I really couldn't say," she replied with brisk unhappiness.

"What if I told you something *has* happened?" I tried, beseechingly. "Something bad. And even if I can't prove it, it might have involved Mr. Hoffman?"

She watched me for a moment, and I watched her back as shadows appeared around her eyes and a great, tired misery overtook her face. At last, she let out a heavy sigh and said, quietly, "I'm very sorry, but there's really nothing I can tell you. Only . . . if something . . . if you really believe that Mr. Hoffman may have . . . *done something*, I urge you to tell the authorities about it."

"Please," I tried again, desperately, wishing I could somehow make her understand the gravity of our situation. I was afraid to say out loud what it was he might have done, and risk having her shoo us and the legal implications of our questions off Hazelton property altogether. "We don't want to go to the authorities unless we're pretty sure we're right, but . . ."

My brilliant argument fizzled out like a dud firework, and Ms. Bagley's expression slammed the rest of the way closed, her manner once again businesslike and impregnable. "I'm very sorry," she repeated, "but for legal reasons, I'm afraid that the best I can do is to confirm that Cedric Hoffman was an instructor here, but his employment at the Hazelton School came to an end prior to the commencement of our fall session last year." She pursed her lips and repeated once more, in a meaningful way, "I'm sorry."

The fruitless conversation at an obvious end, Kaz and I

retreated to the stuffy hallway and started back for the lobby. "What now?" I asked glumly. "Wait till dark, break in, and search the office?"

"Maybe one of the teachers would be willing to gossip." Kaz remained doggedly optimistic. "If Cedric left on bad terms, I'm sure everyone who works here has opinions to share about him. We just need to find someone less discreet."

We didn't have to look very long, as it turned out; rounding the corner to the lobby, we almost collided with Klara, the girl who had been working the copier in the office. It was immediately clear that she had been waiting for us. "I couldn't help but overhear you asking Ms. Bagley about . . . about Professor Hoffman?"

She spoke in a furtive whisper, her voice imbued with an accent—German, I thought, or Austrian—and it occurred to me that between the hardwood floors, paneled walls, and polished stairs, sound probably bounced a good long way through the halls of Hazelton.

"That's right. Did you know him?" Kaz gave her an inquiring look.

She nodded quickly, her mouth a taut line, and I asked, "Why did he leave his job?"

"Not here," she replied in a hiss, glancing left and right exactly as if we were in a cartoon spy movie. "Follow me."

She led us down a labyrinth of corridors, slinking nervously past classrooms in active use, her crepe-soled shoes making not so much as a squeak against the flooring. Finally, she ushered us through a stairwell and out of the building. We stood in the doorway alcove of what appeared to be a side entrance to the school, looking out at an expanse of leaf-strewn lawn that stretched between Hazelton and what looked like a small wedge of forested land. It reminded me uncomfortably of the Walkers' backyard. The clouded sky was darker now, smelling unmistakably of impending rain, and a cold wind hurled itself at us, scraping our faces from time to time with missiles of dried leaves.

Klara stared out at the treetops with pensive, worried eyes, her arms wrapped tightly around herself, while we waited for her to speak. At last, Kaz prompted her, "What can you tell us about Professor Hoffman?"

"Why are you asking about him? What has he done?" she countered, her gaze shifting between us interrogatively. Then she shook her head, putting up her hands. "No, never mind. I think I . . . I'd rather not know." Her face was pale and heart-shaped, her eyes massive, and with her tortured expression she was an Emily Brontë character come to life. "To begin with, he did not exactly *leave* his job here. Not the way that it sounds, at least."

"He was fired?"

Klara shook her head, frustrated. "Not exactly that, either." With an anxious sigh, she added, "I should tell you how it was. How it happened.

"Professor Hoffman taught English here—British literature to the underclassmen, and the history of drama to older students. He was nice, but strange. He would comment all the time about how 'lovely' the girls at Hazelton looked in their uniforms, and every day, at the beginning of class, he would compliment specific girls—always the same ones—telling them how pretty they were." Her voice was soft, but her tone was grave, as though she were reciting an elegy. "Three years ago, there was . . . an incident. One of the girls was down in the stacks, a sort of spillover library in the basement, doing research for a paper; she had a workstation set up, with her books and notes and a cup of iced tea, and she was listening to music—her iPod. She was alone.

"At one point she simply . . . fell unconscious. She said that one minute she was writing in her notebook, and the next thing she knew, she was lying on the floor, and Professor Hoffman was there, with his hands on her . . . her skirt. He said he found her like that, *exposed*, and was trying to cover her up, but she didn't believe him. She was in some pain and insisted on a medical examination, but the doctor found nothing. There were some bruises, but there was no . . . DNA, if you understand me?" She blushed at her own inference, and we nodded. "She was convinced she had been *interfered with* by Professor Hoffman, but she couldn't prove it. There were no witnesses."

"Had she been drugged?" Kaz asked, and Klara nodded.

"She suspected the tea, but by the time she thought of it, it was too late." Anticipating our next question, she continued, "It was from a café in the city, but she had been away from her workstation often to look for books, so anyone could have gone in and out of the library without her being aware."

Kaz and I exchanged a black look as I thought about my conversation with Reiko. *The guy slipped her something so she was unconscious when it happened.* It made me sick to realize that Cedric might actually be a serial rapist, moving from school to school. "This occurred three years ago. . . . What happened prior to last year?"

"The same thing, more or less. Another student of his, this time in one of the classrooms. She was working on a makeup test after regular school hours. Professor Hoffman brought her a cup of coffee and then excused himself from the room. She woke up on the floor, again with him kneeling over her. She had been . . . well, this time there was no doubt she had been . . . attacked, but once again, there was no DNA, no witnesses, no actually incriminating evidence."

"What about the coffee?" I demanded. "He brings her coffee and, whoopsy, she mysteriously blacks out? Isn't that evidence?"

"It was her word against his," Klara said, a spark of anger glimmering in the depths of her brown eyes. "He poured it down the sink before she could stop him, so there was simply no way to test it."

"Fucking *asshole*!" Kaz exploded.

"The girls tried to bring charges, but what they had was all circ-circ-"

"Circumstantial."

"Yes. So when they couldn't get anywhere with the police, the girls' parents threatened to sue Hazelton. The administration tried to dismiss Professor Hoffman, but because the accusations against him couldn't be proved, *he* sued the school instead. Wrongful termination. In the end, Hazelton *paid* him to go away—and they paid the girls' families, too, to make sure they would not talk to the media."

It explained why I'd found no mention of scandal associated with either Cedric's name or the school's, why the man had abandoned his prestigious job and title, and why he was still allowed within a country mile of any occupation involving teenage girls. What it didn't explain was what I should do next. If there was truth in what I was being told, then Cedric was a predator who had gotten away with the same crime at least twice before, leaving nothing behind to convict him.

He had been extremely careful in the attacks on his victims at Hazelton—perhaps he'd even used condoms—but if he was the one who'd assaulted January, I was determined she would be his downfall. All I had to do was somehow find solid proof of a crime I only knew about because I had heard it from a dead girl. No sweat, right?

"He's done it again, hasn't he?" Klara's tone was flat and resigned, and when I nodded my confirmation, she looked away, cursing under her breath. "*Scheißkerl.*" When her eyes returned to mine, they gleamed with moisture. "One of those girls was a friend. A good friend. Even after they bought that *arschloch* off, she still couldn't bear to return to school. She had nightmares and panic attacks. . . ." Klara took a shaky breath. "Whoever he did it to, tell her to make him pay."

"He'll pay," I promised. "You can count on it."

TWENTY-FOUR

"I THOUGHT THE drama kids at Dumbass would be more fun and, like, laid-back—the way they are at Riverside," January remarked morosely one early fall afternoon. The summer heat was taking its time dissipating, fingers of humidity still gripping the city with uncomfortable intimacy, and we were having ice cream at a local place not far from downtown. January's flavor of choice was lemon custard—a nice enough pick, if you go for things that don't have chocolate in them—and my cone was Mackinac Island fudge, a Michigan specialty. "I thought they'd be kinda alternative, you know? Cooler than the rest of the assholes who go there? Instead, they're just more . . . dramatic."

"Sounds like you fit right in."

"Fuck you," she retorted good-naturedly. "I'm serious, though. I'm starting to feel like I'll never have any friends again. You should hear the shit they talk about, Flynn! Fashion magazines and Caribbean vacations and dressage horses . . . like, what in the actual fuck is a 'dressage horse'?"

I made a face. "It sounds like a French horse drag queen."

She cackled. "I made the exact same joke, and this girl glared at *me like I'd just spit on her grandmother's corpse! So you see what I'm dealing with."*

"No one is nice at all? Not even a little?"

"Oh, no, they're all super 'nice.'" She gave a hugely fake, toothpaste-ad smile with the word. "That bitchy-girl kind of nice, where they say something that should be friendly and still manage to make it sound like 'fuck off and die.' Like, 'Wow, January, I wish I had the courage to wear something like that *to school!'"*

"Yikes."

"And the guy who runs the drama club is a total freak."

"How so?"

"I don't know. For one thing, he always wants to explain scenes in their 'original historical context,' which he couldn't possibly make sound less interesting, and he's also a perv. The other day, he spent twenty minutes talking about Louis XIV and the Duke of Orleans, and the entire time he was looking me straight in the boobs."

"Gross. Didn't you say he was, like, old?"

"Yes! He's like sixty! It's like . . . it's like having Santa pat his lap and then lick his lips at you." She performed a parody of this, folding her lips to mimic toothlessness and then slurping her tongue around like a golden retriever while stroking her thigh with her free hand. I couldn't help myself and started laughing. "Yeah, it's really funny when you're not the one Santa wants for his little ho-ho-ho!"

She was laughing, too, though. I nudged her. "Tell him your boyfriend will beat him up if he keeps staring at your bazooms."

"Okay, first of all? I will never *use the word 'bazooms,' and if you value your testicles, you won't, either. Number two? You tell a guy you have a boyfriend, and he just ogles you even more, because*

now you're 'a challenge.' And third, you have nothing to worry about." She made like she was going to touch my nose with her cone, but then she pulled it back at the last second. "Anyway, he's harmless. Just weird."

"If you say so." I shrugged. "I just don't want you to ditch me so you can become the next Mrs. Claus."

She did her gross-old-man impression again, adding in a wink for good measure. "You've gotta be a little naughty this year if you want to get on my Nice List, Mrs. Claus!"

I laughed so hard I almost dropped my ice cream. "Ho-ho-ho!"

The mood inside the Lexus was subdued, to say the least, on the drive back to Ann Arbor. I couldn't stop thinking about Klara's account, what it meant, and how frankly helpless it made me feel. The images gathering in my mind were even darker and more ominous than the storm clouds that finally opened up over I-96 as we were passing the exit to Northville.

"That fucking bastard," Kaz finally hissed, his jaw clenched so tightly I could see a muscle fluttering under his ear. He snapped the windshield wipers on with more force than necessary, and they swung wildly back and forth, throwing the rain across the glass in ropy streaks. "He even joined the search party! What kind of a . . . a *monster* . . ." He stopped and sucked in air, his arms ramrod straight in front of him, hands gripping the wheel. "We have to go to the cops with this. Right now."

"With what?" I asked, giving a pessimistic snort. "They already know about all this, remember? There's no way to prove any of it."

"But it's a *pattern*." Kaz refused to back down. "I mean, it has to be enough for them to at least take him in for questioning, right?"

"At which point he would deny everything and then threaten another lawsuit, for harassment." Frustration made me sound condescending. "Kaz, I don't think they took me seriously when I told them there'd even *been* a rape!" I exclaimed. "They're not going to bring anyone in for questioning about a crime they don't even think happened. And anything I tell them that Reiko told me that January told her is all hearsay, anyway, and it doesn't count for jackshit!"

"So . . . what, then? We just let it go?" Kaz was incredulous and angry. "We just sit on our asses and wait and hope that the police eventually get around to investigating Cedric as a potential suspect? Fuck that!"

"I don't want to give up either, but unless you want to go and threaten him—the same move that might have gotten both January and Reiko killed, by the way—then what other choices do we have?" I wasn't trying to argue with him; pointing all this out only made me feel more useless and miserable.

"We can . . . we can . . . ." Kaz fumbled for an idea and then lapsed into silence. The rain was coming down in sheets, cars racing past us at speeds way too fast for the slippery roads and diminished visibility, and he compensated by slowing down. I'd been distantly hoping we could get back to town in time for me to catch my last class and minimize the extent of my truancy a bit, but it was far too late for that. Finally, Kaz spoke again. "It all fits, Flynn. Everything. We know she stayed late that day; he could have killed her right after rehearsal and then dumped her clothes in her own backyard to divert suspicion from the school, knowing Dumas would be the last place any-one would have seen her alive. Then he put her body in the river somewhere, or buried her in the woods, or . . . who knows, but *somewhere* so no one could ever find it and test the fetus for DNA. He had the motive, the means, and the opportunity, and *damn it* we need to figure out how to get the cops to pay attention!"

"Wait," I said, the beginnings of a terrible idea taking root in my mind. Kaz was absolutely right that we couldn't simply sit around and hope the police eventually heard and lent credence to all the same gossip we had—it felt wrong, and betrayed every sense of justice I had—but I also wasn't anx-ious to phone in tips that they would be unable or unwilling to explore, due to a lack of evidence and the fact that I was probably still technically a suspect. Garcia and Becker seemed to automatically doubt everything that came out of my mouth, and a bunch of unsubstantiated rumors that conveniently impli-cated somebody else probably wouldn't be received with any more credulity than the last unsupportable tidbit I'd shared with them. But if I managed to get my hands on something concrete . . .

I pulled out my phone, connected to the Internet, and did a quick search. "Change of plans—we're not going back to Riverside. I need you to take me somewhere else instead."

I had found an address, which I punched into Kaz's GPS, and we followed the directions all the way to an apartment building on Ann Arbor's north side, not far from the neighbor-hood where Tiana's family lived. It was a boxy, nondescript edifice that had probably been built in the sixties or seventies: three stories of stone and plaster, roughly twelve units to a floor, and each unit with its own tiny balcony. It wasn't a slum by any stretch, but I was still willing to bet that the place had been a huge step down for the guy who lived there.

"Are we here to see someone?" Kaz asked dubiously, looking up through the rain at the orderly balconies with their dark wooden pickets.

"The exact opposite, I hope," I answered, jumping out and sprinting for the entrance. A twenty-yard dash, I was nevertheless soaked by the time I reached the door, but I hardly noticed the chill of my drenched hoodie sticking to my arms and back; for this part of my shaky plan I was flying entirely by the seat of my pants, and unless January's ghost were really out there somewhere, pulling strings from beyond The Veil, this detour might well have been a wasted trip.

I was in luck, however. Someone had wedged a chunk of wood between the security door and its frame, propping it open so tenants wouldn't have to bother with their keys every time they came and went, and a rectangular bank of mailboxes on the wall just inside the vestibule gave me my next piece of vital information: The box for apartment 2D boasted a hand-printed label with the name *C. Hoffman*.

"Why are we at Cedric's apartment building?" Kaz asked nervously. I had barely been aware that he'd followed me in.

"We need evidence, right? Can you think of a better place to look?" I made the equation sound simple enough, even though I well knew that what I meant to attempt was anything but. It was as hazardous as it was foolish, and there were a dozen or more ways for it to go horribly wrong—or to simply fail before it even got off the ground—but, on the other hand, what did we have to lose?

"We're going to *break in* to Cedric's place?" Aghast, Kaz still had the good sense to whisper this horrified question as he tailed me up the stairs to the second floor. The carpeting was threadbare and smelled like mothballs and butt, the wallpaper weirdly thick and textured, but the ugly insulation deadened the sound of our steps and voices. "Flynn, that's insane!"

"Technically, only I'm going to break in," I corrected him, still pretty optimistic, all things considered. "One of us needs to keep watch."

A single hallway ran the length of the second floor, jogging a little to either side to accommodate support beams, a trash chute, and flights of architectural whimsy. Number 2D was easy to find; a solid wooden door fitted with a peephole, a knocker, and a little bell. I had just put my hand on the knob when Kaz grabbed my wrist and pulled me back. "I'm not kidding, Flynn—have you lost your mind? What if he's home?"

"He's not," I assured him confidently. "They have rehearsal after school every day until six. He won't be back for hours." Kaz was still looking at me like I'd just volunteered to join the bomb squad as I gently removed his hand from my arm. Unable to resist, I let my fingers glide slowly across the back of his hand when I released him; just the feeling of his skin against mine sent sparks popping and sizzling up my spine, and I got the guilty rush of an addict stealing one secret gulp of wine. "It's our only shot, Kaz."

He set his mouth in an unhappy line, but didn't argue, so I tried the knob again. Unsurprisingly, it was locked. I'd figured it as a long shot, but if I hadn't at least tried, I'd have felt even stupider. Letting out a breath, Kaz asked, "Now what?"

There was no welcome mat to conceal an extra key, and no

spare hidden above the doorframe, either. It was disappointing, though not totally unexpected, and I devised an even stupider plan B on the spot. Taking a look up and down the hall, I made a mental note of where 2D was located in the building's layout; then, just as quickly as we'd come up the stairs, I went back down, darting through the vestibule, out into the parking lot, and around to the back side of the building.

The balconies were arranged one atop the other, and Cedric's faced the rear lot. Luckily, we were out of sight of passing traffic back there, and owing to the foul weather, there were no people hanging out, either. Looking up at the building again, taking in the tidy grid of apartments that contained so many human existences, I counted up and over until I found the one I wanted.

I had just started hauling myself up to the balcony below Cedric's, elevated a few feet off the ground—and, fortunately for me, with vertical blinds snapped shut across its sliding doors—when Kaz caught up with me again. "*What* are you *doing*?"

He grabbed me by the arm once more and yanked me back down to the blacktop of the parking lot, glaring like I was starting to piss him off. Rain was spraying into my eyes, and I had to squint, but I tried to give him a resolute look as I said, "I can't break down the door, so I'm going in through the balcony."

"What if the balcony is locked, too? Are you going to smash the glass? Take a chance on breaking your hand or cutting your arm open?" His tone was patronizing, and anger stirred to life in the pit of my stomach.

"Yeah, maybe I will," I retorted. In point of fact, I had no intention of smashing anything; if the sliding door was locked, I would curse the fates and then clamber back down the side of the building—but I was betting I wouldn't have to. Unless they live at ground level, very few people worry about keeping their balcony secured. It isn't really worth the risk for casual burglars to go around scaling the outside of apartment complexes and checking doors at random. The odds are too great they might be spotted, pick a place whose owners are home, or break into a student flat filled with nothing but busted Ikea furniture and empty beer cans. Only someone with a lot of determination and a specific purpose would bother to do what I was trying to do, and I doubted that Cedric was expecting me.

Kaz still had me by the elbow, and now his other hand reached out for me, seemingly of its own accord; he placed it on the side of my neck, fingers taut, his thumb brushing my cheek. It was an affectionate gesture, almost proprietary, and his irritated expression gave way immediately to one of worry. "Flynn, someone could see you. You could get caught or arrested, or . . . or you could fall off the balcony and fucking *die*! It's dangerous, don't you get that?"

Between his obvious concern and the touch of his hands, my stomach was coiling and springing like an excited terrier. I wanted him to close the distance between us; I wanted to turn my face into the palm of his hand and kiss it, just to feel his skin against my lips. *Fuck*, I wanted him to feel the same way about me, too—but he didn't, and I had to accept that, like it or not. "I know it's dangerous," I answered him as calmly as I could, "but it's also our best chance at finding evidence—*real* evidence. If I can prove he's got roofies up there, or creepy mementos, or . . . I don't know, a diary of his crimes or something, the police will have to take it seriously!"

"I just . . . I don't want you to get hurt," Kaz replied with difficulty.

"Neither do I." I forced a lopsided smile. The notion that I could get busted—or could potentially just bust open my head— had certainly occurred to me, too. "That's why I need you to stand guard. If Cedric comes back unexpectedly, or if the police show up, call my cell and tell me to get out."

He finally let go. He didn't look happier, but he at least looked resigned to the fact that I intended to do this stupid thing, and he couldn't convince me not to. Glancing around to make sure no neighbors were watching, I took hold of the first-floor balcony again and pulled myself up.

Perched on the railing and standing on my tiptoes, I was just able to reach the bottom of Cedric's balcony, hooking my fingers over the edge of the rectangular platform. Rain pelted my eyes, and my fingers dislodged fat, dirty droplets that splattered revoltingly against my face and coursed down my arms, but I heaved upward again and brought my shoulders level with my hands.

Despite the fact that I don't have much in the way of muscle mass, I also don't have much in the way of weight to support; my arms burned, but I was sure I could do this. Maybe not unequivocally, but at least ninety percent sure. Then again, with my drenched sweatshirt hanging on me like a sack of potatoes lashed around my neck, my legs dangling clumsily in open space, I mentally adjusted that number to eighty.

Instinctively, I tried to brace my feet against something, but they merely pedaled clumsily in the air, increasing the strain on my shoulders. I made a move to reach up with my right hand, and felt the fingers of my left begin to slip hazardously back toward the edge of the slick, painted floor of Cedric's balcony. I brought my right hand back down with a wet slap and sucked in a frightened breath of air. My confidence factor plummeted to sixty percent. Thank God the man didn't live on the third floor.

My fingers were getting stiff, the burn in my arms building to a steady ache, as I adjusted my hold and prepared to try again. Flinging my left hand up this time, I managed to grab onto one of the thick wooden balusters. Its rough surface offered enough friction to give me purchase despite the rain, but when I started to bring my leg up, my hold slipped a bit. I dropped an inch, and a sharp sliver speared the soft flesh of my palm. It hurt as badly as a wasp sting, but I fought the urge to cry out and the instinct to let go, squeezing tight with quaking fingers as I forced my toe up onto the balcony and rebalanced my weight.

Hand over hand, I dragged myself up the wooden posts through sheer force of will, teeth gritted and mind wiped to a self-conscious blank. I got my other leg beneath me, stood, and then swung myself over the rail, collapsing into an ungainly, wet heap on the floor of the balcony between a potted spider plant and a miniature charcoal grill. I was breathing hard, my arms trembling and my hand throbbing, but I'd done it. Or, at least, I hoped I'd done it; there was still the chance the door would be locked, or that my bearings were all wrong and this wasn't the right apartment.

Rising to my feet, I grabbed the handle of the glass door and gave it a tug. It resisted at first, but then, with a click and a scrape, it popped open and slid quietly along its metal track. Furtively, I scanned the black, empty windows of the facing buildings and then slipped inside.

TWENTY-FIVE

ONCE, WHEN WE were in the eighth grade, Micah somehow managed to lock himself out of his house. We spent twenty minutes circling the property, turning over every rock in the yard to see if it concealed a spare key and repeatedly trying to force open the garage door, before I finally discovered the screen on one of his tiny basement windows was loose. With a little brute force, we managed to get the thing open and slither through, dropping into the laundry room with only a handful of scrapes and bruises for our trouble. We got a massive rush out of how clever we'd been in our cunning infiltration, an extra burst of excitement from the once-removed sensation of having violated some kind of basic social rule. We were *almost* just like actual burglars!

That little adventure constituted the entirety of my experience with breaking and entering, prior to the moment I set foot in Cedric Hoffman's apartment. The thrill I'd gotten back then wasn't even in the same ballpark as what came over me when I stepped out of the rain and onto a dark, rectangular floor mat laid down just inside the balcony door.

My heart throbbed frenetically, blood speeding through my

arteries so fast it made me dizzy, and I swallowed hard, as if I had something stuck in my throat. There was a thick silence in the air, the ominous and unnervingly still kind, but I could barely hear it over the *thud thud thud* of my pulse pounding away in my ears. A bit late, it finally occurred to me that Cedric might not live alone, or that he might have called in sick, and my legs went loose and cold underneath me as I stood motionless, straining to listen for signs of life. What would I do, I wondered, if I heard footsteps coming? Besides piss myself, I mean.

But I heard nothing. The heavy, clinging stillness endured, the air practically tingling with it, and at last I eased the sliding door shut behind me. It wasn't until my chest began to hurt that I realized I'd been holding my breath, and as I took in shaky gulps of air, I turned to look around. In the next instant, my heart nearly exploded in my chest when I found myself staring into a narrowed pair of fierce green eyes, glaring at me, practically lit from within by pure hatred.

A surge of adrenaline hit me like a kick to the breastbone, quicksilver panic shooting through my veins, before I realized in the next instant that my hostile nemesis was a cat, crouched on a shelf of Cedric's bookcase. The lithe black animal swished its tail silently as I blinked rain and flop sweat out of my eyes, struggling to get my hyperactive circulatory system to slow back down.

I was standing in the living room. Straight ahead of me was a half wall that separated the space from a small, galley-style kitchen, to the left of which was the front door. A hallway branched off to the left as well, leading, I presumed, to the bedroom and bathroom. The spider plant on the balcony proved to be only a foretaste of Cedric's apparent green thumb—everywhere I looked, I saw something floral or leafy: a ficus towering in the corner by the television set, ferns spilling from pots suspended by ceiling hooks, African violets clustering near my feet to soak in the meager light coming through the glass doors.

Quickly, I removed my shoes and peeled off my drenched socks, leaving them all on the mat. I wasn't sure yet what I intended to do with any evidence I might find—take it with me before Cedric had the chance to destroy it, or leave it where it was for the benefit of the police—but either way, I knew I didn't want the man to realize someone had been inside his home. I was drenched from the rain, and even though I didn't expect him to come back for at least three hours, I couldn't risk the possibility of tracking sodden footprints throughout the apartment. Luckily, the mat was dark enough that it would show nothing once the moisture was absorbed; Cedric would have to step on it in his bare feet to discover how wet it was. At that point, maybe he'd blame the cat for having a weak bladder.

I'd like to pretend that I went about searching the place in an orderly, methodical fashion, but I had no idea where to even start. Aside from drugs that might be used to render someone unconscious—small enough to be concealed almost anywhere—I wasn't certain what I was looking for. January's missing phone? A bloody hacksaw? I would just have to hope that, whatever it was, I would recognize it when I saw it.

A single drawer in the coffee table yielded a treasury of cardboard drink coasters, a wine key, and two decks of playing cards, but little else. The cupboards in the entertainment center were packed with nothing but DVDs and some dusty, ancient VHS cassettes; half of them were adult films, and half of *those* contained the phrases "barely legal" or "naughty schoolgirls" in their titles. Predictable. I shuddered to think what Cedric's browser history might look like.

I gave the kitchen a thorough once-over, sliding knives one at a time out of a block beside the stove to check them for inculpating bloodstains, my stomach tight as a fist. In the junk drawer, under a wild nest of extension cords, loose twine, and rubber bands, I found a thick roll of duct tape. I couldn't decide if this was a coup or not, though; to my eye, it matched the stuff that had been clinging to January's clothes in the meadow—but duct tape was duct tape. How different could it be? And pretty much everyone has a roll of it somewhere in the home. Plus, I didn't think January would have come back there with the man willingly the night she died; neither could I imagine why he would bring her to his apartment rather than simply killing her at Dumas. Either way, I pulled out my iPhone and photographed the suspicious adhesive *in situ*, for posterity.

There was a small closet in the front entryway, and I inspected the pockets of Cedric's coats, rooted around in the toes of his boots and shoes, and even shook out two umbrellas to see if anything had been tucked into them. Nothing.

Looking at my phone's display, I realized to my shock that my search was taking far longer than I expected, and that I had already been up there for over twenty minutes. Even though I knew I was probably safe, I couldn't bring myself to relax; I was somewhere I didn't belong, with no guarantee that one of the neighbors hadn't seen my awkward act of home invasion, and I was itching to leave. Kaz had sent me two nervous texts inquiring after my progress, and I fired back a quick response before heading for the hallway that led to the rest of the apartment.

A stunted passageway, it gave immediate access to three doors. The first turned out to be another small closet, which doubled as a linen cabinet; its interior was half narrow shelves bearing sheets, pillowcases, and towels, while the other half—open space—housed a broom, a vacuum cleaner, and a collapsible ironing board. Immediately across from the closet, the second door was to Cedric's bedroom while, dead ahead, the third gave access to the bathroom.

I went straight for the medicine cabinet, tossing open the mirrored cupboard, and as I took in rows of plastic pill bottles on the grimy, glass shelves, my heart sank. There were dozens of them, in all different colors, shapes, and sizes, and I could already tell I wouldn't have a clue what most of them were. There were half a dozen over-the-counter treatments for allergies, colds, and pain relief alone, but if Cedric had dumped out the real medications and replaced them with roofies, I would never know the difference—and that went double for the prescription meds, with their odd names and ambiguous instructions. Worse, I had to remind myself, even if I *did* find a container that was clearly labeled ROHYPNOL, it *still* wouldn't prove Cedric had committed any sexual assaults, let alone two murders.

With mounting frustration, I went through the process of photographing each bottle, and then replacing it exactly as I had found it. I rummaged quickly through the drawers and other cupboards, but that only increased my awareness of Cedric's dental hygiene and preference for two-ply toilet paper. I gave a quick look into the bathtub, and even dragged a little plastic rake through the cloyingly perfumed cat litter, but struck out both times.

Leaving the bathroom, I hurried into the bedroom, a stuffy

space that was rendered even gloomier by the dark, heavy skies visible through the broad windows above the bed. While the rest of the apartment was neat and clean, almost militaristic in its orderliness, Cedric's private quarters were a nightmare of rumpled sheets, casually discarded underwear, and overflowing wastebaskets. Without much enthusiasm, I started picking through his bureau, trying as best I could to avoid touching anything that had ever been in contact with any of his "intimate parts," but there wasn't much to find. Wedged behind a collection of socks, though, I came across a small flash drive, and the obvious effort to hide it—from whom? I wondered—made my mouth water.

A laptop computer sat open on a small desk in a corner of the room, and I went for it right away, jabbing the USB stick into its port as I fired the machine up. When it blinked to life, a log-in screen confronted me immediately, demanding a password in exchange for access. My heart sank a little lower. Remembering what Klara had told us of "Professor Hoffman's" specialty in British literature and drama, I began trying words inspired by Shakespeare—Hamlet, Elsinore, Romeo, Juliet, Desdemona, Dunsinane. After twenty attempts, and just as many errors, I finally gave up with an aggravated exclamation.

Yanking the flash drive out of the port, I gave my phone another look—forty-five minutes had passed, and I had three more text messages from Kaz. Ignoring them, I crammed the data stick back where I'd found it, and started searching the rest of the desk. I should have made an effort to go through it carefully, but I had been in Cedric's place for the better part of an hour already and I was losing my nerve. It didn't help that by that point I was convinced everything I wanted was doubt-lessly concealed on his inaccessible hard drive.

My phone sprang to life suddenly in my pocket, vibrating urgently against my thigh, and I jumped like I'd received an electric shock. Alarm mounted in me, my chest growing tight, as I fumbled the thing out and saw that Kaz was calling. A burst of fear jump-started my nerves, and I was already jogging back into the living room and heading for my shoes as I asked, "What is it? Is he back already?"

"What the hell is taking you so long?" Kaz demanded, his voice thin and pitched high with anxiety. "Flynn, it's been almost an hour!"

I had reached the glass doors by then, and I paused with a frown, peering out through the rain at as much of the parking lot as was visible through the railing of Cedric's balcony. I could see nothing. Keyed up, I reiterated the question. "Is he back or not? What's going on?"

"Well, no, he's not back *yet*," Kaz answered shrilly, as if this detail were beside the point, "but who knows when he will be? I'm having a heart attack sitting out here waiting for you!"

I heaved a shaky sigh and leaned against the glass, squeez-ing my eyes shut and feeling my frantic pulse begin the slow process of decelerating. "And you figured you'd pass it along or something? I freaked when I saw you were calling—I thought I was about to get busted!"

"I called because you weren't answering my texts, and I got worried," Kaz admitted, sounding guilty. "It turns out there are two entrances to the building, and I've got no idea which one he might use. I've been trying to keep an eye on both of them, but he could get in without me noticing, and then you'd *really* be fucked."

"The play rehearsal ought to continue for at least another couple of hours," I told him, "and I've only got a few places left to check before I'm done, so don't lose your shit, okay? I'll be out of here really soon."

I said it as much to myself as to Kaz, since what he'd revealed really did make me feel a little less secure. After a moment's hesitation, he let out a breathy sound that might have been a nervous laugh. "Sorry. I don't think I have the temperament to be a good lookout man."

"It's okay. Just . . . you know, don't call again unless you actually *see* him. Otherwise I'll be the one having the heart attack, and I don't think Cedric will want to call an ambulance when he finds me lying on the floor of his living room."

Disconnecting, I returned to the bedroom, determined to make good on my promise to finish up quickly and be done with the whole pointless adventure. There were probably a dozen places Cedric could have hidden things that I didn't have the ability to explore—his car, a storage unit, a safe-deposit box—and probably a hundred or so more right there in his apartment that I hadn't even considered. I couldn't spend hours and hours ransacking the place, and I didn't think I had the intestinal fortitude to reenact my unlawful entry, so it was beginning to look as if my photographic essay of Cedric's kitchen and bathroom might be my big haul.

Beside the bed was a little nightstand with two drawers, one large and one small, and I decided it was as reasonable a place as any to stash something one might want to keep private from guests. I was correct, as it turned out, just not quite in the way that I had expected. The large drawer yielded up a trove of Ziploc bags in every imaginable size, and as I lifted some out to see what was in them, a cold thrill pinballed its way up my spine; each bag contained a single item, and each bore a hand-printed label that consisted of a girl's name. They were the same few names over and over, I realized as I sifted through the strange collection—Erica, Alexis, Grace . . . and January.

My breath caught in my throat as I scrabbled through the entire cache, pulling out anything marked with my ex-girlfriend's name; but when I had the bags spread out before me, I was as disappointed as I was disturbed. What I had found was evidence of obsession, but not rape or murder—some blond hairs tangled around a broken bit of elastic in one; in another, an earring I recognized and which January had complained about losing in early September; the lid from a coffee cup in a third. It was a treasury of leavings, things Cedric had scavenged from trash cans and dirty floors, and while it certainly didn't speak in favor of his mental health, neither was it incriminating.

Nevertheless, I photographed the hoard of bags, convinced that each name corresponded to one of Cedric's past—or future—victims, and then moved on. When I opened the smaller drawer, my heart hiccuped hard in my chest as I found myself staring down at a large and preposterously real-looking pistol.

I didn't know much about firearms, but it looked plenty big enough to do the deadly job it was designed for—and, just like that, I couldn't wait to get the hell out of Cedric's place, even if it meant slinking away with nothing to show for myself but a handful of possibly useless pictures. The increasing risk of getting caught suddenly made my quest not feel quite as worth the trouble anymore.

The drawer had just slid shut when my phone vibrated again in my pocket, and my entire body went rigid. It was Kaz. My mouth dry, I answered quietly. "Please tell me you're just having another panic attack."

"I saw a man go inside!" Kaz practically yelped in my ear. "I just came around the corner of the building and saw him go through the door—I didn't get a look at his face, but he was big, and sorta bald, and he started up the stairs, and . . . Flynn, you have to just get out of there! *Now!*"

"I'm on my way," I mumbled, energy starting to spark around me like a Catherine wheel. I jammed the phone back in my pocket and turned, getting ready to sprint for the living room. At that moment, however, my eye finally fell on exactly what I'd been looking for all along.

My jaw dropped, and for a split second I was stunned into paralysis. I had been so focused on identifying all the little nooks, crannies, and cubbies in which Cedric might have been able to conceal something that I had completely ignored what was right there in plain sight. And now I couldn't imagine how I had ever missed it, because the thing grabbed at me like a vortex, pulling my attention away from anything else in the room.

I knew I had no time to waste, that if Cedric *had* been the man Kaz saw entering the building, my lead time on him was already at well under a minute and dwindling fast; but I was looking at proof that the man was a killer, and I couldn't leave it behind. If he realized someone had been in his apartment, he would destroy it immediately.

Darting over to where the thing was mounted on the wall across from Cedric's bed, I tucked my fingers into the sleeves of my hoodie and started trying to work it loose from its moorings.

I didn't want to leave any fingerprints, didn't want to give Cedric the chance to claim it had been planted, but the thick, wet fabric of my sweatshirt made my grip clumsy, and escalating worry made my hands shake.

I was telling myself that Kaz had to be overreacting, that the rehearsal at Dumas couldn't possibly be over yet, but that's when—with a wave of sick-making horror—a terrifying image suddenly leaped from my memory: a poster in the Dumas theater lobby, right where I'd told Kaz to wait for me while I looked for Reiko's friends. The truth of it was so unbelievably awful that I tried to promise myself it wasn't real, even as I understood just how deeply fucked I actually was.

There had been no play rehearsal at Dumas that day—the theater was being used for January's and Reiko's remembrances.

I ripped my find down from the wall, my chest feeling like it had been stabbed full of holes from the inside, and bolted for the living room. I was trying to figure out how I could make it down from the balcony as quickly as possible without breaking anything, but I'd only taken three steps out of the little hallway before a key rattled in the lock of the front door and the dead bolt snapped open with a deafening *click*.

Cedric was home.

TWENTY-SIX

A **WARM BREEZE** *swept in from the backyard, bearing the lingering smells of summer through the screen of our sliding doors—earth, warmth, the mouthwatering scent of someone's nearby barbecue. It was Labor Day weekend, and our freedom officially ended on Tuesday morning with the first day of school, so a sense of imminent loss imbued every tick of the clock. January and I were sprawled on the couch in my living room, watching TV and trying not to think about how little time we had left.*

"Did you enjoy your cute little block party?" she finally asked, her tone playful as she looked up from where her head rested on my chest. We were making a point not to discuss the fact that, pretty soon, we would effectively be having a long-distance relationship in our own hometown, separated by learning institutions as well as several zeros before the decimal point of her new family's net worth.

"Yeah, Micah and I got turned up," I replied with mild sarcasm, rolling my eyes a little. Ever since the advent of that toddler group where I met my best friend, our neighborhood threw block parties straight out of the 1950s for all major warm-weather holidays. The gatherings were all basically the same: potluck dinner, kids running around with sparklers, beer and soda fished from ice-filled coolers,

and music blaring from the Harrisons' crappy sound system. They were actually kind of fun, but there was no possible way to admit that out loud without sounding like a paste-eater. "How was your super-swanky banquet or whatever?"

"Ugh, please don't make me think about it anymore. I spent, like, four straight hours grinning like a mental patient and playing Perfect Obedient Stepdaughter for the cameras. And I barely ate anything, either, because every time I tried to put some food in my mouth a photographer would show up out of nowhere, trying to get a scandalous picture of me fellating a bratwurst or something."

"My mom made enough potato salad to fill a nuclear cooling tower, if you're still hungry," I offered. My parents were off at a movie, and January had been released from Family Photo-Op duty for the night, so we had the place to ourselves. "And Mr. Culbertson talked her into taking home about eighty pounds of some weird egg-plant casserole with asparagus and capers."

"Gee, how could I ever turn that down?" she asked drily, pushing her hair back over one shoulder. For a moment, she gazed up at me silently. "I'm going to miss you, Flynn. This whole thing fucking sucks."

"I know. I'm gonna miss you, too."

Carefully, she pulled herself along my body until we were face-to-face and then leaned in to kiss me. It was gentle at first, sweet, but very quickly became needy and more aggressive. That had been happening a lot lately, and it always made me nervous. I reached up to put my hand on her arm, thinking that maybe I could figure out a non-offensive way to back her off just a little, but she shifted unexpectedly and my fingers closed squarely around her left boob instead.

I jerked my hand away immediately, my face going red and hot, and January ended the kiss. Propping herself up on her elbow, she looked down at me with a strange frown. "They're just boobs, Flynn. They don't bite."

"I—I know," I stammered awkwardly. "I just . . . I don't want you to think I'm like . . . sexually harassing you, or whatever." She was still frowning, so I tried to make it into a joke. "We've had about a million school assemblies where they say I'm not supposed to touch you anywhere without getting your permission first. I'm just trying to be a gentleman!"

"I hereby give you permission not to freak out when your hand accidentally grazes my boob," January responded, too theatrically for her to be entirely serious, and I heaved a secret sigh of relief. The way she'd been looking at me, I'd worried that maybe my compulsive skittishness had begun to make her suspicious; that maybe she'd noticed how I sometimes looked at Matt Bianco during the pool parties she threw at the mansion, and how maybe I hadn't ever really looked at her that way.

"Well, thanks," I said, forcing a smile that I hoped looked far more comfortable than it felt. "I guess it's just that when it comes to sex and, you know, sex stuff, I just . . . I want to wait. I just want it to be right. Special."

January stared at me blankly for so long that I started to sweat, completely unsure of how to read her reaction, and then the corners of her mouth flicked upward. "Flynn, I swear, sometimes I have no idea what goes on in that head of yours. I'm not trying to bewitch you into sex with my aphrodisiac boobs, or whatever! Just for the record, I am totally on board with the waiting plan. I am definitely not ready to lose the V-card yet, and when I am I want things to be special and right, too—with all that soft-focus, mood-lighting,

Hollywood-magic crap we chicks are supposed to want. There's no pressure here, okay? But if you touch my boobs once in a while, I'm not going to call the cops."

She settled back down, putting her head on my chest again, and for a little while we just lay there and listened to the wind chimes tinkling in the backyard. Then she spoke again, her voice so muffled I almost didn't make out what she said.

"When the time is right, though—when it feels right . . . I hope it's with you."

Sweat prickled like a rash across my scalp, the air around me stifling, and my heart chugged like the engine of an ocean liner. Some plastic attachment from Cedric's vacuum cleaner dug painfully into my hip, and I struggled against every single instinct I had to remain utterly motionless.

The minute I'd realized he was coming through the door, I had reacted on autopilot, lunging backward and then yanking open the little hallway closet. The sound of Cedric's absentminded, lumbering entrance had just barely managed to conceal the rasp of the linen cupboard's bifold metal door as it rattled shut behind me along its aluminum track. Or so I hoped. I had been plunged into almost total darkness, the only light leaking through a series of thin, horizontal slats that afforded me no decent view of what was happening just outside my hiding place.

I could hear Cedric moving about in the apartment's little entryway, kicking off his shoes, shrugging out of his coat, hanging it up; then the heavy tread of his footsteps moving into the kitchen. What was I going to do? *What the fuck was I going to do?* I couldn't just stand there, holding my breath until the man went to sleep. Unless he went out again, I was completely and totally screwed. Could I figure out some way to *make* him go? If I could somehow get Kaz to lure him out . . .

As if on cue, my phone buzzed to life, and my heart lurched up into my throat and stuck there. I had never been more grateful that I always kept the ringer off, but the sound made by the vibration was practically deafening to my panicked ears, so loud it might as well have been a band saw in my pocket. I couldn't stop it, either—couldn't risk adding to the noise by moving to shut it off.

Sounds were coming from the kitchen—cupboards banging, a package tearing open with the rough crinkle of reinforced paper, a cascade of something clattering into a ceramic bowl. Impossibly, it masked the thunderous droning of my cell phone, which mercifully died out just before Cedric completed his anvil chorus. After making a series of strange clucking sounds with his tongue, the man then called out, "Dinnertime, Hippolyta, you little minx!"

Hippolyta—the Amazon queen from *A Midsummer Night's Dream*. The Riverside drama club had performed the play only the year before, and the guy who'd played Theseus had constantly called his bride-to-be "Hippo-lighter" to the mean-spirited delight of Micah, January, and myself. I'd have bet anything that the cat's name matched the password needed to access Cedric's computer, and I cursed myself for not thinking to check if the animal had been wearing a tag.

And then, as Cedric left the kitchen, his feet plodding across the linoleum and onto the carpeted living-room floor, I thought of one more careless oversight I had made—one so serious that my blood turned instantly cold and hard in my veins: *My shoes were still sitting on the mat by the balcony doors.*

Before I even had time to entertain the ridiculously optimistic notion that maybe Cedric wouldn't notice them, I heard him stop short. He couldn't have been standing more than ten or fifteen feet from where I was still hunched awkwardly in that darkened closet, clutching tightly onto the telltale item I'd removed from his bedroom wall, and in my mind's eye I could picture him staring at the canvas high-tops that were right there in the open, all but sitting under a spotlight. His feet moved again on the carpet—swiveling?—and his voice sounded out, thin and nervous, "Is someone—? Wh-who's here? Show yourself!"

I stayed quiet, my eyes scrunched shut, pain spearing through my core with every violent beat of my heart, as if there were still maybe some fairy-tale chance he could decide there was no one else in the apartment after all; that perhaps an intruder had already come and gone, leaving behind a pair of shoes as a courtesy. The place was tiny, and although there were plenty of places to hide drugs and diaries full of criminal confessions, there were only a few spots big enough for a human male with size 10 feet, and he would check them all in short order—whether before or after calling the police, I wasn't sure.

Then, as his steps starting pounding decisively in my direction, the same direction as the bedroom, I remembered the gun in his nightstand. I couldn't let him get to it, or I would never walk out of there alive.

There was no time to think, to plan, to consider, only to act. Just as he passed the closet, turning to enter the bedroom, I shoved the door open and yelled, "*Stop!*"

Cedric whirled around, his eyes wide with alarm, and when he saw me, he did a double take. Fear was quickly joined by confusion, surprise, and an obvious trace of anger. "*You!* How did you get in here? What on earth—How *dare* you break into my home!"

"The game is up, Cedric," I announced, quoting every single private-detective movie I'd ever seen. It sounded like a joke, but I was too scared to think straight, too rattled to come up with my own words. My jaw was actually chattering as I spat out, "I know what you did. I know everything!"

"This is . . . I won't stand for this kind of harassment," Cedric blustered, although he didn't move. "Creating a disturbance at my rehearsals is one thing, but *this* . . . I shall call the police!"

"Good—do it! You'll save me the trouble," I shot back, realizing at the exact same moment that the threat had been a double bluff. He'd caught me burgling his home red-handed, and I should by all rights be begging him *not* to involve the police; by doing the opposite, I'd made it clear that I really did know something—that I was, perhaps, truly dangerous. The wariness that crept into his eyes as he regarded me anew made me certain I'd screwed up again. Nervously, I continued, "In fact, why don't you call them right now?"

"You are becoming quite intolerable, Mr. Doherty," he informed me, after a brief pause, his voice suddenly cold and flat, "and now you are a home invader—a juvenile delinquent, a common thug."

"It's better than being a *rapist*," I returned savagely, "and a *murderer*."

His face twitched, but he stifled the reaction quickly. "That is an outrageous allegation, and you had better not repeat it if you—"

"It isn't an allegation, it's the truth! You raped January, and then you killed her when she threatened to tell—and when Reiko confronted you about it, you killed her, too!" I stepped forward, anger blasting through me like a gust of hot desert air. "I had some time to look around before you got home, you sick psychopath, and I *know*."

"I—I don't have to stand here and listen to this kind of slander," Cedric stammered, his face flushed and his jowls trembling. He inched backward. "I am going to call the police right now, so you had better stay where you are!"

He spun around and started moving again, but not for the phone sitting on the edge of the desk—instead, he was making a beeline for the nightstand. My nerves snapping taut as a leather strap, I played my ace card in desperation, screaming out, "*Where did you get this?*"

The tone in my voice made him stop, turn, and look at what I was holding in my hands, what I'd stolen off his wall. It was a portrait of January, so startling in the exactitude of its sure, delicate strokes that when I'd seen Reiko creating it, I'd been amazed by her profound talent. It was the very drawing FBA told me the girl had wanted to complete for January's memorial the night she'd stayed late at the theater—the night she'd been killed. And I had found it in Cedric's bedroom.

His eyes were huge and troubled, his face an unhealthy shade of vermilion. "That's mine! You . . . you put that down this instant!"

"You took this from Reiko," I accused furiously. "You killed her, and you stole it, and then you put it on your *wall*—"

"You have no idea what you're talking about," he spluttered, making a grab for the portrait.

Jerking it back out of his reach, I screamed, "You bought a frame for it! What the hell is wrong with you?"

A thick square of glossy black wood, inset with an ivory matte, now surrounded the carefully penciled face of my ex-girlfriend. The picture was heavy in my sweatshirt-covered hands, and kept slipping as I tried to maintain a hold on it without letting it touch my bare fingers. Panic finally flashed across Cedric's face, and he gasped, "Be careful with that, it is *fragile*!"

"Tell me how you got it," I ordered him. "Admit it!"

"She . . . she gave it to me. Reiko. She knew how much January meant to me, how special our bond was—"

"*Liar!*" I roared. "You filthy, disgusting *liar*! You didn't have any 'bond'—she told me you were a creepy old pervert! She felt *sorry* for you."

"That isn't true. It simply isn't true! We had a . . . a special . . ."

"You forced yourself on her. You *attacked* her, and then you killed her to keep anyone from finding out about it, because you wanted to make sure nothing stopped you from doing it again, you disgusting, twisted—"

"THAT ISN'T TRUE!" he screamed, his chest heaving, and I recoiled, startled by the vehement outburst. "She was special—she was different. From the very beginning there was something between us, something *real*. I don't expect you to understand that. You're too young, too immature, to comprehend—"

"She was *fifteen*, you sick fuck!"

"She had an old soul," he said piously, and I nearly vomited on his carpet.

"It wasn't her *soul* that you roofied—"

"I don't have to explain anything to you!" he interrupted, incandescent with hate. "You know nothing, can prove nothing, and I am done listening to your—"

"I know what happened at Hazelton," I barked acidly, "and when the police hear about it, they're going to be real interested in you. You and this portrait and your sick collection of memorabilia."

He froze, his mouth dropping open, and the color drained from his face. His mouth moved a couple of times, but he didn't make a sound. And then, without warning, he spun on his heels and started sprinting for the nightstand. The sudden movement caught me by surprise, and the distance he had to cover was so short that by the time my reflexes kicked in, it was already too late for me to beat him there—too late for me to make it out the door, down the hall, and all the way to the stairs before he could manage to put a bullet in my spine. So I did the only thing I could; I took the heavily framed portrait of January and threw it at Cedric's head with every bit of strength, determination, and anger I had left.

It revolved in the air, and then—to my amazement—actually caught the man behind his left ear with a satisfying *crack*. The portrait ricocheted to the floor, its glass shattering on impact, while Cedric fell to one knee and pitched forward against the nightstand, propelled by his own, prodigious body weight. Everything on top of the little unit smashed to the ground, and the man landed hard among the debris, sprawling sideways onto the carpet with a sharp cry.

I was on top of him before he had a chance to right himself. Blinded and deafened by wrath, I have no idea what words came out of my mouth, and only a vague notion of how many times I must have hit him. When I became aware of myself again, my arms were sore, my knuckles raw and tender, and my throat ached from screaming obscenities. Blood was smeared across Cedric's broad, puffy face, leaking from his nose and a gash above one eyebrow, his glasses were smashed, and his meaty forearms were flung over his head in self-defense.

"Where is she?" I shouted hoarsely, my eyes swimming, my hands clutching his collar and shaking him as hard as I could. "What did you do with her?"

To my complete surprise, he began to laugh—a bitter, contemptuous laugh that rattled in the back of his throat like gravel pouring down a metal chute. "You're a pathetic child. You think you're a hero, some sort of Galahad defending his fair maiden's honor? You have no idea what she was!" His eyes flickered brightly, gazing up at me from his blood-streaked, sneering face with a kind of manic delight. "She was a temptress, a succubus, and I only gave her what she wanted!" I punched him again, and his lip split open like a rotted peach, the blood rushing over his yellowed teeth making his malicious grin twice as gruesome. "How pitiful you are. A sniveling, snot-nosed *boy*. You would never have been enough for her, you—"

I hit him again, in the side of the head, but the blow landed wrong; after a sudden, sharp twinge, my hand went numb, and I could tell instantly that I'd hurt it seriously. Incensed, I grabbed his throat with my other hand, saliva dripping from my bared teeth as I spat, "She was just a *girl*."

"She was a Venus mantrap," he retorted, unmoved by my

ferocity, "a siren, determined to lure me to my ruin. I knew it. I knew it from the moment I set eyes on her, but I was powerless to resist. I knew exactly what she was, what was inside of her, but still I loved her. So help me, I really and truly loved her. She *made* me do those things! I had no choice. No choice at all."

"She was going to be a scientist." I was crying and exhausted, and if I could have hit him again, I would have, but my right hand was immobilized, a distant ache beginning to throb rhythmically within it. "She was going to move to California and study astronomy and *be* someone, do something important, but you took all of that away from her! From her and Reiko, both."

He came alive then, his face darkening with rage, and he growled, "Don't you dare compare January to that little Japanese *bitch*!" He shoved me off him with such force that I practically flew across the room. I landed on my ass, my head striking the doorjamb so hard that light strobed briefly behind my eyes. Struggling to his knees, Cedric glared at me through a mask of blood, his eyes glowing like hot brands. "There was *nothing* special about that girl, nothing enchanting! She was a vile, foulmouthed *shrew*, who didn't understand January and me any more than you do!" Panting, he spat a streak of pink, bubbling slime onto the carpet. "She threatened me! She came to me spewing filth, accusing me of things in the most appalling language—this . . . this offensive, unladylike *bilge*—and she expected me to grovel, to show her some sort of *respect*!"

"Is that why you killed her?" I asked groggily. The room was tilting madly, and my hand was rapidly turning fat and purple. "Her 'unladylike bilge'?"

"She claimed that she would destroy me, that she would tell the police a number of terrible things she said January had told her about me. I couldn't let her do it, could I? My career would have been over. My *life* would have been over." He grinned again, evilly, and his body shook with smug, proud laughter. "So I stopped her. I begged her to stay quiet—*begged* her, if you please—and once she thought she had the upper hand, I put a screwdriver through her throat and cut out her vulgar, spiteful tongue!" His grin spread wider, bursting with madness, and he began shuffling backward, eyes on me as one hand groped through the air for the drawers of the nightstand. "And now I think it's time I did something about you."

I tried to get up—whether to run away or to attack again I wasn't sure—but the floor wouldn't stay put under my feet. I fell back down with a thud, the room Tilt-A-Whirling around me in a nauseating square dance. At the same time that Cedric took his eyes off me, turning to the nightstand, I heard a distant, frantic hammering at the apartment door. Then my name, shouted with utmost urgency: "Flynn! *Flynn!*"

The door crashed open, feet pounding through the entryway, while Cedric fumbled the gun out into the open, crammed bullets into it with panicky fingers, and jerked back the hammer. He had just managed to take aim when Kaz appeared in the doorway beside me, drawing up short and turning gray from the collar of his peacoat to the roots of his rain-slicked hair as he beheld the tableau in the bedroom.

"Oh, thank G-God someone came!" Cedric stammered unconvincingly, the gun pointed directly at my chest. If he so much as flinched, I would be dead. "This boy, this . . . this thief, he broke into my apartment and attacked me! I was very nearly killed! Please call the police—there's a phone in the living room."

"I've already called them," Kaz reported mechanically, his voice a quaking half whisper. He stood in the doorway like a pillar of salt, transfixed by fear.

"Oh." Cedric's eyes shifted as he recalculated, his mouth jerking into a smile of false gratitude. "Good, thank you! You had best wait in the hall for them. This young man is quite dangerous, and I don't want anything to happen to you."

"I told them—" Kaz's voice choked off, and he went silent. For a weighty moment, he stared blankly at Cedric's weapon, eyes wide and glazed—and then he looked over at me. I saw something shift in his expression then, and he swallowed hard, his voice barely steady when he spoke again. "I told them you asked Flynn to come here. I told them he learned about what you did at Hazelton, that he called you to give you a chance to explain, and that you asked him to come to your place. I told them that I was afraid, that—that I thought you were going to hu-hurt him."

Cedric's gaze flicked between the two of us, his mouth flexing, his right eye beginning to twitch. Gravely, he said, "You should not have done that."

"It doesn't matter, Cedric," I told him. I wish I could say I was stalwart and unflappable in the face of death, that looking down the barrel of a gun freed my inner existentialist badass— but the truth is that I was unreservedly terrified. My legs were jellied, I was a heartbeat away from losing control of my bowels, and my only hope for survival lay in convincing a madman there was no point in killing me. "Even if you tell them he lied, it's already too late. Whatever you do to us now, the cops will have to investigate. You'll never get rid of all your creepy trophies before they get here; and even if you do, I saved photos of them to the cloud, and the police will find them sooner or later. Then they'll uncover the Hazelton story, they'll find the kids I spoke to at Dumas who told me about your obsession with January . . . and they already know you were the last person to see Reiko alive *and* that Reiko knew about January's rape. At that point, they could never believe you killed us in self-defense. No matter what, it's already over for you."

After an agonizingly long moment, Cedric finally spoke. "Well then," he said, his tone brisk and disturbingly hollow, "I suppose I've really got nothing left to lose, do I?"

And he pulled the trigger.

TWENTY-SEVEN

THE NEXT HOUR lasted for about ten years. Most of it was a blur, a series of disconnected images that I could barely organize into a sensible timeline afterward. I remembered the gun going off, the roar of it shocking, much louder than it ever seems on TV; the top of Cedric's head exploding, his body pitching forward as the smoking barrel of the weapon slipped from between his teeth; the grisly red crater in his skull. He'd chosen not to kill me after all, but to turn the weapon on himself. And, to tell the truth, in spite of everything I'd said to him at the very end, I still wasn't entirely convinced that he couldn't have somehow bluffed his way out of trouble with Kaz and me dead.

I remembered speaking with the police, one officer after another, faces shuffling around like a deck of cards. My voice played like a recording, a distant, quiet monotone, as I explained again and again about what had happened that day. I spoke to some EMTs, too, who diagnosed me with a mild concussion, and announced that my hand was most likely broken. My parents were called, and I spent a long time sitting in the back of an open ambulance with them beside me, uniformed men and women cycling through with questions, advice, and veiled accusations. Night had fallen, the rain had stopped, and the bright, brilliant synthesis of light from lampposts, emergency vehicles, and gathered news teams formed a strangely beautiful and abstract smear of color across the slicked asphalt of the parking lot.

It wasn't until I was informed that I could finally leave and was following my parents to where they'd parked their car—not far from the vibrant yellow ring of crime scene tape that held back a steadily growing mass of spectators and media representatives—that I finally saw Kaz for the first time since the police had arrived on the scene.

He broke away from a knot of people outside the building and came sprinting across the parking lot, feet splashing in the puddles that still streaked the ground. "Flynn!"

I turned around just as he caught up to me and, as my parents stood beside the car and watched—bewildered, frightened, and fatigued by their brief involvement in the evening's ordeal—he pulled me into a fierce hug, tight and possessive. Pain scissored clear up to my right elbow, and I jerked backward with a grunt. "Ouch—careful." Glancing awkwardly down at my arm, draped across my solar plexus in the protective cradle of a sling, I explained, "I'm on my way to the hospital to get this x-rayed. They think I broke it on Cedric's face."

His hands on my shoulders and his head bowed, Kaz mumbled something that sounded like *stupid*. I told him I couldn't understand him, and when he looked up at me I was shocked to see tears rolling down his cheeks. "That was *so fucking stupid*, Flynn! What you did . . . you almost died!"

His mouth was trembling, his hazel eyes filled with fear, and

I squirmed uncomfortably as if I were seeing something I shouldn't. "I didn't, though. Thanks to you. You actually . . . you saved my life." I tried on an off-kilter grin. "Just don't think that means I'm your bitch now or something, because I—"

"Stop trying to make this into a joke!" He was really upset, his voice too loud. My parents were paying attention now, glancing at each other as if unsure whether they ought to step in, and I got the feeling some of the looky-loos beyond the crime scene tape were tuning into our little two-man drama as well. "If I hadn't gotten up there when I did, if I had been one minute later . . ."

"But you weren't," I said, as if it were as simple as that—as if I hadn't been thinking obsessively about the exact same thing. Truth was, I wouldn't even have had one full minute left to live if Kaz hadn't shown up the second he did.

"Damn it, Flynn, I thought you were dead." He was crying, his Adam's apple bobbing like a cork and tearing his voice to shreds. "When you didn't answer your phone . . . when I heard the struggling, the shouting . . ."

"It's okay now. It's over, and I'm still here."

"He had a gun, Flynn, a *gun*, and it was *pointed at you*, and I was sure you were about to die and all I could think, the only thing that kept going through my head, was that you'd tried to kiss me and I'd pulled away! I'd thought we had all this time, but then there was this gun, *pointed at you*, and I couldn't stop thinking that I'd never get to kiss you again, *ever*, that I'd had my last chance and I'd blown it, because I thought . . . I thought . . ."

Something clenched hard around my heart, and my breath whooshed out of my lungs as I looked back at him. "Kaz . . ."

"I was wrong, Flynn." He actually started to laugh through his tears. "I don't want to be your friend."

I laughed, too, just as my eyes began to prickle and my vision clouded. "I don't want you to be my friend, either."

And then he pulled me in again and kissed me. It didn't matter that my parents were watching—that, in fact, half the neighborhood was watching, along with a couple of local news teams—I lost myself immediately, and we were alone. His mouth was soft and warm and perfect, like melted chocolate, and I felt it all through me. My entire body hummed to life, and maybe it was because I'd just come so close to dying, but the feeling was so much more intense, so much more real, than anything I'd ever experienced before—even than it had been the first time. My aches and pains, the freezing cold that had woven itself through my very bones while I was sitting outside for an hour in the chill, damp night air . . . it all disappeared in an instant. I was aware of nothing but Kaz and the kiss that fused us together.

When he drew back again, far too soon, he pressed his forehead to mine and gasped for air. With a raspy laugh, he said, "You should . . . you should go to the hospital. But call me as soon as you can, okay? Promise."

I smiled, wider than I had in days. "I promise."

He said good-bye and, with a lingering look, turned and started for his car. I could feel my parents immediately, staring carefully at anything but me, and I kept my own eyes averted and my expression neutral as I crossed to the rear door of my dad's sedan and waited for him to unlock it. I didn't exactly regret casting aside my inhibitions for that kiss, but now that it was over and Kaz was gone, my face was already starting to beat with warmth as I imagined what kinds of questions my parents would be asking me on the way to the emergency room.

The locks blipped open at last, and just as I started to get into the car, my gaze settled on two very familiar people watching me from the edge of the crowd. Standing directly under a streetlamp twenty feet away from me, their stunned, open-mouthed expressions lit up like displays in a museum, were Micah and Tiana.

The X-rays showed that I'd broken one of my metacarpals, and I was fitted with a massive, temporary cast that my dad immediately signed, over my vociferous objections; after that, I was given some phenomenal painkillers and finally sent home. I slept so well I surprised even myself, despite the fact that my parents woke me up repeatedly during the night to ask me my name, my address, and how old I was, just to make sure—as my dad put it—that my cerebellum wasn't "gushing blood like those elevators in *The Shining*."

The questions they had for me about Kaz were disconcertingly respectful and polite—of the *what's his name, how old is he, is he your boyfriend, when do we get to meet him* variety. They kept me home from school the next day, and so Kaz himself dropped by in the afternoon—dressed like a Young Republican on his way to a job interview—and got a chance to answer most of the questions in person. We spent much of the day watching the news coverage, which was split between Cedric Hoffman's death and Senator-elect Jonathan Walker's victory at the polls, and for that reason I didn't see Micah again until Thursday.

My name hadn't been released to the media, but rumors had made their inevitable progress around the halls of Riverside anyway, and when I walked through the doors that morning with an incredibly obvious cast consuming half of my right arm, I instantly became something of a celebrity. Madison Reinbeck came up to me immediately and asked if it was true that I had also been shot while fighting for control of the gun; Lucas Navarro told me he'd heard that I'd been working for the cops and wearing a wire the whole time I was in Cedric's apartment; and Ashley Sobol told me that she'd heard from Mason Collier that if he were really, really drunk, he *might* be willing to let me perform a certain sexual favor for him. I told Ashley to tell Mason I was flattered, but that he'd missed his chance.

And then, much to my surprise, Micah came up to me, materializing at my locker right after the first bell rang. I was so startled that I couldn't think of anything to say. I stood there, afraid to move, like when a bee lands on your arm. After a moment of staring down at his shoes, he finally grunted, "Hey."

"Hey. I thought—" I'd been going to say, *I thought you weren't talking to me*, but it seemed an ungracious way to start what I hoped was a détente, so I shut up.

Micah sighed. "Listen, dude. I just wanted to say that I'm sorry about how I've been acting. I guess—"

"It's okay," I blurted out, so relieved that he finally wanted to put things behind us that I didn't even need to hear an excuse.

"No, you gotta let me finish," he argued glumly, adding, "Ti's gonna cut off my taint if I don't share my feelings or whatever." Another sigh. "When you told me that . . . you know, that you were gay, I freaked out. It was dumb, and I said a bunch of stupid stuff because I was freaked out, and I shouldn't have. You know I don't have a problem with gay people, dude, I mean my aunt's a lesbian, for fuck's sake."

"Right." I'd actually forgotten about that.

"It's just that, like, I kinda tell you *everything*, and I guess . . ." He rolled his eyes at Tiana in absentia, gritted his teeth, and continued, "I guess it *hurt my feelings* that you kept this from me for so long."

"It wasn't because I didn't trust you, or anything," I said, which was mostly true, but not entirely. I'd kept the truth to myself for so long in part because I didn't trust *anyone* with it. I was terrified of what it would do if I set it loose in the world.

"I know. I see that. Honestly, what really got to me was, like, we've known each other since forever, right? I remember when you were afraid of water and we were in Guppies together, and I had to promise not to let you drown." He was talking about the swimming classes our parents made us take when we were in kindergarten—an epic nightmare for me, where each lesson felt like the last thirty minutes of *Titanic*. Micah, of course, was smiling at the memory. "We've had the same teachers, the same bullies, the same clothes—everything, man. I know everything about you, because we went through everything together. You really are like my brother, okay? And for fifteen years, it's like you're the only thing that's just steady, the only thing I *know*, sometimes even better than I know myself." His mouth flipped sideways and another sigh shuddered out of him, and I said a silent prayer to God that Micah Feldman was not about to start crying. "What I'm trying to say is, this is the first thing about you—ever—that I can't . . . you know, relate to. I can't go through it, I can't be a part of it, and it feels . . . it *feels* like there's this gap suddenly between us and there's nothing I can do about it."

He was silent after that, and there was such an air of

humiliated desolation about him that I almost wanted to hug him. I almost did, too, just to make him writhe in discomfort. "Dude. You still know me better than anyone else. And how do you think I felt all those summers you went away to Hebrew camp and came back with stories about stuff I wasn't a part of? I'm not going anywhere, Micah. I still want you to be my best friend."

"Me too," he admitted, and he finally looked up at me with a furtive glance. Then, struggling to sound as if he were only barely interested, he asked, "So . . . that guy with the car, the one who was hoovering your face the other night. Is he, like, your boyfriend, or whatever?"

Innocently, I responded, "What guy? You mean Kaz?"

"*Kaz?*" Micah repeated with a shriek-gasp. "You mean Kaz as in *Fucking Kaz*? Kaz from the toy store, who was always trying to bone down with January?"

"Yeah, well, it turns out that was kind of a misunderstanding."

"Damn, I guess so." Micah shook his head in amazement. "I cannot believe that Fucking Kaz is your boyfriend."

"It's probably time we stopped calling him 'Fucking Kaz.' "

"I'm surprised you can call him anything, the way he eats your face like that," Micah remarked casually. "Did they have to pump his stomach at the hospital to get your lips back?"

"Fuck off," I said, but I was laughing, because I finally realized that my best friend was back.

Despite my buoyant mood that morning, a weird malaise crept over me toward the end of the day. I couldn't stop thinking about that hole in the top of Cedric's head, like a yawning, pink-red mouth with fragments of bone for teeth. Something else was bothering me, too, but it wasn't until after dinner, when my parents turned on the nightly news, that it started to dawn on me what it was.

Cedric and Jonathan still shared the headlines, their stories irrevocably intertwined, and I watched the footage cutting back and forth between the two men in an artless attempt at emphasizing the poignancy of January's and Reiko's fates by highlighting Mr. Walker's promising future. There were clips from the acceptance speech given by the senator-elect as the voting results became clear, the man gravely reminding his constituents about his plans for January's Law while both his son and his campaign manager lurked smugly behind him, a terrible twosome—Tammy more conspicuous than ever by her absence; and there were repeated shots of him and Anson driving off together in a sleek open convertible, waving to the cameras with shit-eating grins on their faces.

All this celebratory folderol gave way to footage of emergency lights flashing against the front of Cedric's apartment building, wobbly, zoomed-in shots of the man's balcony in daylight, and reports of "two unnamed young men" who witnessed the suicide. Revelations about the former teacher's inglorious departure from the Hazelton School were presented in breathless tones, and some details about the investigation into the role he might have played in the disappearance of January McConville and the death of Reiko Matsuda were also disclosed.

An organized search of the city dump had resulted in the triumphant discovery of January's backpack, stained with more blood, which had apparently been found mixed in with other items that sanitation workers had collected from the Dumpsters behind Cedric's apartment building the week after she vanished. It wasn't immediately clear why he hadn't simply left her bag in the meadow with her other things, but the popular speculation was that he had probably been forced to act quickly that night; the clothes had been misdirection, as Kaz had suggested, and he had brought her backpack home with him so he could take his time going through it and removing or destroying anything that might implicate him if it was ever found. Her cell phone, for instance, still remained unaccounted for.

January's bloody clothes silently testified to her having met the same violent and grisly end as her only friend at Dumas and, owing to where Cedric had disposed of Reiko's body, authorities had resumed dragging the river, hoping that the still-missing girl might at last be found. The Huron wasn't particularly deep, nor was it prone to strong currents that might have swept any remains an extraordinary distance from town, and most of those interviewed seemed pretty confident that it was only a matter of time. I wasn't sure how I felt about that—whether I even wanted either the closure or the knowledge such a discovery would surely bring. Just the basic facts of what had been done to Reiko gave me nightmares, and I wasn't exactly anxious to receive confirmation that my ex-girlfriend had suffered the same horrors.

And the truth of the matter was, for as long as January was still out there somewhere, her fate still technically unknown and unknowable, I could pretend. I could hold on to something deep inside me that desperately wanted to believe January was still alive, a survivor after everything she'd gone through, and not just another tragic figure. It was a precious and fragile dream, and I didn't want it shattered—not now, and maybe not ever.

The police, however, were relentless. They had found blood on the floor of the Dumas Academy theater's workshop, inexpertly concealed by a thick layer of spilled paint; and a check of the tools belonging to the drama club turned up more traces of blood on both a screwdriver and the hilt of an X-Acto knife. Representatives of law and order were confident in saying that both weapons had figured in the death of Reiko Matsuda. Rohypnol had been found in the glove compartment of Cedric's car, and duct tape of the type found with January McConville's clothing had been recovered from his apartment. The brand was too common to stand as conclusive proof, but a series of "disturbing images" found on his computer put it beyond doubt that he had sexually assaulted the senator-elect's stepdaughter.

Hearing that, I supposed I was even more grateful in retrospect not to have figured out the man's password that day.

I found myself increasingly depressed as the coverage wore on, rehashing the same grotesque points again and again, and finally it hit me: It had been exactly two weeks since the day I'd come home from school to find a police cruiser sitting in my driveway. Two weeks since I'd first heard January was missing. It was crazy to think how much had occurred in such a short span of time, how drastically my life had changed—how little would ever be the same about Now that had been about Then.

"I'm gonna go out for a little bit," I announced to my parents, who were deep in a murmured conversation about nothing, and they both turned blank looks my way. "I mean, if that's okay."

They didn't speak, exchanging instead a wordless glance

that meant they wanted to say no but couldn't quite figure out how to justify it yet. Finally, my mom tried, "You know, it's a school night—and with everything that's happened . . ."

"I won't be gone long, I promise. There's just something I want to do."

"What's that?" My dad's tone was suspicious, but when I explained where I intended to go, his mood changed considerably. "Do you want me to drive you?"

"I thought I'd take my bike. I . . . kinda want to be alone."

My dad nodded understandingly. "Be back by nine, okay? I know it's a little on the early side, but . . . just humor us? We almost lost our kid a couple days back."

"I'll stay out of trouble," I promised. And at the time, I'd meant it.

TWENTY-EIGHT

THE NIGHT AIR was cold and bracing, streaming against my face like glacial runoff and biting through the tight knit of my beanie, but I pedaled harder and sucked it deep into my lungs. The sky was clear and the moon bright enough to see by, which was lucky—I was on a semirural road with no streetlights, no sidewalks, and no shoulders, and on either side of me rose whip-like trees and shrubs that jabbed out spiky fingers guaranteed to gouge an eye or pierce soft tissue. Three cars passed me, the drivers catching sight of my reflectors with enough time to cor-rect their course and allow me an absurdly wide berth, and I offered silent gratitude to the universe for the lack of sight-limiting hills along this particular route.

The distance I had to go was technically less than four miles, but still I felt like I'd left planet Earth when I hit this semi-desolate stretch of roadway, darkness and quiet settling around me with sudden totality as stars freckled the sky. It was the kind of peace that immediately precedes a werewolf attack in the movies, and I pedaled harder, building up speed until I felt canon-propelled, invincible, untouchable. I felt free. I had snagged myself a quality boyfriend, I had regained my best friend, I had survived not only a brush with death but also the strange, cleansing fire of coming out, and now I was finally going to say good-bye.

The shrine to January's memory had expanded considerably since the last time I'd seen it. The pile of teddy bears, drying flowers, candles, cards, trinkets, pictures, and other bric-a-brac spilled at the curve of the Walkers' drive like pagan offerings at the dolmen of a Celtic princess. The eight-by-ten image of my ex-girlfriend towered above it all, propped on a small stand and backed now by white poster board promising WE WILL NEVER LOSE HOPE! I couldn't help but wonder what January would have made of it. I could almost hear her: *Teddy bears? What am I, eight?*

Hopping off my bike, I dug clumsily in my jacket pocket with my unencumbered left hand until I managed to pull out a small photo. In it, January and I sat at the edge of her pool in the glow of a lantern, our heads bent close together, our laughing faces gilded and magazine-perfect. Tiana had taken the picture the previous summer during one of the many parties at the mansion, and it had immediately become January's favorite photo of the two of us. She'd insisted that Tiana print it out so I could put it up on my wall, just like those images of the night sky that papered her own. There was something important to her about converting it from the digital to the "real," a ceremonial show of respect for what the image represented. At the time, I'd been humoring her, but now I finally got it.

I tucked the snapshot beneath a glass-jarred candle, its flame casting orbital shadows on the detritus that surrounded it, and idly I wondered who had been by that night to light it. How many people had paid tribute to my ex-girlfriend? How many of them had she actually known and considered friends?

My experience with bidding farewell to the departed being extremely limited, I had no idea what exactly I should say or do to honor the moment. What would she have wanted to hear from me? How do you say good-bye to someone when you're still holding on to a pitiful remnant of hope that she might not actually be gone? In an awkward undertone, I started speaking to her out loud, apologizing for the secrets I'd kept and for the fact that I'd failed to see what she was going through; I also told her how I'd confronted Cedric, and how he would never hurt anyone again. It had been too late to help January or Reiko, but at least no one else would suffer at his hands. That's something I was certain she'd have been glad to hear.

When I had finished talking, I kept my finger on the picture's edge for a few solemn moments, and finally whispered, "Good-bye, Jan."

My phone buzzed suddenly in my pocket, interrupting the hushed moment so unexpectedly that I jumped and almost turned January's memorial into a pyre by knocking over the candle. Wrestling my cell free, I saw that I'd received a text, sent from a number I didn't recognize; and as I took in the three-word message, my skin pebbled and my heart skidded to a halt in my chest.

Behind the barn.

TWENTY-NINE

THREADS OF A low mist, thick as cotton candy, clung to the high grasses in back of the Walker mansion. It all but luminesced, undulating with the pale, otherworldly glow of moonlight, and looked exactly like a cheap dry-ice effect from some ridiculous black-and-white monster movie. At least a dozen times I stopped in my tracks, my heart slugging it out like a fighter on the ropes in the final round, wondering what kind of madness had made me even consider doing what I was doing, wondering just what in the hell I was thinking, heading for an abandoned barn in the middle of the night, based on a mysterious and ominous message.

I'd sent four responses back to the unknown texter, each one the same demand—*who are u???*—and each time threatening to ignore the implied directive unless I was given an answer and told just what I was supposed to find "behind the barn." It was clear I was not going to receive an explanation, though. My words simply repeated themselves in succession on the blank white screen of my phone, the lack of a reply quickly beginning to feel eerie and portentous, like the unmoving planchette on a Ouija board when the spirit has left the building.

Only this spirit had a phone number with an area code that wasn't local. This spirit knew about January's secret hideout. And this spirit knew me well enough to know that of course I would follow the implied directive—where else would I go?

Even as my pulse raced in anticipation, I tried to argue against the idea that wanted to take shape in my mind, tried to withhold oxygen from a pathetic wish that would consume me if I gave its tiny flame any room to breathe. The police had asked me numerous times if Cedric had directly taken responsibility for killing both girls, and even though in recounting our conversation word for word so many times, I'd been forced to concede that the man had technically only confessed—in so many plainspoken words—to stabbing Reiko . . . so what? Cedric Hoffman was a rapist and admitted murderer, a lunatic with the motive, means, and opportunity to eliminate both girls. The conclusion spoke for itself.

It could easily have been that I was being led into a trap by some unknown partner of Cedric's who wanted revenge. The deceased drama coach had known about January's meadow, so why not her hideout as well? It could also have been that I was being directed to find her body—hidden all along behind the very barn that Kaz and I had searched the day her clothes were discovered. Was I really prepared to face that?

Or it could be that it was a message from January herself, somehow having survived the traumatic blood loss that left her sweatshirt a gory mess, having lain low while recuperating and rebuilding her strength, and only now reaching out to me when she knew that it was safe—that Cedric was dead and gone for good.

It was a theory so optimistic I'd have been embarrassed to

speak it out loud, but I couldn't help the way my nerves tingled with anxiety as I jumped across the stream and plunged through the border of pine trees. Only when the barn loomed before me like the *Flying Dutchman*, a gray and ghostly hulk that all but writhed with menace, did I stop and check my phone one more time for a response that still hadn't come. It was like the temperature had dropped by about thirty or forty thousand degrees, flesh firming across my back and shoulders while my breath clouded the air, and the total silence that pressed down on me—heavy as endless fathoms of ocean water—left me unsure as to whether or not I had the courage to keep going.

The text could also have been total bullshit, I knew. I'd given my number to FBA and her catty friends, none of whom gave two shits about January, and any one of them could be fucking with me for a few vindictive laughs. It could be Anson, too, having found one more way to amuse himself at the expense of his stepsister's unknown fate.

It could have been anything—and there was only one way I'd know.

My heart thudding like the blades of a helicopter, I began to creep around the side of the barn, each step a demonstration of masterful self-control. The overgrown weeds were all dying now, desiccating quickly as winter approached, and they tangled around my ankles as I slogged through them, grasping at me like hands bursting from the earth. I stopped, started, stopped, and started again, feeling breathless and stupid—wondering if I really had either the fortitude to see this through, or the brains to abort safely while I still could. And then I had reached the point of no return, the back of my neck clammy with sweat, and electricity buzzed and snapped to life in my veins. *Now or never.*

Taking a deep breath, I stepped out behind the barn, tensed and prepared for anything—a corpse, an attack, a barrage of ridicule from Anson, the miraculous sight of a girl who was supposed to be dead—and found myself staring into darkness.

The moon hovered on the other side of the barn, and the forlorn outbuilding cast an inky shadow over the wedge of earth in back of it, rendering it a black void. I stood, frozen, my eyes wide as I waited for them to adjust—as I waited for something, *anything*, to happen. I could hear no movement, no breathing; I felt utterly alone and completely surrounded at the same time, every inch of my skin bristling with awareness.

After what felt like an eternity, familiar forms began at last to distinguish themselves from the stygian gloom before me: weeds and grasses drooping heavily, a tendril of mist slithering its way toward the bordering trees . . . and then something small, rounded, and pale as ivory propped against the back wall of the barn. My heart dove and then launched upward, throbbing with such agony I was afraid I'd pass out; my vision weaved and shimmied, and then refocused, and I emitted a sound somewhere between a sigh and a whimper as I finally made sense of what I was looking at.

Swallowing my heart back to its rightful place, I struggled to steady my breathing. It was not a skull I had found—it was a rock. Looking like a half-melted bowling ball, it sat in a jumble of weeds at the base of the barn and, aside from myself, it was the only thing back there that wasn't undisturbed vegetation. There were no suspicious mounds of freshly turned earth, no tarp-covered heaps or vats of lye or snickering pranksters—just a swath of wild plants and a domed gray boulder braced against the wall.

Doubtfully, I checked my phone again, wondering if a second set of instructions might be forthcoming; but no new messages had come in, and it was clear that I was on my own. I glanced around anyway, feeling eyes on me, all over me, and wondered again what the hell I was doing out there. Had the text been meaningless? A joke?

I gave the rock a skeptical and almost irritated look, feeling mocked by its inscrutability. And then, as I gazed at it, a memory came to me, the skin across my shoulders contracting with goose bumps as the image crystallized in my mind: Micah and I turning over stones in his garden, looking for a hidden key. *Was it possible?*

Wading closer to the back wall of the barn through the sea of damp weeds, I tried not to get too hopeful. What did I really expect to find if I lifted the thing up? A note saying *Now go to the Dumas theater and check under seat 121,* like I'd stumbled into the world's worst episode of *The Amazing Race*? All I could think, though, was that the day we'd searched these fields, even if I *had* thought to check behind the barn, I'd have overlooked that boulder—and the police would have, too. We'd been looking for a body . . . not a secret message.

The rock wasn't heavy, but it was cumbersome, and with only one good hand at my disposal, it took considerable effort to drag it loose from its resting place. When I finally managed to shove it aside, the muscles in my left shoulder sore from the effort, my pulse quickened anew as I saw what I'd uncovered: a strange gap in the earth, about seven inches long and maybe two inches wide, that ran along the base of the building. It looked like the entrance to a den some animal had carved out underneath the floor of the old barn; it was, to my indescribable relief, obviously too small to accommodate a body.

Hunkering down, I pulled out my phone and activated the flashlight app, aiming its glow into the opening and wondering what I would find. At first I could see nothing but the gouged, uneven dirt walls of the burrow, shadows echoing themselves and overlapping into pitch black as the cavity became wider and deeper; but when I angled my phone a different way, I caught a glimpse of something white and shiny. Gingerly, I reached into the hole, silently praying that any snakes or biting insects that might have taken up residence for the coming cold months were already well and duly asleep; on the third try I managed to snag my finger through something that felt like a loop of tissue-thin plastic.

With little difficulty, I tugged the object free and found that my surmise had been correct; I was holding a common grocery bag, its handles tied in a tight knot. It felt almost disappointingly light in weight as it dangled from my pinkie. My bewilderment was growing by the second as I carried my find out into the moonlight, groping the bag with curious fingers, something rubbery rebounding against the pressure while a larger item made the telltale crinkle of starchy plastic, moving and flexing under my touch. Teasing the knot open with care, fighting every instinct to simply rip the bag apart, I looked at what was inside.

An instant later, my world inverted. A precipitous rush of blood thundered into my head, making the night sway around me, and I dropped onto my ass. The bag landed in the grass at my feet and I stared forward in a blank daze, mists roiling turbulently around me and then settling to form a cold and clammy film on my exposed skin. I sucked the frigid vapor into my lungs, numbed and supercharged all at once.

As clearly as if I had been there when it happened—as clearly as if January had taken me into her confidence from the beginning—I could suddenly see how it had all happened. Everything made sense.

Tammy's over-the-top anguish and wish that the baby had been mine; Eddie's proclamation that January had been a "scandal waiting to happen"; Anson's lascivious sneer—*she was fucking around behind your back*—had they known *all along* that January was pregnant? Could they possibly have even known it was the result of a rape? It seemed almost impossible to consider, and yet . . .

As a minor, January couldn't have gotten an abortion without parental consent, and Jonathan, with a U.S. Senate seat in arm's reach, could never have afforded to allow it. A fifteen-year-old girl who also happened to be a national candidate's stepdaughter seeking to terminate a pregnancy would be the kind of thing that would turn up on blogs, newspapers, magazines, and talk shows all over the place. Special interest groups would turn her into a Cause, and her trauma would be broadcast to every home in the country. If, however, the Walkers said no, then sooner or later January's condition would become obvious, and Jonathan would be compelled to explain on the same public platforms why he'd chosen to force his underage stepdaughter to carry her rapist's baby to term. No matter what the decision was, Jonathan would lose enough voter support to cost the election that mattered more to him than even his own family. And trying to get it taken care of on the sly would've been a fool's gamble; the story would be too explosive, too irresistible, for someone in the know not to eventually sell the information to the media.

Damned if they did and damned if they didn't, the Walkers would have had only one choice: to bury the scandal before it could erupt and bury *them*—to listen to Eddie after all, and send January somewhere that she'd no longer be able to "fuck things up" anymore. Probably before she could start to show, they'd have shipped her off, made some lame excuse and sent her to live with a distant relative out of state, or even out of the country. She'd have been forced to bear Cedric's child in secret, to give it up for adoption and lie to everyone she knew about where she'd gone and why, and to swear that she would never, ever reveal the truth. And all for Jonathan's senate seat.

It would have been intolerable to her—her own personal hell.

Just like that, I realized that night in the barn had been more than merely a desperate attempt to obscure the cause of her pregnancy, more even than just a desire to reclaim control over her body by choosing sex with someone she cared about— though it might have been both those things as well. By convincing me that I was the father of her unborn child, she'd have drawn me and my parents into the loop, stretching Jonathan's sphere of influence to its breaking point. He could control Tammy, and therefore to a certain extent her daughter, but not the Doherty family. My parents would probably have gone along with almost any scenario that saw me free from the shackles of teenage fatherhood, but my mother would have been rankled by any attempt to remove January of her agency in the matter, and would have been thrilled to tell Mr. Walker so to his face;

either way, whatever happened, the issue would have irretrievably spread beyond the confines of the man's personal fiefdom. His word would no longer be absolute, and January's chances of prevailing would have increased, even if only marginally.

A strategic maneuver, then, and one worthy of my brilliant girlfriend, January McConville, who wasn't afraid of anything. I took another look at the contents of the bag I'd fished out from the hole underneath the barn—at the torn, plastic pouch with a narrow-gauge rubber hose escaping from a valve on one end, its insides darkened here and there by a crusty black residue. Even if I hadn't been able to immediately recognize what it was that I'd uncovered, the dark matter that gathered in the corners and folds told me the whole story.

It was a blood donor bag.

January, who had volunteered at the Red Cross one day a week all summer long—at Jonathan's insistence—would have known exactly how to draw her own blood, how much she could afford to part with on a daily basis, and where to get the necessary supplies. Given the chilly autumn temperatures, she might even have been able to store her reservoir right there under the barn, adding to it bit by bit, taking the risk that it wouldn't congeal or spoil before she needed it. She could have been planning her escape for a week or even longer, making the awful choice to give up her friends and her future as an astronomer in exchange for control over her own destiny. Our interlude in the barn may have been her last-ditch attempt at creating a situation that might have allowed her to stay.

But it hadn't worked out. And as I looked at the neat slit cut into the bottom of the pouch that had once been filled with blood, I could easily imagine January emptying it out over her clothes—drenching her hoodie and jeans, and then leaving them somewhere she knew they'd eventually be found. Maybe she'd wanted her parents to suffer for failing to support her when she needed them. Maybe she even figured the fact of her pregnancy would be uncovered through the tests run by the medical examiner, and hoped it would ultimately lead to Cedric's exposure as a serial rapist, hoped he might become a suspect in her apparent death; it would explain, after all, why her backpack had been tossed into the Dumpster at his apartment complex.

The discovery of her bag, ever since it had been announced, had been bothering me; why would a man so obsessed that he saved January's hair and drink lids in airtight, moisture-proof plastic bags, literally converting her trash into his treasure, summarily throw out her backpack and everything inside of it? That portrait he'd taken from Reiko and had framed proved that he lacked either the willpower or the basic common sense to dispose of incriminating trophies. If her bloodstained bag had been discovered somewhere near Cedric's apartment, it would have looked bad—but, found at the dump and mixed in with the man's garbage as though he'd tried ineptly to get rid of it, the thing was positively damning, an elegant and diabolical nail that had sealed his coffin shut in the eyes of the public.

Suddenly I was certain, beyond a shadow of a doubt, that I had solved the riddle of January's still-missing body—as certain as I was that the area code of the number that had texted me with instructions to look behind the barn was local to Los Angeles.

With trembling fingers, I pulled out my phone and wrote another text, blinking away tears that distorted the letters on my keypad. It was only one word, but it was all that I could manage: *January?*

An eternity passed, the night growing colder as the stars hardened and the icy mist began to make my teeth chatter, but I finally received an answer. It was one word, but it was all I'd been hoping for.

Good-bye.

EPILOGUE

I HELD MY glass up to the light, one last mouthful of sparkling grape juice swirling at the bottom, and watched a rainbow splinter into fragments through bevels and bubbles. My parents were not averse to allowing me a sip of actual champagne on certain special occasions, but for semi-special ones, I got the training-wheel stuff. To be honest, despite the supposed sophistication, I kind of disliked both versions; sharp and sour, they were like thin jackets that left you freezing and miserable but made you look good. At least the real stuff gave you a buzz.

"Can I help you with the dishes, Mrs. Doherty?" Kaz asked deferentially as he half rose from his seat, hands already reaching for his plate and mine, and my mother—to her credit—rolled her eyes at him.

"Relax, I like you already," she said with a dismissive wave. "Besides, you two better get going or you'll miss your movie." He beamed back at her, proud of the compliment in a way that made me melt a little inside, and I set my glass on the table again so I could lead the way back to my room. As we started up the short hallway to the front of the house, my mom called out, "And can the 'Mrs. Doherty' stuff—it's Kate!"

Two weeks had passed since the night of my discovery behind the barn, and while my life hadn't exactly returned to "normal," it was finally achieving a sense of equilibrium—a new kind of normal, I guess, and one that felt good. It was the first night that Kaz had eaten dinner with my family, for instance, and instead of watching us with frozen smiles as if afraid to say something wrong and offend us both, my parents had actually teased us about our furtive looks and flirtatious nudges under the table. I liked it.

Also, I was something of a living legend at Riverside. Coming out, dating a college guy, getting embroiled in a murder investigation, and facing down a gun-wielding killer had taken me from nondescript to noteworthy in the space of two weeks, and suddenly I was one of the popular kids. The only person who seemed to bear me any ill will, actually, was Mason Collier, who resented my sudden fame and groused nastily to anyone who would listen that I shouldn't be allowed to use the men's locker room anymore, because I "couldn't be trusted."

"Do you really think they like me?" Kaz asked in a doubtful undertone once we reached my bedroom. "Your mom isn't just saying that?"

"Believe me, my mom doesn't say stuff she doesn't mean," I promised, shrugging—with some difficulty—into a sweater, the bulky cast that made a club out of my right hand still turning every change of clothes into a magic trick. "And she's really polite to people she doesn't like. Like, one time, my dad's boss came over for drinks? And he made all these obnoxious, sexist jokes, and the whole night my mom's saying stuff like, 'Well, isn't that interesting?' and 'Can I freshen anyone's coffee?' while giving him this huge smile that was all teeth, like a velociraptor."

"Got it. Dinosaur smile equals no likey."

He was still nervous, I could tell, and not for lack of reason, either; we were about to meet Micah and Tiana for our first official double date. We'd gotten coffee together once already, just so they could all meet each other, but I had sort of monopolized the conversation with my retelling of The Big Showdown With Cedric—much, I believe, to everyone's mutual relief. So tonight was going to be Kind of a Big Deal, and while Micah had relaxed a lot, he still had problems talking to me about Kaz without looking like a student driver trying to merge lanes on a crowded freeway.

But even if there were still the occasional awkward or embarrassing moments as my friends and family adjusted to the idea of my dating a guy, it still meant a ton to me that all of them put effort into getting to know Kaz—that all of them wanted him to feel welcome. For his part, he had steeled his nerves and made a point of telling his parents about me; I wouldn't be getting to meet them anytime soon, but he had been ecstatic to report back that they had actually acknowledged my existence. Even if his mother apparently referred to me exclusively as Kaz's "good friend."

At the front door, my dad performed a cursory check of our preparedness. After ascertaining that we both had working cell phones and cash in case of an emergency, he said, "Okay, well, have fun. Text when you get there. And when the movie's over. And . . . come home right after?"

I nodded, fighting off an eye roll. The night I'd gone to leave that photograph at January's memorial, I hadn't returned to the house until late—well after my curfew—having lost all track of time while I sat thinking in her favorite meadow. It had triggered every paranoid instinct my parents ordinarily suppressed, and even now it was sort of a miracle they were letting me out of the house without a police escort. I was pretty sure they would calm back down eventually; the bad guy was gone, the intrigues were settled, and I had every intention of regaining my nondescript status.

In the days that had passed, I'd received no further communication from the mysterious California number; by the time I screwed up the courage I needed to dial it and see what happened, it was already out of service. A disposable cell, most likely, and one that was probably already on its way to a landfill somewhere.

For an hour or more, I'd sat in January's meadow that night, agonizing over what to do—wondering if I had a duty to tell someone what I'd uncovered, or if I even had the right to. If January really was still out there somewhere, still alive, the road she faced would be a hard one. She was clever, I knew . . . but was she really clever enough to figure out a way to finish school and go to college? To realize the dreams she'd had, to achieve the goals that had driven her for as long as we'd been friends? Or was she maybe just another minimum-wage earner in LA now, already embarked upon her life's career, her destiny settled for her by default? And then there was the fact of her pregnancy, a problem that defied any easy solution. Unless she got her hands on a *really* convincing fake ID, or was willing to risk her life in some back alley somewhere, she was probably going to have to have Cedric's child after all. And what then?

It wasn't fair, and a huge part of me burned with resentment when I thought about Jonathan on his way to Capitol Hill at the expense of everything that had been taken from his stepdaughter—and everything that had been taken from me and Tiana and Micah and everybody else who loved January. My lust for righteousness wanted the story to come out in full detail, for the Walkers to be held publicly to account for failing her, and for her to be able to return to her friends and the possibilities of a bright future.

But that decision wasn't mine to make. I had been taken into the most crucial of confidences, and I simply couldn't violate that trust, no matter how difficult it was to keep silent. She could have gone to the media with her story and blown Jonathan's tightly controlled life apart in one fell swoop, burning down the house and becoming a national news story overnight . . . but she hadn't; she could have disappeared without a trace, and then come back after the election when the stakes weren't quite so high, taking her chances that her parents would be more accommodating at that point—but she hadn't done that, either. She still *could* come back, I told myself, if she really was alive. The door remained open, and she could come back to Ann Arbor any time she wanted. That she hadn't yet meant staying away was her choice. And if someday she did choose to return, I wanted to be part of the reason instead of the cause.

Finally, I'd made the long trek back to where I'd left my bike on the Walkers' drive, the grocery bag containing the empty blood pouch clutched in my hand. On my way home, I stopped at the first public trash can I came across and shoved the evidence all the way to the bottom. When the police eventually gave up on searching the river, they might return to the fields—this time with cadaver dogs. I didn't know if the animals only smelled corpses, or blood as well, but I decided it wasn't worth leaving to chance.

Kaz and I made our way down the front walk to where the Lexus was parked by the curb, and a molding jack-o'-lantern leered up at me from the neighbor's driveway, the final remnant of a Halloween I'd never forget. Thanksgiving was only a week away, and I was actually looking forward to it. In spite of everything, or maybe because of it, I felt like I had a lot to be grateful for: my family, my friends, Kaz, my good memories of January, my crappy bike and my dad's groan-worthy jokes and my mom's velociraptor smiles. That I was still alive to appreciate the smoky fragrance of dried leaves on the night air, to complain about the sticky sourness of fake champagne, to blush whenever Kaz paid me an impromptu compliment or introduced me to one of his friends as "Flynn, my boyfriend."

Before I got into the Lexus, I looked up at the sky, at the scattering of stars that showed above bare tree branches and in between clouds, and I watched my breath stream up and disappear into the night.

Once I buckled my seat belt, and Kaz had put the car in drive, I took his hand in mine and held it all the way to the movie theater.

ACKNOWLEDGMENTS

It takes a village, as they say—and my village has some of the greatest inhabitants. My name may be on the cover of *Last Seen Leaving*, but this book would not be in your hands without the hard work, commitment, and encouragement of many people—all of whom deserve my unending gratitude.

To my amazing agent, Rosemary Stimola (aka Obi-Wan): I know how to say thank you in a dozen languages, and I still can't think of a way to express how grateful I am for all of your confidence, your support, and your counsel. While I was still hoarse from screaming across the Atlantic that *I had an agent*, you presented me with an offer for publication, and my voice hasn't been right since. You believed in my work, and in me, and for that I say: Thank you! *Merci! Tack så mycket! Kiitos! Gracias! Grazie! Danke! Dziękuję! Paldies! Ačiū! Äitah! Спасибо!* Still not enough, but I'm trying.

To my extraordinary editor, Liz Szabla: working with you has been sublime. Your love for this novel and your trust in my writing have made every step of this process a pleasure; thanks to your guidance, the story contained within these pages is stronger and better than I could have ever imagined, and my life has been remarkably stress-free. From the very beginning, every conversation we've had has reinforced my conviction that Flynn and January have been in the perfect hands, and for all that you've done, thank you from the bottom of my heart.

This book would not even be a book at all if not for my publisher, Jean Feiwel; you made my greatest dream come true, and if I were a genie I would return the favor a hundredfold. Until I can make that happen, however, please accept my most sincere gratitude for allowing me to add "Published Author" to my bio.

My admiration for Rich Deas, the creative director for Macmillan Children's Publishing Group and the genius who designed the gorgeous cover art for this book, is boundless. Thank you for your stunning work and for proving that nothing is ever so great that it can't somehow get even better. I am in awe.

My greater Macmillan family has been phenomenal, and every day I find myself more and more grateful for their work in promoting *Last Seen Leaving*. To Molly Brouillette and Caitlin Sweeney: your enthusiasm for this book means everything to me, and I am so incredibly thankful for everything you've done to share it with the world. You are amazing. A thousand thank-yous are also due to Morgan Dubin, Brittany Pearlman, and the rest of the Fierce Reads team for championing this book and for including me in the ranks of some of my all-time favorite authors. I am humbled.

The first person to review a completed draft of this novel was my mom, Amy Roehrig, and, oh boy, does she deserve a lot of thanks. Mom, you read my manuscript in its roughest form and said, "This is the one." And, you know what? As usual, you were right. I've come a long way from the dark, dark house in the dark, dark woods, huh? Thank you for everything. The second person to read the pages that eventually became *Last Seen Leaving* was Mary Pomerantz, and I owe her an enormous debt. Mary, you once rescued me from some serious turmoil with the power of Implied Friday—and I'm not sure, but I believe you might be just a *little* bit magical. Thanks for your feedback and for years of wonderful friendship.

My mother, Kay Nichols, is perhaps most responsible for my love of thrillers and suspense fiction. Mom, our little two-person book club—swapping and rhapsodizing over novels about demented serial killers and grisly murder—is really what made me want to give writing a try. Thank you for always believing in me. My dad, Charlie Roehrig, is the coolest guy I know and also my number one fan. (The feeling is mutual!) Dad, I'm glad I inherited your weird sense of humor, and I'm truly grateful for all those lessons you tried to teach me about discipline and hard work. Took me a few decades, but I finally get it now. My mother-in-law, Māra Trapans, is an incredible human being who felt like family from the moment we met. Thank you so much for your joie de vivre, your warm heart, and for spreading the gospel of kindness at every opportunity. You are an inspiration, and please know that *I* know how big I hit it in the in-law jackpot. *Paldies!*

The rest of my immediate family I am going to list in a big lump, because *Jebus*, you guys. Todd, Debie, Andy, David, Jennifer, Alexis, Olivia, Ann, Gina, Jordan, Pat, Kiersten, Cayden, Liam, Jaime, Nick, Brendan, Dylan, Drew, Dan, Marz, Evie, Maija, Christian, Emma, Amanda, Indra, Daina, Austris, Gunta, and Ieva: I LOVE YOU ALL.

Many, many thanks, too, to my second family—the ones I chose. It is because of you all that I am still barely maintaining these few footholds I have on sanity anymore. Jenn: Neither of us is old enough to have had a friend for *twenty-four years*, and yet . . . here we are. You're the best. Always. Angela: Where do I even begin? Formosa! Jones! Roomie night! Stinkers! *Passions!* Mustache karaoke! Your heart is as big as all outdoors, and I love you to death. Kasey: From London to Los Angeles, we've conquered a lot of territory together, but please always remember that *I'm the best climber.* Natalie: Our exploits are legendary (and possibly on file at the FBI somewhere), but *Tamara* will always be our finest hour. WHERE'S YOUR PEPPERMILL NOW? Tara (aka T-Boz): You will forever be one of my favorite people and not least because of how eagerly you've enabled my unhealthy obsession with horror movies. Leslie: Will you look at this? It's a book! It's *my* book! I can't *believe* it! You were the first person to encourage me to write a novel, and you'll never know how much it meant to me. Thank you.

And, of course, I have saved the best for last. Uldis, when this book hits the shelves, we will have just celebrated eleven years together; they have been the best years of my life, but (no pressure!) I bet the ones to come will be even better. Thank you for being you, for making everywhere feel like home, and for making every day a beautiful adventure. I can't wait to see the rest of the world with you. *Es tevi mīlu, Ulditi.*

GOFISH

CALEB ROEHRIG

What did you want to be when you grew up?
When I was a kid, I had my future narrowed down to three possible careers: artist, actor, or author. At some point, I kind of had to accept that no matter how good my stick figures were—and they are *excellent*—my artistic endeavors would probably not take me terribly far in life. I did act for a while, and even paid the bills (well, most of the bills) (okay, most of *some* of the bills) that way; but I think six-year-old me would be pretty excited to know about this book with my name on it.

When did you realize you wanted to be a writer?
I figured out very early on how much I loved to tell stories. When I was probably four years old, I would climb into my mom's lap and dictate various tales to her, which she would dutifully transcribe into little booklets. I'd illustrate them (with my whizz-bang artistic skills—see above) and then force everyone in the family to read and appreciate them. So I can safely say this has been a lifelong ambition for me.

What was your favorite thing about school?
Art classes were, without question, my favorite thing about school. Math and science never came very easy to me—I could do the same math problem over and over for an hour

and get a different answer every time—and even English classes always seemed to focus more on grammar and structure than on creative writing; but art provided an environment for just self-expression, and was one of the few places where not fitting in was actually sort of an advantage.

What were your hobbies as a kid? What are your hobbies now?

I guess I'd say drawing was a major hobby of mine. I got all these books on how to draw realistic animals and people, and I'd spend hours trying to make it work. As a teenager, I finally started a comic strip journal—a book full of three- to six-panel cartoons recounting real things that had happened to me. Like the time my mom and I got trapped in a car wash, or the time I got tear-gassed while taking a shower (true story!). These days, maybe travel is my hobby? I love to see new places, and I'll take a trip whenever the opportunity arises.

Did you play sports as a kid?

Organized sports were never a good fit for me. I played soccer with my friends when I was a little kid, and in middle school I got into martial arts (fun fact: I had a black belt in tae kwon do by the time I finished the eighth grade!), but I hated team sports.

What was your first job, and what was your worst job?

Oh, man. When I was sixteen, I got hired as a waiter at a Japanese restaurant that was opening in my hometown—only I never actually worked. They just . . . forgot to put me on the schedule, and no matter how many times I called to ask about it, they never ever did. When I finally called to quit after two months of this, they literally had no idea who I was.

My *worst* job was undoubtedly working as a fry cook at a chain restaurant in college; not only did I burn myself every single day, but the verbal abuse and generally toxic environment of the kitchen—combined with a complete lack of any support from the management—made the job miserable. I would work twelve-hour shifts without eating, because they wouldn't feed us and didn't pay me enough that I could afford to order anything off the menu.

What book is on your nightstand now?
I just started reading *The Window* by Amelia Brunskill! It's a debut thriller about a girl looking into the strange circumstances surrounding the death of her twin sister—so it is exactly up my alley, and I cannot wait to see how it turns out.

How did you celebrate publishing your first book?
I was actually on tour the week that *Last Seen Leaving* was released, so I celebrated by buying myself a drink at the bar of the hotel we were staying in! But when the tour ended, my mom threw a party for me, which was really great.

Where do you write your books?
Both *Last Seen Leaving* and my second novel, *White Rabbit*, I wrote while living in Finland. My husband is a linguist, and we moved to Helsinki for about four years for his research, and I had the great privilege of not being allowed to work. So I spent all day, every day, sitting at our kitchen table, typing away.

What sparked your imagination for *Last Seen Leaving*?
Mysteries about missing persons have always fascinated me, because there is an infinite number of intriguing possible answers to the central question, What really happened

to X? So for a long time, I kicked around the notion of writing about a disappearance, but was never able to think about how I would approach it. Meanwhile, I also really wanted to write something with a gay protagonist, because it means so much to me to see the growth of LGBTQ+ representation in literature for young people, and because there was no such thing when I was a teenager—and I cannot begin to explain how much it would have meant to me if there had been. So I had two half ideas, but no clear vision of how to complete them . . . until one day I just tried fitting the two halves together, and the plot of *Last Seen Leaving* came to me!

Who is your favorite fictional character?
This is a really tough question, and I'm going to give two answers. I read a lot of suspense titles, and two of my favorite fictional detectives of all time are Sara Paretsky's V.I. Warshawski, and Sue Grafton's Kinsey Millhone. V.I. is such a bold character, this tough-as-nails feminist badass who won't take no for an answer; and Kinsey is sly, snarky, and resourceful, and it was reading the Millhone series as a teenager that made me want to write mystery novels.

What was your favorite book when you were a kid? Do you have a favorite book now?
My favorite book growing up was *Alice in Wonderland*—I read my copy so many times that both the front and back covers eventually wore off. I'm terrible at picking favorites as an adult, but these days, I would give the hat-tip to either *And Then There Were None* by Agatha Christie or *The Big Sleep* by Raymond Chandler. Both are excellent, twist-filled, atmospheric mystery novels.

Do you ever get writer's block? What do you do to get back on track?

I haven't ever really had writer's "block," per se; I always outline my books in detail before I start drafting, so I'm never at a place where I'm not sure where the story is going or how I intend to get there. I do sometimes find myself unsure how to craft a particular scene or conversation, and in those cases I'll try to walk myself through it by listing out my objectives—what is it that needs to happen here, and why? If that fails, I throw on an old T-shirt and go for a run. I probably do 90 percent of the work of writing a book during my runs, because it gives me time to do nothing but think.

What would your readers be most surprised to learn about you?

A long, long time ago, back when I was a working actor, I was in a movie with Olivia Munn. It was a low-budget horror flick, and we had one scene together (she played a girl who invited me to a party at her sorority), but she is still the most famous person with whom I have ever shared a screen!

When Rufus Holt and his ex-boyfriend Sebastian find Rufus's sister, April, drenched in blood and holding a knife beside her boyfriend's dead body, her guilt seems evident—but April says she didn't do it. Can Rufus clear his sister's name . . . or will he die trying?

Keep reading for an excerpt.

"APRIL!" I GRIP HER BY THE SHOULDERS, HER FLESH FRIGHTENINGLY cold and sticky to the touch, and drag her forward, straightening her up. The knife slips from her right hand as my knee jostles a discarded cell phone resting by her left, and her head lolls and swings on her neck, heavy as a sandbag. Frantically, I give her a hard shake. "April!"

"Holy fuck, dude." Sebastian's eyes are huge with panic as he prowls Fox's body, searching for a pulse. "Holy *fuck*, Rufus, I think he's dead!"

Willing myself not to lose it, I press my fingers against April's carotid, holding my breath. When I feel the faint and erratic undulation of blood moving beneath her pallid skin, I emit a primitive noise of relief and squeeze my eyes shut tight. "She's alive."

"What the fuck happened here, man?" Sebastian asks me, deathly serious. His face is stricken as he backs away from Fox's corpse, the Whitneys' favorite son stretched across the slate floor tiles, his T-shirt so saturated with blood that its true color is impossible to determine. *"What the fuck happened?"*

He jolts to his feet and stumbles a little, eyes still getting wider. His anxiety is so sincere that, I finally realize, if this *is* some twisted prank, he is certainly not in on it. I search my sister's body, looking for wounds or some other sign that she's been hurt, but I can't find anything. The blood doesn't seem to be hers.

"April, wake up," I command sharply, sweeping her auburn hair out of her face and tilting her chin to the light. She mumbles something unintelligible, and I pry one of her eyes open. Her pupil is a tiny dot in a pool of aquamarine, her gaze glassy and unfocused as it drifts up into her skull. "She's on something."

"*Shit*, man!" Sebastian paces agitatedly, but he can't stop staring down at Fox's body. "We have to call someone."

"Not yet," I tell him firmly, giving April another hard shake. With a guilty feeling, I swat her lightly across the face. She gives a sharp snort and her eyelids lift unevenly. "April! April, can you hear me?"

". . . Rufus?" Her voice is a breathy whisper.

"Yeah, it's me."

Fat tears roll down her cheeks as I watch, and then, to my complete surprise, she tosses her arms around me in a flaccid, desperate embrace. Her forehead thuds against my shoulder, and she begins weakly to sob. I let it go on for just a moment before I straighten her back up again, flustered. "April, what happened?"

"I-I don't . . ." She starts to look toward Fox's body, but I take hold of her chin again and force her to face me. I can't afford to lose her concentration now.

"Focus on me, April. Tell me what happened."

She licks her lips, her eyes clouding for a moment before she seems to will them clear again, but her voice is a faded, broken whisper as she moans, "I don't remember. I don't . . . there was . . . all that blood . . ."

With Sebastian's help, I haul her to her feet, and the two of us start walking her through the dining room and living room, hiphop music blasting from speakers I can't see. She's like a newborn colt, her legs rubbery and untrustworthy, and her chin keeps dropping to her chest. I ask her what she's taken, but her answers are unintelligible, and I feel the quick heat of impatience snapping under my skin. I try to quell it, recalling my therapist's advice: *Take a deep breath and step back.* Over April's head, I ask Sebastian, "Do they have a shower? Maybe it'll wake her up."

"There's a bedroom through there," he answers after a beat, his face alarmingly gray, and gestures to a door set in a small vestibule beside the stone-fronted fireplace. "It's got a bathroom. I don't think there's a tub, but—"

"Let's get her in there."

The Whitneys' master suite is cozy in size and luxurious in appointment—Egyptian cotton sheets, a hand-carved headboard, priceless antique armoires—but an open doorway leads to a surprisingly spare bathroom with a shower stall.

I shove April into Sebastian's arms while I kick my shoes aside, strip off my tank top, and crank the cold water to full blast. Then I pull my blood-soaked, half-dead half-sister under the hard spray with me, holding her upright while she squirms and mumbles, pink water sluicing off her and swirling ominously down the drain. Her bare skin becomes slippery as the drying blood loosens up, and I have to hold her tighter. Eventually, her struggling grows more forceful, her protests more lucid, and I slap the water off at last.

With most of the blood washed away, it's even more apparent that she's physically unharmed, her slight, pale frame streaky and textured with goose bumps but otherwise pristine. I sit her down on the lid of the toilet, and she stares at the white tiles of the floor, shivering and blank. Breathing hard from the exertion of holding her up, I ask, "Are you feeling better?"

A long second passes where she just gazes up at me, and then she gives a faint nod. "Yeah."

"Where are your clothes?"

She raises her arm like it weighs two hundred pounds, and points vaguely into the master bedroom. "In there. Is . . . is Fox—"

"Get yourself cleaned up, put your clothes back on, and then I'm gonna need you to tell us what happened tonight, okay?" I try to deliver it like a statement, mimicking the way my mom "asks" me to do chores—*I need you to mow the lawn, okay?*—but my voice is shaking. I clamp down hard against the fear. I cannot lose control. *Take a step back.* "Can you do that for me?"

April nods again, and mumbles, "Yes."

As I herd Sebastian back into the chaos of the living room, shutting the bedroom door behind us, I hear the shower turn on again. My ex-boyfriend gives me an incredulous look, his soft, kissable lips scrunching up like a cat's anus. "You're letting her take a freaking shower, man? She's covered in evidence!"

"This whole *place* is covered in evidence," I fire back, waving my hand around the connected rooms. We've tracked Fox's blood across the pinewood floors, and streaks of it cling to Sebastian's arms and face. I'm standing there, trying to compartmentalize, fighting to think, when I notice his eyes bob up and down the length of my torso and I finally remember that I'm still shirtless. Even in the midst of all the shock and disorder, I feel a wave of wildly inappropriate satisfaction as my ex-boyfriend gets a look at how toned my chest and abs have become in the weeks since he dumped me.

I had this whole plan to turn into a crazy-hot sex god over the summer, to build muscle like an underwear model and then have Lucy take some "candid" photos of me that I could post on Facebook and Instagram and anywhere else Sebastian might see them and realize how awesome I was doing without him—so he could see the newer, hotter Rufus Holt and eat his heart out. My biology proved unequal to the fantasy, however; my upper body hardened a bit, but after putting on exactly two extra pounds of muscle, my narrow-shouldered physique seems to have just plain given up. No matter what I try, I appear to be stuck permanently on lanky. Still, I look way abs-ier than I did the last time Sebastian saw me without a shirt on, and I guess that's all that matters.

"We have to call the police," he insists next.

I shake my head. "Not yet."

"What the fuck do you mean, *not yet?*" Sebastian demands, his voice climbing into the realm of hysteria. "Why not? Fox is fucking *dead*, Rufus!"

"Not until we hear what April has to say! We need to know . . ." *We need to know what we've walked into.* "We need to know what happened first."

Something's not right. On the surface, it sure as hell looks like April killed her boyfriend with a big old knife . . . but why? And why did she call *me* for help? At the risk of sounding selfish, this is the real reason I don't want to involve the police just yet. Instead of her doting parents or her close friends or even our take-charge asshole of a brother, she's involved *me* in this thing, and I want to know exactly where I stand before I start getting all reporty with the cops. My recent history with the law is dodgy, anyway, and I can't exactly afford any misunderstandings.

"Just wait until she's told us, okay? Just *wait*." I try to sound authoritative again as I turn and start for the front door, my brain speeding while I struggle to close off any avenue of thought that doesn't lead directly forward.

"Where are you going?" Sebastian asks, indignant.

"I just want to have a look around outside. I think— Let's just know as much about what's going on here as we can, okay? Before we call anybody?"

Sebastian is silent for a moment, his lips still pursed tightly. He looks more than a little freaked, but he gives me a short nod. "Okay. Okay."

The second the door closes behind me, I sprint to the porch rail, barely covering the three steps before I start to heave. Nothing comes up but an unearthly retching sound, my stomach convulsing, drool running over my bottom lip as I struggle to breathe and fight my nausea into submission. The air outside is still heavy and warm, but it's not until I start sucking in great mouthfuls of it that I realize how good it smells. For all its rarified trappings, the lake house reeks inside with the metallic stench of blood.

I will my stomach to settle, my head to clear. When I'm finally breathing evenly again, I step back and begin a methodical circuit of the house, eyes sweeping left to right as I look for something I can't even begin to anticipate. Nothing special catches my eye, though—just more Solo cups and cigarette butts—and I soon reach the end point of the porch. A set of steps descends to the yard on my right, while on my left, a patio door affords me a full, Technicolor view of the kitchen and Fox's body—still swimming in a lap pool of his own congealing blood.

With a shudder I quickly reverse course, tugging my phone out of my shorts. It's damp from the shower but seems to have avoided the worst of the spray, and it still works. I'm definitely not ready to talk to the cops, but I haven't totally lost my mind, either; I know an adult needs to be involved in this slasher-movie nightmare. But it has to be one that I trust.

My mom answers on the fourth ring, her voice groggy and thick. I can picture her lying on top of her bed, a paperback splayed across her chest, fumbling for her glasses on the nightstand. "Hey, kiddo, what's up?"

"H-hey, Mom, I—" My voice chokes off, the reality of what I have to say slamming into me like a crosstown bus. *April might have murdered her boyfriend.*

"What is it? What's wrong?" She's immediately alert, her hair-trigger panic tripped by my hesitation. "Did you and Lucy have a fight? Do you need a ride?"

"No, it's nothing like that," I assure her in a quiet hurry, feeling my way through my own words. "It's . . . actually, it's, um . . . April?"

"*That girl.*" Mom's tone becomes as hard and sharp as a broken tooth. "What did she do this time? Did she crash your party tonight? Listen, if she said . . . if she said something about my calling Peter—"

"No, Mom, it wasn't—" I stop short, her words hitting their target. "Wait, what do you mean, 'calling Peter?' Did you talk to him?" She stays silent, and I feel the back of my neck prickle. "Mom?"

"I *might* have phoned your sperm donor today," she admits at last in an aggrieved huff. "It was a moment of weakness, and I'm not proud of it."

"Why?" I ask, surprised to find that it's actually still possible for my night to get worse. With one possible exception—me—nothing good has ever resulted from any kind of contact between Peter Covington and Genevieve Holt.

Sixteen years ago, my mother was a bright-eyed, twenty-five-year-old interior designer and art consultant, new to the city of Burlington, Vermont, and the proud owner of a small firm bearing her name. She'd done three years of art school, dropping out when an internship with a major decorator in New York turned into a full-time job she couldn't refuse, and then eventually followed her heart to New England. Thanks to a modest inheritance from my grandparents—a, by all accounts, quirky and lovable couple who ran a country store in a small Maine village, taught their kids to pursue their dreams, and unfortunately died before I could ever meet them—she was able to rent an office, hang out her shingle, and take on private clients.

It wasn't always easy. Work came in when the economy was up, and vanished when it went down, leaving her scrambling to cover the bills; and so, when a law firm by the name of Pembroke, Landau, and Wells offered her a massive chunk of cash to help them choose a few impressively priceless works of art for their offices, she was overjoyed to accept. When she met their junior partner, a Harvard legacy by the name of Peter Covington II, she was quickly swept off her feet. He was tall and handsome, with blond hair and gray eyes, and he was utterly charmed by the bohemian and unpredictable free spirit that was the young Genevieve. They were a total mismatch, his white-collar starchiness at complete odds with her offbeat *joie de vivre*, but—in my mom's mind, at least—the sparks their differences generated were what fueled their romance.

The sparks worked their magic for approximately two weeks before my mom discovered that Peter Covington was in fact married, that he had a toddler at home—a little boy named Hayden—and that most of the things he'd said to her in private were a pack of lies. She ended things immediately, with a fiery speech that she has a tendency to recount verbatim whenever she's had a little too much white wine, and then spent a few months debating whether or not to rat the man out to his wife. When she learned that she was pregnant, it was merely the icing on the cake.

I was born into the midst of an ugly war that continues to this day, erupting in periodic skirmishes as Peter Covington tries to ruin my mother's career and life, and she sues him repeatedly for slander and back child support. Peter's wife, Isabel, amazingly has stuck by him through the whole lengthy ordeal; supposedly, April was born to save their marriage, but I suspect a prenup is the real reason their matrimonial bonds have never been torn asunder.

Peter wouldn't have anything to do with me; in sixteen years, I've never received so much as a birthday card from him. When I was a kid, he fascinated me—my wealthy and elusive father, who lived in a beautiful home and drove a fancy car—but I only made the mistake of calling him Dad once, when I was five years old and he came by our house to deliver some personal message to my mom; his reaction, which was swift, furious, and terrifying, permanently cured me of my misplaced affection. In an emergency, my mother would have turned to the *Cloverfield* monster for help before asking for a favor from Peter Covington—and if she'd called him now, it could only mean one thing.

"How broke are we?" I ask flatly, when her silence becomes unbearable. My thoughts fragment inside my skull. Fox's corpse is practically looming over my shoulder, but the poverty my mom and I struggle against is a black hole with its own inescapable gravity; I can't avoid it, so I might as well dive in instead and give myself a little more time to think about how I'll bring up the *dead body* I've just discovered.

She takes a hesitant breath. "It's not for you to worry about, kiddo."

"Mom."

"I've got it under control, Rufus."

The lie is so threadbare it's impossible to let it pass unchallenged. "You said you'd rather take a bath with a lawn mower than ask that ass-butt for money again! You'd never have called him unless it was really serious." More silence follows, and I bite the inside of my cheek as the bottom drops out of my stomach. *How much worse is this night going to get?* "How bad is it?"

"Ruf—"

"Please, Mom, just . . . tell me." I've made my way to the rear of the cottage now, and I lean tiredly over another porch rail, crickets underscoring the deceptively tranquil view of dark water spreading toward the far shore. The moon glares brightly down at the Whitneys' cottage like the spotlight from a police helicopter, and I duck my head. "Whatever it is, my imagination'll only make it worse."

"We owe the bank about eight grand," my mother confesses miserably, "and, okay, it's kind of . . . urgent." It's only the fourth of the month, and she's already panicked enough to appeal to my father; that means this is an old debt, a compounded one, and she's starting to get desperate. "I can scrape together about a quarter of it if I can get your uncle Connor to pay back the money I loaned him last Christmas. But . . ."

She trails off, my stomach heaves again, and just like that I feel the phantom grip of Fox's cooling fingers at the base of my neck. I called my mom about a *murder* and now we're talking about the chance that we might lose our house? The ground seems to tilt sharply under my feet, pressure grips at my chest, and I struggle for air.

My mom's all I've got; my whole life, it's just been the two of us, holding hands to ride out the storm; and too often, the storm has been *me*. Somewhere inside me lurks a volatile Mr. Hyde, an alter ego driven by an engine of combustible anger I've only recently found any success in mastering. Swept up in the inner hurricane of my rage, I've screamed and ranted, broken dishes and bones, terrorized my teachers—and provided my father with ammunition in his agenda against us. How many phone calls has she gotten from school officials over the years because I lost control and broke the glass on a trophy case or attacked someone in class?

And she's stood by me through all of it. I owe her so much. I owe her everything. How much more can she take? My mouth clicks dryly, my free hand tightening on the wooden rail. "I've been working all year, Mom. I can help—"

"*No.* Absolutely not, no way!" She's so vehement I can practically hear her hand karate-chopping the air. "I will *not* let you spend your money on this, Rufus Holt. Do you hear me? These are my mistakes, not yours, and if—if—"

She stops altogether, and I can picture her again: glasses in her lap, fingers pressed hard against her lips, mouth trembling as she tries not to cry. The lake smears in front of me, black and gray and blue all running together, and I blink hard. None of this is fair. "It affects me, too, Mom. It's my house, too."

"I'll take care of it. If I have to sell my organs on the black market, I will handle it. Okay?" She puts some steel in her tone. "Your shithead sperm donor owes us so much by now I would own this fucking place outright if he'd pay up."

"Don't hold your breath," I mumble weakly.

"I'm sorry, kiddo. All that . . . let's strike it from the record and start over. What did April do this time?"

Reflexively, I turn around and peer back into the cottage through the broad French doors of the family room. The fixtures of the kitchen gleam menacingly at the front of the house, and Sebastian stands near the fireplace, watching me with brightly nervous eyes and radiating an inarticulate terror of being alone inside with a corpse. I know I should tell her what we've found . . . but how can I? She's already in a lousy place; the first thing she'd do would be call the police—or, worse, Peter—and there would go any chance for me to take control of my involvement in the situation.

I'm not exactly one of the Bad Kids, but my history of anger-related behavioral issues are well documented, and cops don't really seem to care much about your GPA when they already remember you from the time you lost your shit in the eighth grade and knocked a bully's tooth out with the back of a chair. Especially when your own father prosecuted the bully's subsequent lawsuit against the school district and publicly called you a "dangerous animal." Thanks to a good therapist and the right medication, my moods have stabilized a lot since then, but the president of the school board is just waiting for the proper excuse to expel me—and having been suspended once this year already, my situation is precarious.

I haven't thought things out, I realize; once my mom learns what's happened, there will be no taking it back. I need to know more. I just need a little more time.

"It's nothing," I mumble at last. "Don't worry about it."

As I disconnect, though, it is with the distinct sensation that—somehow, in some way—the Covingtons have just ruined my life yet again.